2011

MIDNIGHT RIOT

BY BEN AARONOVITCH

Midnight Riot
Moon Over Soho

BEN AARONOVITCH

BALLANTINE BOOKS • NEW YORK

Copyright © 2011 by Ben Aaronovitch

Published in the United States by Del Rey, an imprint of The Random House Publishing Group, a division of Random House, Inc., New York.

DEL REY is a registered trademark and the Del Rey colophon is a trademark of Random House, Inc.

Published in the United Kingdom as *Rivers of London* by Gollancz, a member of The Orion Publishing Group Limited.

ISBN 978-1-61129-446-0

Printed in the United States of America

In memory of Colin Ravey
because some people are too large
to be contained by just the one universe

ACKNOWLEDGMENTS

FIRST OF all, I need to thank Andrew Cartmel for all his support; *"No greater love can a man have than he will lay down his last five pound note for his fellow man."* This is not to slight the efforts of James, the other Andrew, Marc, Kate and Jon. Then once the manuscript was done came the two Johns (aka der management), Betsy at Del Rey and Jo at Gollancz. Lastly I'd like to thank everyone at Waterstone's Covent Garden past and present for their support even when I threatened to bore them to tears.

Yet ah! why should they know their fate?
Since sorrow never comes too late,
And happiness too swiftly flies.
Thought would destroy their paradise.
No more; where ignorance is bliss,
'Tis folly to be wise.

"Ode on a Distant Prospect of Eton College"
by Thomas Gray

Material Witness

IT STARTED at one thirty on a cold Tuesday morning in January when Martin Turner, street performer and, in his own words, apprentice gigolo, tripped over a body in front of the West Portico of St. Paul's at Covent Garden. Martin, who was none too sober himself, at first thought the body was that of one of the many celebrants who had chosen the Piazza as a convenient outdoor toilet and dormitory. Being a seasoned Londoner, Martin gave the body the "London once-over"— a quick glance to determine whether this was a drunk, a crazy or a human being in distress. The fact that it was entirely possible for someone to be all three simultaneously is why good-Samaritanism in London is considered an extreme sport—like BASE jumping or crocodile wrestling. Martin, noting the good quality coat and shoes, had just pegged the body as a drunk when he noticed that it was in fact missing its head.

As Martin noted, to the detectives conducting his interview, it was a good thing he'd been inebriated, because otherwise he would have wasted time screaming and running about—especially once he realized he was standing in a pool of blood. Instead, with the slow methodical patience of the drunk and terrified, Martin Turner dialed 999 and asked for the police.

The police emergency center alerted the nearest Incident Response Vehicle and the first officers arrived on the scene six minutes later. One officer stayed with a suddenly sober

Martin while his partner confirmed that there was a body and that, everything else being equal, it probably wasn't a case of accidental death. They found the head six meters away where it had rolled behind one of the neoclassical columns that fronted the church's portico. The responding officers reported back to control, who alerted the area Murder Investigation Team, whose duty officer, the most junior detective constable on the team, arrived half an hour later. He took one look at Mr. Headless and woke his governor. With that, the whole pomp and majesty that is a Metropolitan Police murder investigation descended on the twenty-five meters of open cobbles between the church portico and the market building. The pathologist arrived to certify death, make a preliminary assessment of the cause and cart the body away for its postmortem. (There was a short delay while they found a big enough evidence bag for the head.) The forensic teams turned up mob-handed and, to prove that they were the important ones, demanded that the secure perimeter be extended to include the whole west end of the Piazza. To do this they needed more uniforms at the scene, so the DCI who was Chief Investigating Officer called up Charing Cross nick and asked if they had any to spare. The shift commander, upon hearing the magic word "overtime," marched into the section house and volunteered everyone out of their nice warm beds. Thus the secure perimeter was expanded, searches were made, junior detectives were sent off on mysterious errands and finally, at just after five o'clock, it all ground to a halt. The body was gone, the detectives had left and the forensic people unanimously agreed there was nothing more that could be done until dawn—which was three hours away. Until then, they just needed a couple of mugs to guard the crime scene until shift change.

Which is how I came to be standing around Covent Garden in a freezing wind at six o'clock in the morning and why it was me that met the ghost.

Sometimes I wonder whether if I'd been the one that went for coffee and not Leslie May my life would have been much less interesting and certainly much less dangerous. Could it have been anyone, or was it destiny? When I'm considering this I find it helpful to quote the wisdom of my father, who once told me, "Who knows why the fuck anything happens?"

COVENT GARDEN is a large piazza in the center of London with the Royal Opera House at the east end, a covered market in the center and St. Paul's Church at the west end. It was once London's principal fruit and veg market, but that got shifted south of the river ten years before I was born. It had a long and varied history, mostly involving crime, prostitution and the theater, but now it's a tourist market. St. Paul's Church is known as the Actors' Church to differentiate it from the Cathedral and was first built by Inigo Jones in 1638. I know all this because there's nothing like standing around in a freezing wind to make you look for distractions, and there was a large and remarkably detailed information plaque attached to the side of the church. Did you know, for instance, that the first recorded victim of the 1665 plague outbreak, the one that ends with London burning down, is buried in its graveyard? I did after ten minutes sheltering from the wind.

The Murder Investigation Team had closed off the west of the Piazza by stringing tape across the entrances to King and Henrietta streets and along the frontage of the covered market. I was guarding the church end, where I could shelter in the portico, and WPC Leslie May, my fellow probationer, guarded the Piazza side, where she could shelter in the market.

Leslie was short, blond and impossibly perky even when wearing a stab vest. We'd gone through basic training at Hendon together before being transferred to Westminster for our probation. We maintained a strictly professional relationship despite my deep-seated yearning to climb into her uniform trousers.

Because we were both probationary constables, an experienced PC had been left to supervise us—a responsibility he diligently pursued from an all-night café on St. Martin's Close.

My phone rang. It took me a while to dig it out from among the stab vest, utility belt, baton, handcuffs, digital police radio

and cumbersome but mercifully waterproof reflective jacket.
When I finally managed to answer, it was Leslie.

"I'm going for coffee," she said. "Want one?"

I looked over at the covered market and saw her wave.

"You're a lifesaver," I said and watched as she darted off
toward James Street.

She hadn't been gone more than a minute when I saw a figure by the portico, a short man in a suit tucked into the shadows behind the nearest column.

I gave the prescribed Metropolitan Police "first greeting."

"Oi!" I said. "What do you think you're doing?"

The figure turned. I saw a flash of a pale, startled-looking
face. The man was wearing a shabby old-fashioned suit complete with waistcoat, watch fob and battered top hat. I thought
he might be one of the street performers licensed to perform
in the Piazza, but it seemed a tad early in the morning for
that.

"Over here," he said and beckoned.

I made sure I knew where my extendable baton was and
headed over. Policemen are supposed to loom over members
of the public, even helpful ones, that's why we wear big boots
and pointy helmets, but when I got closer I found the man was
tiny, five foot nothing in his shoes. I fought an urge to squat
down to get our faces level.

"I saw the whole thing, squire," said the man. "Terrible
thing it was."

They drum it into you at Hendon, before you do anything
else get a name and an address. I produced my notebook and
pen. "Can I ask your name, sir?"

" 'Course you can, squire. My name's Nicholas Wallpenny,
but don't ask me how to spell it because I never really got my
letters."

"Are you a street performer?" I asked.

"You might say that," said Nicholas. "Certainly my performances have hitherto been confined to the street. Though on
a cold night like this I wouldn't be averse to bring some inte-
riosity to my proceedings. If you catch my meaning, squire."

There was a badge pinned to his lapel: a pewter skeleton

caught mid-caper. It seemed a bit goth for a short cockney geezer, but then London is the pick 'n' mix cultural capital of the world. I wrote down street performer.

"Now, sir," I said. "If you could just tell me what it was you saw."

"I saw plenty, squire."

"But you were here earlier this morning?" My instructors were also clear about not cueing your witnesses. Information is supposed to flow in only one direction.

"I'm here morning, noon and night," said Nicholas, who obviously hadn't gone to the same lectures I had.

"If you've witnessed something," I said, "perhaps you'd better come and give a statement."

"That would be a bit of a problem," said Nicholas. "Seeing as I'm dead."

I thought I hadn't heard him correctly. "If you're worried about your safety . . ."

"I ain't worried about anything anymore, squire," said Nicholas. "On account of having been dead these last hundred and twenty years."

"If you're dead," I said before I could stop myself, "how come we're talking?"

"You must have a touch of the sight," said Nicholas. "Some of the old Palladino." He looked at me closely. "Touch of that from your father maybe? Dockman was he, sailor, some such thing, he gave you that good curly hair and them lips?"

"Can you prove you're dead?" I asked.

"Whatever you say, squire," said Nicholas and stepped forward into the light.

He was transparent, the way holograms in films are transparent. Three-dimensional, definitely really there and fucking transparent. I could see right through him to the white tent the forensic team had set up to protect the area around the body.

Right, I thought, just because you've gone mad doesn't mean you should stop acting like a policeman.

"Can you tell me what you saw?" I asked.

"I saw the first gent, him that was murdered, walking down

from James Street. Fine high-stepping man with a military bearing, very gaily dressed in the modern fashion. What I would have considered a prime plant in my corporeal days." Nicholas paused to spit. Nothing reached the ground. "Then the second gent, him what did the murdering, he comes strolling the other way up from Henrietta Street. Not so nicely turned out, wearing them blue workman's trousers and an oilskin like a fisherman. They passed each other just there." Nicholas pointed to a spot ten meters short of the church portico. "I reckon they knew each other 'cause they both nod, but they don't stop for a chat or nothing, which is understandable, it not being a night for loitering."

"So they passed each other?" I asked, as much for a chance to catch up with my note taking as to clarify the point. "And you thought they knew each other?"

"As acquaintances," said Nicholas. "I wouldn't say they were bosom friends, especially with what transpired next."

I asked him what transpired next.

"Well, the second, murdering, gent, he puts on a cap and red jacket and he brings out his stick and as quietly and swiftly as a snoozer in a lodging house he comes up behind the first gent and knocks his head clean off."

"You're having me on," I said.

"No I'm never," said Nicholas and crossed himself. "I swear on my own death and that's as solemn a swear as a poor shade can give. It was a terrible sight, off came his head and up went the blood."

"What did the killer do?"

"Well, having done his business he was off, went down New Row like a lurcher on the commons," said Nicholas.

I was thinking that New Row took you down to Charing Cross Road, an ideal place to catch a taxi or a minicab or even a night-bus if the timing was right. The killer could have cleared central London in less than fifteen minutes.

"That wasn't the worst of it," said Nicholas, obviously unwilling to let his audience get distracted. "There was something uncanny about the killing gent."

"Uncanny?" I asked. "You're a ghost."

"Spirit I may be," said Nicholas. "But that just means I know uncanny when I see it."

"And what did you see?"

"The killing gentleman didn't just change his hat and coat, he changed his face," said Nicholas. "Now, tell me that ain't uncanny."

Someone called my name. Leslie was back with the coffees.

Nicholas vanished while I wasn't looking.

I stood staring like an idiot for a moment until Leslie called again.

"Do you want this coffee or not?" I crossed the cobbles to where the angel Leslie was waiting with a polystyrene cup. "Anything happen while I was away?" she asked. I sipped my coffee. The words—I just talked to a ghost who saw the whole thing—utterly failed to leave my lips.

THE NEXT day I woke up at eleven—much earlier than I wanted to. Leslie and I had been relieved at eight and we'd trudged back to the section house and gone straight to bed. Separate beds, unfortunately.

The principal advantages of living in your station's section house is that it is cheap, close to work and that it's not my parents' flat. The disadvantages are that you're sharing your accommodation with people too weakly socialized to live with normal human beings and who habitually wear heavy boots. The weak socialization makes opening the fridge an exciting adventure in microbiology and the boots mean that every shift change sounds like an avalanche.

I lay in my narrow little institutional bed staring at the poster of Estelle that I'd affixed to the wall opposite. I don't care what they say, you're never too old to wake up to the sight of a beautiful woman.

I stayed in bed for ten minutes, hoping that the memory of my talking to a ghost might fade like a dream, but it didn't, so I got up and had a shower. It was an important day that day and I had to be sharp.

The Metropolitan Police Service is still, despite what people think, a working-class organization and as such rejects totally the notion of an officer class. That is why every newly minted constable, regardless of educational background, has to spend a two-year probationary period as an ordinary plod on the streets. This is because nothing builds character like being abused, spat at and vomited on by members of the public.

Toward the end of your probation you start applying for positions in the various branches, directorates and operational command units that make up the force. Most probationers will continue on as full uniformed constables in one of the borough commands, and the Met hierarchy likes to stress that deciding to remain a uniformed constable doing vital work on the streets of London is a positive choice in and of itself. Somebody has to be abused, spat at and vomited on, and I for one applaud the brave men and women who are willing to step up and serve in that role.

This had been the noble calling of my shift commander, Inspector Francis Neblett. He had joined the Met back in the time of the dinosaurs, risen rapidly to the rank of Inspector and then spent the next thirty years, quite happily, in the same position. He was a stolid man with lank brown hair and a face that looked like it had been struck with the flat end of a shovel. Neblett was old-fashioned enough to wear a uniform tunic over his regulation white shirt, even when out patrolling with "his lads."

I was scheduled to have an interview with him today where we would "discuss" my future career prospects. Theoretically this was part of an integrated career development process that would lead to positive outcomes with regards to both the police service and myself. After this discussion a final decision as to my future disposition would be made. I strongly suspected that what I wanted to do didn't enter into it.

Leslie, looking unreasonably fresh, met me in the squalid kitchenette shared by all the residents on my floor. There was aspirin in one of the cupboards; one thing you can always be certain of in a police section house is that there will always be aspirin. I took a couple and gulped water from the tap.

"Mr. Headless has a name," she said while I made coffee. "William Skirmish, media type, lives up in Highgate."

"Are they saying anything else?"

"Just the usual," said Leslie. "Senseless killing, blah, blah. Inner-city violence what is London coming to. Blah."

"Blah," I said.

"What are you doing up before noon?" she asked.

"Got my career progression meeting with Neblett at twelve."

"Good luck with that," she said.

I KNEW it was all going pear-shaped when Inspector Neblett called me by my first name.

"Tell me, Peter," he said, "where do you see your career going?"

I shifted in my chair.

"Well sir," I said. "I was thinking of CID."

"You want to be a detective?" Neblett was, of course, a career "uniform" and thus regarded plainclothes police officers in much the same way as civilians regard tax inspectors. You might, if pressed, concede that they were a necessary evil but you wouldn't actually let your daughter marry one.

"Yes, sir."

"Why limit yourself to CID?" he asked. "Why not one of the specialist units?"

Because you don't, not when you're still on probation, say that you want to be in a Murder Investigation Team and swan around in a big motor while wearing handmade shoes.

"I thought I'd start at the beginning and work my up, sir," I said.

"That's a very sensible attitude," said Neblett.

I suddenly had a horrible thought; what if they were thinking of sending me to Trident. That was the Operational Command Unit charged with tackling gun crime within the black community. Trident was always on the lookout for black officers to do hideously dangerous undercover work and being mixed race meant that I qualified. It's not that I don't think they do a worthwhile job, it's just that I didn't think I'd be very good at it. It's important for a man to know his limitations and my limitations started at moving to Peckham and hanging around with yardies, postcode wannabes and those weird skinny white kids who don't get the irony in Eminem.

"I don't like rap music, sir," I said.

Neblett nodded slowly. "That's useful to know," he said, and I resolved to keep a tighter grip on my mouth.

"Peter," he said. "Over the last two years I've formed a very positive opinion of your intelligence and your capacity for hard work."

"Thank you, sir."

"And then there is your science background."

I have three C-grade A-levels in Maths, Physics and Chemistry; this is only considered a science background outside of the scientific community. It certainly wasn't enough to get me the university place I wanted.

"You're very useful at getting your thoughts down on paper," said Neblett.

I felt a cold lump of disappointment in my stomach. I knew exactly what horrifying assignment the Metropolitan Police had planned for me.

"We want you to consider the Case Progression Unit," said Neblett.

The theory behind the Case Progression Unit is very sound. Police officers, so the established wisdom has it, are drowning in paperwork, suspects have to be logged in, the chain of evidence must never be broken and the politicians' orders as laid out in PACE, the Police and Criminal Evidence Act, must be followed to the letter. The role of the Case Progression Unit is to do the paperwork for the hard-pressed constable so he or she can get back out on the street to be abused, spat at and vomited on. Thus will there be a bobby on the beat and thus shall crime be defeated and the good *Daily Mail*–reading citizens of our fair nation shall live in peace.

The truth is that the paperwork is not that onerous—any half-competent temp would dispose of it in less than an hour and still have time to do his nails. The problem is that police work is all about "face" and "presence" and remembering what a suspect said one day so you can catch them in a lie on the next. It's about going toward the scream, staying calm and being the one who opens a suspect package. It's not that you can't do both, it's just that it's not exactly common. What Neblett was saying to me was that I wasn't a real copper, not a thief taker, but I might play a valuable role freeing up real coppers. I could tell with a sick certainty that those very words—"valuable role"—were rushing toward the conversation.

"I was hoping for something a bit more proactive, sir," I said.

"This would be proactive," said Neblett. "You'd be performing a valuable role."

POLICE OFFICERS, as a rule, don't need an excuse to go to the pub, but one of the many nonexcuses they have is the traditional end-of-probation booze-up, when members of the shift get the brand new full constables completely hammered. To that end, Leslie and I were dragged across the Strand to the Roosevelt Toad and plied with alcohol until we were horizontal. That was the theory anyway.

"How did it go?" Leslie asked over the roar of the pub.

"Badly," I shouted back. "Case Progression Unit."

Leslie pulled a face.

"What about you?"

"I don't want to tell you," she said. "It'll piss you off."

"Hit me," I said. "I can take it."

"I've been temporarily assigned to the Murder Team," she said.

I'd never heard of that happening before. "As a detective?"

"As a uniformed constable in plainclothes," she said. "It's a big case and they need bodies."

She was right. It did piss me off.

The evening went sour after that. I stuck it out for a couple of hours, but I hate self-pity, especially mine, so I went out and did the next best thing to sticking my head into a bucket of cold water.

Unfortunately, it had stopped raining while we were in the pub, so I settled for letting the freezing air sober me up.

Leslie caught up with me twenty minutes later.

"Put your bloody coat on," she said. "You'll catch your death."

"Is it cold?" I asked.

"I knew you'd be upset," she said.

I put my coat on. "Have you told the tribe yet?" I asked. In addition to her mum, her dad and nan, Leslie had five older sisters, all still resident within a hundred meters of the family home in Brightlingsea. I'd met them once or twice when they'd descended onto London en masse for a shopping expedition. They were loud to the point of constituting a one-family breach of the peace and would have merited a police escort if they hadn't already had one, i.e., Leslie and me.

"This afternoon," she said. "They were well pleased. Even Tanya and she doesn't even know what it means. Have you told yours yet?"

"Tell them what?" I asked. "That I work in an office?"

"Nothing wrong with working in an office."

"I just want to be a copper," I said.

"I know," said Leslie. "But why?"

"Because I want to help the community," I said. "Catch bad guys."

"Not the shiny buttons, then?" she asked. "Or the chance to slap the cuffs on and say 'You're nicked, my son.' "

"Maintain the Queen's Peace," I said. "Bring order out of chaos."

She shook her head sadly. "What makes you think there's any order?" she said. "And you've been out on patrol on a Saturday night. Does that look like the Queen's Peace?"

I went to lean nonchalantly against a lamppost, but it went wrong and I staggered around a bit. Leslie found this much funnier than I thought it really deserved. She sat down on the step of the Waterstone's bookshop to catch her breath.

"Okay," I said. "Why are you in the job?"

"Because I'm really good at it," said Leslie.

"You're not that good a copper," I said.

"Yes I am," she said. "Let's be honest, I'm bloody amazing as a copper."

"And what am I?"

"Too easily distracted."

"I am not."

"New Year's Eve, Trafalgar Square, big crowd, bunch of total wankers pissing in the fountain—remember that?" asked Leslie. "Wheels come off, wankers get stroppy and what were you doing?"

"I was only gone for a couple of seconds," I said.

"You were checking what was written on the lion's bum," said Leslie. "I was wrestling a couple of drunken chavs and you were doing historical research."

"Do you want to know what was on the lion's bum?" I asked.

"No," said Leslie. "I don't want to know what was written on the lion's bum, or how siphoning works or why one side of Floral Street is a hundred years older than the other side."

"You don't think any of that's interesting?"

"Not when I'm wrestling chavs, catching car thieves or attending a fatal accident," said Leslie. "I like you, I think you're a good man, but it's like you don't see the world the way a copper needs to see the world—it's like you're seeing stuff that isn't there."

"Like what?"

"I don't know," said Leslie. "I can't see stuff that isn't there."

"Seeing stuff that isn't there can be a useful skill for a copper," I said.

Leslie snorted.

"It's true," I said. "Last night, while you were distracted by your caffeine dependency, I met an eyewitness who wasn't there."

"Wasn't there," said Leslie.

"How can you have an eyewitness who wasn't there? I hear you ask."

"I'm asking," said Leslie.

"When your eyewitness is a ghost," I said.

Leslie stared at me for a moment. "I would have gone with the CCTV camera controller myself," she said.

"What?"

"Guy watching the murder on CCTV," said Leslie. "He'd be a witness who wasn't there. But I like the ghost thing."

"I interviewed a ghost," I said.

"Bollocks," said Leslie.

So I told her about Nicholas Wallpenny and the murdering gent who turned back, changed his clothes and then knocked poor . . . "What was the victim's name again?" I asked.

"William Skirmish," said Leslie. "It was on the news."

"Knocked poor William Skirmish's head clean off his shoulders."

"That wasn't on the news," said Leslie.

"The murder team will want to keep that back," I said. "For witness verification."

"The witness in question being a ghost?" asked Leslie.

"Yes."

Leslie got to her feet, swayed a bit and then got her eyes focused again. "Do you think he's still there?" she asked.

The cold air was beginning to sober me at last. "Who?"

"Your ghost," she said. "Nicholas Nickleby. Do you think he might be still at the crime scene."

"How should I know," I said. "I don't even believe in ghosts."

"Let's go see if he's there," she said. "If I see him too then it will be like corob . . . like crob . . . proof."

"Okay," I said.

We wandered arm in arm up King Street toward Covent Garden.

There was a great absence of Nicholas the ghost that night. We started at the church portico where I'd seen him and, because Leslie was a thoroughgoing copper even when drunk, did a methodical search around the perimeter.

"Chips," said Leslie after our second circuit. "Or a kebab."

"Maybe he doesn't come out when I'm with someone else," I said.

"Maybe he does shift work," said Leslie.

"Fuck it," I said. "Let's have a kebab."

"You'll be good at the Case Progression Unit," said Leslie. "And you'll be . . ."

"If you say '. . . making a valuable contribution' I will not be held responsible for my actions."

"I was going to say 'making a difference,' " she said. "You could always go to the States; I bet the FBI would have you."

"Why would the FBI have me?" I asked.

"They could use you as an Obama decoy," she said.

"For that," I said, "you can pay for the kebabs."

IN THE end, we were too knackered to get kebabs, so we headed straight back to the section house, where Leslie utterly failed to invite me to her room. I was at that stage of drunk where you lie on your bed in the dark, the room goes whirling around you and you're wondering about the nature of the universe and whether you can get to the sink before you throw up.

Tomorrow was my last day off, and unless I could prove that seeing things that weren't there was a vital skill for the modern police officer, it was hello Case Progression Unit for me.

"I'M SORRY about last night," said Leslie.

Neither of us could face the horrors of the kitchenette that morning, so we found shelter in the station canteen. Despite the fact that the catering staff were a mixture of compact Polish women and skinny Somali men, a strange kind of institutional inertia meant that the food was classic English greasy spoon, the coffee was bad and the tea was hot, sweet and came in mugs. Leslie was having a full English breakfast; I was having a tea.

"It's all right," I said. "Your loss, not mine."

"Not that," said Leslie and smacked me on the hand with the flat of her knife. "What I said about you being a copper."

"Don't worry," I said. "I've taken your feedback on board and having extensively workshopped it this morning, I now feel that I can pursue my core career development goals in a diligent, proactive, but, above all, creative manner."

"What are you planning to do?"

"I'm going to hack HOLMES and see if my ghost was right," I said.

EVERY POLICE station in the country has at least one HOLMES suite. This is the Home Office Large Major Inquiry System, which allows computer illiterate coppers to join the late twentieth century. Getting them to join the twenty-first century would be too much to ask for.

Everything related to a major investigation is kept on the system, allowing detectives to cross-reference data and avoid the kind of cock-up that made the hunt for the Yorkshire Ripper such an exemplary operation. The replacement to the old system was due to be called SHERLOCK but nobody could find the words to make the acronym work, so they called it HOLMES 2.

Theoretically, you can access HOLMES from a laptop, but the Metropolitan Police likes to keep its personnel tied to fixed terminals—which can't be left in trains or sold to pawnshops. When a major investigation occurs, the terminals can be transferred from the suite to incident rooms elsewhere in the station. Leslie and I could have sneaked into the HOLMES suite and risked being caught, but I preferred to plug my laptop into a LAN socket in one of the empty incident rooms and work in safety and comfort.

I'd been sent on a HOLMES familiarization course three months earlier. At the time I'd been excited because I thought they might be preparing me for a role in major investigations, but now I realize they were grooming me for data entry work. It took me less than half an hour to find the Covent Garden investigation. People are often negligent about passwords and Inspector Neblett had used his youngest daughter's name and year of birth, which is just criminal; it also got me read-only access to the files we wanted.

The old system couldn't handle big data files, but because HOLMES was only ten years behind the state of the art, detectives could now attach evidence photographs, document scans and even CCTV footage directly to what's called a "nominal record" file. It's like YouTube for cops.

The Murder Team assigned to the William Skirmish murder had wasted no time grabbing the CCTV footage and seeing if they could get a look at the murderer. It was a big fat file and I went straight for it.

According to the report, the camera was mounted on the corner of James Street looking west. It was low quality, low light footage updated at one frame per second. But despite the poor light it clearly showed William Skirmish walking from under the camera toward Henrietta Street.

"There's our suspect," said Leslie, pointing.

The screen showed another figure, the best you could say was probably male, probably in jeans and a leather jacket, walk past William Skirmish and vanish below the screen. According to the notes this figure was being designated WITNESS A.

A third figure appeared going away from the camera—I hit pause.

"Doesn't look like the same guy," said Leslie.

Definitely not. This man was wearing what looked like a smurf hat and what I recognized as an Edwardian smoking jacket—don't ask me why I know what an Edwardian smoking jacket looks like; let's just say it has something to do with Doctor Who and leave it at that. Nicholas had said it was red but the CCTV image was in black and white. I clicked back a couple of frames and then forward again. The first figure, WITNESS A, dropped out of shot one, two frames before the man in the smurf hat stepped into view.

"That's two seconds to get changed," said Leslie. "That's not humanly possible."

I clicked forward. The man in the smurf hat produced his bat and stepped smartly up behind William Skirmish. The windup was between frames but the hit was clear. In the next frame Skirmish's body was halfway to the ground and a little dark blob, which we decided must be the head, was just visible by the portico.

"My God. He really did knock his head clean off," said Leslie.

Just as Nicholas had said he had.

"Now, that," I said, "is not humanly possible."

"You've seen a head come off before," said Leslie. "I was there, remember?"

"That was a car accident," I said. "That's two tons of metal, not a bat."

"Yeah," said Leslie, tapping the screen. "But there it is."

"There's something wrong here."

"Apart from the horrible murder?"

I clicked back to where Smurf Hat entered the scene. "Can you see a bat?"

"No," said Leslie. "Both his hands are visible. Maybe it's on his back."

I clicked forward; in the third frame, the bat appeared in Smurf Hat's hands as if by magic, but that could just have been an artifact of the one-second lag between frames. There was something else wrong with it too.

"That's much too big to be a baseball bat," I said.

The bat was at least two-thirds as long as the man who carried it. I clicked backward and forward a few times, but I couldn't work out where he was keeping it.

"Maybe he likes to speak really quietly," said Leslie.

"Where do you even buy a bat that size?"

"The Big Bat Shop," said Leslie. "Bats R Us?"

"Let's see if we can get a look at his face," I said.

"Plus Size Bats," said Leslie.

I ignored her and clicked forward. The murder took less than three seconds, three frames; one the windup, two the blow and three the follow-through. The next frame caught Smurf Hat mid-turn, his face in three-quarter profile showing a jutting chin and a prominent hook nose. The frame after showed Smurf Hat walking back the way he'd come, slower than the approach, casual as far as I could tell from the stuttering image. The bat vanished two frames after the murder—again I couldn't see where it had gone.

I wondered if we could enhance the faces and started looking for a graphic function I could use.

"Idiot," said Leslie. "Murder Team will be all over that."

She was right; connected to the footage were links to enhanced pictures of William Skirmish, WITNESS A and the murdering gent in the smurf hat. Contrary to television, there's an absolute limit to how good a close-up you can extrapolate from an old-fashioned bit of videotape. It doesn't matter if it's digital—if the information isn't there, it isn't there. Still, someone at the tech lab had done their best and despite all the faces being blurry, it was at least obvious that all three were different people.

"He's wearing a mask," I said.

"Now you're getting desperate," said Leslie.

"Look at that chin and that nose," I said. "Nobody has a face like that."

Leslie pointed to a notation attached to the image. "Looks like the Murder Team agree with you." There was a list of "actions" associated with the evidence file, one of which was to check local costumiers, theaters and fancy dress shops for masks. It had a very low priority.

"Aha!" I said. "So it might be the same person."

"Who can change their clothes in less than two seconds?" asked Leslie. "Do me a favor."

All the evidence files are linked so I checked to see whether the Murder Team had managed to track WITNESS A as he left the crime scene. They hadn't and, according to the action list, finding him had become a priority. I predicted a press conference and an appeal for witnesses—*police are particularly interested in talking to . . .* would be the relevant phrase there.

Smurf Hat had been tracked all the way down New Row, exactly the route Nicholas had said he'd taken, but vanished off the surveillance grid in St. Martin's Lane. According to the "action" list, half the Murder Team were currently scouring the surrounding streets for potential witnesses and clues.

"No," said Leslie, reading my mind.

"Nicholas . . ."

"Nicholas the ghost," said Leslie.

"Nicholas the corporally challenged," I said, "was right about the murderer's approach, the method of attack and cause of death. He was also right about the getaway route and we don't have a time line where WITNESS A is visible at the same time as Smurf Hat."

"Smurf Hat?"

"The murder suspect," I said. "I need to take this to the Murder Team."

"What are you going to say to the SIO?" asked Leslie. "I met a ghost and he said that WITNESS A put on a mask and did it?"

"No, I'm going to say that I was approached by a potential witness who, despite leaving the scene before I could get his name and address, generated potentially interesting leads that may further the successful outcome of the investigation."

It made Leslie pause at least. "And you think that'll get you out of the Case Progression Unit?"

"It's got to be worth a try," I said.

"It's not enough," said Leslie. "One: they're already generating leads over WITNESS A, including the possibility that he was wearing a mask. Two: you could have got all that information from the video."

"They won't know I had access to the video."

"Peter," said Leslie. "It shows someone's head being knocked off. It's going to be all over the Internet by the end of the day and that's if it's not on the ten o'clock news."

"Then I'll generate more leads," I said.

"You're going to go looking for your ghost?"

"Want to come?"

"No," said Leslie. "Because tomorrow is the most important day of the rest of my career and I am going to bed early with a cocoa and a copy of Blackstone's *Police Investigator's Workbook*."

"Just as well," I said. "I think you scared him away last night anyway."

*   *   *

Equipment for ghost-hunters: thermal underwear, very important; warm coat; thermos flask; patience; ghost.

It did occur to me quite early on that this was possibly the most absurd thing I'd ever done. I took up my first position, sitting at an outdoor table of a café, around ten and waited for the crowds to thin out. Once the café closed, I sauntered over to the church portico and waited.

It was another freezing night, which meant that the drunks leaving the pubs were too cold to assault each other. At one point a hen party went past, a dozen women in oversized pink T-shirts, bunny ears and high heels. Their pale legs were blotchy with the cold. One of them spotted me.

"You'd better go home," she called. "He's not coming."

Her mates shrieked with laughter. I heard one of them complaining that "All the good-looking ones are gay."

Which was what I was thinking when I saw the man watching me from the across the Piazza. What with the proliferation of gay pubs, clubs and chat rooms it is no longer necessary for the single man about town to frequent public toilets and graveyards on freezing nights to meet the man of their immediate needs. Still, some people like to risk frostbite on their nether regions—don't ask me why.

He was about one eighty in height, that's six foot in old money, and dressed in a beautifully tailored suit that emphasized the width of his shoulders and a trim waist. I thought early forties with long, finely boned features and brown hair cut into an old-fashioned side parting. It was hard to tell in the sodium light but I thought his eyes were gray. He carried a silver-topped cane and I knew without looking that his shoes were handmade. All he needed was a slightly ethnic younger boyfriend and I'd have had to call the cliché police.

When he strolled over to talk to me, I thought he might be looking for that slightly ethnic boyfriend after all.

"Hello," he said. He had a proper upper-class accent, like an English villain in a Hollywood movie. "What are you up to?"

I thought I'd try the truth. "I'm ghost-hunting," I said.

"Interesting," he said. "Any particular ghost?"

"Nicholas Wallpenny," I said.

"What's your name and address?" he asked.

No Londoner ever answers that question unchallenged. "I beg your pardon?"

He reached into his jacket and pulled out his wallet. "Detective Chief Inspector Thomas Nightingale," he said and showed me his warrant card.

"Constable Peter Grant," I said.

"Out of Charing Cross nick?"

"Yes, sir."

He gave me a strange smile.

"Carry on, Constable," he said and went strolling back up James Street.

So there I was, having just told a senior Detective Chief Inspector that I was hunting ghosts, which, if he believed me, meant he thought I was bonkers or, if he didn't believe me, meant he thought I was cruising and looking to perpetrate an obscene act contrary to public order.

And the ghost that I was looking for had failed to make an appearance.

Have you ever run away from home? I have on two occasions. The first time, when I was nine, I only got as far as the Argos on Camden Town High Street and the second time, when I was fourteen, I made it all the way to Euston Station and was actually standing in front of the departure boards when I stopped. On both occasions I wasn't rescued or found, or brought back; indeed when I returned home I don't think my mum had noticed I'd gone. I *know* my dad didn't.

Both adventures ended the same way—with my realization that in the end, no matter what, I was going to have to go home. For my nine-year-old self, it was the knowledge that the Argos store represented the outer limit of my understanding of the world. Beyond that point was a tube station and a big building with statues of cats, and farther on more roads and bus journeys that led to downstairs clubs that were sad and empty and smelled of beer.

My fourteen-year-old self was more rational. I didn't know anyone in these cities on the departure boards and I doubted they would be any more welcoming than London. I probably didn't even have enough money to get me farther than Potters Bar and even if I did stow away for free, what was I going to eat? Realistically, I had three meals' worth of cash on me and then it would be back home to Mum and Dad. Anything I did short of getting back on the bus and going home was merely postponing the inevitable moment of my return.

I had that same realization in Covent Garden at three o'clock in the morning. That same collapse of potential futures down to a singularity, a future that I couldn't escape. I wasn't going to drive a fancy motor and say "You're nicked." I was going to work in the Case Progression Unit and make a "valuable" contribution.

I stood up and started walking back to the nick.

In the distance I thought I could hear someone laughing at me.

CHAPTER 2

Ghost Hunting Dog

THE NEXT morning Leslie asked me how the ghost hunting had gone. We were loitering in front of Neblett's office, the place from whence the fatal blow would fall. We weren't required to be there, but neither of us wanted to prolong the agony.

"There are worse things than the Case Progression Unit," I said.

We both thought about that for a moment.

"Traffic," said Leslie. "That's worse than the CPU."

"You get to drive nice motors though," I said. "BMW Five, Mercedes M Class."

"You know, Peter, you really are quite a shallow person," said Leslie.

I was going to protest, but Neblett emerged from his office. He didn't seem surprised to see us. He handed a letter to Leslie, who seemed curiously reluctant to open it.

"They're waiting for you at Belgravia," said Neblett. "Off you go." Belgravia is where the Westminster Murder Team is based. Leslie gave me a nervous little wave, turned and skipped off down the corridor.

"There goes a proper thief taker," said Neblett. He looked at me and frowned.

"Whereas you," he said, "I don't know what you are."

"Proactively making a valuable contribution, sir," I said.

"Cheeky bugger is what you are," said Neblett. He handed

me not an envelope, but a slip of paper. "You're going to be working with a Chief Inspector Thomas Nightingale." The slip had the name and address of a Japanese restaurant on New Row.

"Who am I working for?" I asked.

"Economic and Specialist Crime as far as I know," said Neblett. "They want you in plainclothes, so you'd better get a move on."

Economic and Specialist Crime was an admin basket for a load of specialist units, everything from Arts and Antiques to immigration and computer crime. The important thing was that the Case Progression Unit wasn't one of them. I left in a hurry before he could change his mind, but I want to make it clear that at no point did I break into a skip.

NEW ROW was a narrow pedestrianized street through Covent Garden, with a Tesco's at one end and the theaters of St. Martin's Lane at the other. Tokyo A Go Go was a bentō place halfway down, sandwiched between a private gallery and a shop that sold sporting gear for girls. The interior was long and barely wide enough for two rows of tables, sparsely decorated in minimalist Japanese fashion—polished wooden floors, tables and chairs of lacquered wood, lots of right angles and rice paper.

I spotted Nightingale at a back table, eating out of a black lacquered bentō box. He stood when he saw me and shook my hand. Once I'd settled myself opposite, he asked if I was hungry. I said no, thank you. I was nervous and I make it a rule never to put cold rice into an agitated stomach. He ordered tea and asked if I minded if he continued eating.

I said not at all and he returned to spearing food out of his bentō with quick jabs of his chopsticks.

"Did he come back?" asked Nightingale.

"Who?"

"Your ghost," said Nightingale. "Nicholas Wallpenny: lurker, bug hunter and sneak thief. Late of the parish of St. Giles. Can you hazard a guess to where he's buried?"

"In the cemetery of the Actors' Church?"

"Very good," Nightingale said and grabbed a duck wrap with a quick stab of his chopsticks. "So did he come back?"

"No, he didn't," I said.

"Ghosts are capricious," he said. "They really don't make reliable witnesses."

"Are you telling me ghosts are real?"

Nightingale carefully wiped his lips with a napkin.

"You've spoken to one," he said. "What do you think?"

"I'm awaiting confirmation from a senior officer," I said.

He put the napkin down and picked up his teacup. "Ghosts are real." He took a sip.

I stared at him. I didn't believe in ghosts, or fairies or gods and for the last couple of days I'd been like a man watching a magic show—I'd expected a magician to step out from behind the curtain and ask me to pick a card, any card. I wasn't ready to believe in ghosts, but that's the thing about empirical experience: it's the real thing.

And if ghosts were real?

"Is this where you tell me that there's a secret branch of the Met whose task it is to tackle ghosts, ghouls, faeries, demons, witches and warlocks, elves and goblins . . ." I said. "You can stop me before I run out of supernatural creatures."

"You haven't even scratched the surface," said Nightingale.

"Aliens?" I had to ask.

"Not yet."

"And the secret branch of the Met?"

"Just me, I'm afraid," he said.

"And you want me to what . . . join?"

"Help," said Nightingale. "With this inquiry."

"You think there's something supernatural about the murder?" I asked.

"Why don't you tell me what your witness had to say," he said. "And then we'll see where it goes."

So I told him about Nicholas and the change of clothes by the murdering gent. About the CCTV coverage and that the Murder Team thought it was two separate people. When I'd finished he signaled the waitress for the bill.

"I wish I'd known this yesterday," he said. "But we still might be able to pick up a trace."

"A trace of what, sir?" I asked.

"The uncanny," said Nightingale. "It always leaves a trace."

NIGHTINGALE'S MOTOR was a Jag, a genuine Mark 2 with the 3.8 liter XK6 engine. My dad would have sold his trumpet for a chance to own a car like that and that was back in the sixties when that still meant something. It wasn't pristine, there were some dings on the bodywork, a nasty scratch on the driver's-side door and the leather on the seats was beginning to crack, but when Nightingale turned the key in the ignition and the V6 rumbled, it was perfect where it counted.

"You took sciences at A-level," said Nightingale as we pulled out. "Why didn't you take a science degree?"

"I got distracted, sir," I said. "My grades were low and I couldn't get on the course that I wanted."

"Really. What was the distraction?" he asked. "Music perhaps. Did you start a band?"

"No, sir," I said. "Nothing that interesting."

We headed down through Trafalgar Square and took advantage of the discreet Metropolitan Police flash on the windscreen to cut through the Mall, past Buckingham Palace and into Victoria. I knew there were only two places where we might be going: Belgravia nick, where the Murder Team had their incident room, or Westminster Mortuary, where the body was stashed. I hoped it was the incident room, but of course it was the mortuary.

"But you understand the scientific method though?" asked Nightingale.

"Yes, sir," I said, and thought Bacon, Descartes and Newton—check. Observation, hypothesis, experiment and something else that I could look up when I got back to my laptop.

"Good," said Nightingale. "Because I need someone with some objectivity."

Definitely the morgue, then, I thought.

*   *   *

ITS OFFICIAL name is the Iain West Forensic Suite and it
represents the Home Office's best attempt to make one of its
mortuaries look as cool as the ones in American TV shows.
In order to keep filthy policemen from contaminating any
trace evidence on the body there was a special viewing area
with live autopsies piped in by closed-circuit television. This
had the effect of reducing even the most grisly postmortem
to nothing more than a gruesome TV documentary. I was all
for that, but Nightingale, on the other hand, said that we
needed to be close to the corpse.

"Why?" I asked.

"Because there are other senses than sight," said Nightingale.

"Are we talking ESP here?"

"Just keep an open mind," said Nightingale.

The staff made us don clean suits and masks before letting
us near the slab. We weren't relatives so they didn't bother
with a discreet cloth to cover the gap between the body's
shoulders and his head. I was so glad that I'd skipped bentō
that morning.

I guessed William Skirmish had been an unremarkable
man when he was alive. Middle-aged, just over average height,
his muscle tone was flabby, but he wasn't fat. I found it surprisingly easy to look at the detached head with its ragged
edge of torn skin and muscle instead of a neck. People assume that, as a police officer, your first dead person will be a
murder victim, but the truth is that it's usually the result of a
car accident. My first had been on day two when a cycle
courier had had his head knocked off by a transit van. After
that you don't exactly get used to it, but you do know that it
could be a lot worse. I wasn't exactly enjoying the headless
Mr. Skirmish, but I had to admit it was less intimidating than
I'd imagined it.

Nightingale bent over the body and practically stuck his
face into the severed neck. He shook his head and turned to
me. "Help me turn him over," he said.

I didn't want to touch the body, not even with surgical
gloves on, but I couldn't bottle out now. The body was

heavier than I was expecting, cold and inert as it flopped onto its belly. I quickly stepped away, but Nightingale beckoned me over.

"I want you to get your face as close to his neck as possible, close your eyes and tell me what you feel," said Nightingale.

I hesitated.

"I promise it will become clear," he said.

The mask and eye protectors helped since there was no chance of me accidentally kissing the dead guy. I did as I was told and closed my eyes. At first there was just the smell of disinfectant, stainless steel and freshly washed skin, but after a few moments I became aware of something else, a scratchy, wiry, panting, wet nose, wagging sensation.

"Well?" asked Nightingale.

"A dog," I said. "A little yappy dog."

Growling, barking, yelling, flashes of cobbles, sticks, laughing, maniacal high-pitched laughing.

I stood up sharply.

"Violence and laughter?" asked Nightingale. I nodded.

"What was that?" I asked.

"The uncanny," said Nightingale. "It's like a bright light; when you close your eyes it leaves an afterimage. We call it *vestigium*."

"How do I know I didn't just imagine it?" I asked.

"Experience," said Nightingale. "You learn to distinguish the difference through experience."

Thankfully we turned our back on the body and left.

"I barely felt anything," I said while we were changing. "Is it always that weak?"

"That body's been on ice for two days," said Nightingale. "And dead bodies don't retain *vestigia* very well."

"So whatever caused it must have been very strong," I said.

"Quite," said Nightingale. "Therefore we have to assume that the dog is very important and we have to find out why."

"Maybe Mr. Skirmish had a dog?" I said.

"Yes," said Nightingale. "Let's start there."

We'd changed and were on our way out of the mortuary when fate caught up with us.

"I heard rumors there was a nasty smell in the building," said a voice behind us. "And bugger me if it isn't true."

We stopped and turned.

Detective Chief Inspector Alexander Seawoll was a big man, coming in a shade under two meters, barrel-chested, beer-bellied and with a voice that could make the windows shake. He was from Yorkshire or somewhere like that and, like many Northerners with issues, he'd moved to London as a cheap alternative to psychotherapy. I knew him by reputation and the reputation was don't fuck with him under any circumstances. He bore down the corridor toward us like a bull on steroids and as he did I had to fight the urge to hide behind Nightingale.

"This is my fucking investigation, Nightingale," said Seawoll. "I don't care who you're currently fucking, I don't want any of your X-files shit getting in the way of proper police work."

"I can assure you, Inspector," said Nightingale. "I have no intention of getting in your way."

Seawoll turned to look at me. "Who the hell is this?"

"This is PC Peter Grant," said Nightingale. "He's working with me."

I could see this shocked Seawoll. He looked at me carefully before turning back to Nightingale. "You're taking on an apprentice?" he asked.

"That's yet to be decided," said Nightingale.

"We'll see about that," said Seawoll. "There was an agreement."

"There was an arrangement," said Nightingale. "Circumstances change."

"Not that fucking much they don't," said Seawoll, but it seemed to me he'd lost some of his conviction. He looked down at me again. "Take my advice, son," he said quietly. "Get the fuck away from this man while you still have a chance."

"Is that all?" asked Nightingale.

"Just stay the hell away from my investigation," said Seawoll.

"I go where I'm needed," said Nightingale. "That's the agreement."

"Circumstances can *fucking* change," said Seawoll. "Now, if you gentlemen don't mind, I'm late for my colonic irrigation."

He went back up the corridor, crashed through the double doors and was gone.

"What's the agreement?" I asked.

"It's not important," said Nightingale. "Let's go and see if we can't find this dog."

THE NORTH end of the London Borough of Camden is dominated by two hills, Hampstead on the west, Highgate on the east, with the Heath, one of the largest parks in London, slung between them like a green saddle. From these heights the land slopes down toward the River Thames and the floodplains that lurk below the built-up center of London.

Dartmouth Park, where William Skirmish had lived, was on the lower slopes of Highgate Hill and within easy walking distance of the Heath. He'd had the ground floor flat of a converted Victorian terrace, the corner house of a tree-lined street that had been traffic calmed within an inch of its life.

Farther downhill was Kentish Town, Leighton Road and the estate where I grew up. Some of my schoolmates had lived around the corner from Skirmish's flat, so I knew the area well.

I spotted a face in a first-floor window as we showed our cards to the uniform guarding the door. As in many converted terraces, a once-elegant hallway had been walled off with plasterboard, making it cramped and lightless. Two additional front doors had been jammed side by side into the space at the end. The door on the right was half-open, but symbolically blocked with police tape; the other presumably belonged to the flat with the twitching curtains upstairs.

Skirmish's flat was neat and furnished in the patchwork of styles that ordinary people, the ones not driven by aspirational demons, choose for their homes. Fewer bookcases than I would have expected from a media type, many photographs, but the ones of children were all black-and-white or the faded color of old Instamatic film.

"A life of quiet desperation," said Nightingale. I knew it was a quote but I wasn't going to give him the satisfaction of asking who'd said it.

Chief Inspector Seawoll, whatever else he was, was no fool. We could tell that his Murder Team had done a thorough job; there were smudges of fingerprint powder on the phone, the door handles and frames, books had been pulled off bookcases and then put back upside down. The last seemed to annoy Nightingale more than was strictly appropriate. "It's just care-lessness," he said. Drawers had been pulled out, searched and then left slightly open to mark their status. Anything worthy of note would have been noted and logged into HOLMES, probably by poor suckers like Leslie, but the Murder Team didn't know about my psychic powers and the *vestigium* of the bark-ing dog.

And there was a dog. That or Skirmish had a taste for PAL Meaty Chunks in Gravy and I didn't think his quiet life had been quite *that* desperate.

I called Leslie on her mobile.

"Are you near a HOLMES terminal?" I asked.

"I haven't left the bloody thing since I got here," said Leslie. "They've had me on data entry and bloody statement verification."

"Really," I said, trying not to gloat. "Guess where I am?"

"You're at Skirmish's flat in Dartmouth bloody Park," she said.

"How do you know that?"

"Because I can hear DCI Seawoll yelling about it right through his office wall," she said. "Who's Inspector Nightin-gale?"

I glanced at Nightingale, who was looking at me impa-tiently. "I'll tell you later," I said. "Can you check something for us?"

"Sure," said Leslie. "What is it?"

"When the Murder Team tossed the flat—did they find a dog?"

I heard her tapping away as she did a text search on the relevant files. "No mention of a dog in the report."

"Thanks," I said. "You've made a valuable contribution."

"You're so buying the drinks tonight," she said and hung up.

I told Nightingale about the absence of dog.

"Let's go find a nosy neighbor," said Nightingale. He'd obviously seen the face in the window too.

Beside the front door, an intercom system had been retrofitted above the doorbells. Nightingale barely had time to press the button before the lock buzzed open and a voice said, "Come on up, dear." There was another buzz and the inner door opened, behind a dusty but otherwise clean staircase that led upward, and as we started up we heard a small yappy dog start barking. The lady who met us at the top did not have blue-rinsed hair; actually, I'm not sure what blue-rinsed hair would look like and why did anyone think blue hair was a good idea in the first place? Nor did she have fingerless mittens or too many cats, but there was something about her that suggested that both could be serious lifestyle choices in the future. She was also quite tall for a little old lady, spry and not even slightly senile. She gave her name as Mrs. Shirley Palmarron.

We were quickly ushered into a living room that had last been seriously refurnished in the 1970s and offered tea and biscuits. While she bustled in the kitchen the dog, a short-haired white-and-brown mongrel terrier, wagged its tail and barked nonstop. The dog obviously didn't know which of us it regarded as a greater threat, so it swung its head from one side to the other, barking continuously until Nightingale pointed his finger at it and muttered something under his breath. The dog immediately rolled over, closed its eyes and went to sleep.

I looked at Nightingale, but he just raised his eyebrow.

"Has Toby gone to sleep?" asked Mrs. Palmarron when she returned with a tea tray. Nightingale jumped to his feet and helped her settle it on the coffee table; he waited until our host had sat down before returning to his seat.

Toby kicked his feet and growled in his sleep. Obviously nothing short of death was going to keep this dog quiet.

"Such a noisy thing, isn't he," said Mrs. Palmarron as she poured the tea.

Now that Toby was relatively quiet I had a chance to notice that there was a lack of dogness about Mrs. Palmarron's flat. There were photographs of, presumably, Mr. Palmarron and their children on her mantelpiece, but no chintz or doilies. No dog basket by the fireplace and no hair ground into the corners of the sofa. I got out my notebook and pen.

"Is he yours?" I asked.

"Lord no," said Mrs. Palmarron. "He belonged to poor Mr. Skirmish, but I've been looking after him for a little while now. He's not a bad chap when you get used to him."

"He's been here from before Mr. Skirmish's death?" asked Nightingale.

"Oh yes," said Mrs. Palmarron with relish. "You see, Toby's a fugitive from justice, he's 'on the lam.' "

"What was his crime?" asked Nightingale.

"He's wanted for a serious assault," said Mrs. Palmarron. "He bit a man. Right on his nose. The police were called and everything." She looked down at where Toby was chasing rats in his sleep. "If I hadn't let you hole up here, it would be the pokey for you, my lad," she said. "And then the needle."

I CALLED Kentish Town nick, who put me through to Hampstead nick, who told me that, yes, there had been a call out to a dog attack on Hampstead Heath just before Christmas, but the victim had failed to press charges and that was all there was in the report. They gave me the name and address of the victim: Brandon Coopertown, Downshire Hill, Hampstead.

"You put a spell on the dog," I said as we left the house.

"Just a small one," said Nightingale.

"So magic is real," I said. "Which makes you a . . . what?"

"A wizard."

"Like Harry Potter?"

Nightingale sighed. "No," he said. "Not like Harry Potter."

"In what way?"

"I'm not a fictional character," said Nightingale.

We hopped back into the Jag and headed west, skirting the south end of Hampstead Heath before swinging north to climb the hill into Hampstead Proper. This far up the hill was a maze of narrow streets choked with BMWs and Chelsea Tractors. The houses here had seven-figure prices and if there was any quiet desperation here, then it had to be over the things that money couldn't buy.

Nightingale parked the Jag in a residents-only bay and we walked up Downshire Hill looking for the address. It turned out to be one of a row of grand Victorian semidetached mansions set back from the north side of the road. It was a seriously buff house with gothic trim and bay windows, the front garden was professionally cared for and judging from the absence of an intercom, the Coopertowns owned the whole thing.

As we approached the front door we heard an infant crying, the sort of thready measured crying of a baby that was settling in for a good wail and was prepared to keep it up all day if need be. With a house this expensive, I was expecting a nanny or at the very least an au pair, but the woman who opened the door looked too haggard to be either.

August Coopertown was in her late twenties, tall, blond and Danish. We knew about the nationality because she managed to work it into the conversation almost immediately. Before the baby, she'd had a slim boyish figure, but childbirth had widened her hips and put slabs of fat on her thighs. She managed to work that into the conversation pretty quickly as well. As far as August was concerned, all of this was the fault of the English, who had failed to live up to the high standards a well-brought-up Scandinavian woman comes to expect. I don't know why; perhaps Danish hospitals have gyms attached to their maternity units.

She entertained us in her knocked-through living room stroke dining room with blond wood floors and more stripped pine than I really like to see outside of a sauna. Despite her best efforts, the baby had already begun to make inroads into the ruthless cleanliness of the house. A feeding bottle had rolled between the solid oak legs of the sideboard, there was a discarded romper suit balled up on top of the Bang & Olufsen stereo. I smelled stale milk and vomit.

The baby lay in his expensive crib and continued to cry.

Family portraits were hung in a tasteful grouping over the minimalist granite fireplace. Brandon Coopertown was a good-looking older man in his midforties with black hair and narrow features. While Mrs. Coopertown bustled, I surreptitiously took a photograph with my phone camera. "I keep forgetting you can do that," murmured Nightingale.

"Welcome to the twenty-first century," I said. "Sir."

Nightingale rose politely as Mrs. Coopertown bustled back in; this time I was ready and followed him up.

"May I ask what your husband does for a living?" asked Nightingale.

He was a television producer, a successful one, with BAF-TAs and format sales to the United States—which explained the seven-figure house. He could do even better, but his ascension to the higher planes of international production were entirely hampered by the parochial nature of British television. If only the British could stop making programs that catered only to the domestic audience, or even cast actors who were the least bit attractive.

As fascinating as Mrs. Coopertown's observations on the provinciality of British television were, we felt compelled to ask about the incident with the dog.

"That too is typical," said Mrs. Coopertown. "Of course Brandon didn't want to press charges—he's *English*. He didn't want to make a fuss. The policeman should have prosecuted the dog owner regardless. The animal was clearly a danger to the public—it bit poor Brandon right on his nose."

The baby paused and we all held our breath, but he merely burped once and started crying again. I looked at Nightingale and rolled my eyes over at the baby; perhaps he could use the same spell as he had used on Toby. He frowned at me. Maybe there were ethical issues about using it on babies.

According to Mrs. Coopertown, the baby had been perfectly well behaved until the thing with the dog. Now, well now Mrs. Coopertown thought he must be teething or have colic or reflux. Their GP didn't seem to have a clue and was unforgivably short with her; she thought they might be better off going private.

"How did the dog manage to bite your husband on the nose?" I asked.

"What do you mean?" asked Mrs. Coopertown.

"You said your husband was bitten on the nose," I said. "The dog's very small. How did it reach his nose."

"My stupid husband bent down," said Mrs. Coopertown. "We were out for a walk on the Heath, all three of us, when this dog came running up. My husband bent down to pat the dog and snap, with no warning, it had bitten him on the nose. At first I thought it was quite comical, but Brandon started screaming and then that nasty little man ran over and starts yelling 'Oh what are you doing to my poor dog, leave him alone.' "

"The 'nasty little man' being the owner of the dog?" asked Nightingale.

"Nasty little dog, nasty little man," said Mrs. Coopertown.

"Was your husband upset?"

"How can you tell with an Englishman?" asked Mrs. Coopertown. "I went to get something for the blood and when I got back Brandon was laughing—everything is a joke to you people. I had to call the police myself. They came, Brandon showed them his nose and they started laughing. Everyone was happy, even the nasty little dog was happy."

"But you weren't happy?" I asked.

"It's not a question of happy," said Mrs. Coopertown. "If a dog bites a man, what's to stop it from biting a child or a baby."

"May I ask where you were last Tuesday night," asked Nightingale.

"Where I am every night," she said. "Here taking care of my son."

"And where was your husband?"

August Coopertown: annoying yes, blond yes, stupid no. "Why do you want to know?" she asked.

"It's not important," said Nightingale.

"I thought you were here about the dog," she said.

"We are," said Nightingale. "But we'd like to confirm some of the details with your husband."

"Do you think I'm making this up?" asked Mrs. Coopertown. She had the startled rabbit look that civilians get after five minutes of helping the police with their inquiries. If they stay calm for too long, it's a sign that they're professional villains, or foreign or just plain stupid. All of which can get you locked up if you're not careful. If you find yourself talking to the police, my advice is to stay calm but look guilty; it's your safest bet.

"Not at all," said Nightingale. "But since he's the principal victim, we'll need to take his statement."

"He's in Los Angeles," she said. "He's coming home late tonight."

Nightingale left his card and promised Mrs. Coopertown that he, and by extension all right-thinking policemen, took attacks by small yappy dogs very seriously and that they would be in touch.

"What did you sense in there?" asked Nightingale as we walked back to the Jag.

"As in *vestigium*?"

"*Vestigium* is the singular, *vestigia* is the plural," said Nightingale. "Did you sense *vestigia*?"

"To be honest," I said, "nothing. Not even a vestige."

"A wailing child, a desperate mother and an absent father. Not to mention a house of that antiquity," said Nightingale. "There should have been something."

"She seemed a bit of a neat freak to me," I said. "Perhaps she hoovered up all the magic?"

"Something certainly did," said Nightingale. "We'll talk to the husband tomorrow. Let's get back to Covent Garden and see if we can't pick up the trail there."

"It's been three days," I said. "Won't the *vestigia* have worn off?"

"Stone retains *vestigia* very well. That's why old buildings have such character," said Nightingale. "That said, what with

the foot traffic and the area's supernatural components—
certainly won't be easy to trace."

We reached the Jag. "Can animals sense *vestigia*?"

"It depends on the animal," said Nightingale.

"What if it was one that we think might already be connected to the case?" I asked.

"WHY ARE we drinking in your room?" asked Leslie.

"Because they won't let me take the dog into the pub," I
said.

Leslie, who was perched on my bed, reached down and
scratched Toby behind the ears. The dog whimpered with
pleasure and tried to bury its head in Leslie's knee. "You
should have told them it was a ghost-hunting dog," she said.

"We're not hunting for ghosts," I said. "We're looking for
traces of supernatural energy."

"Did he really say he was a wizard?"

I was really beginning to regret telling Leslie everything.
"Yes," I said. "I saw him do a spell and everything."

We were drinking bottles of Grolsch from a crate that Leslie
had liberated from the station's Christmas party and stashed
behind a loose section of plasterboard in the kitchenette.

"You remember that guy we arrested for assault last week?"

"How could I forget." I'd been shoved into a wall during
the struggle.

"I think you hit your head much harder than you thought,"
she said.

"It's all real," I said. "Ghosts, magic, everything."

"Then why doesn't everything seem different?" she asked.

"Because it was there in front of you all the time," I said.
"Nothing's changed, so why should you notice anything." I
finished my bottle. "Duh!"

"I thought you were a skeptic," said Leslie. "I thought you
were scientific."

She handed me a fresh bottle and I waved it at her.

"Okay," I said. "You know my dad used to play jazz."

" 'Course," said Leslie. "You introduced me once—
remember? I thought he was nice."

I tried not to wince at that and continued, "And you know jazz is about improvising on a melody?"

"No," she said. "I thought it was when you sing about cheese and tying up people's gaiters."

"Funny," I said. "I once asked my dad, when he was sober, how did he know what to play? And he said that when you get the right line you just know because it's perfect. You've found the line and you just follow it."

"And that's got the fuck to do with what?"

"What Nightingale can do fits with the way I see the world; it's the line, the right melody."

Leslie laughed. "You want to be a wizard," she said.

"I don't know."

"Liar," she said. "You want to be his apprentice and learn magic and ride a broomstick."

"I don't think real wizards ride broomsticks," I said.

"Would you like to think about what you just said," said Leslie. "Anyway, how would you know? He could be whooshing around even as we're speaking."

"Because if you have a car like that Jag you wouldn't spend any time mucking about on a broomstick."

"Fair point," said Leslie and we clinked bottles.

COVENT GARDEN, nighttime, again. This time with a dog.

Also a Friday night, which meant crowds of young people being horribly drunk and loud in two dozen languages. I had to carry Toby in my arms or I'd have lost him in the crowd—lead and all. He enjoyed the ride, alternating between snarling at tourists, licking my face and trying to drive his nose into passing armpits.

I'd offered Leslie a chance to put in some unpaid overtime but strangely she'd declined. I did zap her Brandon Coopertown's picture and she'd promised to put his details on HOLMES for me. It was just turning eleven when Toby and I reached the Piazza and found Nightingale's Jag parked as close to the Actors' Church as you could get without being towed away.

Nightingale climbed out as I walked over. He was carrying

the same silver-topped cane as he had when I'd first met him. I wondered if it had any special significance beyond being a handy blunt instrument in times of trouble.

"How do you want to do this?" asked Nightingale.

"You're the expert, sir," I said.

"I looked into the literature on this," said Nightingale. "And it wasn't very helpful."

"There's a literature about this?"

"You'd be amazed, Constable, about what there's a literature on."

"We have two options," I said. "One of us leads him around the crime scene or we let him go and see where he goes."

"I believe we should do it in that order," said Nightingale.

"You think a directed first pass will make a better control?" I asked.

"No," said Nightingale. "But if we let him off the lead and he runs away—that's the end of it. I'll take him for his walk, you stay by the church and keep an eye out."

He didn't say what I should keep an eye out for, but I had a shrewd idea that I knew already. Just as I'd suspected, as soon as Nightingale and Toby vanished around the side of the covered market, I heard someone pssting me. I turned around and found Nicholas Wallpenny beckoning me from behind one of the pillars.

"Over here, squire," hissed Nicholas. "Before he comes back." He drew me behind the pillar where, among the shadows, Nicholas seemed more solid and less worrying. "Do you know what manner of man you're keeping company with?"

"You're a ghost," I said.

"Not myself," said Nicholas. "Him with the nice suit and the silver cad walloper."

"Inspector Nightingale?" I asked. "He's my governor."

"Well, I don't want to tell you your business," said Nicholas. "But I'd find myself another governor if I was you. Someone less touched."

"Touched by what?" I asked.

"Just you ask him about the year of his birth," said Nicholas.

I heard Toby bark and Nicholas suddenly wasn't there anymore.

"You're not making any friends here, Nicholas," I said.

Nightingale returned with Toby and with nothing to report. I didn't tell him about the ghost or what the ghost had said about him; I feel it's important not to burden your senior officers with more information than they need.

I picked up Toby and held him so that his absurd doggy face was level with mine—I tried to ignore the smell of Pal Meaty Chunks in Gravy.

"Listen, Toby," I said. "Your master is dead, I'm not a dog person and my governor would turn you into a pair of mittens as soon as look at you. You're looking at a one-way ticket to Battersea Dogs Home and the big sleep. Your one chance to avoid the big kennel in the sky is to use whatever doggy supernatural senses you have to track . . . whatever it was murdered your owner. Do you understand?"

Toby panted and then barked once.

"Close enough," I said and put him down. He immediately trotted over to the pillar and lifted his leg.

"I wouldn't turn him into a pair of mittens," said Nightingale.

"No?"

"He's a short-haired breed—they'd look terrible," said Nightingale. "Might make a good hat."

Toby snuffled around a spot close to where his master's body had lain. He looked up, barked once and shot off toward King Street.

"Damn," I said. "I wasn't expecting that."

"Get after him," said Nightingale. I was already on my way. Detective Chief Inspectors don't run—that's what they have constables for. I sprinted after Toby who, like all ratlike little dogs, could really shift when he wanted to. Past the Tesco's he went and down New Row with his little legs whirring like a low-budget cartoon. Two years running down drunks in Leicester Square had given me some speed and stamina and I was gaining when he crossed St. Martin's Lane and into St. Martin's Court on the other side. I lost ground when I had to dodge around a crocodile of Dutch tourists leaving the Noel Coward Theatre.

"Police," I yelled. "Get out of the way." I didn't yell "Stop that dog"—I do have some standards.

Toby whirred past the J. Sheekey Oyster Bar and the salt beef and falafel place on the corner and shot across the Charing Cross Road, which is one of the busiest roads in Central London. I had to look both ways before crossing, but luckily Toby had stopped at the bus stop and was relieving himself against the ticket machine.

Toby gave me the smug self-satisfied look employed by small dogs everywhere when they've confounded your expectations or messed on your front garden. I checked which buses used the stop—one of them was the 24, Camden Town, Chalk Farm and Hampstead.

Nightingale arrived and together we counted cameras; there were at least five that had a good view of the bus stop, not to mention the cameras that Transport for London routinely mounts in its buses. I left a message on Leslie's phone suggesting she check the camera footage from the 24 bus first. I'm sure she was thrilled when she got it.

SHE GOT her revenge by calling me at eight o'clock the next morning.

I hate the winter, I hate waking up in the dark.

"Don't you ever sleep?" I asked.

"Early bird gets the worm," said Leslie. "You know that picture you sent me, Brandon Coopertown? I think he boarded a number 24 at Leicester Square less than ten minutes after the murder."

"Have you told Seawoll?"

" 'Course I have," said Leslie. "I love you dearly but I ain't going to fuck up my career for you."

"What did you tell him?"

"That I had a lead on WITNESS A, one of several hundred generated in the last two days, I might add."

"What did he say?

"He told me to check it out," said Leslie.

"According to Mrs. Coopertown, he should be back to-day."

"Even better."

"Can you pick me up?" I asked.

" 'Course," said Leslie. "What about Voldemort?"

"He's got my number," I said.

I had time for a shower and a coffee before meeting Leslie outside. She arrived in a ten-year-old Honda Accord that looked like it had been used in one too many drug raids. She gave me a sour look as Toby scrambled onto the backseat.

"This is just a borrow, you know," she said.

"I wasn't about to leave him in my room," I said as Toby snuffled God knows what from the gaps between the seats. "Are you sure it was Coopertown?"

Leslie showed me a couple of hard copies. The bus security camera was angled to get a good shot of anyone coming up the stairs and there was no mistaking the face—it was him.

"Is that bruising?" I asked. There appeared to be blotches on Coopertown's cheeks and neck. Leslie said she didn't know, but it had been a cold night, so it could have been from drink.

Because it was Saturday, traffic was merely horrendous and we made Hampstead in just under half an hour. Unfortunately, as we pulled into Downshire Hill I spotted a familiar silver shape of the Jaguar nestled among the Range Rovers and BMWs. Toby started yapping.

"Doesn't he ever sleep?" asked Leslie.

"I reckon he was on stakeout all night," I said.

"He ain't my governor," said Leslie. "So I'm going to go do the job. Coming?"

We left Toby in the car and headed for the house. Inspector Nightingale got out of his Jag and intercepted us short of the front gate. I noticed he was wearing the same suit he had been the night before.

"Peter," he said and inclined his head to Leslie. "Constable May. I take it this means your search was successful."

Even the queen of perky wasn't going to defy a senior officer to his face so she told him about the CCTV footage from the bus and how we were 90 percent certain, what with the evidence from our ghost-hunting dog, that Brandon Coopertown, at the very least, was WITNESS A, if not actually the killer.

"Have you checked his flight details with Immigration yet?" asked Nightingale.

I looked at Leslie, who shrugged. "No, sir," I said.

"So he could have been in Los Angeles when the murder was committed?"

"We thought we'd ask him, sir," I said.

Toby started barking, not his usual annoying yap but proper furious barks. For a moment I thought I felt something, a wave of emotion like the excitement of being in a crowd at a football match when a goal is scored.

Nightingale's head snapped round to look at the Coopertowns' house.

We heard a window break and a woman screaming.

"Constable, wait!" shouted Nightingale, but Leslie was already through the gate and into the gardens. Then she stopped so suddenly that Nightingale and I nearly piled into her back. She was staring at something on the lawn.

"Jesus Christ, no," she whispered.

I looked. My brain kept trying to slide away from the idea that someone had thrown a baby from a second-story window. Tried to convince me that what I was seeing was a scrap of cloth or a doll, but it wasn't.

"Call an ambulance," said Nightingale and ran up the steps. I grabbed my phone as Leslie stumbled over to the baby and fell to her knees. I saw her turn the little body over and feel for a pulse. I gave the emergency code and the address on automatic. Leslie bent over and started mouth-to-mouth resuscitation, her mouth covering the baby's mouth and nose in the prescribed manner.

"Grant, get in here," called Nightingale. His voice was steady, businesslike; it got me moving up the stairs and onto the porch. Nightingale must have kicked the front door right off its hinges because I had to run over it to get into the hall. We had to stop to work out where the fuck the noise was coming from.

The woman screamed again—upstairs. There was a thumping sound like somebody beating a carpet. A voice, I thought
it might be a man's but very high-pitched, was screaming—
"Have you got a headache now!"

I don't even remember the stairs; suddenly I was on the
landing with Nightingale in front of me. I saw August Coopertown lying facedown at the far end of the landing, one arm
thrust through a gap in the banisters. Her hair was wet with
blood and a pool was growing under her cheek. A man stood
over her holding a wooden baton at least a meter and a half
in length. He was panting hard.

Nightingale didn't hesitate. He bulled forward, shoulder
down, obviously planning to take the man down in a rugby
tackle. I charged too, thinking I'd go high to pin the man's
arms after he'd gone down. But the man whirled around and
casually backhanded Nightingale with enough force to slam
him into the banisters.

I was staring right at his face. I assumed it must be Brandon Coopertown, but it was impossible to tell. I could see
one of his eyes but a great flap of skin had been peeled back
from around his nose and was covering the other eye. Instead
of a mouth he had a bloody maw full of the white flecks of
broken teeth and bone. I was so shocked that I stumbled and
fell, which was what saved my life; when Coopertown swung
that baton at me, it passed right over my head.

I hit the ground and the bastard ran right over me, one foot
slamming down on my back and blowing the air out of my
lungs. I rolled over as I heard his feet on the stairs and managed to get onto my hands and knees. There was something
wet and sticky under my fingers and I realized that there was
a thick trail of blood leading across the landing and down the
stairs.

There was a crash and a series of thumps from the hallway
below.

"You need to get up, Constable," said Nightingale.

"What the fuck was that?" I asked as he helped me up. I
looked down into the hallway where Coopertown or whoever
the hell it was had fallen—mercifully facedown.

"I really have no idea," said Nightingale. "Try to stay out of the blood trail."

I went down the stairs as fast as I could. The fresh blood was bright red, arterial. I guessed it must have fountained out of the hole in his face. I bent down and gingerly touched his neck, looking for a pulse. There wasn't one.

"What happened?" I asked.

"Peter," said Inspector Nightingale. "I need you to step away from the body and carefully walk outside. We mustn't contaminate the scene any more than we have already."

This is why you have procedure, training and drill, so that you do things when your brain is too shocked to think for itself—ask any soldier.

I stepped outside into the daylight.

In the distance I could hear sirens.

CHAPTER 3

The Folly

INSPECTOR NIGHTINGALE told me and Leslie to wait in the garden and faded back into the house to check there was nobody else inside. Leslie had used her coat to cover the baby and was shivering in the cold. I tried to struggle out of my jacket so I could offer it to her, but she stopped me.

"It's covered in blood," she said.

She was right; there were smears of blood up the sleeves and trailing edge of the hem. There was more blood on the knees of my trousers. I could feel the stickiness where it had soaked through the material. There was blood on Leslie's face, around her lips, from when she'd tried to resuscitate the baby. She noticed me staring.

"I know," she said. "I've still got the taste in my mouth."

We were both trembling and I wanted to scream, but I knew I had to be strong for Leslie's sake. I was trying not to think about it, but the red ruin of Brandon Coopertown's face kept on sneaking up on me.

"Hey," said Leslie. "Keep it together."

She was looking concerned and she looked even more concerned when I started to giggle—I couldn't help myself.

"Peter?"

"Sorry," I said. "But you're being strong for me and I'm being strong for you and don't you get it? This is how you get through the job." I got my giggles under control and Leslie half smiled.

"All right," said Leslie. "I won't freak out if you don't." She took my hand, squeezed it and let go.

"Do you think our backup is *walking* from Hampstead nick?" I asked.

The ambulance arrived first, the paramedics rushing into the garden and spending twenty minutes futilely trying to resuscitate the child. Paramedics always do this with children regardless of how much it damages the crime scene. You can't stop them, so you might as well let them get on with it.

The paramedics had just got started when a transit van's worth of uniforms arrived and started milling around in confusion. The sergeant approached us cautiously, mistaking us for civilians covered in blood and therefore potential suspects.

"Are you all right?" he asked.

I couldn't speak—it seemed like such a stupid question.

The sergeant looked over at the paramedics, who were still working on the baby. "Can you tell me what happened?" he asked.

"There's been a serious incident," said Nightingale as he emerged from the house. "You," he said, pointing at a luckless constable. "Get another body to go round the back and make sure nobody gets in or out that way."

The constable grabbed a mate and legged it. The sergeant looked like he wanted to ask for a warrant card, but Nightingale didn't give him a chance.

"I want the street closed and taped off ten yards in both directions," he said. "The press are going to be all over this any minute, so make sure you've got enough bodies to keep them back."

The sergeant didn't salute because we're the Met and we don't salute, but there was a touch of the parade ground in the way he swiveled around and marched off. Nightingale looked over to where Leslie and I stood shivering. He gave us a reassuring nod, turned on one of the remaining constables and started barking orders.

Soon after that, blankets appeared, a place was found in the transit van and cups of hot tea with three sugars thrust into our hands. We drank the tea and waited in silence for the other shoe to drop.

It took less than forty minutes for DCI Seawoll to reach Downshire Hill. Even with the Saturday traffic it meant he must have had his siren on all the way from Belgravia. He appeared in the side doorway of the van and frowned at me and Leslie.

"You two all right?" he asked.

We both nodded.

"Well, don't fucking go anywhere," he said.

Fat chance of that. A major investigation, once it gets under way, is as exciting as watching reruns of *Big Brother Live,* although possibly involving less sex and violence. Criminals are not caught by brilliant deductive reasoning, but by the fact that some poor slob has spent a week tracking down every shop in Hackney that sells a particular brand of sneaker and then checking the security camera footage on every single one. A good Senior Investigating Officer is one who makes sure their team has dotted every i and crossed every t, not least so that some Rupert in a wig can't drive a defendant's credit card into a crack in the case and wedge it wide open.

Seawoll was one of the best, so first we were taken out separately to a tent that the forensic people had erected near the front gate. There we stripped to our underwear and traded our street clothes for a stylish one-piece bunny suit. As I watched my favorite suit jacket being stuffed into an evidence bag, I realized I'd never bothered to find out whether you ever got things like that back. And if they did give it back to me, would they dry-clean it first? They took swabs of the blood on our faces and hands and then were nice enough to lend us some wipes so we could get the rest off.

We ended up back in the transit van for lunch, which was a couple of shop sandwiches, but this being Hampstead they were pretty high quality. I found myself surprisingly hungry and I was thinking of asking for a second round when DCI Seawoll climbed into the van with us. His weight caused the van to sink down on one side and his presence caused me and Leslie to unconsciously push ourselves into our seat backs.

"How are you two bearing up?" he asked.

We told him that we were fine and ready, in fact dead keen, to get back up on that horse and go to work.

"That's a load of wank," he said. "But at least it's convincing wank. In a couple of minutes we're going to take you down Hampstead nick, where a very nice lady from Scotland Yard is going to take your statements—separately. And while I'm a believer in veracity in all things, I want to make it clear that there isn't to be any fucking mumbo jumbo voodoo X-files shit in any fucking statement. Is that understood?"

We indicated that he had indeed adequately communicated his position.

"As far as anyone else is concerned, normal fucking policing got us into this mess and normal fucking policing will get us out of it." And with a creaking of the van's suspension he left.

"Did he just ask us to lie to a senior officer?" I asked.

"Yep," said Leslie.

"Just checking," I said.

So we spent the rest of the afternoon bearing false witness in separate interview rooms. We were careful to make sure that while our accounts broadly agreed, there were lots of authentic-looking discrepancies. No one can fake a statement the way a policeman can.

After lying, we borrowed some section house castoffs to wear and headed back to Downshire Hill. A serious crime in an area like Hampstead was always going to be big news and the media was out in force, not least because half the presenters could have walked to work that afternoon.

We let a suspiciously quiet Toby out of the Honda Accord, spent an hour or so cleaning up the backseat and then drove all the way back to Charing Cross with the windows down. We couldn't really blame Toby, since we'd been the ones who'd left him in the car all day. We bought him a McDonald's Happy Meal, so I think he forgave us.

We went back to my room and drank the last of the Grolsch. Then Leslie peeled off her clothes and climbed into my bed. I climbed in behind her and put my arms around her. She sighed and spooned against me. I got an erection, but she was much too polite to mention it. Toby made himself comfortable on the end of the bed, using our feet as a pillow, and we all went to sleep like that.

When I woke up the next morning Leslie was gone and my phone was ringing. When I answered it was Nightingale.

"Are you ready to go back to work?" he asked.

I told him I was.

BACK TO work. Back to the Iain West Forensic Bar and Grill where Inspector Nightingale and I were booked in for a guided tour of Brandon Coopertown's horrible injuries. I was introduced to Abdul Haqq Walid, a spry gingery man in his fifties who spoke with a soft Highland accent.

"Dr. Walid handles all our special cases," said Nightingale.

"I specialize in cryptopathology," said Dr. Walid.

"Salaam," I said.

"Assalaamu alaykum," said Dr. Walid, shaking my hand.

I'd been hoping that *this* time we'd use the remote monitoring suite, but Nightingale didn't want a visual record of this stage of the autopsy. Once again in aprons, masks and eye protectors, we entered the lab. Brandon Coopertown, or at least the man we thought was Brandon Coopertown, lay naked on his back on the table. Dr. Walid had already opened up his torso with the standard Y-shaped incision and, after rummaging around for whatever pathologists look for in there, closed him back up again. We had confirmed his identity via the biometrics on his passport.

"Below the neck," said Dr. Walid, "he's a physically fit man in his late forties. It's his face that holds our interest here."

Or rather what was left of his face. Dr. Walid had used clamps to splay open the torn flaps of skin so that Brandon Coopertown's face looked horribly like a pink-and-red daisy.

"Starting with the skull," said Dr. Walid, as he leaned in with a pointer. Nightingale followed suit, but I contented myself with peering over his shoulder. "As you can see, there's extensive damage to the bones of the face; the mandible, maxilla and zygomatic bones have been effectively pulverized and the teeth, those normally reliable survivors, have been shattered."

"A heavy blow to the face?" asked Nightingale.

"That would have been my first guess," said Dr. Walid. "If not for this." He used a clamp to seize one flap of skin, I guessed what had once covered the cheek, and draw it over the face. It reached right across the breadth of the skull and flopped down to cover the ear on the other side. "The skin has been stretched beyond its natural capacity to retain its shape and while there's not much left of the muscle tissue, that too shows lateral degradation. Judging from the lines of stress, I'd say something pushed out his face around the chin and nose, stretching the skin and muscle, pulverizing the bone and then holding it in position. Then whatever was holding it in that shape vanished, the bone and soft tissues lost all their integrity and basically his face fell off."

"Are you thinking *dissimulo*?" asked Nightingale.

"Or a technique very like it," said Dr. Walid.

Nightingale explained, for my benefit, that *dissimulo* was a magic spell that could change your appearance. Actually he didn't use the words "magic spell," but that's what it amounted to.

"Unfortunately," said Dr. Walid, "it essentially moves the muscles and skin into new positions and this can cause permanent damage."

"Never was a popular technique," said Nightingale.

"You can see why," said Dr. Walid, indicating the remains of Brandon Coopertown's face.

"Any signs that he was a practitioner?" asked Nightingale.

Dr. Walid produced a covered stainless steel tray. "I knew you'd ask that," he said. "So here's something I whipped out earlier." He lifted the cover to reveal a human brain. I'm no expert, but it didn't look like a healthy brain to me; it looked shrunken and pitted, as if it had been left out in the sun to shrivel.

"As you can see," said Dr. Walid, "there's extensive degradation of the cerebral cortex and evidence of intracranial bleeding that we might associate with some form of degenerative condition if Inspector Nightingale and I were not already familiar with the true cause."

He sliced it in half to show us the interior. It looked like a diseased cauliflower.

"And this," said Dr. Walid, "is your brain on magic."

"Magic does that to your brain?" I asked. "No wonder nobody does it anymore."

"This is what happens if you overstep your limitations," said Nightingale. He turned to Dr. Walid. "There wasn't any evidence of practice at his house. No books, no paraphernalia, no *vestigia*."

"Could someone have stolen his magic?" I asked. "Sucked it out of his brain?"

"That's very unlikely," said Nightingale. "It's almost impossible to steal another man's magic."

"Except at the point of death," said Dr. Walid.

"It's much more likely that our Mr. Coopertown did this to himself," said Nightingale.

"Then you're saying he wasn't wearing a mask during the first attack?" I asked.

"That seems likely," said Nightingale.

"So his face was mashed up on Tuesday," I said. "Which explains why he looks blotchy on the bus cameras, then he flies to America, stays three nights and comes back here. And all that time his face is essentially destroyed."

Dr. Walid thought it through. "That would be consistent with the injuries and the evidence of the beginnings of regrowth around some of the bone fragments."

"He must have been in some serious pain," I said.

"Not necessarily," said Nightingale. "One of the dangers of *dissimulo* is that it hides the pain. The practitioner can be quite unaware that he's injuring himself."

"But when his face was normal-looking—that was only because the magic was holding it together?"

Dr. Walid looked at Nightingale. "Yes," said Nightingale.

"When you fall asleep what happens to the spell?" I asked.

"It would probably collapse," said Nightingale.

"But he was so badly damaged that once the spell collapsed

his face would fall off. He'd have had to keep the spell up the whole time he was in America." I said. "Are you telling me he didn't sleep for four days?"

"It does seem a bit unlikely," said Dr. Walid.

"Do spells work like software?" I asked.

Nightingale gave me a blank look. Dr. Walid came to his rescue. "In what way?" he asked.

"Could you persuade somebody's unconscious mind to maintain a spell?" I asked. "That way the spell would stay running even when they were asleep."

"It's theoretically possible, but, morality aside, I couldn't do it," said Nightingale. "I don't think any human wizard could."

Any human wizard—okay. Dr. Walid and Nightingale were looking at me and I realized that they were already there and waiting for me to catch up.

"When I asked about ghosts, vampires and werewolves and you said I hadn't scratched the surface, you weren't joking, were you?"

Nightingale shook his head. "I'm afraid not," he said. "Sorry."

"Shit," I said.

Dr. Walid smiled. "I said exactly the same thing thirty years ago," he said.

"So whatever did this to poor old Mr. Coopertown was probably not human," I said.

"I wouldn't like to say for certain," said Dr. Walid. "But that's the way to bet."

NIGHTINGALE AND I did what all good coppers do when faced with a spare moment in the middle of the day—we went looking for a pub. Just round the corner, we found the relentlessly upmarket Marquis of Queensbury looking a little bedraggled in the afternoon drizzle. Nightingale stood me a beer and we sat down in a corner booth below a Victorian print of a bare-knuckle boxing match.

"How do you become a wizard?" I asked.

Nightingale shook his head. "It's not like joining CID," he said.

"You surprise me," I said. "What is it like?"

"It's an apprenticeship," he said. "A commitment, to the craft, to me and to your country."

"Do I have to call you Sifu?"

That got a smile at least. "No," said Nightingale. "You have to call me Master."

"Master?"

"That's the tradition," said Nightingale.

I said the word in my head and it kept on coming out *massa*.

"Couldn't I call you Inspector instead?"

"What makes you think I'm offering you a position?"

I took a pull from my pint and waited. Nightingale smiled again and sipped his own drink. "Once you cross this particular Rubicon there will be no going back," he said. "And you can call me Inspector."

"I've just seen a man kill his wife and child," I said. "If there's a rational reason for that, then I want to know what it is. If there's even a chance that he wasn't responsible for his actions, then I want to know about it. Because that would mean we might be able to stop it happening again."

"That is not a good reason to take on this job," said Nightingale.

"Is there a good reason?" I asked. "I want in, sir, because I've got to know."

Nightingale lifted his glass in salute. "That's a better reason."

"So what happens now?" I asked.

"Nothing happens now," said Nightingale. "It's Sunday. But first thing tomorrow morning, we go see the commissioner."

"Good one, sir," I said.

"No, really," said Nightingale. "He's the only person authorized to make the final decision."

NEW SCOTLAND Yard was once an ordinary office block that was leased by the Met in the 1960s. Since then, the interior of the senior offices had been refitted several times, most recently during the 1990s, easily the worst decade for institutional décor since the 1970s. Which was why, I suppose, the anteroom to the commissioner's office was a bleak wilderness of laminated plywood and molded polyurethane chairs. Just to put visitors at their ease, photographic portraits of the last six commissioners stared down from the walls.

Sir Robert Mark (1972–1977) looked particularly disapproving. I doubt he thought I was making a significant contribution.

"It's not too late to withdraw your application," said Nightingale.

Yes it was, but it didn't mean I wasn't wishing it wasn't. Typically, a constable only sits in the commissioner's anteroom when he's been very brave or very stupid and I really couldn't tell which one applied to me.

The commissioner only made us wait ten minutes before his secretary came and fetched us. His office was large and designed with the same lack of style as the rest of Scotland Yard, only with a layer of fake oak paneling on top. There was a portrait of the queen on one wall and another of the first commissioner, Sir Charles Rowan, on the other. I stood as close to parade ground attention as any London copper can get and nearly flinched when the commissioner offered me his hand to shake.

"Constable Grant," he said. "Your father is Richard Grant, isn't he? I have some of his records from when he was playing with Tubby Hayes. On vinyl, of course."

He didn't wait for me to answer, just shook Nightingale's hand and waved us into our seats. He was another Northerner who'd come up the hard way and done that stint in Northern Ireland that appears to be obligatory for would-be commissioners of the Metropolitan Police, presumably because violent sectarianism is thought to be character building. He wore the uniform well and was judged by the rank and file as possibly not being a total muppet—which put him well ahead of some of his predecessors.

"This is an unexpected development, Inspector," said the commissioner. "There are some who would see this as an unnecessary step."

"Commissioner," said Nightingale carefully, "I believe circumstances warrant a change in the arrangement."

"When I was first briefed about the nature of your section, I was led to believe that it merely served a vestigial function and that the—" The commissioner had to force the word out. "That 'the magic' was in decline and only posed a marginal threat to the Queen's Peace. In fact, I definitely remember the word 'dwindle' being bandied about by the Home Office. 'Eclipsed by science and technology' was another phrase I heard a lot."

"The Home Office has never really understood that science and magic are not mutually exclusive, sir. The founder of my society provided proof enough of that. I believe there has been a slow but steady increase in magical activity."

"The magic's coming back?" asked the commissioner.

"Since the mid-sixties," said Nightingale.

"The sixties," said the commissioner. "Why am I not surprised. This is damned inconvenient. Any idea why?"

"No, sir," said Nightingale. "But then there never was any real consensus as to why it faded in the first place."

"I've heard the word 'Ettersberg' used in that context," said the commissioner.

For a moment there was real pain on Nightingale's face. "Ettersberg was part of it certainly."

The commissioner blew out his cheeks and sighed. "The murders in Covent Garden and Hampstead, these are connected?" he asked.

"Yes, sir."

"You think the situation will get worse?"

"Yes, sir."

"Enough to warrant breaking the arrangement?"

"It takes ten years to train an apprentice, sir," said Nightingale. "It's better to have a spare just in case something happens to me."

The commissioner gave a mirthless chuckle. "Does he know what he's getting himself into?"

"Does any copper?" asked Nightingale.

"Very well," said the commissioner. "On your feet, son."

We stood. Nightingale told to me raise my hand and read me the oath: "Do you Peter Grant of Kentish Town swear to be true to our sovereign Queen and her heirs. And well and truly serve your master for the term of your apprenticehood. And ye shall be in obedience to all the wardens and clothing of that fellowship. In reverence of the secret of the said fellowship, ye shall keep and give no information to no man but of the said fellowship. And in all these things ye shall well and truly behave and secretly keep this oath to your power so help you God, your sovereign and the power that set the universe in motion."

I so swore, although I did almost stumble over the clothing bit.

"So help you God," said the commissioner.

NIGHTINGALE INFORMED me that as his apprentice I was required to lodge at his London residence in Russell Square. He told me the address and dropped me back at the Charing Cross section house.

Leslie helped me pack.

"Shouldn't you be at Belgravia?" I asked. "Doing Murder Team stuff."

"I've been told to take the day off," said Leslie. "Compassionate—don't get on media's radar—leave."

That I could understand. A family annihilation involving charismatic rich people was going to be a news editor's dream story. Once they'd picked over the gruesome details, they could extend the mileage by asking what the tragic death of the Coopertown family told us about our society and how this tragedy was an indictment of modern culture/secular humanism/political correctness/the situation in Palestine—delete where applicable. About the only thing that could improve the story would be the involvement of a good-looking blond WPC out, I might add, unsupervised on a dangerous assignment. Questions would be asked. Answers would be ignored.

"Who's going to Los Angeles?" I asked. Somebody would have to trace Brandon's movement in the States.

"A couple of sergeants I never got a chance to meet," she said. "I only worked there a couple of days before you got me into trouble."

"You're his blue-eyed girl," I said. "Seawoll's not going to hold it against you."

"I still reckon you owe me," she said as she picked up my bath towel and briskly folded it into a tightly packed cube.

"What do you want?" I asked.

Leslie asked if I was likely to get the evening off and I said I could try.

"I don't want to be stuck here," she said. "I want to go out."

"Where do you want to go?" I asked and watched as she unfolded the towel and refolded it into a triangle shape.

"Anywhere but the pub," she said and handed the towel to me. I managed to stuff it into my rucksack but I had to unfold it first.

"What about a film?" I asked.

"Sounds good," she said. "But it's got to be funny."

RUSSELL SQUARE lies a kilometer north of Covent Garden on the other side of the British Museum. According to Nightingale it was at the heart of a literary and philosophical movement in the early years of the last century, but I remember it because of an old horror movie about cannibals living in the underground system.

The address was on the south side of the square where a row of Georgian terraces had survived. They were five stories high counting the dormer conversions, with wrought-iron railings defending steep drops into basement flats. The address I wanted had a noticeably grander flight of stairs than its neighbors, leading to double mahogany doors with brass fittings. Carved above the lintel were the words SCIENTIA POTESTAS EST.

Science points east, I wondered. Science is portentous, yes? Science protests too much. Scientific potatoes rule. Had I stumbled on the lair of dangerous plant geneticists?

I hauled my rucksack and two suitcases up to the landing. I pressed the brass doorbell, but I couldn't hear it ring through the thick doors. After a moment they opened on their own. It might have been the traffic noise, but I swear I didn't hear a motor or any kind of mechanism at all. Toby whined and hid behind my legs.

"That's not creepy," I said. "Not even in the slightest."
I pulled my suitcase through the doors.

The entrance lobby had a mosaic floor in the Roman manner and a wooden and glass booth that, while in no way resembling a ticket booth, indicated that there was an inside and an outside to the building and one had better have permission if one wanted to proceed inside. Whatever this place was, it certainly wasn't Nightingale's private residence.

Beyond the booth, flanked by two neoclassical pillars, was a marble statue of a man dressed in an academic gown and breeches. He cradled a mighty tome in one arm and sextant in the other. His square face held an expression of implacable curiosity and I knew his name even before I saw the plinth, which read:

Nature and nature's laws lay hid in night;
God said "Let Newton be" and all was light.

Nightingale was waiting for me by the statue. "Welcome to the Folly," he said. "Official home of English magic since 1775."

"And your patron saint is Sir Isaac Newton?" I asked.

Nightingale grinned. "He was our founder and the first man to systemize the practice of magic."

"I was taught that he invented modern science," I said.

"He did both," said Nightingale. "That's the nature of genius."

Nightingale took me through a door into a rectangular atrium that dominated the center of the building. Above, there were two rows of balconies and an iron-and-glass Victorian dome at the top. Toby's claws clicked on a floor of polished cream-colored marble. It was very quiet and for all that the place was spotless, I got a strong sense of abandonment.

"Through there is the big dining room that we don't use anymore, the lounge, smoking room, which we also don't use." Nightingale pointed to doors on the other side of the atrium. "General library, lecture hall. Downstairs are the kitchens, sculleries and wine cellar. The back stairs, which are actually at the front, are over there. Coach house and mews are through the rear doors."

"How many people live here?" I asked.

"Just the two of us and Molly," said Nightingale.

Toby suddenly crouched down at my feet and growled. A proper rat-in-the-kitchen growl that was all business. I looked over and saw a woman gliding toward us across the polished marble. She was slender and dressed like an Edwardian maid, complete with a starched white bib apron over a full black skirt and white cotton blouse. Her face didn't fit her outfit, being too long and sharp-boned, with black almond-shaped eyes. Despite her mob cap she wore her hair loose, a black curtain that fell to her waist. She instantly gave me the creeps and not just because I've seen too many Japanese horror films.

"This is Molly," said Nightingale. "She does for us."

"Does what?"

"Whatever needs doing," said Nightingale.

Molly lowered her eyes and did an awkward little dip that might have been a curtsy or a bow. When Toby growled again, Molly snarled back, showing disturbingly sharp teeth.

"Molly," said Nightingale sharply.

Molly demurely covered her mouth with her hand, turned and went gliding back the way she came. Toby gave a little self-satisfied snort that didn't fool anyone but himself.

"And she is . . . ?" I asked.

"Indispensable," said Nightingale.

Before we went up Nightingale led me over to an alcove set into the north wall. There, set on a pedestal like a household god, was a sealed museum case containing a copy of a leather-bound book. It was open to the title page and I leaned over and read *Philosophiae Naturalis Principia Artes Magicis—Autore; J. S. Newton.*

"So, not content with kicking off the scientific revolution, our boy Isaac invented magic?" I asked.

"Not invented," said Nightingale. "But he did codify its basic principles, made it somewhat less hit-and-miss."

"Magic and science," I said. "What did he do for an encore?"

"Reformed the Royal Mint and saved the country from bankruptcy," said Nightingale.

Apparently there were two main staircases; we took the eastern one up to the first of the colonnaded balconies and a confusion of wood paneling and white dust sheets. Two more flights of stairs led us to a fourth-story hallway lined with heavy wooden doors. He opened one, seemingly at random, and ushered me in.

"This is yours," he said.

It was twice the size of my room at the section house, with good proportions and a high ceiling. A brass double bed was shoved into one corner, a Narnia wardrobe in another, a writing desk was between them where it could catch the light from one of the two sash windows. Bookshelves covered two entire walls, empty except for what turned out on later inspection to be a complete set of the eleventh edition of the *Encyclopaedia Britannica* published in 1913, a battered first edition of *Brave New World* and a Bible. What had obviously once been an open fireplace had been replaced with a gas fire surrounded by green ceramic tiles. The reading lamp on the desk had a faux-Japanese print shade and beside it was a Bakelite phone that had to be older than my father. There was a smell of dust and freshly applied furniture polish and I guessed that this room had dreamed the last fifty years away under white dust sheets.

"When you're ready, meet me downstairs," said Nightingale. "And make sure you're presentable."

I knew what that was about so I tried to stretch it, but it didn't take me long to unpack.

STRICTLY SPEAKING, it wasn't our job to pick up grieving parents from the airport. Leaving aside the fact that officially this was Westminster Murder Team's case, it was extremely unlikely that August Coopertown's parents had any information pertinent to the murder. It sounds callous, but detectives have better things to do than impromptu counseling for grieving relatives; that's what Family Liaison Officers are for. Nightingale didn't see it that way, which was why he and I were standing at the arrivals barrier at Heathrow when Mr. and Mrs. Fischer cleared customs. I was the one holding the cardboard sign.

They weren't what I expected; the dad was short and balding and the mum was mousy-haired and tubby. Nightingale introduced himself in what I assumed was Danish and told me to carry the bags back to the Jag—which I was glad to do.

If you ask any police officer what the worst part of the job is, they will always say breaking bad news to relatives, but this is not the truth. The worst part is staying in the room after you've broken the news, so that you're forced to be there when someone's life disintegrates around them. Some people say it doesn't bother them—such people are not to be trusted.

The Fischers had obviously Googled for the closest hotel to their daughter's house and thus booked themselves into a brick-built combination prison block/petrol station on Havistock Hill whose lobby was shopworn, fussy and as welcoming as a job center. I doubt the Fischers noticed, but I could see that Nightingale didn't think it was good enough and for a moment I thought he was going to offer to put them up at the Folly.

Then he sighed and told me to put the luggage down by the reception desk. "I'll deal with things from here," he said and sent me home. I said good-bye to the Fischers and walked out of their lives as fast as I could go.

AFTER THAT I really didn't want to go out, but Leslie persuaded me. "You can't just come to a stop 'cause bad things happen," she said. "Besides, you owe me a night out."

I didn't argue and after all, the good thing about the West End is that there's always somewhere to see a film. We started at the Prince Charles, but they were showing *Twelve Monkeys* downstairs and a Kurosawa double bill upstairs, so we went round the corner to the Leicester Square Voyage. The Voyage is a miniature village version of a multiplex with eight screens, of which at least two were larger than your average plasma screen television. Normally I like a certain amount of gratuitous violence in my cinema, but I let Leslie persuade me that *Sherbet Lemons,* this month's feel-good rom-com with Allison Tyke and Dennis Carter, was just the film to cheer us up. For all I know it might even have worked had we had a chance to see it.

The foyer was dominated by the concessions counter, which stretched across its breadth. There were eight transaction points, each with its own till nestled among a confusion of popcorn dispensers, hotdog grills and cardboard display signs offering kids' boxes tied to the latest blockbuster. Above each transaction point was a wide-screen LCD screen that displayed the films on offer, their age classification, when they were on, how long until they started and how many seats were left in each auditorium. At regular intervals the screen would switch to display a trailer, an advert for mechanically recovered meat or just to tell you what a good time you were having at the Voyage chain of cinemas. That evening there was only one transaction point open and a queue of approximately fifteen waiting to be served. We joined the queue behind a well-dressed middle-aged woman out with four girls between nine and eleven. It didn't bother me and Leslie; if you learn one thing as a copper, it's how to wait.

The follow-up investigation revealed that the single member of staff manning the transaction point that shift was a twenty-three-year-old Sri Lankan refugee named Sadun Ranatunga, one of six people staffing the Leicester Square Voyage that evening. At the time of the incident, two were cleaning out screens one and three in preparation for the next showing, one was on duty to take tickets and the last was dealing with a particularly unpleasant spillage in the gents.

Because Mr. Ranatunga was selling both tickets and popcorn, it took him at least fifteen minutes to wear down the queue to the point where the woman in front of us began to get her hopes up. Her accompanying children, who up till then had been amusing themselves elsewhere, flocked back to the queue so they could get their bid for sweets in early. She was impressively firm, making it clear that the ration was to be one drink and one popcorn or packet of sweets—no

exception and I don't care what Priscilla's mother let you
have when she took you out. No, you can't have nachos, what
are nachos anyway. Behave or you won't get anything.

The tipping point came, according to Charing Cross CID,
when the couple next in line asked for a concessionary price.
The couple, who were identified as Nicola Fabroni and Eu-
genio Turco, a pair of heroin addicts from Naples who had
come to London to dry out, had leaflets from the Piccadilly
English Language School that they claimed made them bona
fide students. As recently as the week before, Mr. Ranatunga
would have just let it slide, but that afternoon his manager
had informed him that the Head Office had decreed that
Leicester Square Voyage had been selling far too many concessionary tickets and that in future staff should decline any
request that seemed suspect. In compliance with this directive,
Mr. Ranatunga regretfully informed Turco and Fabroni that
they would have to pay full price. This did not go down well
with the couple, who had budgeted their evening on the basis
that they could scam into the cinema. They remonstrated with
Mr. Ranatunga, who was adamant in his refusal, but since both
parties were doing this in their second language it used up valuable time. Finally, and with ill grace, Turco and Fabroni paid
the full price with a pair of grubby five-pound notes and handful of ten-pence pieces.

Apparently Leslie had kept her copper's eye on the Italians
right from the start while I, easily distracted remember, had
been wondering whether I could sneak Leslie back to my
room at the Folly. That's why it came as a bit of a surprise
when the respectable middle-class woman in the good coat
standing in front of us lunged across the counter and tried to
strangle Mr. Ranatunga to death.

Her name was Celia Munroe, resident of Finchley, who
had brought her daughters Georgina and Antonia and their
two friends Jennifer and Alex to the West End as a special
treat. The dispute started when Ms. Munroe proffered five
Voyager Film Fun vouchers as part payment for the tickets.
Mr. Ranatunga regretfully indicated that the vouchers were
not valid at this particular cinema, Ms. Munroe asked why

this might be so, but Mr. Ranatunga was unable to say why since his management had never bothered to brief him on the promotion in the first place. Ms. Munroe expressed her dissatisfaction with a degree of forcefulness that surprised Mr. Ranatunga, me and Leslie and, according to her later statement, Ms. Munroe herself.

It was at that point that Leslie and I decided to intervene, but we hadn't even had time to step forward and ask what the problem was when Ms. Munroe made her move. It happened very quickly and as is often the case with unexpected events it took us a few moments to register what was going on. Fortunately we were both sufficiently street seasoned not to freeze and we each grabbed a shoulder and tried to drag the woman off poor Mr. Ranatunga. Her grip on his neck was so strong that Mr. Ranatunga was pulled back across the counter as well. By now one of the girls was hysterical and apparently the eldest, Antonia, started beating me across the back with her fists, but I didn't feel it at the time. Ms. Munroe's lips were drawn back in a rictus of rage, the tendons standing out on her neck and forearms. Mr. Ranatunga's face was darkening, his lips turning blue.

Leslie got her thumbs into the pressure points on Ms. Munroe's wrists and she let go in such a hurry that we both went sprawling backward onto the floor. She landed on top of me so I tried to pin her arms but not before she got a vicious elbow into my ribs. I used my weight and strength advantage to tip her off and roll her facedown into the popcorn-smelling carpet. Of course, I didn't have my cuffs with me so I had to hold her with both hands behind her back. Legally speaking, once you've laid hands on a suspect you pretty much *have* to arrest them. I gave her the caution and she went limp. I looked over at Leslie, who had not only tended to the injured man but had corralled the children and called in the incident to Charing Cross.

"If I let you up," I asked, "are you going to behave?"

Ms. Munroe nodded. I let her roll over and sit up where she was.

"I just wanted to go to the pictures," she said. "When I was young, you just went to the local Odeon and 'a ticket please' and you gave them money and they gave you a ticket. When did it become so complicated, when did these disgusting nachos arrive, I mean what the fuck is a nacho anyway?" One of the girls giggled nervously at the profanity.

Leslie was writing in her official notebook. You know in the caution when it says "anything that you do or say may be used in evidence against you," this is what they're talking about.

"Is that boy hurt?" She looked at me for reassurance. "I don't know what happened. I just wanted to talk to someone who could speak English properly. I went on holiday to Bavaria last summer and everyone spoke English, really well. I bring my kids down to the West End and everyone's foreign, I don't understand a word they're saying."

I suspected that some total bastard at the CPS could parlay that into a racially aggravated crime. I caught Leslie's eye and she sighed, but she stopped taking notes.

"I just wanted to go to the pictures," repeated Ms. Munroe.

Salvation arrived in the form of Inspector Neblett, who took one look at us and said, "I just can't let you two out of my sight, can I?" He didn't fool me; I knew he'd been rehearsing that line the whole way over.

Nonetheless, we all trooped back to the nick to complete the arrest and do the paperwork. And that's three hours of my life I won't get back in a hurry. We ended up, like all coppers on overtime, in the canteen, where we drank tea and filled in forms.

"Where's the Case Progression Unit when you need it," said Leslie.

"Told you we should have seen *Seven Samurai,*" I said.

"Did you think there was something odd about the whole thing?" asked Leslie.

"Odd how?"

"You know," said Leslie. "Middle-aged woman suddenly goes bonkers and attacks someone in a cinema, in front of her children. Are you sure you didn't feel any . . ." She waved her fingers.

"I wasn't paying attention," I said. Looking back I thought there might have been something, a flash of violence and laughter, but it felt suspiciously retrospective—a memory I'd conjured up after the fact.

Mr. Munroe arrived with a lawyer and the parents of the other children around nine and his wife was released on police bail less than an hour later. Considerably earlier than Leslie and I finished the paperwork. I was too knackered by then to try anything clever, so I said good-bye and caught a lift in the fast response car back to Russell Square.

I had a brand new set of keys, including one for the trades-man entrance round the back. That way I didn't have to sneak past the disapproving gaze of Sir Isaac. The main atrium was dimly lit, but as I climbed the first flight of stairs I thought I saw a pale figure gliding across the floor below.

You know you're staying somewhere posh when the "Breakfast Room" is a completely different room and not the same place you had dinner only dressed up with different china. It faced southeast to catch the thin January light and looked out over the coach house and mews. Despite the fact that only Nightingale and I were eating, all the tables had been laid and bore laundry-white tablecloths; you could have seated fifty people in there. Likewise, the serving table sported a line of silver-plated salvers with kippers, eggs, bacon, black pudding and a bowl full of rice, peas and flaked haddock that Nightingale identified as kedgeree. He seemed as taken aback by the amount of food as I was.

"I think Molly may have become a little overenthusiastic," he said and helped himself to the kedgeree. I had a bit of everything and Toby got some sausages, some black pudding and a bowl of water.

"There's no way we can eat all this," I said. "What's she going to do with all the leftovers."

"I've learned not to ask these questions," said Nightingale.

"Why's that?"

"Because I'm not sure I want to know the answers," he said.

*   *   *

MY FIRST proper lesson in magic took place in one of the labs at the back of the first floor. The other labs had once been used for research projects, but this one was for teaching; indeed, it looked just like a school chemistry lab. Waist-high benches with gas taps for Bunsen burners at regular intervals and white porcelain basins sunk into the varnished wooden tops. There was even a poster of the periodic table on the wall—missing, I noticed, all the elements discovered after World War 2.

"First we need to fill up a sink," said Nightingale. He selected one and turned the tap at the base of its long swan-necked spout. There was a distant knocking sound, the black swan neck shook, gurgled and then coughed up a gout of brown water.

We both took a step backward.

"How long since you used this place?" I asked.

The knocking grew louder, faster and then water poured from the spout, dirty at first but then clear. The knocking faded away. Nightingale put the plug in and let the basin fill three-quarters up before closing the tap.

"When you're attempting this spell," he said, "always have a basin of water ready as a safety precaution."

"Are we going to make fire?"

"Only if you do it wrong," said Nightingale. "I'm going to make a demonstration and you must pay close attention, as you did when searching for *vestigia*. Do you understand?"

"*Vestigia*," I said. "Got it."

Nightingale held out his right hand palm upward and made a fist. "Watch my hand," he said and opened his fingers. Suddenly, floating a few centimeters above his palm, there was a ball of light. Bright, but not so bright that I couldn't stare right at it.

Nightingale closed his fingers and the globe vanished. "Again?" he asked.

Up until then I think a bit of me had been waiting for the rational explanation, but when I saw how casually Nightingale produced that werelight I realized that I had the rational explanation—magic worked. The next question, of course, was—how did it work?

"Again," I said.

He opened his hand and the light appeared. The source seemed to be the size of a golf ball, with a smooth pearlescent surface. I leaned forward, but I couldn't tell whether the light emanated from inside the globe or from its skin.

Nightingale closed his palm. "Be careful," he said. "You don't want to damage your eyes."

I blinked and saw purple blotches. He was right. I'd been fooled by the soft quality of the light into staring too long. I splashed some water in my eyes.

"Ready to go again?" asked Nightingale. "Try to focus on the sensation as I do it—you should feel something."

"Something?" I asked.

"Magic is like music," said Nightingale. "Everyone hears it differently. The technical term we use is *forma,* but that's no more helpful than 'something,' is it?"

"Can I close my eyes?" I asked.

"By all means," said Nightingale.

I did feel a "something," like a catch in the silence at the moment of creation. We repeated the exercise until I was sure I wasn't imagining it. Nightingale asked me if I had any questions. I asked him what the spell was called.

"Colloquially it's known as a werelight," he said.

"Can you do it underwater?" I asked.

Nightingale plunged his hand into the sink and despite the awkward angle demonstrated a werelight without any apparent difficulty.

"So it's not a process of oxidization, is it," I said.

"Focus," said Nightingale. "Magic first, science later."

I tried to focus, but on what?

"In a minute," said Nightingale, "I'm going to ask you to open your hand in the same manner as I have demonstrated. As you open your hand I want you to make a shape in your mind that conforms to what you sensed when I created my werelight. Think of it as a key that opens a door. Do you understand?"

"Hand," I said. "Shape, key, lock, door."

"Precisely," said Nightingale. "Start now."

I took a deep breath, extended my arm and opened my fist—nothing happened. Nightingale didn't laugh, but I would have preferred it if he had. I took another breath, tried to "shape" my mind, whatever that meant, and opened my hand again.

"Let me demonstrate again," said Nightingale. "And then you follow."

He created the werelight, I felt for the shape of the *forma* and tried to replicate it. I still failed to create my own light, but this time I thought I felt an echo of the *forma* in my mind like a snatch of music from a passing car.

We repeated several times until I was certain I knew what the shape of the *forma* was, but I couldn't find the shape in my own mind. This process must have been familiar to Nightingale, because he could obviously tell what stage I was at.

"Practice this for another two hours," he said. "Then we'll stop for lunch and then two more hours after that. Then you can have the evening off."

"Just do this?" I asked. "No learning of ancient languages, no magic theory?"

"This is the first step," said Nightingale. "If you can't master this, then everything else is irrelevant."

"So this is a test?"

"That's what an apprenticeship is," said Nightingale. "Once you've mastered this *forma,* then I can promise you plenty of study. Latin, of course, Greek, Arabic, technical German. Not to mention you'll be taking over all the legwork on my cases."

"Good," I said. "Now I'm incentivized."

Nightingale laughed and left me to it.

CHAPTER 4

By the River

THERE ARE some things you don't want to be doing less than ten minutes after waking up and doing a ton down the Great West Road is one of them. Even at three in the morning with the spinner going and a siren to clear the way and the roads as empty of traffic as London roads ever get. I was hanging on to the door-strap and trying not to think about the fact that the Jag, with its many vintage qualities of style and craftsmanship, was sadly lacking in the airbag and modern crumple zone department.

"Have you fixed the radio yet?" asked Nightingale.

At some point the Jag had been fitted with a modern radio set that Nightingale cheerfully admitted he didn't know how to use. I'd managed to get it turned on, but got distracted when Nightingale put us around the Hogarth roundabout fast enough to smack my head against the side window. I took advantage of a relatively straight bit of road to key into Richmond Borough command, which was where Nightingale said the trouble was. We caught the tail end of a report delivered in the slightly strangulated tone adopted by someone who's desperately trying to sound like they're not panicking. It was something about geese.

"Tango Whiskey Three from Tango Whiskey One; say again?"

TW-1 would be the Richmond Duty inspector in the local

control room, TW-3 would be one of the Borough's incident response vehicles.

"Tango Whiskey One from Tango Whiskey Three; we're down by the White Swan, we're being attacked by the bloody geese."

"White Swan?" I asked.

"It's a pub in Twickenham," said Nightingale. "By the bridge to Eel Pie Island."

Eel Pie Island I knew, a collection of boatyards and houses on a river islet barely five hundred meters long. The Rolling Stones had once played a gig there; so had my father, that's where I knew it from.

"And the geese?" I asked.

"Better than watchdogs," said Nightingale. "Ask the Romans."

TW-1 wasn't interested in the geese; she wanted to know about the crime. There'd been multiple 999 calls twenty minutes earlier, reporting a breach of the peace and possible fighting between groups of youths. Which in my experience could turn out to be anything from a hen night gone wrong to foxes turning over rubbish bins.

TW-3 reported seeing a group of IC1 males dressed in jeans and workman's jackets fighting with an unknown number of IC3 females on Riverside Road. IC1 is the identification code for white people, IC3 is black people and if you're wondering, I tend to jump between IC3 and IC6—Arabic or North African; it depends on how much sun I've caught recently. Black versus white was unusual but not impossible, but I'd never heard of boys versus girls before; neither had TW-1, who wanted a clarification.

"Female," reported TW-3. *"Definitely female, one of them is stark naked."*

"I was afraid of that," said Nightingale.

"Afraid of what?" I asked.

There was a rush of emptiness outside the Jag as we shot across the Chiswick Bridge. Upstream of Chiswick, the Thames throws a loop northward around Kew Gardens and we were cutting across the base and aiming for Richmond Bridge.

"There's an important shrine nearby," said Nightingale. "I think the boys might have been after that."

When he said shrine, I guessed he wasn't talking about the rugby stadium.

"And the girls are defending the shrine?"

"Something like that," said Nightingale. He was a superb driver with a level of concentration that I always find a comfort at high speed, but even Nightingale had to slow down when the streets narrowed. Like a lot of London, Richmond Town center had been laid out back when town planning was something that happened to other people.

"Tango Whiskey One from Tango Whiskey Four; I'm on Church Lane by the river and I've got five or six IC1 males climbing into a boat—in pursuit."

TW-4 would be Richmond's second Incident Response Vehicle, meaning that just about every available body was now dealing.

TW-3 reported that there was no sign of the IC3 females, naked or otherwise, but they could see the boat and that it was heading for the opposite bank.

"Call them and tell them we're on our way," said Nightingale.

"What's our call sign? I asked.

"Zulu One," he said.

I keyed the microphone. "Tango Whiskey One from Zulu One; show us dealing."

There was a bit of a pause while TW-1 digested this. I wondered if the duty inspector knew who we were.

"Zulu One from Tango Whiskey One; copy that." The inspector sounded flat, neutral. He knew who we were all right. *"Be advised that the suspects seem to have crossed the river and may now be on the south bank."*

I tried to acknowledge, but it came out strangulated when Nightingale put us the wrong way down the one-way system on George Street, which you're not supposed to do even with your lights and siren on. Not least because of the risk of coming face-to-face with something heavy and designed to clean streets in the middle of the night. I braced my legs in the footwell as our headlights lit up a two-meter cherry-red Valentine's heart in the window of Boots.

TW-3 called in: *"Be advised that the suspect boat is now on fire, I can see people jumping off."*

Nightingale put his foot down, but mercifully we turned a corner and were back going the right way down the street. On the right was Richmond Bridge, but Nightingale went straight across the mini-roundabout and down the road that ran beside the Thames. We heard TW-1 calling in the LFB's fire boat—twenty minutes away at least.

Nightingale threw the Jag into a right-hand turn that I hadn't even noticed and suddenly we were racing through pitch darkness, jolting along a track with gravel pinging off the bottom of the chassis. A sudden turn to the left and we were running right along the water's edge following the river as it curved north again. A line of cabin cruisers was moored close to the opposite bank and beyond them I could see yellow flames— our burning boat. This was no modern pleasure cruiser; it looked more like a half-length narrowboat, the kind owned by homeopathic entrepreneurs and that was supposed to have handpainted gunwales and a cat asleep on the roof. If this boat had a cat, though, I hoped it could swim because the boat was on fire from stem to stern.

"There," said Nightingale.

I looked ahead and saw figures caught on the fringes of our headlights. I called it in to TW-1: "Confirm suspects on the south bank near . . . where the hell are we?"

"Hammerton's Ferry," said Nightingale and I passed it on.

Nightingale braked the Jag and we pulled up opposite the burning boat. There were flashlights in the glove compartment, vulcanized monstrosities with old-fashioned filament bulbs; mine proved reassuringly heavy in the hand when Nightingale and I stepped out into the darkness.

I swept my light along the path, but the suspects, assuming that's what they were, had scarpered. Nightingale seemed more interested in the river than the path. I used my flashlight to check the water around the narrowboat, which I saw was drifting slowly downstream, but there was nobody in the water.

"Shouldn't we check there's no one left on board," I said.

"There had better be no one on that boat," said Nightingale, loudly, as if speaking to the river rather than me. "And I want that fire put out right now," he said.

I heard a giggle out in the darkness, I pointed my light in that direction, but there was nothing to see except the boats moored on the far bank. I turned back to see the burning boat being sucked down into the river as if someone had grabbed hold of the bottom and yanked it under the surface. The last of the flames guttered out and then, like an escaping rubber duck, it bobbed up to the surface, the fire entirely dowsed.

It took me a moment to find my voice.

"What did that?" I asked.

"River spirits," said Nightingale. "Stay here while I check farther up the bank."

I heard another laugh from across the water. Then, very clearly and not three meters from where I was standing, someone, definitely a woman and a Londoner, said, "Oh shit!" Then the sound of metal being torn.

I ran over. At that point, the bank was a muddy slope held together with tree roots and bits of stone reinforcement. As I got close, I heard a splash and got my light on it just in time to see a sleek curved shape vanish beneath the surface. I might have thought it was an otter if I was stupid enough to think otters were hairless and grew as big as a man. Just below my feet was a square cage made out of chickenwire, part of an anti-erosion project I learned later, one side of which had been torn open.

Nightingale returned empty-handed and said that we might as well wait for the fireboat to come and take the remains of the narrowboat under tow. I asked him if there was such a thing as mermaids.

"That wasn't a mermaid," he said.

"So there are such things as mermaids," I said.

"Focus, Peter," he said. "One thing at a time."

"Was that a river spirit?" I asked.

"*Genii loci,*" he said. "The spirit of a place, a goddess of the river if you like." Although not the Goddess of the Thames herself, Nightingale explained, because her taking a direct part in any aggro would be a violation of the agreement. I asked whether this was the same agreement as "the agreement" or a different agreement entirely.

"There are a number of agreements," said Nightingale. "A great deal of what we do is making sure everyone keeps to them."

"There's a goddess of the river," I said.

"Yes—Mother Thames," he said patiently. "And there's a god of the river—Father Thames."

"Are they related?"

"No," he said. "And that's part of the problem."

"Are they really gods?"

"I never worry about the theological questions," said Nightingale. "They exist, they have power and they can breach the Queen's Peace—that makes them a police matter."

A searchlight stabbed out of the darkness and swept over the river once, twice, before swinging back to fix on the remains of the narrowboat—the London Fire Brigade had arrived. I smelled diesel exhaust as the fireboat gingerly maneuvered alongside, figures in yellow helmets waiting with hoses and boathooks. The searchlight revealed that the superstructure had been completely gutted by the fire, but I could see that the hull had been painted red with black trim. I could hear the firemen chatting to each other as they boarded and made the narrowboat safe. It was all reassuringly mundane. Which brought me to another thought. Nightingale and I had scrambled out of bed, into the Jag and headed west before there was any indication that this was nothing more than the tail end of an average Friday night.

"How did you know this was our shout?" I asked.

"I have my own sources," said Nightingale.

One of the Richmond IRVs arrived with the duty inspector on board and we all indulged in a bit of bureaucratic strutting to establish our respective bona fides. Richmond won on points, but only because one of them had a flask full of coffee. Nightingale briefed the locals—it was a gang thing, he said. Some IC1 youths, no doubt drunk, had stolen a boat, sailed down from beyond Teddington Lock and picked a fight with a local group of IC3 youths, some of whom were female. When they tried to escape, the Teddington gang had managed to accidentally set their boat on fire, had abandoned ship and escaped on foot down the Thames pathway. Everybody nodded their heads—it sounded like a typical Friday night in the big city. Nightingale said he was sure that nobody had drowned, but the Richmond Duty Inspector decided to call in a search and rescue team just in case.

Then, our two inspectors having marked their respective trees, we went our separate ways.

We drove back up to Richmond, but stopped well short of the bridge. Dawn was at least an hour away, but as I followed Nightingale through an iron gate I could see that the road we'd been on cut through a municipal garden that sloped down to the river. There was an orange glow ahead of us, a hurricane lantern hung on the lower branches of a plane tree; it illuminated a row of redbrick arches built into the revetment that supported the roadway. Looking inside these artificial caves, I glimpsed sleeping bags, cardboard boxes and old newspaper.

"I'm just going to have a chat with this troll," said Nightingale.

"Sir," I said. "I think we're supposed to call them rough sleepers."

"Not this one we don't," said Nightingale. "He's a troll."

I saw movement in the shadow of one of the arches, a pale face, ragged hair, layers of old clothes against the winter cold. It looked like a rough sleeper to me.

"A troll, really?" I asked.

"His name is Nathaniel," said Nightingale. "He used to sleep under Hungerford Bridge."

"Why did he move?" I asked.

"Apparently he wanted to live in the suburbs."

Suburban troll, I thought, why not?

"This is your snout, isn't it," I said. "He tipped you off."

"A policeman is only as good as his informants," said Nightingale. I didn't tell him that these days they were supposed to be referred to as Covert Human Intelligence Sources. "Stay back a bit," he said. "He doesn't know you yet." Nathaniel ducked back into his lair as Nightingale approached and crouched politely at the threshold of the troll's cave. I stamped my feet and blew on my fingers. I'd been sensible enough to grab my uniform sweater, but even with that on under my jacket, three hours by the river in February was edging me into brass monkey territory. If I hadn't been so busy jamming my hands into my armpits, I might have noticed that I was being watched much sooner. Actually, if I hadn't spent the last couple of weeks trying to separate *vestigia* from ordinary random paranoia I wouldn't have noticed at all.

It started as a flush, like embarrassment, like the time at the eighth-grade disco when Rona Tang marched across the no-man's-land of the dance floor and informed me, in no uncertain terms, that Fumne Ajayi wanted me to dance with her, but there was no way I was going to dance with a conspiracy of teenaged girls watching me while I did it. It was the same scrutiny—defiant, mocking, curious. I checked behind myself first, as you do, but I could see nothing but sodium streetlights up the road. I thought I felt a puff of warm breath against my cheek, a sensation like sunlight, mown grass and singed hair. I turned and stared out over the river and for a moment I thought I saw movement, a face, something . . .

"Seen something?" asked Nightingale, making me jump.

"Jesus Christ," I said.

"Not on this river," said Nightingale. "Not even Blake thought that was possible."

We returned to the Jag and the fickle embrace of its 1960s heating system. As we returned through Richmond town center, the right way round the one-way system this time, I asked Nightingale whether Nathaniel the troll had been helpful.

"He confirmed what we suspected," he said. That the boys in the boat had been followers of Father Thames, had come downstream to raid the shrine at Eel Pie Island and been caught by followers of Mother Thames. They were doubtless well tanked up and probably did set their own fire while trying to make their escape. Downstream, the Thames was the sovereign domain of Mother Thames; upstream, it belonged to Father Thames. The dividing line was at Teddington Lock, two kilometers downstream from Eel Pie Island.

"So you think Father Thames is making a grab for turf?" I asked. It made these "gods" sound like drug dealers. Traffic was noticeably heavier heading back—London was waking up.

"It's hardly surprising that the spirits of a locality would exhibit territoriality," said Nightingale. "In any case I think you might have a unique insight into this problem. I want you to go and have a word with Mother Thames."

"And what do I and my unique insight say to Mrs. Thames?"

"Find out what the problem is and see if you can find an amicable solution," said Nightingale.

"And if I can't?"

"Then I want you to remind her that, whatever some people may think, the Queen's Peace extends to the whole Kingdom."

NOBODY GOT to drive the Jag except Nightingale, which was understandable; if I had a car like that I wouldn't let anyone else drive it either. However, I did have access to a ten-year-old Ford Escort in electric blue that had ex–Panda car written all over it. Obviously Nightingale shopped at the same used-car showroom as Leslie. You can always tell an old cop car because however hard you scrub, it always smells of old cop.

SHOREDITCH, WHITECHAPEL, Wapping—the old and the new East End mashed up together by money and intransigence. Mother Thames lived east of the White Tower in a converted warehouse just short of the Shadwell basin. It was the other side of the slipway from the Prospect of Whitby, an ancient pub that was a legendary jazz venue back in the day. My dad had sat in there with Johnny Keating, but had managed, with his finely tuned ability to sabotage his own career, to miss performing with Lita Roza—I think they got Ronnie Hughes to replace him.

To the main road the warehouse showed a blind face of London brick pierced by modern windows, but on the Thames side the old loading wharves had been converted into a car park. I parked between an orange Citroën Picasso and a firebrick-red Jaguar XF with an Urbandance FM sticker in the windscreen.

As I stepped out, I had the clearest sense of *vestigia* so far. A sudden smell of pepper and seawater as quick and shocking as the scream of a gull. Hardly surprising since the warehouse had once been part of the Port of London, the busiest port in the world.

A bitterly cold wind was sweeping up the Thames, so I hurried for the entrance lobby. Somewhere someone was playing music with the bass turned up to health and safety violating levels. The melody, assuming there was one, wasn't audible, but I could hear the bass line in my chest. Above it suddenly there was a trill of feminine laughter, wicked and gossipy. The neo-Victorian lobby was guarded by a top-of-the-line entry phone. I pressed the number Nightingale had given me and waited. I was about to try the number again when I heard the slap of flip-flops on tile approaching the door from the other side. Then it opened to reveal a young black woman with cat-shaped eyes, wearing a black T-shirt that was many sizes too big for her with the words WE RUN TINGZ printed on the front.

"Yeah," she said. "What do you want?"

"I'm Detective Constable Grant," I said. "I'm here to see Mrs. Thames."

The girl looked me up and down and having judged me against some theoretical standard folded her arms across her breasts and glared at me. "So?" she asked.

"Nightingale sent me," I said.

The girl sighed and turned to yell down the communal hallway. "There's some geezer here says he's from the Wizard." Printed on the back of her T-shirt was TINGZ NUH RUN WE.

"Let him in," called a voice from deep inside the building. It had a soft but distinctive Nigerian accent.

"You'd better come in," said the girl and stood aside.

"What's your name?" I asked.

"My name's Beverley Brook," she said and cocked her head as I walked past.

"Pleased to meet you, Beverley," I said.

It was hot inside the building, humid, tropical almost, and sweat prickled on my face and back. I saw the front doors in the communal corridor were wide open and the heavy bass beat came floating down the wrought iron staircase that linked the floors. Either this was the most neighborly block of flats in English history or Mother Thames controlled the whole building.

Beverley led me into a ground floor flat and I tried to keep my eyes off the long legs that emerged slender and brown below the hem of the T-shirt. It was even hotter inside the flat proper and I recognized the smell of palm oil and cassava leaf. I knew exactly the style of home I was in from the walls painted hint of peach to the kitchen full of rice and chicken and Morrisons own brand custard cream biscuits.

We stopped at the threshold to the living room and Beverley beckoned me down so she could murmur in my ear—"You show some respect now." I breathed in cooked hair and cocoa butter. It was like being sixteen again.

During the 1990s when the architect who built this place had been commissioned, he had been told that he was designing luxury apartments for thrusting young professionals. No doubt he envisioned power suits, suspenders and people who would furnish their home with the bleak minimalist style of a Scandinavian detective novel. In his worst nightmare he probably never considered the idea that the owner would use the generous proportions of the living room as an excuse to cram in at least four World of Leather three-piece suites. Not to mention a plasma television, currently showing soccer with the mute on and a huge plant in a pot that I recognized with a start as being a mangrove tree. An actual mangrove *tree* whose knobbly kneed roots spilled over the edges of the pot and had gone questing through the shag pile carpet. I looked up and saw that the topmost branches had thrust up through the ceiling, I could see where the white plaster had flaked away to reveal the pine joists.

Arrayed on the leather sofa was as fine a collection of middle-aged African women as you'd find in a Pentecostal church, all of whom gave me the same once-over that Beverley had. Seated incongruously among them was a skinny white woman in a pink cashmere twinset and pearls who looked perfectly at home, as if she'd wandered in on her way into town and never left. I noticed that the heat wasn't bothering her. She gave me a friendly nod.

But none of this was important, because also in the room was the Goddess of the River Thames.

She sat enthroned on the finest of the executive armchairs. Her hair was braided and threaded with black cotton and tipped with gold so that it stood above her brow like a crown. Her face was round and unlined, her skin as smooth and perfect as a child's, her lips were full and very dark. She had the same black cat-shaped eyes as Beverley. Her blouse and wrap skirt were made from the finest gold Austrian lace, the neckline picked out in silver and scarlet, wide enough to display one smooth plump shoulder and the generous upper slopes of her breasts.

One beautifully manicured hand rested on a side table, at the foot of the table stood burlap sacks and little wooden crates. As I stepped closer, I could smell saltwater and coffee, diesel and bananas, chocolate and fish guts. I didn't need Nightingale to tell me I was sensing something supernatural, a glamour so strong it was like being washed away by the tide. In her presence I found nothing strange that the Goddess of the River was Nigerian.

"So you are the wizard's boy," said Mama Thames. "I thought there was an agreement?"

I found my voice. "I believe it was more of an arrangement."

I was fighting the urge to fling myself to my knees before her and put my face between her breasts and go blubby, blubby, blubby. When she offered me a seat, I was so hard it was painful to sit down.

I caught Beverley snickering behind her hand. So did Mama

Thames, who sent the teenager scuttling for the kitchen. This I know for a fact: the reason African women have children is so that there's someone else to do the housework.

"Would you like some tea?" asked Mama Thames.

I declined politely. Nightingale had been very specific, don't eat or drink anything under her roof. "Do that," he'd said, "and she'll have her hooks in you." My mum would have taken such a refusal as an insult, but Mama Thames just inclined her head graciously. Perhaps this too was all part of the arrangement.

"Your master," she said. "He is well?"

"Yes, ma'am," I said.

"He does seem to get better as he gets older, does our Master Nightingale," she said. Before I could ask what she meant, she had asked after my parents. "Your mother is a Fula—yes?" she asked.

"From Sierra Leone," I said.

"And your father no longer plays, I believe?"

"You know my father?"

"No," she said and gave me a knowing smile. "Only in the sense that all the musicians of London belong to me, especially the jazz- and bluesmen. It's a river thing."

"Are you on speaking terms with the Mississippi, then?" I asked. My father always swore that jazz, like the blues, was born in the muddy water of the Mississippi. My mother swore that it came from the bottle, like all the devil's best work. I'd been joking a little bit, but it suddenly occurred to me that if there was a Mother Thames, why not a god of Old Man River and, if that was so, did they talk? Did they have long phone calls about silting, watersheds and the need for flood management in the tidal regions? Or did they e-mail or text or twitter?

With that reality check, I realized that some of the glamour was wearing off. I think Mama Thames must have sensed it, too, because she gave me a shrewd look and nodded. "Yes," she said. "I see how it is now. How clever of your master to choose you—and they say you can't teach an old dog new tricks."

Two weeks of similarly impenetrable remarks from Nightingale meant that I had developed a sophisticated countermeasure to gnomic utterances—I changed the subject.

"How did you come to be Goddess of the Thames?" I asked.

"Are you sure you want to know?" she asked, but I could tell that she was flattered by my interest. It's a truism that everybody loves to talk about themselves. Nine out of ten confessions arise entirely out of human beings' natural instinct to tell their life stories to an attentive listener. Even if it involves how they came to bludgeon their golf partner to death. Mama Thames was no different; in fact, I realized, gods had an even greater need to explain themselves.

"I came to London in 1957," said Mama Thames. "But I wasn't a goddess then. I was just some stupid country girl with a name that I have forgotten, here to train as a nurse, but if I am honest I have to say I was not a very good nurse. I never liked to get too close to the sick people and there were too many Igbo in my class. Because of those stupid patients I failed all my exams and they threw me out." Mama Thames kissed her teeth at the barefaced cheek of them. "Into the street just like that. And then my beautiful Robert, who had been courting me for three years, says to me, 'I can no longer wait for you to make up your mind and I am going to marry a white bitch Irish woman.'"

She kissed her teeth again and it was echoed around the room by all the other women.

"I was so heartbroken," said Mama Thames, "that I went to kill myself. Oh yes, that is how bad the man broke my heart. So I went to Hungerford Bridge to throw myself in the river. But that is a railway bridge and the old footbridge that ran along the side—very dirty in the those days. All sorts of things used to live on that bridge, tramps and trolls and goblins. It is not the sort of place a decent Nigerian girl wants to throw herself off. Who knows what might be watching. So I went to Waterloo Bridge, but by the time I got there it was sunset and everywhere I looked it was so beautiful that I thought I just cannot bring myself to jump. Then it was dark, so I went home for my dinner. The next morning I got up nice and early and caught a bus to Blackfriars Bridge. But there is that damn statue of Queen Victoria at the north end and even if she is looking the other way, think how embarrassed you would be if she were to turn round and see you standing on the parapet."

The rest of the room shook their heads in agreement.

"There was no way on Earth that I was going to throw myself off Southwark Bridge," said Mama Thames. "So after another long, long walk, where did I find myself?"

"London Bridge?"

Mama Thames reached out and patted me on the knee. "This was the old bridge, the one that was sold soon afterward to that nice American gentleman. Now, there was a man who knew how to show a river a good time. Two barrels of Guinness and a crate of Rhum Barbancourt, that's what I call an offering."

There was a pause while Mama Thames sipped her tea. Beverley entered with a plate of custard creams and placed them within easy reach. I had a biscuit in my hand before I realized what I was doing and put it back. Beverley snorted.

"In the middle of the Old London Bridge was a chapel, a shrine to St. Birinus and I thought, good Sunday Christian that I was, that this would be the right place to jump off. I stood there looking west just as the tide began to turn. London was still a port back then, dying, but like an old man with a long exciting life, full of stories and memories. And terrified that he was going to be old and frail with no one to look after him. Because there was no life left in the river, no Orisa, no spirit, nothing to care for the old man. I heard the River call me by the name I have forgotten and it said, 'We see you are in pain, we see you are weeping like a child because of one man.'

"And I said, 'Oh River, I have come such a long way, but I have failed as a nurse and I have failed as a woman and this is why my man does not love me.'

"And then the River said to me, 'We can take the pain away, we can make you happy and give you many children and grandchildren. All the world will come to you and lay its gifts at your feet.'

"Well," said Mama Thames. "This was a tempting offer, so I asked, 'What must I do? What do you want from me?' And the River answered, 'We want nothing that you were not already willing to give.'

"So I jumped into the water—splash! And I sank all the way to the bottom and let me tell you there are things down there that you wouldn't believe. Let's just say that it needs to be dredged and let it go at that."

She languidly waved her arm toward the river. "I walked out of the river over there on the Wapping Stair where they used to drown pirates. I have been here ever since," she said. "This is the cleanest industrial river in Europe. Do you think that happened by accident, Swinging London, Cool Britannia, the Thames Barrier, do you think that all happened by accident?"

"The Dome?" I asked.

"Now the most popular music venue in Europe," she said. "The Rhine Maidens come to visit me to see how it's done." She gave me a significant look and I wondered who the hell the Rhine Maidens were.

"Perhaps Father Thames sees things differently," I said.

"Baba Thames," spat Mama. "When he was a young man he stood where I stood, on the bridge, and made the same promise I did. But he hasn't been below Teddington Lock since the Great Stink of 1858. He never came back, not even after Bazalgette put the sewers in. Not even for the Blitz, not even when the city was burning. And now he says this is his river."

Mama Thames pulled herself upright in her chair as if posing for a formal portrait.

"I am not greedy," she said. "Let him have Henley, Oxford and Staines. I shall have London and the gifts of all the world at my feet."

"We can't have your people fighting each other," I said. The "royal we" is very important in police work, it reminds the person you're talking to that behind you stands the mighty institution that is the Metropolitan Police, robed in the full majesty of the law and capable, in manpower terms, of invading a small country. You only hope when you're using that term that the whole edifice is currently facing in the same direction as you are.

"It's Baba Thames who is trespassing below the lock," said Mama Thames. "I am not the one that needs to back off."

"We'll be the ones that talk to Father Thames," I said. "We expect you to keep your people under control."

Mama Thames tilted her head to one side and gave me a long slow look. "I'll tell you what," she said. "I'll give you until the Chelsea Flower Show to bring Baba to his senses; after that we shall take matters into our own hands." Her use of the "royal we" was a great deal less tentative than mine.

The interview was over, we exchanged pleasantries and then Beverley Brook showed me to the door. As we got to the atrium, she deliberately let her hip graze mine and I felt a sudden hot flush that had nothing to do with the central heating.

She gave me an arch little look as she opened the door for me.

"Bye-bye, Peter," she said. "See you around."

WHEN I got back to the Folly, I found Nightingale in the Reading Room on the first floor. This was a scattering of upholstered green leather armchairs, footstools and side tables. Glass-fronted mahogany bookcases lined two walls, but Nightingale had admitted to me that in the old days people had generally come here for a nap after lunch. He was doing the *Telegraph* crossword.

He looked up as I sat down opposite. "What did you think?"

"She certainly thinks she's the Goddess of the Thames," I said. "Is she?"

"That's not a terribly useful question," said Nightingale.

Molly silently arrived with coffee and a plate of custard creams. I looked at the biscuits and gave her a suspicious look, but she was unreadable as ever.

"In that case," I said. "Where does their power come from?"

"That's a much better question," said Nightingale. "There are several conflicting theories about that; that the power comes from the belief of their followers, from the locality itself or a divine source beyond the mortal realm."

"What did Isaac think?"

"Sir Isaac," said Nightingale, "had a bit of a blind spot when it came to divinity—he even questioned whether Jesus Christ was truly divine. Didn't like the idea of the trinity."

"Why was that?"

"He had a very tidy mind," said Nightingale.

"Does the power come from the same place as magic?" I asked.

"All of this will be much easier to explain once you've mastered your first spell," he said. "I believe you could get a good two hours of practice in before afternoon tea."

I slunk off in the direction of the lab.

I DREAMED that I was sharing my bed with Leslie May and Beverley Brook, both lithe and naked on either side of me, but it wasn't nearly as erotic as it should have been because I didn't dare embrace one for the fear that I'd mortally offend the other. I had just devised a strategy to get my arms around both at the same time when Beverley sank her teeth into my wrist and I woke with a terrible cramp in my right arm.

It was bad enough to make me fall out of bed and thrash around being uselessly stoic for a good two minutes. There's nothing like excruciating pain for waking you up, so once it was clear I wasn't going back to sleep I left my room and went looking for a snack. The basement of the Folly was a warren of rooms left over from when it boasted dozens of staff, but I knew that the back stairs bottomed out next to the kitchen. Not wanting to disturb Molly, I padded down the steps as quietly as I could, but as I reached the basement I saw that the kitchen lights were on. As I got closer I heard Toby growl, then bark and then a strange rhythmic hissing sound. A good copper knows when not to announce his presence so I crept to the kitchen door and peered in.

Molly, still dressed in her maid's outfit, was perched on the edge of the scarred oak table that dominated one side of the kitchen. Beside her on the table was a beige ceramic mixing bowl and sitting, some three meters in front of her, was Toby. Since the door was behind her shoulder, Molly didn't see me watching as she dipped her hand into the mixing bowl and lifted out a cube of chopped meat—raw enough to be dripping.

Toby barked with excitement as Molly teased him with the meat for a moment before sending it flying toward him with an expert flick of her wrist. Toby did an impressive jump from a sitting position and caught the meat in midair. At the sight of Toby chewing industriously, while turning tight little circles, Molly began to laugh—the rhythmic hissing sound I'd heard earlier.

Molly picked up another cube of meat and waved it at Toby, who did a little dance of doggy anticipation. This time Molly faked him out, hissing at his confused twirling and then, when she was sure he was watching, popping the bloody piece of meat into her own mouth. Toby barked crossly but Molly stuck out an unnaturally long and prehensile tongue at him.

I must have gasped or shifted my weight because Molly leaped off the table and spun to face me. Eyes wide, mouth open to reveal sharp pointed teeth, blood, bright red against her pale skin, dribbling down her chin. Then she clamped her hand over her mouth and with a look of startled shame ran silently from the kitchen. Toby gave me an irritated growl.

"It's not my fault," I told him. "I just wanted a snack."

I don't know what he was complaining about; he got the rest of the bowl of meat—I got a glass of water.

CHAPTER 5

Action at a Distance

APART FROM the cramp and a definite improvement in the strength of my grip, my efforts to create my own werelight were frustrating. Every other morning Nightingale would demonstrate the spell and I'd spend up to four hours a day opening my hand in a meaningful manner. Fortunately, I got a break three weeks into February when Leslie May and I were due to give evidence against Celia Munroe, the perpetrator of the Leicester Square Cinema assault.

That morning we both dutifully turned up in our uniforms, magistrates like their constables to be in uniform, at the requisite time of 10:00 A.M. in the firm and certain knowledge that the case would be delayed at least until 2:00 P.M. As forward thinking and ambitious constables, we'd brought our own reading material; Leslie had the latest *Blackstone's Police Investigator's Manual* and I had Horace Pitman's *Legends of the Thames Valley*, published in 1897.

City of Westminster Magistrates' Court is around the back of Victoria Station on the Horseferry Road. It's a bland box of a building built in the 1970s; it was considered to be so lacking in architectural merit that there was talk of listing it so that it could be preserved for posterity as an awful warning. Inside, the waiting areas maintained the unique combination of cramped busyness and barren inhumanity that was the glory of British architecture in the second half of the twentieth century.

There were two benches outside the court. We sat on one while the accused, Celia Munroe, her lawyer and a friend she'd brought along for moral support shared the other with Mr. Ranatunga and Mr. Ranatunga's brother. None of them wanted to be there and all of them blamed us.

"Any word from Los Angeles?" I asked.

"Brandon Coopertown was a man on the edge," said Leslie. "Apparently all of his American deals had fallen through and his production company was about to fold."

"And that house?" I asked.

"About to go the way of all flesh," said Leslie. I looked blank. "Mortgage was six months in arrears," she said. "And his income this year barely scraped thirty-five thousand."

That was a good ten grand more than I was getting as a full constable—my sympathy was limited.

"It's starting to look like a classic family annihilation," said Leslie, who'd been reading up on her forensic psychology. "Father faces a catastrophic loss of status, he can't live with the shame and decides that without him his wife and kid's lives are meaningless. He snaps, tops a fellow media professional, tops his family and tops himself."

"By making his face fall off?" I asked.

"No theory is ever perfect," said Leslie. "Particularly since we can't even find a reason for William Skirmish being in the West End that night."

"Maybe he was on the pull," I said.

"He wasn't on the pull," said Beverley. "And I should know."

Because William Skirmish's "victim timeline" had become barely relevant to the case, the job of completing it had been handed to the Murder Team's most junior member, i.e., Leslie. Since she'd spent such a lot of time and effort on reconstructing William Skirmish's last hours she was perfectly willing, in fact overjoyed, to share it with me in excruciating detail. For she'd checked out William Skirmish's romantic leanings and found no history of trawling the West End for sex—serially monogamous, that was our William—all of them guys he'd met through work or mutual friends. She'd also traced every single CCTV that he'd passed by that night and as far as Leslie could tell he'd walked from his house to Tufnel Park Station and caught the tube to Tottenham Court Road—from there he'd walked straight to Covent Garden, via Mercer Street, and his fatal encounter with Coopertown. No deviation or hesitation—as if he had an appointment.

"Almost as if something was messing with his head," she said. "Right?"

So I told her about the *dissimulo* spell and the theory that something had invaded Coopertown's mind, forced him to change his face, kill William Skirmish and then his family. This led, naturally, to a description of my visit to Mama Thames, the magic lessons and Molly "God knows what she is" Maid.

"Should you be telling me this?" asked Leslie.

"I don't see why not," I said. "Nightingale's never told me not to. Your boss believes this stuff is real too, he just don't like it very much."

"So something was messing with Coopertown's mind— right?" asked Leslie.

"Right," I said.

"So whatever that was," said Leslie, "could have been interfering with William Skirmish's mind as well. It could have made him come down west just so he could have his head knocked off. I mean if it can mess with one person's mind why not another, why not yours or mine?"

I remembered the horror of Coopertown's face as he lurched toward me across the balcony—the smell of blood. "Thank you for that thought, Leslie," I said. "I shall certainly treasure it forever, probably late at night when I'm trying to sleep."

Leslie glanced at where Celia Monroe sat demurely. "She had the same kind of sudden mad rage," she said. "What if her mind had been messed with too?"

"Her face didn't fall off," I said.

Celia Monroe caught us looking at her and flinched. "What if Coopertown was the big splash," said Leslie, "and she was just an echo. There could have been other incidents going on all over the place, but we just happened to be there when this one blew."

"We could check the crime reports and see if anything fits," I said. "See if there's a cluster."

"That would be Westminster and Camden," said Leslie. "That's a lot of crime."

"Limit it to physical assaults and first offenses," I said. "The computer should do most of the work."

"What are you going to be doing?" she asked.

"I shall be learning to make light," I said loftily.

Two DAYS later, Nightingale called me downstairs just as I left the bathroom; practice was canceled and so, it seemed, was breakfast. Nightingale was wearing what I recognized as his "working suit," light brown herringbone tweed, double-breasted, leather patches on the elbows. He had his original Burberry trench coat folded over his arm and he was carrying his silver-topped cane—something I'd never seen him do in daylight before.

"We're going to Purley," he said, and to my surprise threw me the keys to the Jag.

"What's in Purley?" I asked.

"I'm not going to tell you," he said. "I'd rather you gathered your own impressions."

"Is this police business or apprentice stuff?" I asked.

"Both," said Nightingale.

I climbed behind the wheel of the Jag, turned the ignition and took a moment to savor the sound of the engine. It's important not to rush the good things in life.

"Whenever you're ready," said Nightingale.

She didn't handle as well as I had expected, but the way the engine responded to my foot on the accelerator made up for any other faults, including the oversteer and the heater that periodically blew hot stale air into my face.

I took us across Lambeth Bridge; weekday traffic in London is always bad and we stop-started all the way past the Oval, through Brixton and on to Streatham. Beyond that we were into the South London suburbs, hectares of Edwardian two-story terraced housing interspersed with interchange-able high streets. Occasionally we passed irregular rectangles of green space, the remnants of ancient villages that had grown together like spots of mold on a petri dish.

The A23 morphed into the Purley Way and we passed a pair of tall chimneys crowned with the IKEA logo. Next stop was Purley, famous place Purley, know what I mean?

A red VW Transporter with LFB trimming was waiting for us in the car park at Purley Station. As we pulled up beside it, a big man got out of the side door and raised his hand in greeting. He was in his forties, he had a broken nose and hair cut down to a brown fuzz. Nightingale introduced him as Frank Caffrey.

"Frank works out of the New Cross station; he's our Fire Brigade liaison."

"Liaison for what?" I asked.

"This," said Frank and handed me a canvas satchel; it was unexpectedly heavy and I almost dropped it. Something metal clonked inside.

"Be careful," said Nightingale.

I opened the flap and had a look. Inside were two metal cylinders the size of aerosol cans, but much heavier. They were white with *No. 80 WP Gren.* stenciled around the body. At the top there was a spring release trigger held in place by a large metal pin. I'm not a military buff, but I know a hand grenade when I see one. I looked at Nightingale, who gave me an irritable wave.

"Put them away," he said.

I closed the satchel and settled it gingerly over my shoulder.

Nightingale turned back to Frank. "Are your people ready?" he asked.

"Two fire engines on standby—just in case."

"Good man," said Nightingale. "We should be done in about half an hour."

We got back into the Jag and Nightingale directed me across the station bridge and down a couple of identical streets until he said, "This one here."

We found a parking spot round the corner and walked the rest of the way.

Grasmere Road ran parallel to the railway and looked utterly normal, a string of detached and semidetached houses built in the 1920s with mock Tudor façades and bay windows. There was nobody about, the kids were all at school, their parents were at work and we kept the pace casual, at least as casual as I could manage with a pair of grenades banging against my hip. Anyone watching would have taken us for a pair of feral estate agents out marking their territory.

Nightingale made a sudden left turn through the gate of a particular house and headed for the wooden door-sized gate that blocked access to the side passage. Without slowing down he thrust his right arm, palm forward, at the gate and with a tiny sound the lock popped out of the wood and clattered on the pathway beyond.

We stepped through the open gate and stopped in the blind spot. Nightingale nodded at the gate and I propped it closed with a big terra-cotta flowerpot. There was still soil in the flowerpot with a shriveled black stalk poking out. I checked the similar pots lined up on the sunny side of the path; they were all dead too. Nightingale stooped down, grabbed a handful of soil and crumbled it beneath his nose. I followed his lead; the soil smelt of nothing, sterile, as if it had been left on a windowsill for too long.

"They've been here awhile," said Nightingale.

"Who has?" I asked, but he didn't answer.

The house backed onto the railway tracks, so we had to worry only about neighbors on two sides. The garden wasn't a jungle, but the lawn looked like it hadn't been mown for months and sections of once-neat flower beds were as dead as the flowerpots. The French doors that led out to the garden patio were locked and the curtains firmly drawn. We worked our way round to the kitchen; blinds were down across the windows and the door was bolted from the inside. I watched closely, expecting Nightingale to do the lock popping thing again, but instead he just smashed the window with his cane.

He reached through the pane, pulled the bolt and opened the door. I followed him inside.

Apart from the dim light it was a perfectly normal suburban kitchen. Swedish countertops, gas hob and oven, microwave, faux stoneware jars marked sugar, tea and coffee. The fridge-freezer was switched off, notes and bills stuck to the doors with magnets. The newest bill was six months old. Next to it a note read: *Grandad?* Below that was a schedule that included nursery collection times.

"There are kids living here," I said.

Nightingale looked grim. "Not anymore," he said. "That was one of the things that alerted us."

"This isn't going to turn out well, is it?" I asked.

"Not for the family that was living here," he said.

We crept into the hallway. Nightingale indicated that I should check upstairs, I extended my baton and kept it ready as I climbed the steps. The window over the stairs had had sheets of black construction paper crudely taped over to block the sunlight. One of the sheets had a child's drawing of a house, square windows, a pig's tail of smoke from a misshapen chimney and mummy and daddy stick figures standing proudly off to one side.

As I stepped onto the gloomy landing, a word formed in my mind, two syllables, starts with a V and rhymes with dire. I froze in place. Nightingale said that everything was true, after a fashion, and that had to include vampires, didn't it? I doubted they were anything like they were in books and TV, and one thing for certain, they absolutely weren't going to sparkle in the sunlight.

There was a door on my left. I forced myself to go through it. A child's bedroom, a boy young enough to still have Legos and action figures scattered on the floor. The bed was neatly made with no-nonsense blue-and-purple matching pillowcases and duvet cover. The boy had liked Ben 10 and Chelsea FC enough to put their posters on his walls. There was a smell of dust, but none of the mildew and damp that I would associate with a long-abandoned house. The master bedroom was the same, the bed neatly made up, an air of dry dustiness, but no cobwebs in the corners of the ceiling. The digital alarm clock by the bed had stopped despite being plugged into the mains. When I picked it up, white sand trickled out from a bottom seam. I replaced it carefully and made a mental note to check it later.

The main room at the back of the house was the nursery. Beatrix Potter wallpaper, a cot, playpen, a hypoallergenic wooden mobile from Galt's Educational Toys shivered in the draft from the open door. As with the other rooms, there was no sign of a struggle or even a rapid departure; everything was neatly squared away. Unnatural in a child's bedroom. Equally unnatural was the lack of shower mold in the bathroom and the dusty nonsmell of the water in the cistern.

The last room on the top floor was what an estate agent would call a "half bedroom," suitable for small children or midgets with agoraphobia. This had been converted into a mini-office with a two-year-old Dell PC and unsurprisingly an IKEA filing cabinet and desk lamp. When I touched the computer I got a flash of dust and ozone, a *vestigium* that I recognized from the master bedroom. I popped open the side of the case and found the same white sand inside. I rubbed it between my fingers; it was very fine, powdery even, but definitely granular and flecked with gold. I was about to pull the motherboard when Nightingale arrived in the doorway.

"What the hell are you waiting for?" he hissed.

"I'm checking the computer," I said.

He hesitated, pushed his hair back off his forehead. "Leave it," he said. "Only one last place to look."

I'd have to remember to come back with an evidence bag and grab the whole computer.

There was a door in the hallway that led to a set of narrow stairs heading down. The steps were worn hardwood planks that I guessed had been laid down when the house was built, a bare bulb dangled just inside the door, half blinding me and making the gloom at the base of the stairs more intense.

The basement, I thought, why am I not surprised.

"Well," said Nightingale. "We're not getting any younger."

I was happy to let him go first.

I shivered as we went down the narrow stairs; it was cold, like descending into a freezer, but I noticed that when I breathed out, my breath didn't mist. I put my hand under my armpit, but there was no temperature differential. This wasn't physical cold, this had to be a type of *vestigia*. Nightingale paused, shifted his weight and flexed his shoulders like a boxer preparing to fight.

"Are you feeling this?" he asked.

"Yes," I whispered. "What is it?"

"*Tactus disvitae*," he said. "The smell of antilife—they must be down here."

He didn't say what and I didn't ask. We started down the stairs again.

The basement was narrow and well lit, I was surprised to find, by a fluorescent tube that ran half its length. Someone had mounted shelves along one wall and optimistically assembled a workbench underneath. More recently an old mattress had been thrown down on the concrete floor and on that mattress lay two vampires. They looked like tramps, old-fashioned tramps, the kind that dressed up in ragged layers of clothes and growled at you from the shadows. The sensation of cold intensified as Nightingale and I got closer. They looked like they were asleep, but there were no breathing sounds and none of the fug a sleeping human being would produce in a confined space.

Nightingale handed me a framed family photograph, obviously looted from a living room mantelpiece, and transferred his cane to his right hand.

"I need you to do two things," he said. "I need you to confirm their identities and check them both for a pulse. Can you do that?"

"What are you going to be doing?"

"I'm going to cover you," he said. "In case they wake up."

I considered this for a moment. "Are they likely to wake up?"

"It's happened before," said Nightingale.

"How often before?" I asked.

"It gets more likely the longer we're down here," said Nightingale.

I crouched down and reached out gingerly to draw back the collar of the closest one's coat. I was careful not to touch the skin. It was the face of a middle-aged man, white with unnaturally smooth cheeks and pallid lips. I checked him against the photograph and although the features were the same, he bore no true resemblance to the smiling father in the picture. I shifted round to get a look at the second body; this one was female and her face matched that of the mother. Mercifully, Nightingale had chosen a photo without the children in it. I reached out to feel for a pulse and hesitated.

"Nothing lives on these bodies," said Nightingale. "Not even bacteria."

I pressed my fingers against the male's neck. His skin was physically cool and there was no pulse. The female was the same. I stood up and backed away. "Nothing," I said.

"Back upstairs," said Nightingale. "Quickly now."

I didn't run, but I wouldn't call what I did up those stairs casual either. Behind me Nightingale came up backward, his cane held at the ready. "Get the grenades," he said.

I took the grenades from the satchel; Nightingale took one and showed me what to do. My hand was shaking a little and the pin proved harder to pull than I expected—I guess that's a safety feature on a grenade. Nightingale pulled the pin on his own grenade and gestured down the basement stairs.

"On the count of three," he said. "And make sure it goes all the way down to the bottom." He counted and after three we threw the grenades down the stairs and I, stupidly, stood watching it bounce down to the bottom until Nightingale grabbed my arm and dragged me away.

We hadn't even reached the front door when I heard a double thump beneath our feet. By the time we were out of the house and into the front garden white smoke was billowing out of the basement.

"White phosphorous," said Nightingale.

A thin scream began from somewhere inside. Not human but close enough.

"Did you hear that?" I asked Nightingale.

"No," he said. "And neither did you."

Concerned neighbors rushed out to see what was happening to their property values, but Nightingale showed them his warrant card. "Don't worry, we made sure nobody was inside," he said. "Lucky we were passing, really."

The first fire engine pulled up less than three minutes later and we were hustled away from the house. The Fire Brigade recognize only two kinds of people at a fire, victims and obstacles and if you don't want to be either, it's best to stay back.

Frank Caffrey arrived on the scene and exchanged nods with Nightingale before striding over to the leading fireman to get briefed. Nightingale didn't have to explain how it would go down; once the fire was out, Frank, as Fire Investigation Officer, would examine the scene and declare that it was caused by something plausible and sanitize any evidence to the contrary. No doubt there were equally discreet arrangements for dealing with the remains of the bodies in the basement and the whole thing would pass off as just another daytime house fire. Probably an electrical fault, lucky no one was in there at the time, makes you think about getting a smoke detector, doesn't it?

And that, ladies and gentlemen, is how we deal with vampires in old London Town.

IT'S HARD to describe what success felt like. Even before I managed to produce my first spell, I slowly became aware that I was getting closer. Like a car engine turning over on a cold morning, I could sense something catching on my thoughts. An hour into my practice I stopped, took a deep breath and opened my hand.

And there it was, the size of a golf ball and as brilliant as the morning sun—a globe of light.

And that's when I found out why Nightingale insisted that I kept a sink filled with water while I did the exercise. Unlike his globe of light, mine was yellow and giving off heat, loads of heat. I yelled as my palm burned and stuck my hand in the sink. The globe sputtered and went out.

"You burned your hand, didn't you?" said Nightingale. I hadn't heard him come in.

I pulled my hand out of the water and had a look. There was a pinkish patch on my palm, but it didn't look that serious.

"I did it," I said. I couldn't believe it, I'd done real magic. It wasn't some stage trick by Nightingale.

"Do it again," he said.

This time I held my hand directly over the sink, formed the key in my mind and opened my hand.

Nothing happened.

"Don't think about the pain," said Nightingale. "Find the key, do it again."

I looked for the key, felt the engine turn over and opened my hand to release the clutch.

It burned me again, but it definitely wasn't as hot and my hand was much closer to the water. Still, I checked my palm—this time it was going to blister for sure.

"And again," said Nightingale. "Reduce the heat, keep the light."

I was surprised how easy I found it to obey. Key, power, release—more light, less heat. Warmth this time, not heat, and a yellow tone like an old 40-watt bulb.

Nightingale didn't have to tell me again.

I opened my palm and produced a perfect globe of light.

"Now hold it," said Nightingale.

It was like balancing a rake on your palm; the theory is simple, but the practice lasts five seconds tops. My beautiful globe popped like a soap bubble.

"Good," said Nightingale. "I'm going to give you a word and I want you to say this word every time you do the spell. But it's very important that the spell's effect is consistent."

"Why's that?"

"I'll explain why in a minute," said Nightingale. "The word is *lux*."

I did the spell again, key, motor. I spoke the word on the release. The globe sustained for longer—it was definitely getting easier.

"I want you to practice this spell," said Nightingale. "And just this spell for at least another week. You'll have the urge to experiment, to make it brighter, to move it around . . ."

"You can move it around?"

Nightingale sighed. "Not for the next week. You practice until the word becomes the spell and the spell becomes the word. So that to say *'Lux'* is to make light."

"Lux?" I said. "What language is that?"

Nightingale looked at me in surprise.

"It's Latin for light," he said. "They don't teach Latin in secondary moderns anymore?"

"Not at my school they didn't."

"Not to worry," said Nightingale. "I can tutor you in that as well."

Lucky me, I thought.

"Why use Latin?" I asked. "Why not use English or make up your own words."

"Lux, the spell you just did, is what we call a form," said Nightingale. "Each of the basic forms you learn has a name— *lux, impello, scindere*—others. Once these become ingrained you can combine the forms to create complex spells the way you combine words to create a sentence."

"Like musical notation?" I asked.

Nightingale grinned. "Exactly like musical notation," he said.

"So why not use musical notation?"

"Because in the main library there are thousands of books detailing how to do magic and all of them use the standard Latin forms," said Nightingale.

"Presumably all this was invented by Sir Isaac?" I asked.

"The original forms are in the *Principia Artes Magices,*" said Nightingale. "There have been changes over the years."

"Who made the changes?"

"People who can't resist fiddling with things," said Nightingale. "People like you, Peter."

So Newton, like all good seventeenth-century intellectuals, wrote in Latin because that was the international language of science, philosophy and, I found out later, upmarket pornography. I wondered if there was a translation.

"Not of the *Artes Magices,*" said Nightingale.

"Wouldn't want the hoi polloi learning magic, would we?"

"Quite," said Nightingale.

"Don't tell me," I said. "In the other books, it's not just the forms. Everything is written in Latin."

"Except for the stuff that's in Greek and Arabic," said Nightingale.

"How long does it take to learn all the forms?" I asked.

"Ten years," said Nightingale. "If you work at it."

"I'd better get on."

"Practice for two hours and then stop," said Nightingale. "Don't do the spell again until at least six hours have passed."

"I'm not tired, you know," I said. "I can keep this up all day."

"If you overdo it, there are consequences," said Nightingale.

I didn't like the sound of that at all. "What kind of consequences?"

"Strokes, brain hemorrhages, aneurysms . . ."

"How do you know when you've overdone it?"

"When you have a stroke, brain hemorrhage, aneurysm . . ." said Nightingale.

I remembered Brandon Coopertown's shrunken cauliflower brain and Dr. Walid saying, "This is your brain on magic."

"Thank you for the safety tip," I said.

"Two hours," said Nightingale from the doorway. "Then meet in the study for your Latin lesson."

I waited until he had gone before opening my hand and whispering, *"Lux!"*

This time the globe gave off a soft white light and no more heat than a sunny day.

Fuck me, I thought. I can do magic.

CHAPTER 6

The Coach House

DURING THE day, if I wasn't in the lab or studying, or out, it was my job to listen for the bell and answer the front door when it rang. This happened so infrequently that the first time it occurred it took me a minute to work out what the noise was.

It turned out to be Beverley Brook in a electric blue quilted jacket with the hood up.

"You took your time," she said. "It's freezing out here."

I said she should come in, but she looked shifty and said she couldn't.

"Mum says I'm not to; she says that it's inimical to the likes of us."

"Inimical?"

"There's like magic force fields and stuff," said Beverley.

That would make sense, I thought; it would certainly explain why Nightingale was so relaxed about security.

"Why are you here, then?"

"Well," said Beverley. "When a mummy river and a daddy river love each very much . . ."

"Funny."

"Mum says that there's some weird stuff at the UCH you should check out."

"What kind of weird stuff?"

"She said it was on the news."

"We don't have a TV," I said.

"Not even freeview?"

"No kind of TV at all," I said.

"Brutal," said Beverley. "You coming out or what?"

"I'll go see what the inspector says," I said.

I found Nightingale in the library, making notes on what I strongly suspected was tomorrow's Latin homework. I explained about Beverley and he told me to check it out. By the time I got back to the lobby, Beverley had risked coming just inside the door, although she stood as close to the threshold as she could get. Surprisingly, Molly was standing beside her, their heads close together as if exchanging confidences. When they heard me coming they separated with suspicious speed—I felt my ears burning. Molly scurried past me and vanished into the depths of the Folly.

"Are we taking the Jag?" asked Beverley as I put my coat on.

"Why, are you coming with me?" I asked.

"I have to," said Beverley. "Mum told me to facilitate."

"Facilitate what?"

"The woman that called it in is an acolyte," said Beverley. "She won't talk to you without me there."

"Okay," I said. "Let's go."

"Are we taking the Jag?"

"Don't be stupid," I said. "UCH is walking distance."

"Aw," said Beverley. "I wanted to take the Jag."

So we took the Jag and got caught in a traffic jam on the Euston Road and then spent another twenty minutes looking for a parking space. It took us, I estimated, twice as long to drive as it would have to walk.

UNIVERSITY COLLEGE Hospital takes up two whole blocks between Tottenham Court Road and Gower Street. Founded in the nineteenth century, its main claim to fame was as the teaching hospital for the University College of London and the birthplace of one Peter Grant, apprentice wizard. Since that momentous day in the mid-eighties, half the site had been redeveloped into a gleaming blue-and-white tower that looked as if a bit of Brasilia had crash-landed in the middle of Victorian London.

The lobby was a wide clean space with lots of glass and white paint marred only by the large numbers of sick people shuffling around. Police officers spend a lot of time in casualty, since you're either asking people where they got their knife wounds from, dealing with the violently drunk or being stitched up yourself. It's one of the reasons why so many coppers marry nurses—that and nurses understand about unreasonable shift systems.

Beverley's acolyte was a nurse, a pale skinny one with purple hair and an Australian accent. She stared at me suspiciously.

"Who's this," she asked Beverley.

"This is a friend," she said, and put her hand on the woman's arm. "We tell him everything."

The woman relaxed and gave me a smile full of hope. She looked like one of the Pentecostal teenagers from my mum's second-from-last church. "Isn't it wonderful to be part of something real," she said.

I agreed that being part of something real was indeed wonderful, but it would be groovy if she could tell me what she'd seen. I actually used the word "groovy" and she didn't even flinch, which was worrying on so many levels.

According to her, a cycle courier had been brought in by ambulance following a road traffic accident and while he was being treated he'd kicked the attending doctor in the eye. The doctor had been stunned rather than seriously injured and the cycle courier had run out of casualty before security could nab him.

"Why bring it to us?" I asked.

"It was the laughing," said the nurse. "I was going back to the treatment bay when I heard this screeching laugh, like a mynah bird. Then I heard Eric, Dr. Framline, that's the doctor who was injured, I heard him swearing and then the cycle courier comes charging out of the bay and there was something wrong with his face."

"Wrong how?" I asked.

"Just wrong," she said. Displaying precisely the characteristics that make eyewitnesses such a useful part of any police investigation. "He went past so fast I didn't see much, but it just looked . . . wrong."

She showed me the treatment bay where it happened, a white-and-beige cubicle with an examination bed and a curtain for privacy. The *vestigium,* note that I'm using the singular here, slapped me in the face as soon as I walked in. Violence, laughter, dried sweat and leather. It was the same as poor William Skirmish when he was lying in the mortuary, only minus the annoying yappy dog.

Two months previously, I would have walked into that treatment bay, shivered, thought "That's weird" and walked right back out again.

Beverley stuck her head in and demanded to know whether I'd found anything.

"I need to borrow your phone," I said.

"What happened to yours?" she asked.

"I blew it up in a magic accident," I said. "Don't ask."

Beverley pouted and handed over a surprisingly chunky Ericsson. The casing had latex seals and the buttons were large and protected by a layer of clear plastic. "It's designed to go underwater," she said. "Don't ask."

"Can you get your acolyte to find out Dr. Framline's address for me?"

Beverley shrugged. "Sure," she said. "But, you talk, you pay!"

While Beverley was distracted with her task, I took her phone outside to Beaumont Place, a quiet pedestrianized road that ran between the old and the new bits of the hospital, and called Nightingale. I described the incident and the *vestigium* and he agreed that it was worth stepping up the search for the courier.

"I want to keep an eye on the doctor," I said.

"Interesting," said Nightingale. "Why?"

"I'm thinking of the sequence of events around Skirmish's murder," I said. "Toby bites Coopertown on the nose, that's when it starts, but Coopertown doesn't go postal until later when he runs into Skirmish in Covent Garden."

"You think it was set off by a chance meeting?"

"That's just it," I said. "Leslie says that the Murder Team haven't found a reason for Skirmish to even be in Covent Garden that night. He gets a bus down to the West End, meets Coopertown and gets his head knocked off. No meetings, no friends—nothing."

"You think both parties were affected?" asked Nightingale. "You think an outside agency made them meet?"

"Is such a thing possible?"

"Anything's possible," said Nightingale. "If your dog was affected along with his master *and* Coopertown, then it would explain why he was so sensitive to the *vestigia*."

I noticed Toby was my dog now. "So it's possible?"

"Yes," said Nightingale, but I could tell he was skeptical.

"What if the cycle courier is playing Toby's role and the doctor is taking Coopertown's?" I asked. "At the very least it wouldn't hurt to keep an eye on the doctor until the courier is caught."

"Can you handle that?" asked Nightingale.

"No problem," I said.

"Good," said Nightingale, and said he'd coordinate the search for the cycle courier. I hung up as Beverley Brook sauntered over from the hospital, the swing of her hips dragging at my eyes. She grinned when she caught me looking and handed me a slip of paper—Dr. Framline's address.

"What next, guv?" she asked.

"Where can I drop you?" I asked.

"No no no," Beverley said quickly. "Mum says I was to facilitate."

"You've facilitated," I said. "You can go home now."

"I don't want to go home," she said. "Mum's got the whole entourage round, Ty and Effra and Fleet, not to mention all the old ladies. You don't know what it's like."

Actually, I knew exactly what it was like, but I wasn't going to tell Beverley that.

"Come on, I'll be good," she said giving me the big-eye. "I'll let you borrow my phone."

I gave in before she escalated to the trembling lip. "But you have to do what I say."

"Yes, guv," she said and saluted.

You can't do a stakeout in a vintage Jag, so, much to Beverley's disappointment, we drove back to the Folly to swap it for the ex-Panda. The Folly's garage is out the back of the building and takes up the entire bottom floor of the converted coach house. From the mews, you can see where the original doors, wide and high enough to accept a coach and four, had been bricked in and replaced with a more modest sliding door. The Jag and the ex-Panda rattled around inside a space big enough for four carriages.

Unlike the entrance hall, the coach house didn't seem to bother Beverley at all. "What happened to the inimical magic force fields?" I asked.

"Not in here," she said. "Bit of protection on the garage door and that's it."

Nightingale had left the building, but Molly met me in the lobby with a Tesco carrier bag full of sandwiches wrapped in grease paper and tied up with string. I didn't ask what was in them, but I doubted it was chicken tikka masala. Back in the coach house, I threw my bag and sandwiches in the back of the ex-Panda, made sure Beverley had her seat belt on and headed off to harass a junior doctor.

DR. FRAMLINE LIVED in a two-story Victorian terrace off the Romford Road in Newham. It was farther east than I like to go, but not a bad neighborhood. I found a parking space with decent sightlines of the front door and got out. I knew no force on earth was going to keep Beverley in the car, so I let her come with me on the strict understanding that she'd keep her mouth shut.

There was only one doorbell and the small front garden was given over to gravel, the dustbins and a couple of empty bright red plant pots, so I was thinking that either Dr. Framline owned the whole place or he was sharing with friends. I pressed the bell and a cheerful voice said it was on its way. The voice belonged to a plump round-faced woman of the sort that develops a good personality because the alternative is suicide.

I showed my warrant card. "Good afternoon. My name's Peter Grant, I'm from the police and this is my colleague Beverley Brook, who's a river in South London." You can get away with stuff like that with civilians because their brains lock in place on the word "police."

Actually, I think I may have overdone it, because the woman frowned at Beverley and asked, "Did you just say she was a river?" Which is why you should never show off when on duty.

"It's an office joke," I said.

"She seems a bit young to be police," said the woman.

"She's not," I said. "She's on work experience."

"Can I see your identification again?" asked the woman.

I sighed and handed it over. Beverley snickered.

"I can give you the number of my superior if you like," I said. This normally does the trick since members of the public are generally lazier than they are suspicious.

"Are you here about what happened at the hospital?" asked the woman.

"Yes," I said relieved. "That's exactly why we're here."

"Only Eric's gone into town," she said. "You just missed him, he went fifteen minutes ago."

Of course he has, I thought, no doubt to some spot less than five hundred meters from where Beverley and I started out. "Do you know where he was going?"

"Why do you want to know?"

"We think we have a line on the man who attacked him," I said. "We just need him to confirm a few details. If we do this quickly, we may be able to make an arrest tonight."

That perked her up and got me not just the name of the gastropub Dr. Framline was heading for, but also his mobile number. Beverley had to trot to keep up with me as we headed back to the car.

"What's the rush?" she asked as we climbed in.

"I know the pub," I said. "It's on the corner of Neal and Shelton Street." I pulled out without waiting for Beverley to buckle up. "Right across from there is the pedestrian space outside Urban Outfitters."

"Urban Outfitters, eh," said Beverley. "That explains the Dr. Denim shirt."

"My mum bought me that," I said.

"And you think that's less embarrassing?"

I gunned the ex-Panda, or at least I came as close to gunning it as you can with a ten-year-old Ford Escort, and went through a set of lights on red. There was a yell behind me. "Cycle couriers like to hang out there," I said. "It's convenient for the pubs and cafés, but also close to most of their clients."

Rain began to splatter on the windshield and I had to ease up—the streets were getting wet. How long would it take Dr. Framline to reach Covent Garden by public transport, not less than an hour, but he had a head start and this was London where the tube was often faster than the car.

"Call Dr. Framline," I told Beverley.

She grumbled, dialed, listened and said, "Voice mail. He's probably underground."

I gave her Leslie's number. "Remember," she said. "You talk you pay."

"That's the way it works," I said.

Beverley held the phone to my ear so I could keep both hands on the controls. When Leslie picked up, I could hear the incident room at Belgravia in the background—proper police work.

"What happened to your phone?" she asked. "I've been trying to ring you all morning."

"I broke it doing magic," I said. "Which reminds me—I need you to book me out an airwave." Airwave was the all-singing, all-dancing digital radio handset for coppers.

"Can't you get one from your nick?" she asked.

"You're joking," I said. "I don't think Nightingale's got the hang of airwave yet. Or even radios, for that matter. In fact, I think he might be a bit hazy on telephones."

She agreed to meet us at Neal Street.

The rain was sheeting down as I crawled up the semi-pedestrianized length of Earlham Street and stopped on the corner where we could get a good view of the pub and the cycle courier hangout. I left Beverley in the car and popped across to check inside the pub, which was deserted; obviously Dr. Framline hadn't arrived yet.

My hair was soaked through when I got back in the car, but I had a towel in my stakeout bag and I used it to squeeze most of the water out. For some reason, Beverley found this hilarious.

"Let me do that," she said.

I handed her the towel and she leaned over and started rubbing my head, one of her breasts pushed against my shoulder and I had to resist an urge to put my arm around her waist. She dug her fingers into my scalp.

"Don't you ever comb this?" she asked.

"I can't be bothered," I said. "I just shave down to stubble every spring."

She ran her palm down the back of my head and let it rest, lightly, on the back of my neck. I felt her breath close on my ear.

"You really got nothing from your dad, didn't you?" Beverley sat back in her own seat and tossed the towel into the back seat. "You're mum must have been disappointed. I bet she thought you'd have big curls."

"It could have been worse," I said. "I could have been a girl."

Beverley unconsciously touched her own hair, which was straightened and side parted into wings that reached to her shoulders. "You don't know the half of it," she said. "Which is why you ain't going to get me out into that." She nodded at the rainswept streets.

"If you're supposed to be a goddess . . ."

"Orisa," said Beverley. "We're Orisa. Not spirits, not local geniuses—Orisa."

"Why can't you do something about the weather?" I asked.

"For a start," she said with exaggerated slowness, "you don't mess with the weather and for second, this is North London and this manor belongs to my older sisters."

I'd found a seventeenth-century map of the rivers of London. "That would be the Fleet and the Tyburn?" I asked.

"You can call her Tyburn if you want to spend the rest of the day dangling from a noose," said Beverley. "If you ever meet her, you better make sure you call her Lady Ty. Not that you ever want to meet her. Not that she ever wants to meet you."

"So you don't get on with them?" I asked.

"Fleet is okay," she said. "But nosy. Ty is just stuck-up, lives in Mayfair, goes to posh people's parties, 'knows people that matter.' "

"Mum's favorite?"

"Only because she fixes stuff with the politicians," said Beverley. "Has tea on the terrace at the Palace of Westminster. I get to sit in a car with Nightingale's errand boy."

"If I remember, you're the one that didn't want to go home," I said.

I spotted Leslie's car pulling up behind us; she flashed her lights and got out. I quickly leaned back to open the passenger door for her. Rain hit me in the face hard enough to make me splutter and Leslie practically threw herself onto the backseat.

"I think it's going to flood," she said, and seized my towel to dry her face and hair. She jerked her head at Beverley. "Who's this?" she asked.

"Beverley, this is PC Leslie May," I turned to Leslie. "This is Beverley Brook, river spirit and winner of the London regional all-comers continuous talking championship five years running." Beverley punched me in the arm. Leslie gave her an encouraging smile. "Her mother is the Thames, you know."

"Really," said Leslie. "Who's your dad, then?"

"That's complicated," said Beverley. "Mum said she found me floating down the brook by the Kingston Vale dual carriageway."

"In a basket?" asked Leslie.

"No, just floating," said Beverley.

"She was spontaneously created by the midichlorians," I said. Both women gave me blank looks. "Never mind."

"Has your man arrived yet?" asked Leslie.

"Nobody's arrived since we got here," I said.

"Do you know what he looks like?" said Leslie.

I realized that I didn't have the faintest idea what Dr. Framline looked like; I'd been expecting to interview him at home before I followed him. "I have a description," I said. Leslie gave me a pitying look and pulled out an A4 hard copy of the photo from Dr. Framline's driver's license. "He'd be a decent copper," she told Beverley, "if he could just keep his mind on the details."

She handed me something that looked like the chunky mutant offspring of a Nokia and a walkie-talkie, an airwave handset; I stuffed it in the inside pocket of my jacket. The handset is a bit heavier than a mobile phone and was going to make me lopsided.

"Is that him?" asked Beverley.

We peered out into the rain and saw a couple approaching from the Covent Garden end of Neal Street. The man's face matched the photograph apart from the bruising around his left eye and the railway track of adhesive strips holding the cut on his cheek together. He held an umbrella over himself and his companion, a stocky woman in a lurid orange waterproof. They were both smiling and seemed happy.

We watched in silence as they reached the gastropub and, with a pause to shake out his umbrella, went inside.

"Remind me why we're here again?" asked Leslie.

"Have you found the cycle courier yet?" I asked.

"No," said Leslie. "And I don't think my governor likes your governor treating him as his errand boy."

"Tell him welcome to the club," I said.

"You tell him," said Leslie.

"So what's in the sandwiches?" asked Beverley.

I opened the Tesco bag and unwrapped the packets to find crusty white bread with roast beef and dill pickle garnished with horseradish, very nice, but once it had been fried calves' brains, so I tend to approach Molly's sandwiches with caution. Leslie, who eats without fear and thinks eels in jelly are a delicacy, dove in, but Beverley hesitated.

"If I eat these, you're not going to expect an obligation, are you?" asked Beverley.

"Don't worry about it," I said. "I have an air freshener in the bag."

"I'm serious," said Beverley. "There's a geezer at my mum's flats who turned up to repossess some furniture in 1997; one cup of tea and a biscuit later and he's never left. I used to call him Uncle Bailiff. He does odd jobs around the place, fixes stuff and keeps the place clean and my mother will never let him go." Beverley jabbed me in the chest with her finger. "So I want to know what your intentions are with this sandwich."

"I assure you my intentions are honorable," I said, but part of me was thinking about how close I came to eating that custard cream back at Mama Thames's flat.

"Swear it on your power," said Beverley.

"I don't have any power," I said.

"Good point," said Beverley. "Swear it on your mum's life."

"No," I said. "This is childish."

"Fine," said Beverley. "I'll get my own food." She got out of the car and stomped away, leaving the door open. I noticed that she'd waited for the rain to ease up before throwing a fit.

"Is that true?" asked Leslie.

"Which bit?" I asked.

"Spells, food, obligations, wizards—the bailiff," said Leslie. "For God's sake, Peter, that's false imprisonment at the very least."

"Some of it's true," I said. "I don't know how much. I think becoming a wizard is about discovering what's real and what isn't."

"Is her mum really the goddess of the Thames?"

"She thinks she is and I've met her and I'm beginning to think she might be," I said. "She's got real power, so I'm going to treat her daughter as the real thing until I find out different."

Leslie leaned over the seat back and looked me in the eyes.

"Can you do magic?" she asked softly.

"I can do one spell," I said.

"Show me."

"I can't," I said. "If I do it now I'll blow the airwave sets, and the stereo and possibly the ignition system. That's how I busted my phone—I had it in my pocket when I did my practice."

Leslie tilted her head to the side and gave me a cool look.

I was about to protest when Beverley banged on my window—I rolled it down.

"I just thought you ought to know that it's stopped raining," she said. "And there's a cycle courier walking down the street."

Leslie and I piled out of the car, which shows how inexperienced we really were at basic surveillance, remembered that we were trying to be unobtrusive and pretended to be having casual chat with each other. In our defense, we'd just spent two years in uniform and being obtrusive is what a uniformed constable is all about.

Beverley must have had good eyes because the courier was at the Shaftesbury Avenue end of Neal Street and approaching at a slow deliberate pace. He was pushing his bike, which was suspicious, and I saw that the back wheel was bent out of shape. I felt a deep sense of unease, but I couldn't tell if that was me or something external.

In the near distance, a dog started barking. Behind us, a mother told off a child that wanted to be carried. I could hear rain draining into a gutter somewhere and I found myself straining to hear—I'm not sure what. Then I heard it, a thin, strangled high-pitched giggle that seemed to float in from far away.

The cycle courier looked normal enough, dressed in painfully tight yellow and black Lycra, a messenger bag with a radio attached to its shoulder strap and a street helmet in blue and white. He had a narrow face and a mouth that was a thin line under a sharp nose, but his eyes were worryingly blank. I didn't like the way he was walking; the twisted back wheel scraped the forks and the man's head seemed to bob unnaturally on his neck in time with every revolution. I decided it would be a bad idea to let him get any closer.

"Bastard!" A shout behind me and a rattling crash.

I turned, saw nothing until Leslie pointed to the glass

double doors of Urban Outfitters, where a man was being slammed violently against the inside of the doors. He was jerked out of sight and then smashed against the doors again—hard enough to pop one of the hinges and make a gap large enough for the man to escape. He looked like a tourist or foreign student, well dressed in the European style, dirty blond hair cut the respectable side of too long, a blue Swissair complimentary knapsack still hooked over one shoulder. He shook his head as if bewildered and flinched back as his attacker smacked open the doors and strode toward him.

This was a short plump man with thinning brown hair and round wire-framed glasses. He was wearing a white shirt with a manager's tag clipped to the pocket. He was sweating and his shining face was red with rage.

"I've fucking had it," he screamed. "I try to be polite, but no, you've got to fucking treat me like I'm some fucking slave."

"Oi," shouted Leslie. "Police." She advanced on them, warrant card in her left hand, her right hand resting on the handle of her extendable baton. "What seems to be the problem?"

"He attacked me," said the young man. Definitely an accent, German, I thought.

The enraged shop manager hesitated and turned to look at Leslie, his eyes blinking behind his specs. "He was talking on the phone," said the manager. The violence seemed to have drained out of him. "While he was at the till. It's not even like he got a call—he dialed it himself while he was paying. I'm expected to have a mutually beneficial and courteous interaction with him and the fucker ignores me and makes a phone call."

Leslie stepped between the two men and gently edged the manager backward. "Why don't we go inside," she said. "And you can tell me all about it." It really was a delight to watch her work.

"I mean why?" said the manager. "What was so important it couldn't wait?"

Beverley smacked me in the arm. "Peter," she said. "Over there."

I turned just in time to see Dr. Framline charge up the street brandishing a stick half as tall as he was. Behind him came his date from the gastropub, yelling his name in confusion. I ran as fast as I could, passing the woman quickly, but there was no way I could make Dr. Framline before he reached his target.

The courier didn't even put an arm up to defend himself when Dr. Framline clubbed him hard on the shoulder with the stick. I saw the man's right arm jerk brokenly and his hand lose its grip on the bike, which began to topple sideways.

"The more you take," yelled the doctor, raising the stick again, "the better it is for you."

I hit him low, getting my shoulder into the sweet spot just above his hips so that he went sideways and down and broke my fall instead of the other way round. I heard the bike hit the street and then the stick skittering across the pavement. I tried to pin Dr. Framline, but he seemed amazingly strong and jammed an elbow into my chest hard enough to leave me gasping for breath. I made a grab for his legs and got a knee in the face that made me swear.

"Police," I shouted. "Stop fighting." And amazingly he did. "Thank you," I said; it seemed only polite. I tried to get up, but somebody fetched me such a blow that I was facedown on the pavement again before it even registered I'd been hit. In a street fight, no matter how hurt you are, the pavement is not your friend, so I rolled over and tried to get back up again. As I did, I saw the cycle courier grab the outsized stick off the ground and swing at Dr. Framline. The doctor flinched out of the way, but the stick caught him on the upper part of his arm; he slipped over and went down gasping in pain.

A wave of emotion washed over me, elation, excitement, an undertone of violence, like that of the home crowd at a soccer match when their team gets a chance at the goal.

I saw the *dissimulo* as it happened that time: the courier's chin seemed to bulge and I heard the distinct cracking of bone and teeth as it jutted forward into a sharp point. The lips twisted into a snarl as the nose stretched until it was almost as long. It wasn't a real face, it was a caricature man-in-the-moon face that no human could have in real life. The mouth opened and I could see inside to the red ruin of his jaw.

"That's the way to do it!" he shrieked and lifted his stick.

Leslie's baton hit him in the back of the head, he staggered, Leslie hit him again and with a gurgling sigh he fell forward in front of me. I crawled forward and rolled him over but it was too late. His face slumped like wet papier-mâché. I saw the skin tearing around the nose and chin and then a great dripping flap peeled open and lolled over his forehead. I tried to make myself do something, but nothing in my first-aid training had prepared me for someone's face flopping open like a starfish.

I slid my palm under the flap of skin, flinching at the warm wetness and tried to fold it back over the face, I had some vague idea that I should at least try to stop the bleeding.

"Let me go," yelled Dr. Framline. I looked over and saw that Leslie already had him in handcuffs. "Let me go," he said. "I can help him." Leslie hesitated.

"Leslie," I said and she started uncuffing the doctor.

Too late. The courier went suddenly rigid, his back arched and a tide of blood welled up from his neck and forced it-self out through the rips in his skin and the gaps between my fingers.

Dr. Framline scrambled over and jammed his fingers into the courier's neck. He shifted their position looking for a pulse, but I could see in his expression that there was none. Finally he shook his head and told me to let go. The courier's face flopped open again.

Somebody was screaming and I had to check it wasn't me. It could have been me. I certainly wanted to scream, but I re-membered that right then and there Leslie and I were the only coppers on the scene and the public doesn't like it when the police start screaming; it contributes to an impression of things not being conducive to public calm. I got to my feet and found that we'd attracted a crowd of onlookers.

"Ladies and gentlemen," I said. "Police business. I need you to stand back."

The crowd stood back—being covered in blood can have that effect on people.

WE PRESERVED the scene until the backup arrived, but two-thirds of the crowd had their phones out and were taking video and stills of me, Leslie and the mutilated remains of the cycle courier. The images had already hit the Internet before the ambulance arrived and the paramedic covered the poor sod with a sheet. I spotted Beverley hanging around near the back of the crowd and when she saw that she'd caught my eye, she gave me a little wave, turned and walked away.

Leslie and I found a place under a shop awning and waited for the forensic tent, the swabs and the replacement bunny suit.

"We can't keep doing this," said Leslie. "I'm running out of clothes."

We laughed—sort of. It's not that it gets easier the second time, it's just that by then you know you're still going to wake up the next morning the same person who went to sleep.

A DS from the Murder Team arrived and took charge. She was a squat, angry-faced, middle-aged woman with lank brown hair who looked like she fought Rottweilers for a hobby. This was the legendary Detective Sergeant Miriam Stephanopoulos, Seawoll's right-hand woman and terrifying lesbian. The only joke ever made at her expense goes: "Do you know what happened to the last police officer who made a joke about DS Stephanopoulos?" "No, what did happen to him?" "Nobody else knows either." I said it was the only joke, not a good one.

She seemed to have a soft spot for Leslie, though, so we got processed much faster this time, but as soon as we were done we were bundled into an unmarked car and driven to Belgravia. Nightingale and Seawoll debriefed us in an anonymous conference room at which nobody took notes, but at least we were offered tea.

Seawoll glared at Leslie; he wasn't happy. Leslie glared at me; she wasn't happy that Seawoll wasn't happy. Nightingale wasn't anything except distracted, he only seemed interested when I reported my sense impressions just prior to the attack. After the briefing, we trooped over to the Westminster mortuary where, surprisingly, both Seawoll and Stephanopoulos attended the autopsy. Leslie and I made a point of standing behind them in the hope they wouldn't notice us.

The cycle courier lay on the table with his face splayed open in a way that was becoming horribly familiar. Dr. Walid was giving his conclusion that, somehow, person or persons unknown had managed to trick the victim into changing his face with magic and then set him to attacking random strangers. DS Stephanopoulos gave Seawoll a sharp look at the word "magic," but her boss gave a small shake of his head that said—later, not here.

"His name was Derek Shampwell," said Dr. Walid. "Age twenty-three, Australian citizen, had been in London for three years, no criminal record, hair analysis shows intermittent marijuana use over the last two years."

"Do we know why he was singled out?" asked Seawoll.

"No," said Nightingale. "Although all the cases seem to start with a sense of grievance; Coopertown was bitten by someone's pet, Shampwell was struck by a motor vehicle while riding."

Seawoll glanced at Stephanopoulos. "Hit-and-run on the Strand, sir, in a CCTV blind spot."

"A blind spot?" asked Seawoll. "On the Strand?"

"Thousand-to-one chance," said Stephanopoulos.

"May," barked Seawoll without turning round. "You think there are related cases?"

"Including the incident Grant and I witnessed in the cinema and the one that took place just prior to Shampwell's death, I've identified fifteen cases where the perpetrators have shown uncharacteristic levels of aggression," said Leslie. "All people with clean records, no psychiatric history and all within half a mile of Cambridge Circus."

"How many do we know were actually," Seawoll paused, "possessed?"

"Just the ones whose faces fell off," said Nightingale.

"Just so we're clear," said Seawoll. "The commissioner wants this kept quiet, so PC May liases with PC Grant for the low-level stuff, but anything significant, anything at all, you talk to me. Do you have a problem with this, Thomas?"

"Not at all, Alexander," said Nightingale. "It all seems eminently sensible."

"His parents are flying in tomorrow," said Dr. Walid. "Is it all right if I sew his face back together?"

Seawoll glared at the body. "Fuck," he said.

Nightingale was silent on the drive back to the Folly, but at the foot of the stairs he turned to me and told me to get a good night's sleep. I asked him what he was going to do and he said he'd do some research in the library—see if he couldn't narrow down what was doing the killing. I asked if I could help.

"Train harder," he said. "Learn faster."

As I went upstairs, I met Molly gliding down. She paused and gave me an inquiring look.

"How should I know?" I said. "You know him better than I do."

YOU DON'T tell your governor that you need a broadband connection, cable for preference, because you want to watch soccer. You tell him that you need the Internet so you can access HOLMES directly instead of having constantly to rely on Leslie May. The soccer coverage, movies on demand and multiplayer console games are all merely serendipitous extras.

"Would this involve physically running a cable into the Folly?" asked Nightingale when I tackled him during practice in the lab.

"That's why they call it cable," I said.

"Left hand," said Nightingale and I dutifully produced a werelight with my left hand.

"Sustain it," said Nightingale. "We can't have anything physically entering the building."

I'd got to the point where I could talk while sustaining a

werelight, although it was a strain to make it look as casual as I did. "Why not?"

"There's a series of protections woven around the building," said Nightingale. "They were last set up after the new phone lines were put in in 1941. If we introduce a new physical connection with the outside, it would create a weak spot."

I stopped trying to be casual and concentrated on maintaining the werelight. It was a relief when Nightingale told me to stop.

"Good," he said. "I think you're almost ready to move on to the next form."

I dropped the werelight and caught my breath. Nightingale wandered over to the adjoining bench, where I'd dismantled my old mobile phone and set up the microscope I'd found in a mahogany case in one of the storage cupboards.

He touched the brass and black lacquer tube. "Do you know what this is?" he asked.

"An original Charles Perry number five microscope," I said. "I looked it up on the Internet. Made in 1932." Nightingale nodded and bent down to examine the insides of my phone.

"You think magic did this?" he asked.

"I know it was the magic," I said. "I just don't know how or why."

Nightingale shifted uncomfortably. "Peter," he said. "You're not the first apprentice with an inquiring mind, but I don't want this getting in the way of your duties."

"Yes, sir," I said. "I'll keep it to my free time."

"You're about to suggest the coach house," said Nightingale.

"Sir?"

"For this cable connection," said Nightingale. "The heavy defenses tended to disturb the horses, so they skirt the coach house. I'm sure this cable connection of yours will be very useful."

"Yes, sir."

"For all manner of entertainments," continued Nightingale.

"Sir."

"Now," said Nightingale. "The next form—*impello*.

"And now," said Nightingale. "You start on Latin."

I COULDN'T tell whether the coach house had originally been built with a second floor, to house footmen or whatever, which had then been knocked through in the 1920s, or whether the floor had been added by sticking a new ceiling on the garage when they bricked up the main gate. At some point someone had bolted a rather beautiful wrought iron spiral staircase to the courtyard wall. When I'd first ventured up, I was surprised to find that a good third of the sloping roof on the south-facing side had been glazed; the glass was dirty on the outside and some of the panes were cracked, but it let in enough daylight to reveal a jumble of shapes shrouded by dust sheets. Unlike those in the rest of the Folly, these sheets were furry with dust—I didn't think Molly had ever cleaned in there.

If the chaise longue, Chinese screen, the mismatched side tables and the collection of ceramic fruit bowls that I found under the sheets weren't enough of a clue, I also found an easel and a box full of squirrel hair paintbrushes gone rigid with disuse. Somebody had used the rooms as a studio; judging from the empty beer bottles neatly lined up against the south wall, probably apprentices like me—that or a wizard with a serious alcohol problem.

Stacked in the corner and carefully wrapped in brown paper and string were a series of canvases, a number of still lifes painted in oils, a rather amateurish portrait of a young woman whose discomfort was palpable despite the sloppy execution. The next was much more professional, an Edwardian gentleman reclining in the same wickerwork chair I'd found under a dust sheet earlier. The man was holding a silver-topped cane and for a moment I thought he might be Nightingale, but the man was older and his eyes were an intense blue. Nightingale senior perhaps? The next, probably by the same painter, was a nude with a subject that so shocked me that I took it to the skylight to get a better look. I hadn't made a mistake: there was Molly, reclining pale and naked on the chaise longue, staring out of the canvas with heavy-lidded eyes, one hand dipping into a bowl of cherries placed on a table by her side. At least I hope they were cherries; the painting was in the Impressionist style, so the brushstrokes were bold, making it hard to tell. They were definitely small and red, the same color as Molly's lips.

I carefully rewrapped the paintings and put them back where I'd found them. I did a cursory check of the room for damp, dry rot and whatever it is that makes wooden beams crumbly and dangerous. I found that there was still a shuttered loading door at the courtyard end of the room and mounted above it a hoisting beam. Presumably to serve a hayloft for the coach horses.

As I leaned out to check it was still solid, I saw Molly's pale face in one of the upper windows. I didn't know what I found stranger, that somebody had persuaded her to get her kit off or that she hadn't changed in appearance in the last seventy years. She withdrew without apparently seeing me. I turned and looked around the room.

This, I thought, will do nicely.

At one time or other, most of my mum's relatives had cleaned offices for a living. For a certain generation of African immigrants, cleaning offices became part of the culture, like male circumcision and supporting the Arsenal Football Club. My mum had done a stint herself and had often taken me with her to save on babysitting. When an African mum takes her son to work, she expects her son to work, so I quickly learned how to handle a push broom and a window cleaner. So the next day after practice, I returned to the coach house with a packet of marigold gloves and my uncle Tito's Numatic vacuum cleaner. Let me tell you—a thousand watts of suckage makes a big difference when cleaning a room and the only thing I had to worry about was causing a rift in the space-time fabric of the universe. I found the window cleaners online and a pair of bickering Romanians scrubbed up the skylight while I rigged up a pulley to the hoisting beam. Just in time for the TV to be delivered along with the fridge.

I had to wait a week for the cable to be hooked up, so I caught up on my practice and started narrowing down the location of Father Thames. "Finding him will be a good exercise for you," Nightingale had said. "Give you a good grounding in the folklore of the Thames Valley." I asked for a clue and he told me to remember that Father Thames had traditionally been a peripatetic spirit, which, according to Google, meant *walking or traveling about, itinerant,* so not really a lot of help. I had to admit that it was expanding my knowledge of the folklore of the Thames Valley, most of which was contradictory, but would no doubt be helpful at the next pub quiz I took part in.

To inaugurate my reentry into the twenty-first century I ordered some pizza and invited Leslie round to see my etchings. I had a long soak in the claw-footed porcelain tub that dominated the communal bathroom on my floor and swore, not for the first time, that I was definitely going to install a shower. I'm not a peacock, but on occasion I like to dress to impress, although like most coppers I don't wear much in the way of bling. The rule being never wear something round your neck that you don't want to be strangled with. I laid in some Beck's because I knew Leslie preferred bottled beer and settled in to watch sports TV while I waited for her to turn up.

Among the many other modern innovations that I'd introduced to the coach house was an entry phone installed on the garage's side door, so that when Leslie arrived all I had to do was buzz her in.

I opened the door and met her at the top of the spiral staircase—she'd brought company.

"I brought Beverley," said Leslie.

"Of course you did," I said.

I offered them beer. "I want you to make it clear that nothing I eat or drink here puts me under obligation," said Beverley. "And no mucking me about this time."

"Fine," I said. "Eat, drink, no obligations, scout's honor."

"On your power," said Beverley.

"I swear on my power," I said.

Beverley grabbed a beer, hopped onto the sofa, found the remote and started channel surfing. "Can I on-demand a movie?" she asked. There followed a three-way argument for what we were going to watch that I lost at the start and Leslie won in the end by the simple expedient of grabbing the remote and switching to one of the free movie channels.

Beverley was just complaining that none of the pizzas had pepperoni when the door opened a fraction and a pale face peered in. It was Molly. She stared at us and we stared back.

"Would you like to come in?" I asked.

Molly slipped silently inside and drifted over to the sofa, where she sat next to Beverley. I realized that I'd never been this close to her before; her skin was very pale and perfect in the same way that Beverley's was. She refused a beer, but tentatively accepted a piece of pizza. When she ate she turned her face away and held her hand so that it obscured her mouth.

"When are you going to sort out Father Thames?" asked Beverley. "Mum's getting impatient and the Richmond posse is getting restless."

"Richmond posse," said Leslie and snorted.

"We've got to find him first," I said.

"How hard can it be," said Beverley. "He's got to be close to the river. Hire a boat, go upstream and stop when you get there."

"How would we know when we got there?"

"I'd know."

"Then why don't you come with us?"

"No way," said Beverley. "You're not getting me up past Teddington Lock. I'm strictly tidal, I am."

Suddenly Molly's head whipped round to face the door and a moment later somebody knocked. Beverley looked at me, but I shrugged—I wasn't expecting anyone. I hit mute on the remote and got up to answer the door. It was Inspector Nightingale, dressed in the blue polo shirt and blazer that I recognized as being the closest thing he ever got to casual dress. I stared at him stupidly for a moment and then invited him in.

"I just wanted to see what you'd done with the place," he said.

Molly shot to her feet as soon as Nightingale came into the room, Leslie got up because he was a senior officer and Beverley stood either from some vestigial politeness or in anticipation of a quick getaway. I introduced Beverley, whom he'd met only briefly when she was ten.

"Would you like a beer, sir?" I asked.

"Thank you," he said. "Call me Thomas, please."

Which was just not going to happen. I handed him a bottle and indicated the chaise longue. He sat carefully and upright at one end. I sat at the other end while Beverley flopped into the middle of the sofa, Leslie sat slightly to attention and poor Molly bobbed a couple of times before perching right on the edge. She kept her eyes resolutely downcast.

"That's a very large television," said Nightingale.

"It's a plasma TV," I said. Nightingale nodded sagely while, out of his sight, Beverley rolled her eyes.

"Is there something wrong with the sound?" he asked.

"No," I said. "I have it on mute." I found the remote and we got ten seconds of *Beat the Rest* before I got the volume under control.

"That's very clear," said Nightingale. "It's like having your own cinema."

We sat in silence for a moment, everyone, no doubt, appreciating the theater-quality surround sound.

I offered him a slice of pizza, but he explained that he'd already eaten. He asked after Beverley's mother and was told that she was fine. He finished his beer and stood up.

"I really must be on my way," he said. "Thank you for the beer."

We all stood up and I walked him to the door. When he left, I heard Leslie sigh and flop back on the sofa. I almost shouted when Molly suddenly slid past me in a rustle of fabric and slipped out the door.

"Awkward," said Beverley.

"You don't think she and Nightingale . . . ?" asked Leslie.

"Ew," said Beverley. "That's just wrong."

"I thought you and her were friends?" I asked.

"Yeah, but she's like a creature of the night," said Beverley. "And he's old."

"He's not that old," said Leslie.

"Yes he is," said Beverley, but however many hints I dropped that evening, she wouldn't say any more.

CHAPTER 7

The Puppet Fayre

IT BEGAN when I started a practice session without taking my phone out of my jacket pocket. I even noticed a little flare in intensity when I formed the werelight, but I'd only been reliably casting for two days, so it didn't register as significant. It was only later, when I tried to call Leslie and found my phone was busted, that I opened up the case and saw the same trickle of sand as I'd noticed in the vampire house. I took it down to the lab and pried out the microprocessor. As it came loose, the same fine sand streamed out of its plastic casing; the gold pins were intact, as were the contacts, but the silicon bit of the silicon chip had disintegrated. The cupboards in the lab were full of the scent of sandalwood and the most amazing range of antique equipment, including the Charles Perry microscope, all put away with such precision and tidiness that I knew no student had been involved. Under the microscope, I found the powder to be mostly silicon with a few impurities that I suspected was germanium or gallium arsenide. The chip that handled RF conversion was superficially intact, but had suffered microscopic pitting across its entire surface. The patterns reminded me of Mr. Coopertown's brain. This was my phone on magic, I thought. Obviously I couldn't do magic and carry a mobile phone, or stand near a computer, or an iPod or most of the useful technology invented since I was born. No wonder Nightingale drove a 1967 Jag. The question was, how close did the magic have to be—I was formulating some experiments to find out when Nightingale distracted me with my next form.

We sat down on opposite sides of the lab bench and Nightingale placed an object between us. It was a small apple. *"Impello,"* he said and the apple rose into the air. It hung there, rotating slowly, while I checked for wires, rods and anything else I could think of. I poked it with my finger, but it felt like it was embedded in something solid.

"Seen enough?"

I nodded and Nightingale brought out a basket of apples. A wicker basket with a handle and a checked napkin no less. He placed a second apple in front of me and I didn't need him to explain the next step. He levitated the apple, I listened for the *forma,* concentrated on my own apple and said, *"Impello."*

I wasn't really that surprised when nothing happened.

"It does get easier," said Nightingale. "It's just that it gets easier slowly."

I looked at the basket. "Why do we have so many apples?"

"They have a tendency to explode," said Nightingale.

THE NEXT morning I went out and bought three sets of eye protectors and a heavy-duty lab apron. Nightingale hadn't been kidding about the exploding fruit and I'd spent the afternoon smelling of apple juice and the evening picking pips out of my clothing. I asked Nightingale why we didn't train with something more durable, like ball bearings, but he said that magic required the mastery of fine control right from the start.

"Young men are always tempted to use brute force," Nightingale had said. "It's like learning to shoot a rifle; because it's inherently dangerous, you teach safety, accuracy and speed—in that order."

We went through a lot of apples in that first session. I was getting them in the air, but sooner or later—splat! There was a brief phase when it was fun and then it got boring. After a week of practice I could levitate an apple without it exploding nine times out of ten. I wasn't a happy little wizard though.

What was worrying me was where the power was coming

from. I never was very good at electricity, so I didn't know how much power it took to make a werelight, but levitating one small apple against the Earth's gravity—that was essentially the standard definition of one newton of force and it should be using one theoretical joule of energy every second. The laws of thermodynamics are pretty strict about this sort of thing and they say that you never get something for nothing. Which meant that that joule was coming from somewhere, but from where? From my brain?

"So it's like ESP," said Leslie during one of her periodic visits to the coach house. Officially she was there to liaise with me on the case but really she was mainly there for the wide-screen TV, takeout and the unresolved sexual tension. Besides, apart from the fifteen cases Leslie had found, nothing had come to our attention.

"Like that guy on that show who could move things around," she said.

"It doesn't feel like I'm moving things around with my mind." I said. "It's like I'm making shapes with my mind that affect something else that makes stuff happen at the other end. Do you know what a theremin is?"

"It's that weirdo sci-fi musical instrument with the loops," she said. "Right?"

"Pretty much," I said. "The point is, it's the only musical instrument you don't physically touch; you make shapes with your hands and you get a sound. The shapes are completely abstract, so you have to learn to associate a particular shape with a note and tone before you can get the thing to make a tune."

"What does Nightingale say?"

"He says that if I stopped letting myself get distracted I might spend less time covered in bits of apple."

AT THE end of March, the clocks go forward one hour to mark the start of British Summer Time. I woke up late to find the Folly feeling weirdly empty, the chairs in the breakfast room still tucked beneath the tables and the buffet counter unlaid. I found Nightingale reading the previous day's *Telegraph* in one of the overstuffed armchairs that lined the second-floor balcony.

"It's the change in the clocks," he said. "Twice a year she takes the day off."

"Where does she go?"

Nightingale pointed up toward the attic. "I believe she stays in her room."

"Are we going on a road trip?" I asked. Nightingale was wearing his sports jacket over a cream-colored Aran sweater. His driving gloves and the keys to the Jag were lying on a nearby occasional table.

"That depends," he said. "Do you think you know where the Old Man of the Thames is today?"

"Trewsbury Mead," I said. "He'll have arrived there around about the Spring Equinox, which was last week, and he'll stay until All Fools' Day."

"Your reasoning?" asked Nightingale.

"It's the source of his river," I said. "Where else is he going to go in the spring?"

Nightingale smiled. "I know a nice little transport café off the M4—we can have breakfast there."

TREWSBURY MEAD, early afternoon under a powder blue sky. According to the Ordnance Survey, this is where the Thames first rises 130 straight-line kilometers west of London. Just to the north is the site of either an Iron Age hill fort or a Roman encampment, the exact nature of which is awaiting an episode of *Time Team*. Apparently there is a soggy field, a stone to mark the spot and a chance, after a particularly wet winter, that you might see some water. You approach down a minor road that turns to gravel once past the private houses it was built to serve; the line of the river is marked by a dense stand of trees and the source of the Thames is beyond that.

In the field beyond was the Court of the Old Man of the River. We could hear it before we saw it: the rumble of diesel generators, steelwork clanking, the bass beat of music thumping, loudspeakers barking, girls screaming, glimpse of neon over the treeline and the whole round-the-corner thrill of a traveling funfair. I had a sudden bank holiday memory of holding my father's hand in one fist and clutching a precious handful of pound coins in the other. Never enough and quickly gone.

We left the Jag by the side of the road and walked the rest of the way. Beyond the line of trees I could see the tops of the big wheel and that ride where they fling you into the air on the end of a rope that I really don't see the point of. The track crossed a streambed on a modern concrete culvert that had recently been scored by the passage of heavy trucks and for a moment we were in the shade of the trees.

The first line of parked caravans began as soon as we were back in the sunlight. Most of them were old-fashioned with humpbacked roofs and mean little doors and windows; a few were modern with sloped fronts and go-faster stripes. I even caught sight—through the thickets of propane bottles, deck chairs, guy ropes and sleeping Rottweilers—of the horseshoe roof of a wooden gypsy caravan, something I thought was only for tourists. Although the caravans seemed to be parked randomly, I was struck by the notion that there was a pattern, a deep structure that nagged at the edge of perception. There was definitely a perimeter and nothing illusive about the heavyset man who guarded it from the doorway of his caravan.

The man had thick black hair greased into a quiff and a set of long sideburns that had last been fashionable when my dad was doing regular sessions with Ted Heath in the late fifties. He also had a totally illegal twelve-bore shotgun propped up against the side of his caravan.

"Afternoon," said Nightingale and kept walking past.

The man nodded. "Afternoon," said the man.

"Good weather we're having," said Nightingale.

"Looks to be fair," said the man in an accent either Irish or Welsh, I couldn't tell, but definitely Celtic. I felt a prickle on the back of my neck. A London copper doesn't like to intrude upon a traveler camp with anything less than a van full of bodies in riot gear—it's considered disrespectful otherwise.

The residential caravans formed a semicircle around the

fair proper. There the big beasts of the fairground world roared and clanked and blared out "I Feel Good" by James Brown. Every copper knows that the funfairs of Great Britain are run by the Showmen, a collection of interwoven families so clannish that they officially constitute a separate ethnic group of their own. Their family names were painted on the generator trucks and blazoned across the tops of billboards. I counted at least six different names on six different rides and half a dozen more as we walked through the fair. It seemed that each family had brought one ride to the spring fair at Trewsbury Mead.

Skinny young girls ran past, trailing laughter and streamers of red hair. Their older sisters paraded in white hot pants, bikini tops and high heel boots, checking out the older boys through Max Factor lashes and clouds of cigarette smoke. The boys tried to hide their awkwardness by playing butch or walking the moving rides with studied indifference. Their mums worked the booths painted with the rough murals of last decade's film stars and festooned with banners and Health and Safety warnings. Nobody seemed to be paying for the rides or the cotton candy, which probably explained why the kids were so happy.

The fair proper formed another semicircle and at its center was a rough-hewn wooden corral like those you see in Westerns and in the center of that was the source of the mighty River Thames. Which looked to me like a small pond with ducks in it. And standing at the fence rail was the Old Man of the River himself.

There was once a statue of Father Thames at the Mead, now transported to the more reliably wet stretch of the river at Lechlade, which showed a muscular old man with a William Blake beard reclining on his plinth with a shovel over his shoulder, crates and bundles arranged at his feet—fruits of industry and trade. Even I can spot a bit of Empire spin when I see it, so I didn't really expect him to look like that, but I think I was still expecting something grander than the man at the fence.

He was short, with a pinched face dominated by a beaky

nose and a heavy brow. He looked old, in his seventies at least, but there was a sinewy vigor in the way he moved and his eyes were gray and bright. He wore an old-fashioned double-breasted suit in dusty black, the jacket unbuttoned to show off a red velvet waistcoat, a brass watch fob and a folded pocket handkerchief the bright yellow of a spring daffodil. A battered homburg was jammed on his head, wisps of white hair escaping from underneath, and a cigarette dangled from his lip. He stood leaning on the fence, one foot on the lowest rail, talking out of the side of his mouth to a crony, one of several frighteningly spry old men who shared the fence with him, gesturing at the pond or taking a long pull on his cigarette.

He glanced up as we approached, frowning at the sight of Nightingale before turning his attention to me. I felt the force of his personality drag at me; beer and skittles it promised, the smell of horse manure and walking home from the pub by moonlight, a warm fireside and uncomplicated women. It was a good thing that I'd had practice with Mama Thames and mentally prepared on the walk up, because otherwise I would have marched right up and offered him the contents of my wallet. He winked at me and turned his full attention on Nightingale.

He called out a greeting in a language that could have been Skelta or Welsh or even authentic pre-Roman Gaelic for all I knew. Nightingale answered in the same language and I wondered whether I was going to have to learn that one too. The cronies shuffled along to make a space at the fence—only wide enough for one, I noticed. Nightingale joined Father Thames and they shook hands. With his height and good suit, Nightingale should have looked like the lord of the manor mixing with the commoners, but there was no deference in the way Father Thames sized him up.

Father Thames was doing most of the talking, emphasizing his words with little twirls and flicks of his fingers. Nightingale leaned on the fence deliberately minimizing the height difference, nodding and chuckling, I could tell, at all the right moments.

I was considering whether to edge forward so that I could

understand what they were saying more clearly, when one of the younger men at the fence caught my eye. He was taller and thicker set than Father Thames, but with the same long sinewy arms and narrow face.

"You don't want to be bothering with that," he said. "It'll be a good half hour before they get past the pleasantries." He reached out a large calloused hand to shake mine. "Oxley," he said.

"Peter Grant," I said.

"Come and meet the wife," he said.

The wife was a pretty woman with a rounded face and startling black eyes. She met us on the threshold of a modest 1960s caravan that was parked in its own little space to the left of the funfair.

"This is my wife, Isis," said Oxley and to her, "This is Peter, the new apprentice."

She took my hand, her skin was warm but with the same unreal perfection that I'd noticed on Beverley and Molly. "Delighted," she said. Her accent was pure Jane Austen.

We sat on folding chairs around a card table with a cracked linoleum top, decorated with a single daffodil arranged in a slender vase of fluted glass.

"Would you like some tea?" Isis asked and when I hesitated said, "I, Anna Maria de Burgh Coppinger Isis, solemnly swear on the life of my husband," which got a chuckle from Oxley, "and the future prospects of the Oxford rowing team that nothing you partake of in my house will place you under any obligation." She crossed her heart and gave me a little girl smile.

"Thank you," I said. "Tea would be nice."

"I can see you're wondering how we met," said Oxley.

I could see he wanted to tell the story. "I presume she fell into the river," I said.

"You would presume wrong, sir," said Oxley. "Back in the day, I had great fondness for the theater and would often smarten myself up and row up to Westminster for an evening's entertainment. Quite the peacock I was back then and attracted, I like to think, many an admiring gaze."

"What with him traversing the cattle market at the time," said Isis, returning with the tea. The cups and teapot were modern porcelain, a very clean design with a stylish platinum strip around the lip, not chipped at all, I noticed. I suspected I was getting the VIP treatment and I wondered why.

"I first set eyes on my Isis at the old Royal on Drury Lane, this being the new one that burned down not long after. I was in the upper tier and she was in a box with her dear friend Anne. I was smitten, but alas, she already had her fancy man." He paused long enough to pour the tea. "Although he suffered a terrible disappointment, I can tell you."

"Hush, my love," said Isis. "The young man doesn't want to hear about that."

I picked up my teacup; the brew was very pale and I recognized the aroma of Earl Grey. I hesitated with the cup at my lips, but trust has to start somewhere so I took a resolute sip. It was a very fine cup of tea indeed.

"But I am like the river," said Oxley. "I may run, but I am always there."

"Except during droughts," said Isis and offered me a slice of Battenberg cake.

"I'm always lurking under the surface," said Oxley. "I was, even then. Her friend had a very nice house at Strawberry Hill, beautiful place and back in those days not surrounded by mock Tudor semis. If you've seen the place, then you'll know that it's built like a castle and my Isis was a princess held captive in its tallest tower."

"Having a long weekend at a friend's house, actually," said Isis.

"My chance came when they held a great masquerade at the castle," said Oxley. "Dressed in my finest, my features cleverly disguised with a swan mask, I slipped in through the tradesmen's entrance and soon found myself mingling with the fine people inside."

I figured that I was already in trouble for the tea so I might as well have the cake too. It was shop-bought and very sweet.

"It was a grand ball," said Oxley. "Lords and ladies and gentlemen, all dressed in Josephine gowns or tight breeches and velvet waistcoats, and every one of them thinking wicked thoughts while safe behind their masks. And most wicked was my Isis, for all that she was wearing the mask of the queen of Egypt."

"I was Isis," said Isis. "As you well know."

"So I boldly stepped up and marked her card for every dance," said Oxley.

"Which was a cheek and an effrontery," said Isis.

"I saved you from the left feet of many a swain," said Oxley.

She put her hand on his cheek. "Which I cannot deny."

"The thing you have to remember about a masquerade is that at the end of the night, the masks have to come off," said Oxley. "At least in polite company, but I had been thinking . . ."

"Always a worrying development," said Isis.

"Why did the masquerade have to end?" said Oxley. "And as the son follows the father, I let action follow the thought and seized my darling Isis, threw her over my shoulder and was away across the fields toward home."

"Oxley," said Isis. "The poor boy is an officer of the law. You can't be telling him you kidnapped me; he'd be honorbound to arrest you." She looked at me. "It was entirely voluntary I can assure you," she said. "I was twice married and a mother and I'd always known my own mind."

"It is certain that she proved to be an experienced woman," he said and, much to my embarrassment, winked at me.

"You wouldn't think he was once a man of the cloth," said Isis.

"I was a terrible monk," he said. "But that was a different life." He rapped the table. "Now that we've fed, watered and bored you senseless, why don't we talk some business. What is it that the Big Lady wants?"

"You understand that I'm strictly the go-between in this," I said. We actually did a course on conflict resolution at Hendon and the trick is to always stress your neutrality while allowing both parties to think you're secretly on their side. There were role-playing exercises and everything—it was one of the few things I was better at than Leslie. "Mama Thames feels that you may be looking to move downstream of Teddington Lock."

"It's all one river," said Oxley. "And he's the Old Man of the River."

"She claims he abandoned the tideway in 1858," I said. More precisely during the Great Stink, note the capitals, when the Thames became so thick with sewage that London was overwhelmed with a stench so terrible that Parliament considered relocating to Oxford.

"Nobody stayed in London that summer who could move away," said Oxley. "It wasn't fit for man or beast."

"She says he never came back," I said. "Is that true?"

"That is true," said Oxley. "And in truth the Old Man has never loved the city, not since it killed his sons."

"Which sons were these?"

"Oh, you know who they are," said Oxley. "There was Ty and Fleet and Effra. All drowned in a flood of muck and filth and finally put out of their misery by that clever bastard Bazalgette. Him that made the sewers. I met him, you know, very grand man with the finest set of chops this side of William Gladstone. Knocked him on his arse for the murdering bastard that he was."

"You think he killed the rivers?"

"No," said Oxley. "But he was their undertaker. I've got to hand it to the daughters of the Big Lady, for they certainly must be hardier than my brothers."

"If he doesn't want the city why is he pushing downstream?" I asked.

"Some of us still have a hankering for the bright lights," said Oxley and smiled at his wife.

"I daresay it would be nice to attend the theater again," she said.

Oxley refilled my cup. A crackly voice on a loudspeaker somewhere behind me yelled, "Let's get this party started." James Brown was still feeling nice, sugar and spice now.

"And you want to fight Mama Thames's daughters for the privilege?"

"You think they're too fearsome for us?" asked Oxley.

"I don't think you want it badly enough," I said. "Besides, I'm sure arrangements could be made."

"An excursion by coach, perhaps?" asked Oxley. "Will we need passports?"

Despite what you think you know, most people don't want to fight, especially when evenly matched. A mob will tear an individual to pieces and a man with a gun and a noble cause is happy to kill ever so many women and children, but risking a fair fight—not so easy. That's why you see those *pissed* young men doing the dance of "don't hold me back" while desperately hoping someone likes them enough to hold them back. Everyone is always so pleased to see the police arrive, because we have to save them whether we like them or not.

Oxley wasn't a drunk young man, but I could see he was just as keen to find someone to hold him back. Or maybe his father?

"Your father," I said. "What does he really want?"

"What any father wants," said Oxley. "The respect of his children."

I nearly said that not all fathers were worthy of respect, but I managed to keep my gob shut and anyway not everyone had a dad like mine.

"It would be nice if everyone could chill for a bit," I said. "Keep everything relaxed while the inspector and I sorted something out."

Oxley looked at me over his teacup. "It is spring," he said. "Plenty of distractions upstream of Richmond."

"Lambing season," I said. "And whatnot."

"You're not what I expected," said Oxley.

"What were you expecting?"

"I was expecting Nightingale to choose someone more like himself," said Oxley.

"Upper class?"

"Solid," said Isis, preempting her husband. "Workman-like."

"Whereas you," said Oxley, "are a cunning man."

"Much more like the wizards we used to know," said Isis.

144 Ben Aaronovitch

"Is that a good thing?" I asked.

Oxley and Isis laughed. "I don't know," said Oxley. "But it will be interesting finding out."

IT WAS strangely hard to leave the fair, my legs felt heavy as if I was wading out of a swimming pool. It wasn't until we were back at the Jag and the funfair sounds had started to fade that I felt I had escaped.

"What is that?" I asked Nightingale as we climbed into the car.

"Seducere," he said. "The Compulsion or, as the Scots say, 'the Glamour.' According to Bartholomew, many supernatural creatures do it as a form of self-defense."

"When do I learn how to do it?" I asked.

"In about ten years," he said. "If you pick up the pace a bit."

As we headed back through Cirencester for the M4, I told Nightingale about my meeting with Oxley.

"He's the Old Man's consigliere, isn't he?" I asked.

"If you mean his *consiliarius,* his advisor," said Nightingale, "then yes. Probably the second most important man at the camp."

"You knew he'd talk to me, didn't you?"

Nightingale paused to check for traffic before pulling out onto the main road. "It's his job to press for an advantage," he said. "You had the Battenberg cake, didn't you?"

"Should I have refused?"

"No," said Nightingale. "He wouldn't try to trap you while you're under my protection, but you can't always take common sense for granted when dealing with these people. It makes no sense for the Old Man to suddenly be pushing downstream. Now that you've met them both—what do you think?"

"They both have genuine power," I said. "But it feels different; hers is definitely from the sea, from the port and all that. His is all from the earth and the weather and leprechauns and crystals, for all I know."

"That would explain why the border's at Teddington Lock," he said. Teddington is the highest point the tide reaches, the river below that point is called the tideway. It's also the part of the Thames administered directly by the Port of London—I doubted that was a coincidence.

"Am I right?" I asked.

"I believe you are," he said. "I think there may always have been a split between the tideway and the freshwater river. Perhaps that's why it was so easy for Father Thames to abandon the city."

"Oxley was hinting that the Old Man doesn't really want anything to do with the city," I said. "That he just wanted some respect."

"Perhaps he would be content with a ceremony," said Nightingale. "An oath of fealty perhaps."

"Which is what?"

"A feudal oath," said Nightingale. "A vassal pledges his loyalty and service to his liege lord and the lord pledges his protection. It's how medieval societies were organized."

"Medieval is what it would get if you tried to make Mama Thames swear loyalty and service to anyone," I said. "Let alone Father Thames."

"Are you sure?" asked Nightingale. "It would be purely symbolic."

"Symbolic just makes it worse," I said. "She'd see it as a loss of face. She sees herself as the mistress of the greatest city on earth and she's not going to kowtow to anyone. Particularly not some yokel in a caravan."

"It's a pity we can't marry them off," said Nightingale.

We both laughed out loud at that and bypassed Swindon.

Once we were on the M4, I asked Nightingale what he and the Old Man had talked about.

"My contribution to the conversation was cursory at best," said Nightingale. "A great deal of it was technical, groundwater overdrafts, aquifer delay cycles and aggregate catchment area coefficients. Apparently all these will affect how much water goes down the river this summer."

"If I was to go back two hundred years and have that same conversation," I said, "what would the Old Man have talked about then?"

"What flowers were blooming," said Nightingale. "What kind of winter we'd had—the flight of birds on a spring morning."

"Would it have been the same Old Man?"

"I don't know," said Nightingale. "It was the same Old Man in 1914, I can tell you that for certain."

"How do you know that?"

Nightingale hesitated, then he said, "I'm not quite as young as I look."

My phone rang. I really wanted to ignore it, but the tune was "That's Not My Name," which meant it was Leslie. When I answered, she wanted to know where the hell we were. I told her we were just going through Reading.

"There's been another one," she said.

"How bad?"

"Really bad," she said.

I put the spinner on the roof as Nightingale put his foot down and we topped 120 mph back into London with the setting sun behind us.

THERE WERE three fire engines parked up in Charing Cross Road and the traffic was backing up as far as Parliament Square and the Euston Road. We arrived at St. Martin's Close to the smell of smoke and the chatter and squawk of emergency radios. Leslie met us at the tape line and handed us bunny suits. I could see while we were changing that half of J. Sheekey's frontage had been burned out and that there were three forensic evidence tents set up in the alley. Three bodies at least.

"How many inside?" asked Nightingale.

"None," said Leslie. "They all went out the back emergency doors—minor injuries only."

"Something to be thankful for," said Nightingale. "You're sure this is our case?"

Leslie nodded and led us over to the first tent. Inside, we

found that Dr. Walid had got there before us and was crouched beside the body of a man dressed in the distinctive saffron robes of a Hare Krishna devotee. The body lay on its back where he'd fallen, legs straight, arms stretched out to either side as if he'd participated in one of those trust-building exercises where you let yourself fall backward—only no one had been there to catch him. His face was the same bloody ruin as Coopertown's and the cycle courier's had been.

That answered that question.

"That's not the worst of it," she said, and beckoned us over to the second tent. This one had two bodies; the first was a dark-skinned man in a black frock coat, his hair stuck up in clumps stiff with blood. He'd been hit hard enough to crack open the skull and expose a section of his brain. The second body was another devotee of Krishna; a random Good Samaritan had obviously tried to help by putting him in the recovery position, but with his face split open the gesture had been futile.

I was aware of a thudding in my ears and a shortness of breath. Blood, presumably from the blow struck to the other man, had splattered the devotee's robes and made a bloody tie-dye pattern on the orange cloth. The interior of the forensic tent was stifling and I started sweating inside my bunny suit. Nightingale asked a question but I didn't really hear Leslie's answer. I stepped outside the tent, gagged once, swallowed it and stumbled to the tape line where, to my own amazement, I managed to keep my Battenberg cake down.

I wiped my mouth on the cold plastic sleeve of the bunny suit and leaned against the wall. Opposite me was a poster for the Noel Coward Theatre, where they were showing a farce called *Down With Kickers!*

Two victims with their faces half off meant that the "possession" had affected two individuals at the same time. There was one more tent left. I asked myself, how much worse could that be?

Stupid question.

The third body was seated with legs crossed, but like a child, not a yogi; for all that his hands were resting on his

knees, palms upward. His robes were drenched in blood and
ribbons of red ropy stuff covered his shoulders and upper
arms. His head was completely gone, leaving a ragged stump
of a neck. There was a flash of white buried among the torn
muscle—I assumed it was his spine.

Seawoll had been waiting for us in the tent. He grunted
when Leslie led us in. "Somebody's just making fun of us
now."

"It's escalating," I said.

Nightingale gave me a sharp look but said nothing.

"But what's escalating?" asked Leslie. "And why can't you
stop it?"

"Because, Constable," said Nightingale coldly, "we don't
know what it is."

THERE WERE plenty of witnesses and suspects and people
who were helping the police with their inquiries. We paired
off to conduct the interviews as fast as possible; I worked
with Seawoll while Nightingale paired with Leslie. That way
there'd be someone in the room who could spot a *vestigium*
when it slapped him in the face. DS Stephanopoulos handled
the collection of physical evidence and collating the CCTV
coverage.

It was a bit of a privilege to watch Seawoll work. He wasn't
nearly so intimidating with the suspects as he was with other
policemen. His interrogation technique was gentle, never
chummy, always formal, but he never raised his voice. I took
notes.

The sequence of events, as we reconstructed them, was
depressingly familiar, but on a larger scale than we'd seen
before. It had been a mild spring Sunday afternoon and St.
Martin's Close had been moderately crowded. The Close itself
is a pedestrianized alleyway that has access to three separate
stage doors, the back entrance to Brown's and the famous J.
Sheekey Oyster Bar. It's where the theater staff go for a coffee
and a crafty smoke between performances.

J. Sheekey is a thespian landmark, which isn't surprising if
you sell food late at night within walking distance of the

most famous theaters in the West End. Sheekey also employs uniformed doormen in top hats and black frock coats and that's where the trouble had started that afternoon.

At two forty-five, about the same time I was sitting down for tea with Oxley and Isis, six members of the International Society for Krishna Consciousness entered the Close from the Charing Cross Road end. This was a common route for the *bhaktas,* the aspirant devotees to God, as they traversed from Leicester Square to Covent Garden. They were being led by Michael Smith, the identity later confirmed through fingerprint evidence, a reformed crack addict, alcoholic, car thief and suspected rapist, who had lived an unblemished life since joining the movement nine months previously. ISKON, as the International Society for Krishna Consciousness likes to be known, is aware that there is a fine line between drawing attention to yourself and provoking active hostility from passersby. The intention is that through dancing and chanting in public, converts may be attracted to the movement, and not to provoke an angry confrontation. Thus "dwell time" in a particular locality had to be judged carefully to avoid trouble. Michael Smith had proved particularly good at judging what the devotees could get away with and that was why he was leading the saffron crocodile that afternoon.

Which was why, according to Willard Jones, former Llandudno lifeguard and lucky survivor, everyone had been surprised when they came to a halt outside J. Sheekey's and Michael Smith said he wanted to hear some noise. Still, making a noise and attracting attention was what they were on the street for, so they started making a noise.

"A harmonious noise," said Willard Jones. "In this age of materialism and hypocrisy, no other form of spiritual realization is as effective as the chanting of the maha-mantra. It is like the genuine cry of the child for his mother . . ." He went on like this for some time.

What was not harmonious was the cowbell that Willard Jones knew was a genuine cowbell because his father and brothers were genuine failing Welsh hill farmers. "If you've ever heard a cowbell," said Jones, "you'd realize that they are not designed to be harmonious."

At approximately two-fifty, Michael Smith produced a huge cowbell from somewhere about his person and started ringing it with great sweeping movements of his arm. On duty as uniformed doorman that day was Gurcan Temiz of Tottenham via Ankara. As a typical Londoner, Gurcan had a high tolerance threshold for random thoughtlessness; after all, if you live in the big city there's no point complaining that it's a big city, but even that tolerance has its limit. Ringing a huge cowbell outside the restaurant and disturbing the patrons certainly constituted the limit, so Gurcan stepped up to remonstrate with Michael Smith. Who clubbed him repeatedly with the bell around the head and shoulders. According to Dr. Walid, the fourth blow was the one that killed him. Once Gurcan Temiz was on the ground two more devotees, Henry MacIlvoy of Wellington, New Zealand, and William Cattrington of Hemel Hempstead, rushed over and proceeded to kick the victim. This didn't cause the damage it might have, because both devotees were wearing soft plastic sandals.

At that point an incendiary device exploded behind the bar inside J. Sheekey. The clientele, despite being a mix of thespians and tourists, evacuated the premises in an orderly but rapid fashion. Those who went out the back fire exits dispersed via Cecil Court, those going out the front streamed past the bodies of Gurcan Temiz, Henry MacIlvoy and William Cattrington, who were already dead. Most registered that there were bodies, that there was blood, but they were all vague about the details. Only Willard Jones had a clear view of what happened to Michael Smith.

"He just sat down," said Jones. "And then his head exploded."

There are a couple of mundane things that can make your head explode, a high-velocity rifle shot for one, so the murder team spent some time eliminating them from our inquiries. Meanwhile, I'd figured out what had caused the explosion inside J. Sheekey, which was just as well because by that time the Anti-Terrorist Squad and MI5 were starting to sniff around the case, which nobody wanted.

THE ANSWER came from the experiments I'd been conducting, semicovertly, into why my phone broke. I had no intention of using my laptop or even another phone as a guinea pig, so a quick trip to Computers for Africa, who refurbish abandoned computers and donate them abroad, netted me a bagful of chips and a motherboard that I suspected came from an Atari ST. I used masking tape to set marks at twenty-centimeter intervals along the length of a bench and once I had a chip placed at every mark I carefully positioned my hand and cast a werelight. The trick in science is to try to change only one variable at a time, but I felt I'd gained enough fine control to consistently produce the same intensity of werelight each time. I spent an entire day conjuring up lights and then checking each chip for damage under the microscope. All to no avail, except pissing off Nightingale, who said that if I had that much time to waste I should be able to tell him the difference between prepositions of the accusative and the ablative kind.

Then he distracted me by teaching my first *adjectivum*, which is a *forma* that changes some aspect of another *forma*. This *adjectiva* was called *iactus*, which, combined with *impello*, should have, theoretically, allowed me to float an apple around the room. After two weeks of exploding apples, I'd got to the point where I could reliably whoosh an apple down the length of the lab with a fair degree of accuracy. Nightingale said that the next stage was catching things that were thrown toward me, which took us back to exploding apples and that's where we were the day the clocks went forward and we paid our respects to Father Thames.

It was while I was in the interview room watching Seawoll gently pluck the facts from Willard Jones's testimony that I had my breakthrough. Magic, it turned out, was just like science in that sometimes it was a question of spotting the bleeding obvious. Just as Galileo spotted that objects accelerate under gravity at the same rate regardless of their weight, I spotted that the big difference between my mobile phone and the various microchips I'd been experimenting on was that my mobile phone was connected up to its battery when it got fried.

Just connecting up my collection of secondhand microchips to a battery seemed far too random and time-consuming, but luckily you can get ten generic calculators for less than a fiver—if you know where to go. Then it was just a matter of laying them out, casting the werelight for precisely five seconds and sticking them under the microscope. The one placed directly under my hand was toast and there were decreasing levels of damage out to the two-meter mark. Was I emitting power as a waste product that was damaging the electronics or was I sucking power out of the calculators and that's what was doing the damage? And why was the damage principally to the chips and not the other components? Crucially, despite the unresolved questions, it implied that I could now carry my mobile phone and do magic—providing I took the battery out first.

"But what does all that mean?" asked Leslie, once I'd filled her in.

I took a pull on my Beck's and waved the bottle at the TV. "It means that I've just figured out how the fire was started."

The next morning, Leslie e-mailed me the fire report and after I'd checked that, I tracked down a retail equipment store that could deliver a till just like the one used in J. Sheekey Oyster Bar. Because of Nightingale's no visitors in the Folly rule, not counting the coach house, I had to carry the bloody thing from the tradesman's entrance down into my lab all by myself. Molly watched me staggering past and covered her smile with her hand. I figured Leslie didn't count as a visitor in this instance, but when I called and invited her over for the demonstration she said she was busy running errands for Seawoll. Once I had everything in position, I asked Molly to ask Nightingale to meet me in the lab.

I cleared an area in the corner, away from any gas pipes, and mounted the till on a metal trolley and plugged it in. When Nightingale arrived I handed him a lab coat and eye protectors and asked him to stand on a mark six meters from the till. Then, before I did anything else, I removed the battery from my mobile phone.

"And the purpose of this is what, exactly?" asked Nightingale.

"If you just bear with me, sir," I said. "It'll all become clear."

"If you say so, Peter," he said and folded his arms. "Should I be wearing a helmet as well?"

"That's probably not necessary, sir," I said. "I'm going to count down from three and on zero I'd like you to do the strongest magic consistent with safety."

"The strongest?" asked Nightingale. "You're sure about this?"

"Yes, sir," I said. "Ready?"

"Ready when you are."

I counted down and on zero Nightingale blew up the lab—at least that's what it felt like. A ball of burning fire, like a werelight spell gone horribly wrong, formed over Nightingale's outstretched palm. A wave of heat washed over me and I smelled crisping hair and I almost threw myself behind a bench before I realized that the heat wasn't physical. It couldn't have been or Nightingale would have been on fire. Somehow the heat was all contained within the sphere above his hand—what I'd felt was *vestigia* on a grand scale.

Nightingale looked at me and calmly raised an eyebrow. "How long do you want me to keep this up?"

"I don't know," I said. "How long can you keep it up?"

Nightingale laughed. I caught a flicker of movement in my peripheral vision and I turned to find Molly standing in the doorway, eyes shining with reflected fire and fixed on Nightingale.

I turned back just in time for the till to explode. The top blew right off and a spray of burning plastic fountained out, black smoke billowed upward and raced across the ceiling. Molly gave a delighted shriek and I ran forward with the fire extinguisher and sprayed the CO_2 over the till until it went out. Nightingale shut down his sphere of flaming death and switched on a set of extractor fans I didn't even know the lab was equipped with.

"Why did it explode?" he asked.

"The rapid breakdown of the components releases a volatile gas, hydrogen or something," I said. "I only got a C in chemistry, remember; the gas mixes with air inside the casing, there's an electrical spark and boom. The question I need you to answer is—does doing a spell suck magic out of an object or put magic into an object?"

The answer was of course—both.

"You don't normally cover this until you've mastered the primary *forma,*" said Nightingale. Magic, as Nightingale understood it, was generated by life. A wizard could draw on his own magic or on magic that he'd stored by enchantment, which sounded interesting but not relevant to exploding cash tills. However, life protected itself, and the more complex it was, the more magic it produced, but the harder it was to draw off. "It's impossible to draw on magic from another human being," said Nightingale. "Or even a dog, for that matter."

"The vampires," I said. "They sucked the life out of everything in the house, didn't they?"

"The vampires are obviously parasitical in that way, but we don't know how they do it," said Nightingale. "Nor do we know how people like your friend Beverley Brook draw power from their environment either."

"The vampire house is where I first noticed the effect on the microchips," I said.

"As machines become more like men," said Nightingale, "I suppose it follows that they might start producing magic of their own. I'm not sure I see how this helps us." I tried not to wince at the pseudoscience and decided now was not the time to get into that.

"In the first instance," I said, "it means we know that whatever is doing this is sucking down enormous amounts of power and in the second instance it gives us another thing to look for."

"And we can call off the Anti-Terrorist Squad," said Nightingale.

"And that," I said.

*   *   *

NOT THAT we were finding anything. In the meantime, Sea-woll's Murder Team was assigned a particularly pointless stabbing in a pub off Piccadilly Circus. I had a sniff around, but there were no *vestigia* and a stupid but comprehensible motive. "Cheating boyfriend," Leslie explained one night when she came round to watch a DVD. First boy meets girl, girl sleeps with second boy, first boy stabs second boy and runs away. "We think he's hiding in Walthamstow," she said. And many would say that was punishment enough.

The murders outside J. Sheekey were blamed on Michael Smith, who had supposedly shot three people in the head with an illegal firearm before killing himself with the same gun. The media might have taken more of an interest had not a soap star been caught with an equally famous soccer player in the loos of a club in Mayfair. The resulting media whiteout blotted out any real news for two weeks and was, according to Leslie, far too convenient to be a coincidence.

I spent April practicing my *forma,* my Latin and experimenting with new ways to blow up microchips. Every afternoon I'd take Toby out for a walk in the area around Covent Garden and Cambridge Circus to see if either of us picked up a sniff, but nothing. I called Beverley Brook a couple of times, but she said that her mother had told her not to have anything to do with me until I'd done something about Father Thames.

May started in typical bank holiday fashion with two days of rain and three of drizzle until the next Sunday dawned bright and fair. It's on a day like this that a young man's mind turns to romance, ice cream and Punch and Judy shows.

It was the day of the Covent Garden May Fayre, which celebrates the first ever recorded performance of Punch and Judy with a brass band parade, a special puppet mass at the Actors' Church and as many Punch and Judy shows as can be crammed into the church grounds. While I'd been a probationary constable at Charing Cross, I'd always been on crowd control that day, so I called up Leslie and asked if she wanted to try the fayre from the civilian point of view. We got ice cream and Cokes from the Tesco Metro and dodged around the tourists until we reached the front portico of the church. A single "professor's" booth had been set up not half a meter from where poor old William Skirmish had had his head knocked off.

"Four months ago," I said out loud.

"It hasn't been boring," said Leslie.

"You're not the one who's had to learn Latin," I said.

Mats had been put down for the kids to sit on while we adults stood at the back. A man in jester's motley stepped forward and warmed up the audience. He explained that over the centuries there had been many versions of the Punch and Judy show, but today, for our education and our entertainment, the renowned Professor Phillip Pointer would perform *The Tragical Comedy, or Comical Tragedy, of Punch and Judy* as told to John Payne Collier by Giovanni Piccini in 1827.

The story started with Punch being bitten on the nose by Toby the dog.

CHAPTER 8

The Grade-School Version

TOBY THE dog bites Punch, who beats Mr. Scaramouch, Toby's owner, to death. He then goes home and throws his baby out the window and beats his wife Judy to death. He falls off his horse and kicks the doctor in his eye. The doctor attacks him with a stick, but he grabs that and beats the doctor to death. He rings a sheep bell outside a rich man's house and when the rich man's servant remonstrates with him, Punch beats him to death. At that point my ice cream melted and slopped all over my shoes.

The Tragical Comedy, or Comical Tragedy, of Punch and Judy as told to John Payne Collier by Giovanni Piccini in 1827. Not very hard to get hold of once you know what you're looking for. After the show, Leslie and I showed the Professor our warrant cards and he was happy to hand over the hard copy of the script. We took it over to the Roundhouse on the corner of New Row and Garrick Street and settled in to read it with two double vodkas.

"It can't be a coincidence," I said.

"You think?" asked Leslie. "Something is using real people to act out this stupid puppet show."

"Your governor's not going to like this," I said.

"Well, I'm not going to tell him," said Leslie. "Let your governor tell my governor that the fucking ghost of Mr. Punch is knocking off people on his patch."

"You think it's a ghost?" I asked.

"How should I know," she said. "That's what you magic cops are for."

THE FOLLY has three libraries; one I didn't know about back then, number two was a magical library where the direct treatises on spells, *forma* and alchemy were kept, all of them written in Latin and so all Greek to me, and number three was the General Library on the first floor next to the Reading Room. The division of labor was clear from the start; Nightingale checked the magic library and I hit the books in the Queen's English.

The General Library was lined with enough mahogany to reforest the Amazon basin. On one wall, the stacks went all the way to the ceiling and you reached the top shelves by using a ladder that slid along on shining brass rails. A row of beautiful walnut cabinets held the index cards that were the closest thing the library had to a search engine. I caught a whiff of old cardboard and mildew when I opened the drawers and it comforted me to think that Molly didn't go so far as to regularly open them up and clean inside. The cards were arranged by subject with a master index arranged by title. I started by looking for references to Punch and Judy, but found none. Nightingale had given me another term to search for: revenant. A couple false passes with the index cards led me to Dr. John Polidori's *Meditations on the Matter of Life and Death,* which, according to the frontispiece, had been published in 1819. The same page had a notation in Latin written in an elegant looping hand: *vincit qui se vincit* August 1821. I wondered what it meant.

According to Polidori, a revenant was an unquiet spirit who returns from the dead to wreak havoc on the living, usually in reprisal for some slight or injustice, real or perceived, that the person suffered during their life.

"It certainly fits our profile," I told Nightingale over lunch; Beef Wellington, boiled potato and sautéed parsnip. "These little grievances going all postal—it fits the profile of the echoes as well."

"You think it's infecting them?"

"I think it's a field effect, like radiation or light from a bulb," I said. "I think the echoes are inside the field, their brains get charged up with negative emotions and off they go."

"Wouldn't more people be affected, in that case?" asked Nightingale. "There were at least ten other people in the cinema foyer including you and Constable May and yet only the mother was affected."

"Could be that it reinforces anger that's already there," I said. "Or acts as a catalyst. It wouldn't be an easy thing to prove scientifically."

Nightingale smiled.

"What is it?" I asked.

"You remind me of a wizard I used to know called David Mellenby," said Nightingale. "He had the same obsession."

"What happened to him?" I asked. "And did he leave any notes?"

"I'm afraid he died in the war," said Nightingale. "He never did get a chance to do half the experiments he wanted to. He had this theory about how the *genii locorum* works that would have appealed to you."

"What was his theory?" I asked.

"I believe I will make telling you that contingent on you mastering your next *forma,*" he said. "I did notice that there were discrepancies between the script and Mr. Punch's actions. I'm thinking of Pretty Polly."

As laid down in the *Tragical Comedy,* after killing his wife and kid Mr. Punch sings a happy little song about the benefits of wife murdering and that done he presses his suit with Pretty Polly. A character who says nothing, but seems "nothing loth" when our cheerful little serial killer starts kissing her.

"We don't know he's following that particular script," I said.

"True," said Nightingale. "Piccini was relating an oral tradition and those are almost never reliable."

According to the possibly unreliable Piccini, the next victim was due be a blind beggar who coughs in Mr. Punch's face and is thrown off the stage for his presumption. The script didn't specify if he survived the experience or not. "If our revenant Punchinella is following form," I said, "then the most likely target is going to be a tinny for the RNIB."

"What's a tinny?"

"A person with a collecting tin," I said miming a shake. "People put their spare change in it."

"Blind man begging for money," he said. "It would be more useful to know who the revenant was and where he's buried."

"Presumably if we know who he is, then we can deal with his issues and lay him to rest peacefully," I said.

"Or," said Nightingale, "we dig up his bones and grind them into dust, mix them with rock salt and then scatter them out at sea."

"Would that work?"

"Victor Bartholomew says that's the way to do it." Nightingale shrugged. "He wrote the book on dealing with ghosts and revenants—literally."

"I think we may be overlooking a blindingly obvious source of information," I said.

"Really?"

"Nicholas Wallpenny," I said. "All the attacks have originated near the Actors' Church, which I'm guessing means that our revenant is located nearby. Nicholas might know him—for all we know, they hang out."

"I'm not sure ghosts 'hang' quite the way you imagine," said Nightingale and with a quick glance to be sure that Molly wasn't watching, he slipped his half-full plate under the table. Toby's tail banged against my legs as he snuffled it down.

"We need a bigger dog," I said. "Or smaller portions."

"See if he won't talk to you tonight," said Nightingale. "But remember that our Nicholas wasn't a reliable witness when he was alive—I doubt his veracity has improved since his demise."

"How did he die?" I asked. "Do you know?"

"Died of drink," Nightingale said. "Very enjoyable."

*   *   *

SINCE TOBY was our official ghost-hunting dog and because he had begun to waddle alarmingly when he walked, I took him with me. It's a half-hour stroll from Russell Square and the Folly to Covent Garden. Once you're past Forbidden Planet and across Shaftesbury Avenue, the direct route takes you down Neal Street where the cycle courier had died, but I figured if I started avoiding certain streets just because somebody's died on them I'd have to move to Aberystwyth.

It was late evening and not all that warm, but there was still a crowd of drinkers outside the gastropub. London had come late to the idea of outdoor café society and it wasn't going to allow a bit of chill to get in the way now—especially since it had become illegal to smoke indoors.

Toby did pause close to the point where Dr. Framline had attacked the courier, but only long enough to pee on a bollard.

Even at closing time, Covent Garden was packed; the post-performance crowd was emerging from the Royal Opera House and looking for somewhere to have a bite to eat and a pose, while clusters of young people on school-sponsored holidays from all over Europe exercised their time-honored right to block the pavement from one side to the other.

Once the cafés, restaurants and pubs in the covered market shut down, the Piazza emptied quickly and soon there were few enough people about for me to risk a bit of ghost chasing.

There was disagreement among the authorities as to what the true nature of a ghost was. Polidori insisted that ghosts were the detached souls of the deceased who clung to a locality; he theorized that they fed off their own spirit and would, unless this spirit was replenished through magic, eventually fade away to nothing. Richard Spruce's *The Persistence of Phantasmagoria in Yorkshire,* published in 1860, broadly agreed with Polidori, but added that ghosts might draw on the magic in their environment in a similar manner to a moss leaching sustenance from its rocky home. Peter Brock, writing in the 1930s, theorized that ghosts were nothing more than recordings etched into the magical fabric of their surroundings in much the same way music is recorded on a vinyl disk. I personally figured that they were like crude copies of the dead person's personality that were running in a degraded fashion in a kind of magical matrix where packets of "information" were passed from one magic node to the next.

Since both my encounters with Nicholas had started in the portico of the Actors' Church, that was where I started. Coppers don't look at the world the same way other people do. You can tell a policeman by the way he looks around a room. It's a chilly, suspicious gaze that makes him immediately recognizable to others who know what to look for. The strange thing is how fast you pick it up. I was still a Police Community Support Officer, had only been doing it a month, when I visited my parents' flat and realized that even if I didn't know already that my father was an addict, I would have spotted the fact the moment I was in the door. You have to understand that my mum is a cleaning fanatic and you could eat dinner off her living room carpet, but still all the signs were there if you knew what to look for.

It had become the same with *vestigia*. When I put my hand on the limestone blocks that made up the portico, the sensations, the cold, the vague sense of presence, an odor in the nostrils that might be sandalwood, were the same—only now, like a copper reading a street, I had some inkling of what they meant. I also expected them to be much stronger. I tried to think back to the last time I'd touched the stones; had the impressions been the same?

I checked to make sure nobody was watching. "Nicholas," I said to the wall. "Are you in there?"

I felt something through my palm, a vibration I thought, like a distant tube train. Toby whined and scrambled backward, claws skittering on the cobbles. Before I could take my own step backward Nicholas's face, white and transparent, appeared in front of me.

"Help me," he said.

"What's wrong?" I asked.

"He's eating me," said Nicholas and then his face was sucked backward into the wall. For a moment I felt a strange tugging sensation on the back of my head and threw myself back. Toby barked once and then turned and shot off in the direction of Russell Square. I landed heavily on my back, which hurt, so I lay there feeling stupid for a moment and then got back on my feet. Cautiously I approached the church and gingerly laid my palm on the stone again.

It felt cold and rough and there was nothing else. It was as if the *vestigia* had been sucked out of the stones the same way it had back at the vampire house. I snatched my hand away and backed off. The Piazza was dark and quiet. I turned and strode into the night, looking out for Toby as I went.

He'd run all the way back to the Folly; I found him in the kitchen curled up in Molly's lap. She comforted the dog and gave me a stern look.

"He's supposed to face danger," I said. "If he stays he works."

JUST BECAUSE I had an active case didn't mean I was excused practice. I'd persuaded Nightingale to show me the fireball spell, which was, not surprisingly, a variation on *lux*, with *iactus* to move it about. Once Nightingale was convinced I could do the first part without burning my hand off, we went down to the firing range in the basement to practice. Not that I had known we had a firing range until then. At the bottom of the back stairs you turned left instead of right, through a set of reinforced doors that I'd always assumed led to a coal store, and into a room fifty meters long with a wall of sandbags at one end and a line of metal lockers at the other. A row of vintage Brodie helmets hung from pegs above a line of khaki gas mask cases. There was a poster, white lettering on a blood-red background, KEEP CALM AND CARRY ON, which I thought was good advice. There was a stack of cardboard silhouettes at the target end, brittle with age but still legible as German soldiers with coal scuttle helmets and fixed bayonets. Under Nightingale's direction, I set up a row of them against the sandbags and trotted back to the firing line. Before we started, I checked to make sure I wasn't carrying my brand new mobile phone.

"Watch carefully," said Nightingale. Then he flung out his hand, there was a flash, a sound like a sheet being ripped in half and the target on the extreme left-hand side was blown into flaming fragments.

I turned at the sound of excited clapping and found Molly hissing with delight and standing on her tiptoes like a small child at the circus.

"You didn't say the Latin," I pointed out.

"You practice this in silence," he said. "From the outset. This spell is a weapon. It has a single purpose and that is to kill. Once you've mastered it, you are under the same obligations as any other armed constable, so I suggest you familiarize yourself with the current guidelines on firearms use."

Molly yawned, covering her mouth to hide how wide it opened. Nightingale gave her a bland look. "He has to live in the world of men," he said.

Molly shrugged as if to say—*whatever.*

Nightingale demonstrated again at one-quarter speed and I attempted to follow suit. The fireball I had already practiced, but when it came time to apply *iactus* it felt slippery as if, unlike the apples, there was nothing to get a purchase on. When I flung out my arm in the approved dramatic fashion my fireball drifted gently down the length of the firing range, burned a small hole in the target and embedded itself in the sandbags behind.

"You have to release it, Peter," said Nightingale. "Or it won't go off."

I released the fireball and there was a muffled thump from behind the target—a whisp of smoke curled up toward the ceiling. Behind me, Molly sniggered.

We did an hour of practice, at the end of which I was capable of flinging a fireball down the range at the dizzying speed of a bumblebee who'd met his pollen quota and was taking a moment to enjoy the view.

We broke for morning tea and I broached my idea for

recovering Nicholas—assuming that enough of the ghost remained to be recovered after "something" had "eaten" him.

"Polidori refers to a spell that can summon ghosts," I said. "Does it work?"

"It's more of a ritual than a spell," said Nightingale. In an attempt to stop Molly from overwhelming us with food, we'd taken to having tea in the kitchen, the thinking being that if she didn't have to lay six tables in the breakfast room we might get only two portions. It worked, but they were big portions.

"What's the difference?"

"You keep asking the kind of questions," said Nightingale, "that really shouldn't be coming up for another year or so."

"Just the basics—the grade-school version."

"A spell is a series of *forma* strung together to achieve an effect, while a ritual is what it sounds like; a sequence of *forma* arranged as a ritual with certain paraphernalia to help move the process along," said Nightingale. "They tend to be older spells from the early part of the eighteenth century."

"Are the ritual bits important?" I asked.

"I honestly don't know," said Nightingale. "These spells don't get used very often, otherwise they'd have been updated in the 1900s."

"Can you show me how to do it?" I asked. Toby spotted me buttering a tea cake and sat up attentively. I broke off a bit and fed it to him.

"There's another problem," said Nightingale. "The ritual as it stands requires an animal sacrifice."

"Well," I said, "Toby's looking good and fat."

"Modern society tends to frown on that sort of behavior, especially the modern church on whose grounds, incidentally, we'd have to carry it out."

"What's the sacrifice for?"

"According to Bartholomew, at the point of death the animal's intrinsic magic becomes available to 'feed' the ghost and help bring it into the material plane," said Nightingale.

"So it uses the animal's life essence as magic fuel?" I asked.

"Yes."

"Can you sacrifice people?" I asked. "Take their magic that way?"

"Yes," he said. "But there's a catch."

"What's the catch?"

"You get hunted down even unto the ends of the Earth and summarily executed," said Nightingale.

I didn't ask who would be called upon to do the hunting and the executing.

Toby barked, demanding sausages.

"If all we need is a source of magic," I said, "I think I've got an acceptable substitute."

ACCORDING TO Bartholomew, the closer to the ghost's grave site the better, so I spent a couple of hours going through the parish records while Nightingale persuaded the rector that we were interested in catching some church vandals. It's a very strange church, a great big rectangular stone barn designed by Inigo Jones. The east portico, where I'd first met Nicholas Wallpenny, was fake—the actual entrance being at the western end of the church and giving out onto the churchyard, which had been made over into gardens. Access was via a pair of high wrought-iron gates on Bedford Street. Nightingale managed to talk the rector into lending him the keys.

"If you're planning a stakeout," said the rector, "shouldn't I stay behind just in case?"

"We're worried that they might be following you," said Nightingale. "We want them to think the coast is clear so we can catch them in the act."

"Am I in danger?" asked the rector.

Nightingale looked him in the eye. "Only if you stay in the church tonight," he said.

The gardens were enclosed on three sides by the brick backs and shuttered windows of the terraced houses built at the same time as the rest of the Piazza. Cut off from the traffic noise, they formed a calm green space watched over by the true portico of the church. Cherry trees, pink with flowers in the May sunlight, were planted along the path. It was, as Nightingale said, quite the loveliest spot in London. It was just too bad that I was going to be coming back at midnight to perform a necromantic ritual.

The parish burial records were sketchy and the best approximate position I could get for Wallpenny's grave was over on the north side of the gardens, somewhere near the middle. Since Nicholas had been loath to show himself with Nightingale around, he was going to be stationed by the gate on Bedford Road, safely within screaming-for-help range. There was still the occasional trill of birdsong as I entered just after midnight. The night was clear, but you couldn't see any stars through the haze. The iron of the gate was cold under my hand as I swung it closed and headed for the grave. I had a Canadian survival light that came with a headband; I used it to read the crib notes in my standard issue police notebook.

You cannot scratch a pentagram into soft springy turf with anything less than a backhoe and in any case I wasn't about to vandalize such a lovely lawn. Instead, I drew the star and circle with charcoal dust using a burlap sack with a hole cut in one corner like an icing piper. I laid it on nice and thick. Polidori had quite a lot to say about the dangers of breaking the pentagram when summoning a spirit. Having your soul dragged out and sent screaming down to hell was only the start of it.

At each cardinal point of the pentagram I put one of my calculators. I'd suggested that I bring Toby along just in case the substitution didn't work, but when it was time to leave the Folly the dog was nowhere to be found. I'd picked up a packet of chemical glow sticks from a local camping shop and these I cracked and placed where the crib sheet called for candles. The conjurer, in this case me, was supposed to impart some of his essence, which was late eighteenth-century magic speak for "put some magic into" the circle around the pentagram. There's a particular *forma* created for just that purpose, but I hadn't had time to learn it—instead Nightingale suggested that I just create a werelight in the center.

I took a deep breath, created the werelight and floated it into the center of the pentagram. I adjusted my light and started to read the conjuration from my notebook. The original had gone on for four manuscript pages, but with Nightingale's help I'd managed to shave it down some.

"Nicholas Wallpenny," I said. "Hear my voice, accept my gifts, rise and converse."

And suddenly he was there, as shifty-looking as ever.

"I knew you was special as soon as I laid eyes on you," he said. "Your governor not around, is he?"

"Over there," I said. "Beyond the gate."

"Mind you keep him there," said Nicholas. "I was right about the murdering gent, weren't I?"

"We think it's the spirit of Punchinella," I said.

"You what?" said Nicholas. "Mr. Punch? I think you must have had one too many. Get thee to a lushery."

"You wanted my help last night," I said.

"Did I?" asked Nicholas. "But that would make me a blower and a slag and ain't nobody ever said that Nicholas Wallpenny ever put the jack on a cove lest he get a visit from the punishers." He gave me a significant look. A "blower" was old London slang for an informer and "punishers" were likewise slang for men hired to beat people up—presumably for "blowing."

"That's a relief," I said. "How's . . . death treating you?"

"Fair enough," said Nicholas. "Can't complain, certainly a lot less crowded than it once was. This being the Actors' Church and all, we're never short for an evening's entertainment. We've even had the occasional guest artiste for the further edification. We had that famous Henry Pyke, that's Pyke with a Y mind you—he's very particular, he's popular with the ladies on account of his long nose."

I didn't like the way Nicholas looked, tense, nervous and as if he would be sweating if he could still sweat. I considered backing off, but the cruel fact is that informants, dead or alive, are there to be used up if necessary.

"This . . . Henry Pyke, is he planning a long run?" I asked.

"Best to say that he's bought the theater," said Nicholas.

"Sounds good," I said. "Any chance of me catching a show?"

"Well, Constable, I wouldn't be so damned keen to get on the bill if I was you," said Nicholas. "Mr. Pyke can be strangely hard on his costars and I daresay he's got a role in mind for you."

"Still I wouldn't mind getting to meet . . ." I said but suddenly Nicholas was gone.

The pentagram was empty, with just my werelight burning at its center. Before I could snuff it out I felt something grab me by the head and try to drag me bodily into the pentagram. I panicked, pulling and twisting frantically to try to escape. Nightingale had been emphatic about not stepping into the pentagram and I had no intention of finding out why. I yanked my head back, but I felt my heels scrape in the turf as I was dragged forward—toward the pentagram. Then I saw it, below my own werelight: a dark shadow in the center of the pentagram, like the mouth of a pit dug into the earth. I could see the roots of the grass and the worms frantically trying to burrow back into the sides, the layers of topsoil and London clay fading into the darkness.

I was almost on the brink when I realized that whatever was pulling me was working through my own spell. I tried to shut down the werelight, but it stayed lit—glowing now with a sullen yellow color. I'd pushed my shoulders so far back that I was practically lying vertical and still my heels plowed forward.

I heard Nightingale yelling and looked over to see him running flat out toward me. I had a horrible feeling that he wasn't going to make it in time, so in my desperation I had one more thing to try. It's not easy to concentrate when you're being dragged into oblivion, but I forced myself to take a deep breath and make the correct *forma*—the werelight suddenly burned a fiery red. I made the shape with my mind that I hoped would pour in the magic, but I couldn't tell whether it was working. My heels dug through the edges of the pentagram and I felt a rush of excitement, a hunger for violence and a whole ocean of shame and humiliation and lust for revenge.

I dropped the fireball half a meter and let go.

There was a disappointingly quiet thump, like the sound a heavy dictionary would make if you dropped it. Then the ground lifted up underneath my legs and knocked me tumbling backward. I hit the branches of the cherry tree behind me and caught a glimpse of a column of earth shooting upward like a freight train leaving a tunnel before I fell out of the tree and the ground got its licks in.

Nightingale grabbed my collar and pulled me away as cherry blossoms and clods of earth rained down around us. A big chunk landed on my head and shattered, sending dirt trickling down the back of my neck.

Then there was silence, nothing but the sound of distant traffic and a nearby car alarm going off. We waited half a minute to catch our breath and just in case something else was going to happen.

"Guess what," I said. "I've got a name."

"You're damned lucky to still have a head," said Nightingale. "What's the name?"

"Henry Pyke," I said.

"Never heard of him," said Nightingale.

Predictably, my headband light had died, so Nightingale risked a werelight. Where the hole had been was now a shallow dish-shaped depression three meters across. The turf was completely destroyed, ground into a mix of dead grass and pulverized soil. Something round and dirty and white was resting near my foot. It was a skull, I picked it up.

"Is that you, Nicholas?" I asked.

"Put that down, Peter," said Nightingale. "You don't know where it's been." He surveyed the mess we'd made of the garden. "The rector's not going to be happy about this," he said.

I put the skull down and as I did, I noticed something else embedded in the ground. It was a pewter and brass badge depicting a dancing skeleton—I recognized it as the one Nicholas Wallpenny had "worn." He must have been buried with it.

"We did say we were hunting vandals," I said.

I picked up the badge and felt just the tiniest flash of tobacco smoke, beer and horses.

"Perhaps," said Nightingale. "But I doubt he's going to accept that as an explanation."

"A gas leak, maybe," I said.

"There's no gas main running under the church," said Nightingale. "He may become suspicious."

"Not if we tell him the gas leak story is a cover for digging up an unexploded bomb," I said.

"A UXB?" asked Nightingale. "Why make it that complicated?"

" 'Cause then we can bring in a digger and have a good rummage around," I said. "See if we can't disinter this Henry Pyke and grind him up into grave dust."

"You've got a devious mind, Peter," said Nightingale.

"Thank you, sir," I said. "I do my best."

Besides a devious mind, I also had a bruise the size of a dinner plate on my back and a couple more beauties on my chest and legs. I told the doctor I saw in casualty that I'd had an argument with a tree. He gave me a funny look and refused to prescribe any painkillers stronger than Nurofen.

So we had a name—Henry Pyke. Nicholas had hinted that Pyke wasn't buried at the Actors' Church, but we checked the records just in case. Nightingale called the General Registry Office at Southport while I scoured for Pykes on genepool, familytrace and other online genealogy sites. Neither of us got very far except to establish that it was a common name and strangely popular in California, Michigan and New York State. We convened in the coach house so that I could continue to use the Internet and Nightingale could watch the rugby.

"Nicholas said he was an entertainer," I said. "He might even have been a Punch and Judy man, a 'professor.' The Piccini script was published in 1827, but Nicholas said that Pyke was an older spirit, so I'd guess late eighteenth, early nineteenth century. But records from that period are useless."

Nightingale watched the All Blacks roll right over the

Lions's fullback to score, and judging by his long face, the margin of victory was suitably dire. "If only you could speak to some keen theatergoers from that period," he said.

"You want to summon more ghosts?" I asked.

"I was thinking of someone who was still alive," he said. "In a manner of speaking."

"Are you talking about Oxley?" I asked.

"And his darling common-law wife, Isis, also known as Anna Maria de Burgh Coppinger, mistress of John Montagu, the fourth Earl of Sandwich and live-in lover of the famous Shakespearean scholar Henry Ireland. Departed this vale of tears 1802, presumably for the greener pastures of Chertsey."

"Chertsey?"

"That's where the Oxley River is," he said.

IF I was going to see Oxley again, then I figured I might as well kill two birds with one stone. I called Beverley on her waterproof mobile and asked her if she was up for a field trip. Just in case her mum's prohibition was still in force, I was going to tell her that it was in aid of "dealing" with Father Thames, but I never got the chance to say it.

"Are we taking the Jag?" she asked. "No offense, but your other car stinks."

I told her yes and she was buzzing on the entry phone fifteen minutes later. Obviously she'd been lurking about the West End already.

"Mum's got me sniffing around," she said as she climbed into the Jag. "Looking for your revenant." She was wearing a black embroidered bolero over a red turtleneck sweater and black leggings.

"Would you know a revenant if you saw one?" I asked.

"I don't know," she said. "There's a first time for everything."

I wanted to watch her tuck her long legs under the dash, but I figured the temperature was high enough already. My dad had once told me that the secret to a happy life was never to start something with a girl unless you were willing to follow wherever it leads. It's the best piece of advice he's ever given me and probably the reason I was born. I concentrated on getting the Jag out of the garage and setting course for the southwest and the wrong side of the river again.

In 671 A.D., an abbey was founded on the high ground south of the River Thames in what is now Chertsey. It was your classic Anglo-Saxon establishment, half center of learning, half economic powerhouse and a refuge for those sons of the nobility who thought there was more to life than stabbing people with swords. Two hundred years later, the Vikings, who never got tired of stabbing people with swords, sacked the abbey and burned it down. It was rebuilt, but the inhabitants must have done something to piss off King Edgar the Peaceable, because in 964 A.D. he kicked them out and replaced them with some Benedictines. This order of monks believed in a life of contemplation, prayer and really big meals and because they liked to eat, this meant they never saw a stretch of arable land they didn't want to improve. One of their improvements, sometime in the eleventh century, was to dig a separate channel for the Thames from the Penton Hook to the Chertsey Weir to provide water power for their grinding mills. I say the monks "dug," but of course they drafted in some peasants for the hard labor. This artificial tributary of the Thames is marked on the maps as the Abbey River, but was once known as the Oxley Mills Stream.

I hadn't told Beverley where we were going, but she twigged what we were up to as soon as we swung off the Clockhouse roundabout and headed down the London Road for glorious Staines.

"I can't be coming down here," she said. "This is off my patch."

"Relax," I said. "This is sanctioned."

It's a weird thing that despite being born and raised in London, there are large stretches of the city that I've never seen. Staines was one of those and to me it looked low rise and countrified. After we crossed Staines Bridge, I found myself on an anonymous stretch of road with tall hedges and fences blinding me on both sides. I slowed down as we approached a roundabout and wished that I'd invested in a GPS system.

"Go left," said Beverley.

"Why?"

"You're looking for one of the sons of the Old Man?" she asked.

"Oxley," I said.

"Then go left," she said with absolute certainty.

I took the first exit off the roundabout with that weird sense of dislocation you get when driving under someone else's direction. I saw a marina on my left—bobbing rows of white-and-blue cruisers with the occasional longboat to break up the monotony.

"Is that it?" I asked.

"Don't be stupid," she said. "That's the Thames, keep going straight." We crossed a short modern bridge over what Beverley assured me was Oxley River and reached a strange little roundabout. It was like driving into the land of the munchkins, an estate made of little streets lined with pink stucco bungalows. We turned right, parallel to the river—I drove slowly in case some little bugger jumped out into the middle of the road and started singing.

"Here," said Beverley and I parked the car. When I got out she stayed in her seat. "I think this is a bad idea."

"They're really very nice people," I said.

"I'm sure they're very civilized and all that," she said. "But Ty is not going to like this."

"Beverley," I said. "Your mum told me to sort things out; this is me sorting things out—this is you facilitating me sorting things out. Only that's not going to happen unless you get out of the car."

Beverley sighed, unbuckled and climbed out. She stretched and arched her back, making her breasts strain alarmingly against her sweater. She caught me staring and winked. "Just getting the kinks out," she said.

Nightingale had said that eating Isis's Battenberg cake had been a bad idea, so I couldn't see him approving of me fraternizing with the local water nymphs. So I kept my eyes off Beverley's round bum and tried to think professional thoughts. Besides, there was always Leslie—or more precisely, the remote hope of Leslie—at some point in the future.

I rang the doorbell and stepped back politely.

I heard Isis call from inside, "Who is it?"

"Peter Grant," I said.

Isis opened the door and beamed at me. "Peter," she said. "What a pleasant surprise." She spotted Beverley behind me and although she didn't lose her smile, a wariness came into her eyes. "And who is this?" she asked.

"This is Beverley Brook," I said. "I thought it was about time proper introductions were made. Beverley, this is Isis."

Beverley extended a cautious hand, which Isis shook. "Pleased to meet you, Beverley. We're out back—you'd better come through." Although she didn't do anything as undignified as break into a run, Isis did walk at the brisk pace of a wife determined to reach her husband with the shocking news ahead of the guests. I got a brief glimpse of tidy little rooms with floral wallpaper and chintz before we emerged from the kitchen door.

The bungalow backed straight onto the river and Oxley had built himself a wooden wharf that projected over a wide spot in the river. A pair of magnificent weeping willows, one at each end, screened the pool from the outside. It felt as cool and timeless as the inside of a country church. Oxley was standing naked in the pool with the brown water lapping at his thighs. He was grinning up at Isis who was making frantic— behave yourself—gestures from the edge of the wharf. He looked past at me and Beverley as we walked out.

"What's this?" he asked. I saw his shoulders tense and I swear the sun went behind a cloud—although that could have been a coincidence.

"This," I said, "is Beverley Brook. Say hello, Beverley."

"Hello," said Beverley.

"I thought it was about time you met the other half," I said.

Oxley shifted his weight; behind me, I felt Beverley take a step backward.

"Well, isn't this nice," said Isis brightly. "Why don't we all have a nice cup of tea."

Oxley opened his mouth as if to speak, appeared to think better of it and, turning to his wife, said, "Tea would be nice."

I breathed out, Beverley giggled nervously and the sun came out again. I took Beverley's hand and led her forward. Oxley had a laborer's physique, lean and covered in hard ropy muscle—Isis obviously liked her bit of rough. Beverley, interestingly, seemed more interested in the water.

"This is a nice place," she said.

"Would you like to come in?" asked Oxley.

"Yes, please," said Beverley and to my utter amazement she whipped off her sweater and bolero in one sinuous movement, stepped out of her leggings and with a memorable flash of naked brown limbs threw herself into the water. Isis and I had to step back smartly to avoid being drenched.

Oxley winked at me and looked at his wife. "Are you coming in too, my love?"

"We have another guest," said Isis primly. "Some of us still have manners."

Beverley surfaced and stood in the river up to her waist with a cheeky grin and bare breasts. Her nipples, I couldn't stop myself noticing, were large and stiff. She turned her gaze on me, heavy-lidded and suggestive. If her mother had been like the undertow of the sea, then Beverley was as irresistible as a swift clear river rushing through a hot summer's afternoon.

I'd already started unbuttoning my shirt when I felt Isis's hand on my arm.

"You really are the most extraordinarily gullible young man," she said. "What on earth are we going to do with you?"

Oxley ducked under the surface. Beverley looked at me with her head cocked to one side, a sly smile on her lips, and then she slipped down into the water.

Isis offered me a seat at the plastic garden table and then, muttering under her breath, collected up Beverley's discarded clothes, folded them neatly and draped them over a drying rail by the back door. Oxley and Beverley had been out of sight for more than a minute. I looked at Isis, who seemed unperturbed.

"They're going to be at least another half hour," she said and made us tea. I kept an eye on the water as she bustled, but there weren't even bubbles. I told myself they must have swum out of the pool and surfaced beyond the trees somewhere, but I wasn't very convincing even to myself. She gave me the now standard assurances as she poured and offered me a slice of Madeira—I said no, thank you. I asked her if she remembered a Henry Pyke. She thought the name was familiar.

"I'm certain there was an actor of that name," she said. "But there were always so many actors, so many beautiful men. My good friend Anne Seymour had a mulatto footman who could have been your brother. He was a terror for the kitchen maids." She leaned forward and looked me in the eyes. "Are you a terror to the kitchen maids, Peter?"

I thought of Molly. "I'd have to say no," I said.

"No, I can see that," she said and sat back in her chair. "He was murdered," she said abruptly.

"The footman?" I asked.

"Henry Pyke. Or that was the rumor. Another victim of the notorious Charles Macklin."

"Who was he?"

"A most terrible Irishman," said Isis. "But a splendid actor. He'd killed a man once already at the Theatre Royal in a dispute about a wig, stabbed him in the eye with his cane."

"Lovely," I said.

"Had that Irish temper, you see," said Isis. Macklin had been a successful actor in his youth who retired in his prime to run a gin house that promptly went out of business. Forced back onto the boards, he was an ever-popular fixture at the Theatre Royal. "They loved him there," said Isis. "You always saw him in his favorite seat in the pit just behind the orchestra. I remember Anne liked to point him out."

"And he killed Henry Pyke?"

"According to the gossip he did, for all that there were half a dozen witnesses who said he did not," she said.

"Were these witnesses friends of Macklin?"

"And admirers too," said Isis.

"Do you know where Henry Pyke is buried?" I asked.

"Sorry," she said. "It was just a bit of scandal at the time.

Though I would have thought St. Paul's, since that would have been the proper parish."

She meant St. Paul's of Covent Garden, of course—the Actors' Church. Things kept coming round to that one bloody spot.

There was a splash and Beverley came running onto the wharf as if there was a set of stairs hidden under the water. She was as dark and sleekly naked as a seal and you could have fired a shotgun past my ear and I still wouldn't have looked away. She turned back to the river and jumped up and down like a kid.

"I beat you," she said.

Oxley stepped out of the river with as much dignity as a naked middle-aged white man could be expected to have. "Beginner's luck," he said.

Beverley threw herself into the chair next to mine; her eyes were bright and water was pearling on her arms and the smooth skin of her shoulders and the slopes of her breasts. She smiled at me and I tried to keep my eyes on her face. Oxley padded over and sat down opposite and without preamble, and ignoring a look from Isis, grabbed himself a piece of Madeira.

"Did you enjoy your swim?" I asked.

"There are things down there you wouldn't believe, Peter," she said.

"Your hair's wet," I said.

Beverley touched her straightened hair, which was beginning to frizz. I kept watching as she suddenly remembered she was stark naked. "Oh shit," she said and gave Isis a panicked look. "Sorry," she said.

"Towels are in the bathroom, dear," said Isis.

"Laters," said Beverley and ran for the back door.

Oxley laughed and reached for another slice of cake. Isis slapped his hand. "Go and put some clothes on," she said. "You appalling old man." Oxley sighed and went into the bungalow; Isis watched him fondly as he went.

"They're always like that after a swim," she said.

"Do you go swimming too?" I asked.

"Oh yes," said Isis and blushed ever so slightly. "But I'm still a creature of the riverbank. There's a balance in them between the water and the land, the more time they spend with us, the more like us they become."

"And the more time you spend with them?"

"Don't be in a hurry to go into the water," said Isis. "It's not a decision you want to rush into."

BEVERLEY WAS quiet all the way back up west. I asked her whether she wanted to be dropped off somewhere.

"Can you take me home," she said. "I think I need to talk to my mum."

So I had to drive all the way across town to wonderful Wapping with Beverley too subdued to talk, which was unsettling in its own right. When I dropped her off outside the flats, she paused before she got all the way out and told me to be careful. When I asked her what I should be careful of, she shrugged and before I could stop her she kissed me on the cheek. I watched her walk away from the car, the hem of her sweater clinging to her backside, and thought—what the fuck was that about?

Don't get me wrong, I fancied Beverley Brook, but I was a little suspicious, not least because both she and her mother seemed capable of getting an erection out of moss if the mood took them. Isis's caution about getting into the water with somebody who wasn't a hundred percent human was just the icing on the cake.

Rush hour was starting to build as I drove back to the Folly. The day had clouded over and rain began to spatter the windshield. I was fairly certain that Oxley and Beverley had made a connection. When I saw them standing side by side in the river they'd looked . . . comfortable was the best word, or maybe familiar in the sense of cousins. Bartholomew, who could bore for England on the subject of *genii locorum*, was adamant that the "nature spirits," as he called them, would always take some of the characteristics of the locus they represented. Father and

Mama Thames were spirits of the same river—if I could edge them closer together, then their true nature should take its course.

And if that meant spending a few days watching Beverley in the river, that was a price I was willing to pay.

I considered checking in with Leslie but instead I locked up the garage and walked across the park to Russell Square tube station. I bought some flowers from a stall by the station and, for no apparent reason, headed in to catch a train to somewhere else.

CHAPTER 9

The Judas Goat

I'D GOT the tube all the way to Swiss Cottage and was a quarter of the way up Fitzjohn's Avenue when I started to question what I was doing. It wasn't just that I'd abandoned my motor for public transport; it was also that I was walking up one of the steepest hills in London when I could have taken the train to Hampstead and walked downhill instead. It was still bright and the afternoon sunlight cut through the gaps between the trees that lined the avenue. The flowers in my hand were roses, a purple variety that was so dark as to be almost black. I wondered who they might be for.

It was warm enough that I unclipped my tie and stuffed it into my jacket pocket. I didn't want to arrive sweaty, so I took my time and ambled along in the shade of the plane trees planted along the pavement. It was the kind of day where a tune gets stuck in your head and you can't help singing it out loud; in this case it was a blast from my past, "Digging Your Scene" by the Blow Monkeys. Given that it was released when I was still in nappies, it was a wonder that I knew all the words. I'd sung "I'd just like to be myself again" in the third chorus when I reached my destination. The house was a tall gothic confection with a mock tower at each corner and sash windows painted white. Marble-clad steps led up to an imposing front door, but I ignored them and made my way to the side gate—I knew where I was going. I checked my jacket was straight and rubbed the toes of my shoes on the backs of my calves; satisfied, I pushed open the gate and stepped through.

Honeysuckle had been planted along the side wall of the house, making a sweet-scented corridor that opened up into a wide sunny garden. A neatly mown lawn bordered with formal beds planted with surfinia, petunias, marigolds and tulips. Two huge terra-cotta pots bursting with spring flowers guarded steps down to a sunken patio that pooled the afternoon sunlight around a fountain. Even I could see that this wasn't some piece picked up in a garden store or hypermarket. It was a delicate marble birdbath with a central statue of a nude carrying water, Italian Renaissance maybe; I didn't have enough art history to know. It was antique and battered, the marble chipped in places and the nymph had a discolored streak running from her shoulder to her groin from the water trickling out of her gourd.

The water smelled sweet and enticing, just the thing after my long slow walk up the hill. A handsome middle-aged woman was waiting for me by the fountain. She was dressed in a yellow cotton sundress, straw hat and open-toed sandals. As I drew closer, I saw she had her mother's eyes, black and slanted like a cat's, but that she was lighter than Beverley with a nice straight media-friendly nose.

There was once a gallows, close to where Marble Arch now stands, where they used to hang the criminals of old London town. The gallows was named after the village, which was named after the river that ran through it and the river was named Tyburn. Tyburn's inhabitants profited so greatly from the grisly spectacles that they built viewing stands to bring in the punters. They hung poor Elizabeth Barton there and Gentleman Jack, for all that he escaped four times before, and the Reverend James Hackman for the murder of pretty Martha Ray. I knew all this because after Beverley dropped her sister's name into the conversation as the one who *knows people who matter,* I made a point of finding out.

"I thought it was time you and I had a little chat," said Tyburn.

I offered her the flowers, which she took with a delighted

laugh. She pulled my head down and kissed me on the cheek. She smelt of cigars and new car seats, horses and furniture polish, Stilton, Belgium chocolate and behind it all the hemp and the crowd and the last drop into oblivion.

I'd traced the sources, as well as I could anyway, of all the lost rivers of London. Some, like the Beverley Brook, the Lea or the Fleet, were easy to find, but the location of the Tyburn, the legendary Shepherd's Well, had got lost in the mad Victorian steam-powered expansion of London in the latter half of the nineteenth century. This fountain was obviously at the source, but the fountain itself, I suspected, had been looted by an enterprising official in the last days of the Empire.

I was thirsty—I would have liked a drink.

"What would you like to talk about?" I asked.

"For a start," said Tyburn, "I'd like to know what your intentions are with regards to my sister."

"My intentions?" I asked. My mouth was very dry. "Are purely honorable."

"Really?" she said and crouched down to retrieve a vase from behind the fountain. "Is that why you took her to see the pikeys?"

Pikey is a word for Gypsies that a well brought up young policeman is not supposed to use. "That was just a preliminary, exploratory, investigation," I said. "And Oxley and Isis are not pikeys."

Tyburn stroked the back of her hand down the back of the marble water carrier and the trickle from the gourd thickened into a strong stream from which she filled the vase. "Still," she said, as she unwrapped the roses. "Not the sort of people one wants one's sister associating with."

"We don't get to choose our family," I said cheerfully. "Thank God we can choose our friends."

Tyburn gave me a sharp look and started arranging the roses. The vase was unremarkable, fat bottomed like a volumetric flask and made from green lacquered fiberglass, the sort of thing you can pick up cheaply at a yard sale. "I've got nothing against the Old Man or his people but this is the twenty-first century and this is my town and I haven't busted a gut for thirty years so that some 'gentleman of the road' can move back in and take what's mine."

"What do you think is yours?" I asked.

She ignored me and, having arranged the last of the roses, placed the vase on the patio wall close by. When I'd bought them, the roses had been the last of the stock and were beginning to wilt on the stand. Once Tyburn placed them in the vase, they perked up, becoming full, rich and even darker.

"Peter," she said. "You've seen the way the Folly is organized, or rather not organized. You know that it has no official standing in government and its relationship with the Metropolitan Police is entirely a matter of custom and practice and, God help me, tradition. It's all held together with spit and sealing wax and the old boy network. It's a typical British mash up and the one time it was asked to step up it failed horribly. I have access to files you don't even know exist, Peter, about a place in Germany called Ettersberg—you might want to ask your mentor about that."

"Technically he's my master," I said. "I swore a guild oath as his apprentice." My tongue felt thick and dry as if I'd just spent the night sleeping with my mouth open.

"I rest my case," she said. "I know it's against the national character, but don't you just wish we were little bit more organized about these things, just a tad more grown up. Would it kill us to have an official branch of government that handled the supernatural?"

"A Ministry of Magic?" I asked.

"Ha bloody ha," said Tyburn.

I wanted to know why she hadn't offered me a cup of tea. I'd brought her flowers and figured that the least I could expect in return would be a nice cup of tea or a beer or even a drink of water. I cleared my throat and it came out a bit wheezy. I glanced at the fountain and the water streaming into the basin.

"Do you like it?" she asked. "The basin is a rather crude seventeenth-century knockoff of an Italian design, but the central figure was excavated when they were building Swiss Cottage station." She rested her hand on the statue's face.

"The marble's from Belgium, but the archaeologists assure me that it was carved locally."

I was having trouble working out why I didn't want to drink the water. I've drunk water before, when beer or coffee or Diet Coke weren't available, I've drunk it from bottles, occasionally from a tap. When I was a kid, I used to drink from the tap all the time, used to run back into the flat all hot and sweaty from playing and didn't even bother putting it in a glass—just turned the tap on and stuck my mouth underneath it. If my mum caught me doing it, she used to scold me, but my dad just said that I had to be careful; "What if a fish jumped out," he used to say. "You'd swallow it before you knew it was there." Dad was always saying stuff like that and it wasn't until I was seventeen that I realized that it was because he was stoned all the time.

"Stop that," I mumbled.

She gave me a pretty smile. "Stop what?"

I don't mind getting drunk, but there always comes a moment in the evening when I find myself watching myself bumping into things and thinking—I'm bored of this, can I have full control of my brain back, please? I was getting equally irritated by my sudden need to deliver flowers to Hampstead and drink water from strange fountains. I tried to take a step backward, but the best I could manage was a minor shuffle.

Tyburn's smile vanished. "Why don't you have a nice drink?" she asked.

She'd gone too far and she knew it and she knew I knew she knew it too. Whatever influence she'd put on me must have been too subtle to handle a suggestion that obvious. Plus I've always wondered about that fish.

"Good idea," I said. "There's a pub down the road. Let's go there."

"You cunning bastard," she said and I didn't think she was talking about me. She leaned in closer and stared into my eyes. "I know you're thirsty," she said. "Drink the water."

I felt my body lurch forward toward the fountain. It was involuntary, just like when you get a twitch in your leg or the hiccups, but now it was my whole body working to a purpose that wasn't mine—it was terrifying. I realized then that the Old Man and Mama Thames hadn't even been trying to control me and had they wanted to, they could have had me doing cartwheels around the room. There had to be a limitation to the power or else what was to stop Mama Thames or the Old Man walking into Downing Street and dictating terms? I think people would notice if that happened—the Thames would be a lot cleaner, for a start.

It had to be Nightingale, I realized. The counterweight, the human balance to the supernatural, and that meant that they couldn't control him. The only thing that separated Nightingale from an ordinary guy was his magic, which meant that the magic must supply a defense. It was a stretch, but it isn't easy thinking things through when the personification of a historic London river is trying to mentally overwhelm you.

To try to buy time I attempted to throw myself backward. It didn't work, but it did stop my next lurch toward the fountain. Nightingale hadn't taught me a block yet, so I reached for *impello* instead. Lining up the *forma* in my mind was so much easier than I expected—later I speculated that whatever it was Tyburn was doing acted on the instinctive bit of my brain, not the "higher" functions—that I got carried away.

"*Impello,*" I said and tried to lift the statue off its pedestal.

Tyburn's eyes widened at the sound of cracking marble. She whirled to look and as her eyes left mine I staggered back—suddenly free. I felt the shape in my mind slip out of control and the statue's head disintegrated in a spray of marble chips. I felt a blow on my shoulder and a sharp cut on my face, and a chunk of marble the size of a small dog slammed into the patio tiles by my feet.

I saw that the birdbath had also cracked and that water was escaping to spread across the patio like a bloodstain. Tyburn turned back to look at me. There was a cut on her forehead and her sundress was torn just above her hip.

She'd gone very quiet and that was not a good sign. I'd seen that quiet before, on my mum and on the face of a woman whose brother had just been knocked down by a drunk driver. People are conditioned by the media to think that black women are all shouting, and head shaking and girlfriending and "oh no you didn't" and if they're not sassy, then they're dignified and downtrodden and soldiering on and "I don't understand why folks just can't get along." But if you see a black woman go quiet the way Tyburn did, the eyes bright, the lips straight and the face still as a death mask, you have made an enemy for life, do not pass Go, do not collect two hundred.

Do not stand around and try to talk about it; trust me, it won't end well. I took my own advice and backed away. Tyburn's black eyes watched me go and as soon as I was safely in the side passage I turned and legged it as fast I could. I didn't exactly run down the hill to Swiss Cottage, but I did make it a brisk walk. There was a pay phone near the bottom, which I needed since the battery had been in my mobile during my statue demolition. I called the operator, gave my identification number and got a call routed to Leslie's mobile. She wanted to know where I'd been, because apparently it had all gone pear-shaped without me.

"We saved the blind guy," she said. "No thanks to you." She refused to give me any details because, "Your boss wants you down here yesterday." I asked her where "here" was and she told me the Westminster Mortuary, which made me cross because we may have saved the blind man, but some poor bastard had obviously still lost his face. I told her I'd be there as soon as possible.

I caught a lift in the local area car down to the Swiss Cottage tube and hopped a Jubilee Line train into town. I doubted that Lady Ty had the manpower or the inclination to have the stations covered and one of the few advantages of blowing out my phone was that it couldn't be lojacked, ditto any trackers she might have stashed about my person. I'm not being paranoid, you know. You can buy those things off the Internet.

Rush hour was just building up when I got on the train and the carriage was crowded just short of the transition between the willing suspension of personal space and packed in like sardines. I spotted some of the passengers eyeing me up as I took a position at the end of the carriage with my back to the connecting door. I was sending out mixed signals; the suit and reassuring countenance of my face went one way, the fact that I'd obviously been in a fight recently and was mixed race went the other. It's a myth that Londoners are oblivious to one another on the tube; we're hyper aware of each other and are constantly revising our what-if scenarios and counterstrategies. What if that suavely handsome yet ethnic young man asks me for money, do I give or refuse; if he makes a joke, do I respond and if so, will it be a shy smile or a guffaw? If he's hurt in a fight, does he need help? If I help him, will I find myself drawn into a threatening situation, or an adventure, or a wild interracial romance? Will I miss supper? If he opens his jacket and yells "God is great," will I make it down the other end of the carriage in time?

And all the time most of us were devising friction-free strategies to promote peace in our time, our carriage and please God at least until I get home. It's called, by people over sixty, common courtesy and its purpose is to stop us from killing each other. It was like *vestigia;* you weren't always aware of it, but you instinctively shaped your behavior in response to the accumulation of magic around you. This is what kept ghosts going, I realized; they lived off the *vestigia* like LEDs off a long-life battery, powering down to ration it out. I remembered the dead space that was the vampire house in Purley. According to Nightingale, vampires were ordinary people who became "infected," no one was sure how or why, and started feeding off the magic potential, including the *vestigia,* of their surroundings.

"But it's not enough to sustain a living being," Nightingale had said. "So they go hunting for more magic." The best source of that, according to Isaac Newton, was human beings, but you can't steal magic from a person, or any life more complex than slime molds, except at the point of death and even then it wasn't easy. I'd asked the obvious question—why the blood drinking? He said that nobody knew. I asked him why hadn't anyone done any experiments and he gave me a strange look.

"There were some experiments done," he'd said after a long pause. "During the war, but the results were considered unethical and the files were sealed."

"We were going to use vampires during the war?" I'd asked, and been surprised by the look of genuine hurt and anger on Nightingale's face. "No," he'd said sharply and then with more moderation, "Not us—the Germans."

Sometimes when someone tells you not to go somewhere, it's better not to go there.

The *genii locorum,* like Beverley, Oxley and the rest of the dysfunctional family Thames, were also living beings on one level, also got their power from their surroundings. Bartholomew and Polidori both suggested that they drew sustenance from *all the diverse and myriad life and magic within their domains.* I was skeptical, but I was willing to accept that they lived in symbiosis with their "domains," whereas vampires were clearly parasitical. What if that was mirrored by ghosts? If Nicholas Wallpenny was in some way part of the *vestigia* he inhabited and drew power from, a symbiote, then the revenant could be a parasite, a ghost vampire. That would explain the shrunken cauliflower brains of the victims—they'd had the magic sucked out of them.

Which meant that the summoning I'd done with the calculators had achieved nothing more than feeding Henry Pyke's appetite for magic. But I also wondered if you couldn't attract a revenant by spilling magic around, like laying a chum line for a shark. By the time the train pulled into Baker Street, I was already beginning to formulate a plan.

The tube is a good place for this sort of conceptual breakthrough because, unless you've got something to read, there's bugger all else to do.

THIS TIME when I arrived at Westminster Mortuary, I didn't even have to show my warrant card. The guards on the gate just waved me through. Nightingale was waiting for me in the locker room. While I was kitting out, I gave him a brief explanation of my meeting with Tyburn.

"It's always the children," said Nightingale. "They're never satisfied with the status quo."

"How did you save the blind man?" I asked.

"Apparently, they're not blind," said Nightingale. "They

are, in fact, visually impaired. A very forceful young lady pointed this out to me at some length while we were waiting at the hospital."

"How did you save the visually impaired man, then?"

"I wish I could take the credit," said Nightingale. "It was his guide dog; as soon as the sequestration began . . ."

"Sequestration?" I asked.

Apparently this was the term that Dr. Walid had invented to describe what happened when a normal human being was taken over by our revenant. It's a legal term that refers to the legal process by which a person's property is seized in order to pay off debts or because it's considered to be the proceeds of crime. In this case, the property sequestrated was the person's body.

"As soon as sequestration commenced," said Nightingale, "the guide dog, who I believe is called Malcolm, went berserk and dragged the potential victim away. Inspector Seawoll already had his people covering charity collections in the area and one of them intervened before our poor sequestrated Punch could follow the blind man."

"Another triumph for intelligence-led policing," I said.

"Quite," said Nightingale. "It was your friend Constable May who was on the scene first."

"Leslie? I bet she wasn't happy about that," I said.

"In her words, 'Why does this shit always fucking happen to me,' " said Nightingale.

"So who was our sequestration victim when he was alive?" I asked.

"Who says he's dead?" said Nightingale.

He led me down the corridor where they had a room kitted out as a mobile intensive care unit, which is, when you think about it, a disturbing thing to find in a mortuary. Leslie was slumped in a chair in the corner of the room. She raised her hand in a hello when we entered. The bed was surrounded on both sides by machines huffing, going beep or just silently blinking. In the bed was Terrence Pottsley, aged twenty-seven, of Sedgefield, County Durham, a stock control manager for Tesco's, next of kin most definitely not informed as yet. A thicket of stainless steel was growing out of his face—a medical scaffold they call it. Dr. Walid hoped that would allow successful reconstructive surgery once the issue of Pottsley's sequestration was resolved.

"And I complained when I had my braces in," said Leslie.

"Is he awake?" I asked.

"Apparently he's being kept in what they call a 'medical coma,'" said Nightingale. "Did Oxley know who we're dealing with?"

"Isis did," I said. "She remembers Henry Pyke as a failed actor who may have been murdered by Charles Macklin—a much more successful actor."

"That would explain the resentment," said Nightingale.

"Was he arrested?" asked Leslie.

"Records are sketchy," I said. "Pyke might have been arrested . . ."

"Not Pyke," said Leslie. "Macklin. To get away with one murder is like an accident, but to get away with two seems a little bit fucking improbable. Not to mention unfair."

"Macklin lived on to a ripe old age," said Nightingale. "He was a fixture of Covent Garden life. I knew he'd committed murder, but I'd never heard of Henry Pyke."

"Can we have our discussion somewhere else?" said Leslie. "This guy's making me nervous."

Since we were, mostly, coppers, that meant a pub or the canteen—the canteen was closer. I waited for Dr. Walid to join us before outlining my strategy.

"I have an idea," I said.

"This better not be a cunning plan," said Leslie.

Nightingale looked blank, but at least it got a chuckle from Dr. Walid.

"It is in fact," I said, "a cunning plan."

Nightingale had been carrying around a hard copy of the Piccini script. I laid it out and drew attention to the scene that followed Punch's disposal of the blind beggar. In it, the constable arrives to arrest Punch for murdering his wife and baby.

"I make myself the constable in the next scene."

"You're volunteering to have your head beaten in?" asked Dr. Walid.

"If you read the script, you'll see that the constable actually survives the encounter," I said. "As does the officer who arrives immediately after."

"And I take it that would be me," said Nightingale.

"Just so long as it's not me," said Leslie.

"I'm not sure I can see this working," said Nightingale. "Henry Pyke has no reason to engineer an encounter with us, however well we fit his little play."

Dr. Walid put his finger on the script and said, "Punch asks 'And who sent for you?' to which the constable replies, 'I'm sent for you.' Punch doesn't get a choice, this is his destiny catching up with him. 'I don't want Constable,' he says."

"I think you've got Punch all wrong," said Leslie. "You're assuming he's like a kind of supernatural serial killer who's locked into acting out a Punch and Judy show. But what if he's something else?"

"Like what?" I asked.

"Like the manifestation of a social trend, crime and disorder, a sort of superyob. The spirit of riot and rebellion in the London mob."

We all looked at her in amazement.

"You forget I did A-levels too, you know," said Leslie.

"Do you have another plan?" I asked.

"No," said Leslie. "I just want you to be careful. Just because you think you know what you're doing doesn't mean you actually know what you're doing."

"I'm glad we clarified that," I said.

"You're welcome," she said. "Even if you catch up with Henry, what then?"

It was a good question—I looked at Nightingale.

"I can track his spirit," said Nightingale. "If I get close enough I can track him all the way back to his old bones."

"And then what?" asked Leslie.

I looked at Nightingale. "We dig them up and grind them into dust, mix them with rock salt and then scatter them out at sea," I said.

"And that'll work?" she asked.

"Has before," said Dr. Walid.

"You'll need a warrant," said Leslie.

"We don't need a warrant for a ghost," I said.

Leslie grinned and pushed the script over to my side of the table. She tapped the page with her spoon and I read the line: *Constable: Don't tell me. You have committed murder, and I have a warrant for you.* "If you want to play the part, you're going to need all the props."

"A warrant for a ghost," I said.

"That at least will not pose a difficulty," said Nightingale. "Although it does mean we'll have to postpone the capture operation until late tonight."

"You're going ahead with this?" asked Leslie. She looked at me with concern. I gave my best shot at insouciance, but I suspect it came out looking more like unfounded optimism.

"I believe, Constable, that this is our only option," said Nightingale. "I'd be most grateful if you could brief Inspector Seawoll and ask him to stand ready in Covent Garden at eleven."

"As late as that?" I asked. "Henry Pyke might not wait that long."

"We won't get our warrant until eleven at the earliest," said Nightingale.

"And if this doesn't work?"

"Then it'll be Leslie's turn to come up with a plan," said Nightingale.

WE DROVE back to the Folly, where Nightingale vanished into the magic library to, presumably, bone up on his revenant tracking spells while I went upstairs to my room and took my uniform out of the cupboard. I had to hunt around for my helmet and eventually found it under the bed with my silver whistle, absurdly still part of the modern uniform, inside. Since my latest phone hadn't survived the destruction of Tyburn's fountain, I retrieved the police issue airwave from my desk and slotted in its batteries. As I packed it in my carryall with my uniform jacket, I realized that the room still looked like somebody's spare bedroom, somewhere that I was just staying in until something better came along.

I slung the carryall over my shoulder and turned to find Molly watching me from the doorway. She cocked her head to one side.

"I don't know," I said. "But we'll be eating out."

She frowned.

"I'm the one who's going to be out front," I said, but it didn't seem to impress her. "He'll be fine."

She gave me a last skeptical look before gliding away. By the time I was out of my room she was nowhere to be seen. I went downstairs and waited for Nightingale in the Reading Room. He emerged half an hour later dressed in his "working" suit and carrying his cane. He asked me whether I was ready and I said that I was.

It was a beautiful warm spring evening, so rather than take the Jag we strolled down past the British Museum before cutting through Museum Street and into Drury Lane. Even though we'd taken our time, we still had hours to spare, so we popped into a curry house near the Theatre Royal with the promising name of the House of Bengal for dinner.

As I checked a menu mercifully free of potatoes, thick crust pastry, suet and gravy, I realized why Nightingale liked to eat out so much.

Nightingale had the lamb in wild lemon and I made do with a chicken madras hot enough to make Nightingale's eyes water. It was a little on the mild side for me. Indian cooking has no terrors for a boy raised on groundnut chicken and jelof rice. The motto of West African cooking is that if the food doesn't set fire to the tablecloth the cook is being stingy with the pepper. Actually there's no such motto—from my mum's point of view it was simply inconceivable that anybody would want to eat anything that didn't burn the inside of your mouth out.

We ordered a beer while we waited and Nightingale asked me how my diplomatic efforts were progressing. "Leaving aside your little contretemps with Tyburn."

I told him about the visit to Oxley's river and Beverley's response. I left out the whole wanting-to-jump-in-myself aspect of the visit. I said that I'd thought it had gone well and had established that there was a mutual connection between the two sides. "It's something we can build on," I said.

"Conflict resolution," said Nightingale. "Is this what they teach at Hendon these days?"

"Yes, sir," I said. "But don't worry, they also teach us how to beat people with phone books and the ten best ways to plant evidence."

"It's good to see the old craft skills are being kept up," said Nightingale.

I sipped my beer. "Tyburn's not a big fan of the old ways," I said.

"Peter," he said. "Of all of Mother Thames's children, you had to pick a fight with Lady Ty." He waved his fork. "That is why we do not throw magic around until we are trained."

"What was I supposed to do?"

"You could have talked your way out of it," he said. "What do you think Ty is—a gangster? Did you think she was going to 'plug a cap' in your head? She pushed you to see where you'd go and you blew up."

We ate our curries for a while. He was right—I'd panicked.

"It's 'pop a cap in my ass,' " I said. "Not plug—pop."

"Ah," said Nightingale.

"You don't seem that worried about it, sir," I said. "The Lady Ty business."

Nightingale finished a mouthful of lamb and said, "Peter, we're about to offer ourselves up as Judas goats to a powerful revenant spirit who's killed eight people that we know of." He dug into his rice. "I'm not going to worry about Lady Ty until after we've lived through that."

"If I remember rightly," I said, "I'm the Judas goat, the 'constable' in this scenario. And considering that it's my backside hanging out in the air, sir. Are you sure you can track him?"

"Nothing is certain, Peter," he said. "But I'll do my best."

"And if we can't run him into his grave?" I asked. "Do we have a plan B?"

"Molly can do hemomancy," said Nightingale. "It's very impressive."

I sorted through my slim store of Greek. "Divination through the agency of blood?"

Nightingale chewed thoughtfully and swallowed. "Perhaps that's not the best term for it," he said. "Molly can help you extend your sense of *vestigia* out some distance."

"How far out?"

"Two to three miles," said Nightingale. "I only did it the once, so it's hard to tell."

"What was it like?"

"Like stepping into a world of ghosts," said Nightingale. "It may even be *the* world of ghosts, for all that I know. It might be possible to find Henry Pyke that way."

"Why can't we do it that way now?" I asked.

"Because the odds are five to one against you surviving the experience," said Nightingale.

"So yeah," I said. "Probably best not to do it that way now, then."

IF MY profession—that's thief catcher, not wizard—could be said to have started anywhere in London, then it started in Bow Street with Henry Fielding—magistrate, satirical author and founder of what came to be known as the Bow Street Runners. His house was right next door to the Royal Opera House back when it was just the Theatre Royal and Macklin was supplementing his gin-running activities with a bit of acting on the side. I know all this because Channel 4 did a TV drama about it starring the bloke who played the Emperor in the Star Wars films. When Henry Fielding died, his position as magistrate was taken by his blind younger brother, John, who strengthened the Bow Street Runners further, but obviously not to the point where they could stop Macklin beating Henry Pyke to death practically on their doorstep. No wonder Henry was pissed off. I know I would be.

It became London's first true police station and in the nineteenth century it moved across the road and became the Bow Street Magistrates' Court—probably the most famous court in Britain after the Old Bailey. Oscar Wilde was sent down there for being a public nuisance, William Joyce, Lord Haw

Haw himself, started his short walk to the hangman's noose from Bow Street and the Kray twins were remanded there for the murder of Jack "the Hat" MacVitie. It was sold in 2006 to a land magnate who turned it into a hotel, because while history and tradition have a fine voice in London, money has a sweet siren song all its own.

The original house had been replaced by an indoor flower market with an arched iron-and-glass roof. Eliza Doolittle, as played by Audrey Hepburn in *My Fair Lady,* would have bought her violets there before moving off to display the worst cockney accent this side of Dick Van Dyke. When they rebuilt the Royal Opera House in the 1990s, it swallowed up most of the surrounding block, including the flower market. Which was why we found ourselves round the backstage entrance of the Opera House where, apparently, Nightingale knew a guy who could get us in.

It wasn't so much a stage door as a heavy goods entrance; I've seen warehouses with smaller loading bays and there was an industrial-sized lift for getting enormous scenery pallets from floor to floor. Terry, a balding little man in a beige cardigan, who was Nightingale's guy on the inside, said that they weighed upward of fifteen tons and when they weren't being used were stored in a depot in Wales—he didn't say why it had to be Wales.

"We've come to see the magistrate," said Nightingale.

Terry nodded gravely and led us through a series of narrow white-painted corridors and HSE-specified fire doors that reminded me uncomfortably of Westminster Mortuary. We finished up in a low-ceilinged storeroom that Nightingale assured us was the ground floor of the flower market.

"Directly where the parlor of Number Four once stood," he said and turned to our guide. "Don't worry, Terry, we can see ourselves out."

Terry gave us a cheery wave and left. The room was lined with ugly steel and hardboard shelving stuffed with cardboard boxes and delivery wraps full of napkins, cocktail sticks and packs of twelve serving trays. The center of the room was empty, with just a few scuff marks to show where a line of shelves had once stood. I tried to feel for *vestigia,* but all I got at first was dust and ripped plastic. Then I sensed it, right on the edge of perception: parchment, old sweat, leather and spilled port.

"A ghost magistrate," I said. "To provide a ghost warrant?"

"Symbols have power over ghosts," said Nightingale. "They often have more effect than anything we can bring to bear from the physical world."

"Why's that?"

"To be honest, Peter," said Nightingale, "I remember the class where we studied it and I know I read the relevant passages in Bartholomew—I may even have written an essay, but I'm damned if I remember any of the why."

"How are you planning to teach me this stuff if you don't know it yourself?"

Nightingale gently tapped his cane against his chest. "I was going to refresh my memory before we got to that part of your education," he said. "I know at least two of my masters did the same thing and back then we had specialist teachers."

I realized suddenly that Nightingale was looking for reassurance, which I found extremely worrying. "Just make sure you stay ahead of me," I said. "How do we find the magistrate?"

Nightingale smiled. "We just need to get his attention," he said. He turned and addressed the empty center of the room. "Captain Nightingale to see the colonel."

The smell of old sweat and spilled drink grew stronger and a figure appeared in front of us. This ghost seemed more transparent than my old friend Wallpenny, thinner and more ghostly, but his eyes glittered as they turned on us. Sir John Fielding had worn a black bandage to hide his blind eyes and Nightingale had called on the "colonel," so my guess was that this was Colonel Sir Thomas De Veil—a man so routinely corrupt that he managed to shock eighteenth-century London society, generally considered by historians to be the most corrupt epoch in the history of the British Isles.

"What do you want, Captain?" asked De Veil. His voice was thin and distant and around him I could sense rather than see the faint outlines of furniture, a desk, a chair, a bookcase.

Legend had it that De Veil had a special private closet where he conducted "judicial examinations" of female witnesses and suspects.

"I'm looking for a warrant," said Nightingale.

"On the usual terms?" asked De Veil.

"Of course," said Nightingale. He drew a roll of heavy paper from his jacket pocket and proffered it to De Veil. The ghost reached out a transparent hand and plucked it from Nightingale's fingers. For all that he did it casually, I was certain that the effort of moving a physical object must be costing De Veil something. The laws of thermodynamics were very clear on the subject—all debts must be paid in full.

"And which miscreant are we looking to apprehend?" asked De Veil and placed the paper on the transparent desk.

"Henry Pyke, your honor," said Nightingale. "He goes by the name of Punch and also by the name of Punchinella."

De Veil's eyes glittered and his lips twitched. "Are we arresting puppets now, Captain?"

"Let us say that we are arresting the puppet master, your worship," said Nightingale.

"And the charge?"

"Murder of his wife and child," said Nightingale.

De Veil tilted his head. "Was she a shrew?" he asked.

"I beg your pardon, your worship?" said Nightingale.

"Come now, Captain," said De Veil. "No man strikes his wife without provocation—was she a shrew?"

Nightingale hesitated.

"A most terrible shrew," I said. "Begging your worship's pardon. But the babe was an innocent."

"A man can be driven to terrible acts by the tongue of a woman," said De Veil. "As I can testify for myself." He winked at me and I thought, nice, there's an image that will never fade. "However, the babe was innocent and for this he must be arrested and brought before his peers." A quill appeared in De Veil's ghostly hand and with a flourish he scratched out a warrant. "I trust you've remembered the prerequisite," said De Veil.

"My constable will take care of the formalities," said Nightingale.

Which was news to me. I looked to Nightingale who made the *lux* gesture with his right hand. I nodded to show that I understood.

De Veil made a show of blowing the ink dry before rolling the warrant into a tube and handing it back to Nightingale.

"Thank you, your worship," he said and then to me, "In your own time, Constable."

I created a werelight and floated it over to De Veil who cupped it gently in his right hand. Although I was still maintaining the spell, the light dimmed as, I presumed, De Veil sucked up the magic. I kept it going for a minute before Nightingale made a cutting motion with his hand and I ended the spell. De Veil sighed as the light faded and nodded his thanks to me. "So little," he said wistfully and vanished.

Nightingale handed me the roll of paper. "You are now duly warranted," he said. I unrolled the warrant and found, as I had suspected, that the paper was still blank. "Let's go and arrest Henry Pyke," said Nightingale.

Once we were well clear of the storeroom, I slapped the battery back into the airwave handset and called Leslie. "Don't worry about us," she said. "We're quite happy to be waiting around for you to get your finger out." Behind her I could hear voices, glasses and Dusty Small's latest single. I didn't have any sympathy, she was obviously in the pub. I suggested that it might be time for her and the rest of the backup team to go on standby.

Police work is all about systems and procedures and planning—even when you're hunting a supernatural entity. When Nightingale, Seawoll, Stephanopoulos, Leslie and I worked out the details of the operation, it took less than fifteen minutes because what we were doing was a standard identify, contain, track and arrest. It was my job to identify Henry Pyke's latest victim; once I'd done that, Nightingale would do his magic trick and track Henry's spirit back to his grave. Seawoll's people would provide containment in case things went pear-shaped, while Dr. Walid stood by with a mobile trauma team to help any poor bastard who had the bad luck to have their face fall off. DS Stephanopoulos was ready, meanwhile, with a van full of builders on time and a half and, I found out later, a mini-JCB to dig up the grave wherever they might find it. She had another van full of uniformed bodies to handle crowd control in case Henry Pyke turned out to be buried under something inconveniently populated, such as a pub or a cinema. Seawoll was technically in charge of the whole thing, which I'm sure put him in a wonderful mood.

Everything was supposed to be in place by the time Nightingale and I emerged from the Royal Opera House's stage door and stepped back onto Bow Street. Given that Henry Pyke was beaten to death by Charles Macklin less than ten meters up the road, we both figured that this would be the ideal spot to start our little fishing expedition. So reluctantly I opened my carryall and donned my uniform jacket and my bloody stupid helmet. For the record—we all hate the bloody helmet, which is useless in a fight and makes you look like blue biro with the top still on; the only reason we're still wearing it is because the alternative designs all seem to be worse. Still, if I was going to act the part of a constable, I supposed I'd better look like one.

It was coming up to midnight and the last of the evening opera devotees had trickled out of the House and headed for the tube station and the taxi stands. Bow Street was as quiet and as empty as any street in central London ever gets.

"You're sure you can track him?" I asked.

"You do your bit," he said. "And I'll do mine."

I tightened the strap on my helmet and checked in with the airwave. This time I got Seawoll, who told me to stop faffing around and get on with it. I turned to ask whether I looked the part, which is why I was looking straight at the man in the good suit when he stepped out of the shadows by the stage door and shot Nightingale in the back.

CHAPTER 10

The Blind Spot

HE WAS a middle-aged white man in a good quality but otherwise nondescript bespoke suit. He held what looked like a semiautomatic pistol in his right hand and a Kobb's Opera guide in his left. He wore a white carnation in his buttonhole.

Nightingale fell down quickly. He just slipped to his knees and flopped forward onto his face. He let go of his cane and it rattled on the paving stones.

The man in the good suit looked at me, his eyes pale and colorless in the sodium light of the streetlamps, and winked. "That's the way to do it," he said.

You can run away from a man with a handgun, especially in poor lighting conditions, providing you remember to zigzag and can open the range fast enough. I'm not saying that option wasn't tempting, but if I ran, there was nothing to stop the gunman stepping forward and shooting Nightingale in the head. I was trained to placate the gunman while edging backward; talking establishes a rapport and keeps the suspect's focus on the officer so that the civilians can get clear. Ever see *The Blue Lamp* with Jack Warner and Dirk Bogarde? During our training at Hendon, they made us watch the scene where PC Dixon, Warner's character, is shot dead. The film was written by an ex-copper who knew what he was talking about; Dixon dies because he's a dinosaur who stupidly advances on an armed suspect. Our instructors were clear: don't crowd, don't threaten, keep talking and backing away, a suspect has to be particularly stupid, political or, in one memorable case, protected by diplomatic immunity to think that killing a police officer will, in any way, make their situation any better. At the very least, you're buying enough time for an armed response team to arrive and blow the silly bugger's head off.

I didn't think that backing off was an option; this was obviously one of Henry Pyke's sequestrated puppets and wouldn't hesitate to shoot me or Nightingale no matter how calmly I was talking.

Actually to be honest I didn't think at all, my brain went— Nightingale down—gun—spell!

"*Impello!*" I said as calmly as I could and levitated the man's left foot one meter upward. He screamed as his body was catapulted upward and to the right. I must have lost concentration because I heard a distinct crack of a bone breaking in his ankle. The gun fell out of his hand and his arms flailed as he tumbled to the ground. I stepped forward and kicked the gun down the street and kicked him once in the head, hard, just to make sure.

I should have cuffed him, but Nightingale was lying on the road behind me making wet breathing sounds. It was what they call a "sucking chest wound" and they're not being metaphorical in their description. There was an entry wound ten centimeters below Nightingale's right shoulder but at least when I'd gently rolled him on his side I couldn't find an exit wound. My first-aid training was unequivocal about sucking chest wounds—it said that every second you spend faffing around is another second that the London Ambulance service hasn't arrived.

I knew that the backup teams couldn't have heard the gunshot because they'd have been there already and I'd blown my airwave when I levitated the gunman off his feet. Then I remembered the silver whistle in the top pocket of my uniform jacket. I fumbled it out and put it in my mouth and blew as hard as I could.

A police whistle on Bow Street. For a moment I felt a connection, like a *vestigium,* with the night, the streets, the whistle and the smell of blood and my own fear, with all the other uniforms of London down the ages who wondered what the hell they were doing out so late. Or it could just have been me, panicking; it's an easy mistake to make.

Nightingale's breath started to falter.

"Keep breathing," I said. "It's a habit you don't want to break."

I heard sirens coming closer—it was a beautiful sound.

THE TROUBLE with the old boy network is you can never be really sure whether it's switched on or not and whether it's operating in your interest or some other old boy's. I began to suspect that it wasn't operating in my interest when they brought a cup of coffee and a biscuit to the interview room. Fellow police officers being interviewed in a friendly manner get to go to the canteen and fetch their own coffee. You only get room service when you're a suspect. I was back in Charing Cross nick, so it wasn't as if I didn't know the way to the canteen.

Inspector Nightingale was still alive, they told me that much before they sat me down on the wrong side of the interview table. He'd been taken to the brand new trauma center at UCH and was listed as "stable," a term that covered a multitude of sins.

I checked the time. It was three thirty in the morning, less than four hours after Nightingale had been shot. If you work for any time in a large institution, you start to get an instinctive feel for its bureaucratic ebb and flow. I could feel the hammer coming down, and since I'd only been a copper for two years, the fact that I could feel it coming meant that it was a very big hammer indeed. I had a shrewd idea about who'd put the hammer in motion, but there was nothing I could do but stay sitting on the wrong side of the interview table with my cup of bad coffee and my two chocolate biscuits.

Sometimes you have to stand still and take the first blow, that way you see what the other man has in his hand, expose his intentions and, if that sort of thing is important to you, put yourself unequivocally on the right side of the law. And if the blow is so heavy that it puts you down? That's just the risk you have to take.

The blunt instrument chosen caught me by surprise, although I made sure I kept my face neutral when Seawoll and Detective Sergeant Stephanopoulos entered the interview room and sat down opposite me. Stephanopoulos slapped a folder down on the table. It was far too thick to have been generated in the last couple of hours, so most of it must have been padding. She gave me a thin smile as she ripped the cellophane off the audio cassettes and slotted them into a dual tape machine. One of those tapes was for me or my legal representative to prevent me being quoted out of context; the other was for the police to prove that I had copped to the charge without them having to beat me around the back, thighs and buttocks with a sock full of ball bearings. Both of the tapes were redundant because where I sat was neatly framed in the viewfinder of a CCTV camera mounted just above the door. The live feed went to the observation room down the corridor where, judging from the theatrical way Seawoll and Stephanopoulos had made their entrance, someone of ACPO rank was watching—Deputy Assistant Commissioner at the very least.

The tape machine was turned on, Seawoll identified me, himself and Stephanopoulos as being present and reminded me that I was not under arrest but merely helping police with their inquiries. Theoretically I could stand up and walk out anytime I liked, providing I didn't mind kissing my career in the police good-bye. Don't think I wasn't tempted.

Seawoll asked me, for the record, to outline the nature of the operation that Nightingale and I had been running when he was shot.

"You really want that on the record?" I asked.

Seawoll nodded so I gave the full account, our theory that Henry Pyke was a revenant, a vampire ghost bent on revenge, who was acting out the traditional story of Punch and Judy, using real people as puppets, and that together we had devised a way to put ourselves into the story so that Nightingale could track Henry Pyke's bones and destroy them.

Stephanopoulos couldn't suppress a wince when I talked about magical aspects of the case—Seawoll was unreadable. When we got to the shooting, he asked me whether I recognized the gunman.

"No," I said. "Who was he?"

"His name is Christopher Pinkman," said Seawoll, "and he denies that he shot anyone. He claims that he was walking home from the Opera when two men attacked him in the street."

"How does he explain the gun?" I asked.

"He claims there wasn't a gun," said Seawoll. "He stated that the last thing he remembers was leaving the Opera; the very next thing he remembers is being kicked in the head by you."

"That and the excruciating pain from the fractured bones in his lower leg," said Stephanopoulos. "Plus some serious bruising and contusions from when he was thrown to the ground."

"Was he tested for gunshot residue?" I asked.

"He teaches chemistry at Westminster School," said Stephanopoulos.

"Bugger," I said. The gunshot residue test was notoriously unreliable and if the suspect handled chemicals for a living, then no forensic witness on earth was going to testify in court that it was likely, let alone conclusive, that he'd fired a gun. A horrible suspicion formed in my mind.

"You did find a gun—right?" I asked.

"No firearm was recovered from the scene," said Stephanopoulos.

"I kicked it along the pavement," I said.

"No firearm was recovered," said Stephanopoulos slowly.

"I saw it," I said. "It was a semiautomatic pistol of some sort."

"Nothing was found."

"Then how did Nightingale get shot?" I asked.

"That," said Seawoll, "is what we were hoping you could tell us."

"Are you suggesting that I shot him?"

"Did you?" asked Stephanopoulos.

My mouth was suddenly dry. "No," I said. "I didn't shoot

him and if there's no gun, what I am supposed to have not shot him with?"

"Apparently you can move things around with your mind," said Stephanopoulos.

"Not with my mind," I said.

"Then how?" asked Stephanopoulos.

"With magic," I said.

"Okay, with magic," said Stephanopoulos.

"How fast can you move something?" said Seawoll.

"Not as fast as a bullet," I said.

"Really," said Stephanopoulos. "How fast is that?"

"Three hundred and fifty meters per second," I said. "For a modern pistol. Higher for a rifle."

"What's that in old money?" said Seawoll.

"I don't know," I said. "But if you lend me a calculator I can work it out."

"We want to believe you," said Stephanopoulos, playing the role of most unlikely "good cop" in the history of policing. I made myself pause and take a deep breath. I hadn't done any advanced interview courses, but I knew the basics and the conduct of this interview was far too sloppy. I looked at Seawoll and he gave me the "at last he wakes up" look so beloved of teachers, senior detectives and upper-middle-class mothers.

"What do you want to believe?" I asked.

"That magic is real," Seawoll said, and gave me a knowing smile. "Can you give us a demonstration?"

"That's not a good idea," I said. "There could be side effects."

"Sounds a bit too convenient to me," said Stephanopoulos. "What kind of side effects?"

"Probably destroy your mobile phones, palm pilot, laptop or any other electronic equipment in the room," I said.

"What about the tape recorder?" asked Seawoll.

"That too," I said.

"And the CCTV?"

"Same as the tape recorder," I said. "You can protect the phones by disconnecting them from their batteries."

"I don't believe you," said Stephanopoulos, and leaned

forward aggressively, neatly masking from the camera behind her the fact that she was popping the battery from her very ladylike Nokia slimline.

"I think we're going to want a demonstration," said Seawoll.

"How much of a demonstration?" I asked.

"Show us what you're made of, son," said Seawoll.

It had been a really long day and I was knackered, so I went for the one *forma* I can reliably do in a crisis—I made a werelight. It was pale and insubstantial under the fluorescent strip lighting. Seawoll wasn't impressed, but Stephanopoulos's heavy face broke into such a wide smile of unalloyed delight that for a moment I saw her as a young girl in a pink room full of stuffed unicorns. "It's beautiful," she said.

One of the tapes unspooled messily inside the tape machine while the other just stopped dead. I knew from my experiments that I needed to up the strength of the werelight to take out the camera. I was going for a brighter light when the "shape" in my mind went wrong and suddenly I had a column of light hitting the ceiling. It was a bright blue color and focused. When I moved my hand the beam played across the walls—it was like having my own personal searchlight.

"I was hoping for something a bit more subtle," said Seawoll.

I shut the light down and tried to remember the "shape," but it was like trying to remember a dream, slipping away even as I grabbed for it. I knew I was going to have to spend a long time in the lab trying to recapture that form, but as Nightingale had said right at the beginning—knowing the *forma* is there is half the battle.

"Did that do for the camera?" asked Seawoll. I nodded and he gave a sigh of relief. "We've got less than a fucking minute," he said. "I haven't seen this much shit rolling downhill since de Menezes got shot, so my advice to you, son, is to find the deepest hole you can crawl into and stay there until this shitfall is over and the crap lies crisp and deep and even."

"What about Leslie?" I asked.

"I wouldn't worry about Leslie," said Seawoll. "She's my responsibility."

Which meant that Seawoll had stepped in as Leslie's patron and made it clear that anyone trying to get to her would have to go through him first. Since my patron was currently lying on a bed at the UCH and breathing through a tube, Nightingale was unlikely to do the same for me. I like to think that Seawoll would have extended his protection to me if he could have, but I'll never know for sure. He didn't tell me that I should look out for myself—that was a given.

"What the fuck do we do next?" asked Seawoll.

"You're asking me?"

"No I'm fucking asking the table," said Seawoll.

"I don't know," I said. "Sir. There's loads of stuff I don't know."

"Then you'd better start educating yourself, Constable," said Seawoll. "Because I don't know about you, but I don't think Mr. Henry Pyke is going to stop now—do you?"

I shook my head.

Stephanopoulos grunted and tapped her watch.

"I'm going to spring you," he said. "Because we need to put an end to this fucking spiritual shit before some ACPO wallah panics and decides to bring in the Archbishop of Canterbury."

"I'll do my best," I said.

Seawoll gave me a look that implied that my best had better be fucking good enough. "When we start again," he said, "I need you to make sure your brain is engaged before you put your mouth into gear. Just like after the thing in Hampstead—clear?"

"Crystal," I said.

The door to the interview room slammed open and a man stuck his head inside. He was middle-aged, with graying hair, broad-shouldered and with extraordinarily bushy eyebrows. Even if I hadn't recognized him from his Web profile I would have known Deputy Assistant Commissioner Richard Folsom was one of the big beasts of the jungle. He crooked his finger at Seawoll and said, "Alex, a word, please."

Seawoll looked at the ruined tape machine. "Interview suspended," he said and gave the time. Then he rose and meekly followed Folsom out of the room. Stephanopoulos gave me a halfhearted attempt at her famous evil glare, but I was wondering whether she still had her My Little Pony collection.

Seawoll returned and told us that we would be continuing the interview in an adjacent interview room, one where the monitoring equipment was still working. There we continued the time-honored tradition of brazenly lying through our teeth while telling nothing but the truth. Nightingale and I had reason to believe, through an entirely conventional informer, that the group, because it had to be more than one person, who had perpetrated a series of senseless attacks in and around the West End, would be on Bow Street and were investigating when we were ambushed by unknown assailants.

"Deputy Assistant Commissioner Folsom is particularly worried about any threat to the Royal Opera House," said Seawoll. Apparently he was a bit of a connoisseur, having been introduced to Verdi soon after having risen to the rank of commander. A sudden attack of culture snobbery is a common affliction among policemen of a certain rank and age; it's like a normal midlife crisis, only with more chandeliers and foreign languages.

"We think that the focus of activity may be on Bow Street," I said. "But as of yet our investigations have discovered no tangible link to the Royal Opera House."

By six o'clock, we ended up with a statement of events that Seawoll could sell to Folsom and I was falling asleep in my chair. I expected to be suspended, at least warned that I was facing disciplinary action or an investigation by the Independent Police Complaints Commission, but it was just coming up to seven when they let me go.

Seawoll offered me a lift, but I refused. I walked up St. Martin's Lane shaky with tension and lack of sleep. The weather had turned during the night. There was a chill wind under a dirty blue sky. The rush hour starts late on a Saturday and the streets retained some of their early morning quiet as I crossed New Oxford Street and headed for the Folly. I was expecting the worst and I wasn't disappointed. There was at least one unmarked police car that I could see parked across the street. I couldn't see anyone inside, but I gave a little wave just in case.

I went in through the front door because it's better to face things head-on and I was too knackered to walk round to the Mews at the back. I was expecting police, but what I got were a pair of soldiers in battle dress and carrying service rifles. They wore woodland DP jackets and maroon berets with parachute regiment badges. Two were blocking my way past the cloakroom booths while two more were tucked away either side of the main doors, ready to catch anyone suicidal enough to attack two fully armed paras in the flank. Somebody was taking the physical security of the Folly very seriously.

The paras didn't raise their rifles to block me, but they did take on that air of menacing nonchalance that must have enlivened the streets of Belfast no end in the years before the peace agreement. One of them nodded his head toward the alcove where, in the Folly's more elegant days, the doorman would wait until needed. Another para with sergeant's stripes resided there with a mug of tea in one hand and a copy of the *Daily Mail* in the other. I recognized him—it was Frank Caffrey, Nightingale's Fire Brigade liaison. He gave me a friendly nod and beckoned me over. I checked the flashes on Frank's shoulders. This was the 4th Battalion of the Parachute regiment, which I knew was part of the TA. Frank must have been a reservist, which certainly explained where he got phosphorous grenades from. I suspected that this was another part of the old boy network, but in this instance I was pretty sure that Frank was Nightingale's boy. I didn't see any officers around. I expect that they were back at the barracks turning a blind eye while the NCOs sorted things out.

"I can't let you in," Frank said. "Not until your governor gets better or they name an official replacement."

"On whose authority?" I asked.

"Oh, this is all part of the agreement," said Frank. "Nightingale and the regiment go back a way; you might say there were some debts."

"Ettersberg?" I asked, guessing.

"Some debts can never be repaid," said Frank. "And there are some jobs that have to be done."

"I have to get in," I said. "I need to use the library."

"Sorry, son," he said. "The agreement is clear, no unauthorized access beyond the main perimeter."

"The main perimeter," I said. Frank was trying to tell me something but sleep deprivation was making me stupid. He had to repeat himself before I realized that he was hinting that the garage was outside that perimeter.

I stepped back out into the pale sunlight and made my way round to the garage and let myself in. There was a battered Renault Espace with such patently fraudulent plates that I knew it could only belong to the paratroopers. I took a moment to check that the Jag was locked before pulling a dustcover from under a workbench and throwing it over the vintage car. I tramped wearily up the stairs to the coach house, only to find that Tyburn had beaten me there.

She was rummaging through the trunks and other old stuff that I'd piled at the far end. The picture of Molly and the portrait of the man I'd assumed was Nightingale's dad were propped up against the wall. I watched as she knelt down and reached under the divan to pull out another trunk.

"They used to call this a cabin trunk," she said without turning round. "It's made low enough to slide under your bed. That way you could pack the things you needed for your voyage separately."

"Or more likely your valet would," I said. "Or your maid."

Tyburn lifted a carefully folded linen jacket from the cabin and laid it on the divan. "Most people didn't have servants," she said. "Most people made do." She found what she was looking for and stood up. She was wearing an elegant Italian black satin trouser suit and sensible black shoes. There was still a mark on her forehead where a marble fragment had cut her. She showed me her prize, a drab brown cardboard sleeve containing what I recognized as a 78 rpm record. "Duke Ellington and Adelaide Hall, 'Creole Love Call' on the original Black and Gold Victor label," she said. "And he has it stuffed in a trunk in the spare room."

"Are you going to sell it on eBay?" I asked.

She gave me a cold look. "Are you here to pick up your things?"

"If that's all right with you?"

She hesitated. "Help yourself," she said.

"You're too kind," I said.

Most of my clothes were stuck in the Folly, but because Molly never cleaned the coach house I managed to scrounge up a sweatshirt and a pair of jeans that had fallen behind the sofa. My laptop was where I'd left it, perched on a pile of magazines. I had to hunt around for the case. Tyburn kept her cool gaze on me the whole time. It was like being watched in the bath by your mother.

Sometimes, as Frank had pointed out, there are things you have to do no matter what the cost. I straightened and faced Tyburn. "Look," I said. "I'm sorry about the fountain."

For a moment I thought it might work, I swear I saw something in her eyes, a softening, a recognition—something—but then it was gone, replaced by the same flat anger as before.

"I've been investigating you," she said. "Your father's a junkie, has been for thirty years."

It shouldn't hurt when people say these things to me. I've known my dad was an addict since I was twelve. He was quite matter-of-fact about it once I'd found out and keen to make sure I understood what it meant—he didn't want me following in his footsteps. He was one of the few people in the UK who still got his heroin on prescription, courtesy of a GP who was a big fan of London's least successful jazz legend. He's never been clean, but he's always been under control and it shouldn't hurt me when people call him a junkie, but of course it does.

"Damn," I said. "He's kept that really quiet. I'm shocked."

"Disappointment runs in your family, doesn't it," she said. "Your chemistry teacher was so disappointed in you that he wrote a letter to the *Guardian* about it. You were his blue-eyed boy—figuratively speaking."

"I know," I said. "My dad keeps the clipping in his scrapbook."

"When they sack you for gross misconduct," said Tyburn, "will he keep that clipping as well?"

"Deputy Assistant Commissioner Folsom," I said. "He's your boy, isn't he?"

Tyburn gave me a thin smile. "I like to keep track of the rising stars," she said.

"Got him twisted around your little finger?" I asked. "It's amazing what people will do for a bit of slap and tickle."

"Grow up, Peter," said Tyburn. "This is about power and mutual self-interest; just because you still do most of your thinking with your external genitalia doesn't mean everyone else does."

"I'm glad to hear that, because somebody has to tell him to trim those eyebrows," I said. "Did the gun come from you?"

"Don't be absurd," she said.

"It's your style. Get somebody else to solve your problems for you. Machiavelli would be proud."

"Have you ever read any Machiavelli?" she asked. I hesitated and she drew the correct conclusions. "I have," she said. "In the original Italian."

"And why did you do that?"

"For my degree," she said. "At St. Hilda's Oxford. History and Italian."

"Double first, of course," I said.

"Of course," she said. "So you understand why I don't find Nightingale's shabby gentility impressive in any way."

"So did you provide the gun?" I asked.

"No, I did not," she said. "I didn't need to engineer this failure. It was only a matter of time before Nightingale screwed up. Although even I wasn't expecting him to be stupid enough to get himself shot. Still, it's an ill wind."

"Why aren't you inside right now?" I asked. "Why are you stuck in the coach house? It's very impressive in there, got a library you wouldn't believe and you could make a fortune hiring it out to film companies as a period location."

"All in good time," she said.

I fumbled my keys out of my pocket. "Here, I can lend you

my keys," I said. "I'm sure you can talk your way past the paras." She turned away from my outstretched hand.

"The one good thing to come out of this," she said, "is that now we get a chance to make a rational choice about how these matters are handled."

"You can't go in," I said. "Can you?"

I thought of Beverley Brook and her "inimical" wards.

She gave me the Duchess look, the old money stare that soccer players' wives never get the knack of and for a moment it rolled off her, the stink of the sewer and money and the deals done over brandy and cigars. Only, Tyburn being modern, there was a whiff of cappuccino and sun-dried tomatoes in there as well. "Have you got what you came for?" she asked.

"The TV's mine," I said.

She said I could pick it up whenever I liked. "What did he see in you?" she asked and shook her head. "What makes you the keeper of the secret flame?"

I wondered what the hell the secret flame was. "Just lucky, I guess."

She didn't dignify that with a reply. She turned her back on me and returned to rummaging in the trunks—I wondered what she was really looking for.

On my way out through the coach yard I heard a muffled barking behind me and looked back. A pale mournful face was watching me from a second floor window, Molly, holding Toby tightly to her chest. I stood and gave them what I hoped was a reassuring wave and then headed off to see if Nightingale was still alive.

THERE WAS an armed police officer stationed outside Nightingale's room. I showed him my warrant card and he made me leave all my bags outside. A modern ICU can be surprisingly quiet; the monitoring equipment only makes a noise when something goes wrong and since Nightingale was breathing on his own, there was no Darth Vader wheezing from a respirator.

He looked old and out of place among the polyester

bedcovers with their crisp easy-to-clean pastel colors. One limp arm was exposed and hooked up to half a dozen wires and tubes, his face was drawn and gray and his eyes closed. But his breathing was strong, even and unaided. There was a bowl of grapes on the sideboard and a bunch of blue wildflowers had been stuffed, a bit randomly I thought, into a vase.

I stood next to the bed for a while thinking that I should say something, but nothing came to mind. Checking first to make sure that no one was likely to see me, I reached out and squeezed his hand—it was surprisingly warm. I thought I felt something, a vague sense of wet pine, wood smoke and canvas, but it was so faint that I couldn't tell whether it was *vestigia* or not. I caught myself swaying on my feet, I was that tired. There was an institutional armchair in the corner of the room. Made of laminated chipboard and polyester-covered fire retardant foam, it was far too uncomfortable to sleep in. I sat down, let my head flop to one side and was gone in less than thirty seconds.

I woke up briefly to find Dr. Walid and a pair of nurses bustling around Nightingale's bed. I stared at them stupidly until Dr. Walid saw me and told me to go back to sleep—at least I think that's what he said.

I woke again to the smell of coffee. Dr. Walid had brought me a cardboard jug of latte and enough tubular sachets of sugar to make a significant dent in my grocery budget.

"How is he?" I asked.

"He was shot in the chest," said Dr. Walid. "That sort of thing's bound to slow you down."

"Is he going to be all right?"

"He's going to live," said Dr. Walid. "But I can't say whether he'll make a full recovery or not. It's a good sign that he's breathing unaided, though."

I sipped the latte and it burned my tongue.

"They locked me out of the Folly," I said.

"I know," said Dr. Walid.

"Can you get me back in?"

Dr. Walid laughed. "Not me," he said. "I'm just a civilian advisor with a bit of esoteric expertise. With Nightingale incapacitated, unlocking the Folly is a decision that has to be made by the commissioner, if not higher up."

"Home Secretary?" I asked.

Dr. Walid shrugged. "At the very least," he said. "Do you know what you're going to do?"

"Do you have access to the Internet?" I asked.

IN A teaching hospital like the UCH, if you walk through the right doors it stops being a hospital and becomes a medical research and administrative center. Dr. Walid had an office there and, I was shocked to learn, students. "I don't teach them the esoteric stuff," he explained, but he was, not wanting to blow his own trumpet, a world-renowned gastroenterologist. "Everyone needs a hobby," he said.

"Mine is going to be job hunting," I said.

"I'd have a shower first," said Dr. Walid. "If you're planning any interviews."

Dr. Walid's office was an awkwardly narrow room with a window at the thin end and shelves covering the entire length of both long walls. Every surface was piled with folders, professional journals and reference books. At one end of the narrow shelf that served as a desk, a PC bobbed uncertainly in a sea of hard copy. I dumped my bags and plugged the laptop into the mains to recharge the batteries. The modem was hidden behind a stack of *Gut; an international journal of Gastroenterology and Hepatology*. A jaunty subtitle revealed that *Gut* had indeed been voted best journal of gastroenterology by gastroenterologists worldwide. I didn't know whether to be worried or reassured by the implication that there were many more magazines devoted to the smooth functioning of my intestines. The socket for the modem looked suspiciously jury-rigged and definitely not standard NHS issue. When I asked Dr. Walid about it, he merely said that he liked to keep certain of his files secure.

"From who?" I asked.

"Other researchers," he said. "They're always looking to pirate my work." Apparently the hepatologists were the worst. "What do you expect from people who deal with so much bile," said Dr. Walid, and then looked disappointed that I didn't get the joke.

Content that work was possible, I let Dr. Walid show me to the staff bathroom down the corridor, where I showered in a cubicle big enough, and equipped for, a paraplegic, his wheelchair, a care assistant and her guide dog. There was soap provided, a generic lemon-smelling antibiotic cake that felt ferocious enough to strip off the upper layer of my epidermis.

While I showered, I thought about the mechanics of how Nightingale got shot. Despite the lurid fantasies of the *Daily Mail,* you can't just walk into a random pub and buy a handgun, especially not a high-end semiautomatic like the one carried so inexpertly by Christopher Pinkman the night before. Which meant that there was no way that Henry Pyke had maneuvered Pinkman into place in the time between our arrival at the Royal Opera House and our emergence from the stage door less than twenty minutes later. Henry Pyke must have known that we were planning to trap him on Bow Street and that left three options: he foresaw the future, he read somebody's mind, or somebody who knew about the plan was one of his sequestrated puppets.

I dismissed precognition out of hand. Not only am I a big fan of causality, but Henry Pyke had never done anything else that suggested knowledge of the future. According to my research in the mundane library at the Folly, there was no such thing as mind reading, at least not in the sense of hearing someone's thoughts as if they were narrating a voice-over on television. Which meant that somebody had told Henry Pyke, or told somebody who was sequestrated by Henry Pyke, what the plan was. Nightingale didn't. I didn't. Which left the Murder Team. Given that Stephanopoulos and Seawoll were reluctant to talk about magic with its official practitioners, I couldn't see them discussing it with their people and Leslie would have followed their lead.

I stepped out of the shower feeling pleasantly raw and dried myself off with a towel that had been repeatedly washed into the texture of sandpaper. The clothes I'd retrieved from the coach house weren't exactly fresh, but at least they were cleaner than what I'd been wearing. After a few missed turnings in the featureless corridors, I relocated Dr. Walid's office.

"How you feeling?" he asked.

"Human," I said.

"Close enough," he said. After that he pointed out the location of the coffee machine and left me to get on with it.

Ever since mankind stopped wandering around aimlessly and started cultivating its own food, society has been growing more complex. As soon as we stopped sleeping with our cousins and built walls, temples and a few decent nightclubs, society became too complex for any one person to grasp all at once, and thus bureaucracy was born. A bureaucracy breaks the complexity down into a series of interlocking systems; you don't need to know how the systems fit together or even what function your bit of the system has, you just perform your bit and the whole machine creaks on. The more diverse the functions performed by an organization, the more complex the interlocking systems and subsystems become. If you are responsible, as the Metropolitan Police are, for preventing terrorist attacks, sorting out domestic rows and keeping motorists from killing random strangers, then your systems are very complex indeed. One part of the system is the requirement that every OCU, that's Operational Command Unit, have access to HOLMES2 and CRIMINT databases either through a dedicated HOLMES suite or via specialized software installed on an authorized laptop. This is handled by the Directorate of Information who, because their responsibility is only to their bit of the system, don't make a distinction between the Serious and Organized Crime Group (OCU) and the Folly, which was made an OCU only because nobody knew how else to drop it into the Met's organizational chart. Now, this meant nothing to Inspector Nightingale, but to yours truly it meant that not only could I install a legal copy of the HOLMES2 interface into my laptop, I was also provided with the same access privileges as the head of the Homicide and Serious Crime Command (OCU).

Which was just as well, because one of my suspects was Chief Inspector Seawoll and that's a target you don't take aim at unless you're certain it's going to go down on the first hit. DS Stephanopoulos, who'd also known about the operation in advance, was an equally hard target unless I wanted to be joke number two—*Do you know what happened to the DC who accused Stephanopoulos of being the unwitting tool of a malicious revenant spirit?* Dr. Walid was suspect number three, which was why I didn't tell him what I was up to. Leslie was suspect number four, and suspect number five, and the one that frightened me the most, was of course myself. There was no way of proving it, but I was reasonably certain that between killing William Skirmish and throwing his child out the window, Brendan Coopertown had had no inkling that he was anything other than the same man he'd always been.

After my shower I'd spent some time staring at my face in the mirror, working up the courage to open my mouth and look inside. In the end I closed my eyes and dug my fingers into my cheeks—I've never been so happy to fondle a bicuspid in my life. All that meant for certain was that Henry Pyke hadn't stretched my face out *yet*.

I booted up HOLMES and typed in my access code and password. Technically, both belonged to Inspector Nightingale and, technically, both should have been revoked as soon as he became inactive, but obviously nobody had got round to doing it yet—inertia being another key characteristic of civilization and bureaucracy. I started at the beginning with the murder of William Skirmish, Covent Garden, January 26.

I found what I was looking for three hours and two coffees later, when I was reviewing the Framline case. That attack had started with the cycle courier being knocked off his bike on the Strand and being taken to UCH for treatment, where he attacked Dr. Framline. A uniformed PC had actually taken a statement from him at the scene of the accident while they were waiting for the ambulance to arrive. He'd claimed that a driver had overtaken him and deliberately forced him off the road. Leslie had told me that the accident had taken place in a rare CCTV blind spot on the Strand, but according to the initial report the courier had been forced off the road outside Charing Cross Station. There hasn't been a camera blindspot outside a London rail terminus since the IRA declared them legitimate targets in the 1990s. I went rummaging in the bowels of the HOLMES archive, where some demented soul on the Murder Team had uploaded the relevant footage from every single operable camera from Trafalgar Square to the Old Bailey. None of it was labeled properly and it took me a good hour and a half to find the video I was looking for. The cycle courier hadn't specified what make of car had crowded him, but there was no mistaking the battered Honda Accord that deliberately ran him off the road. The video resolution wasn't good enough to show the driver or the license plate, but even before I tracked its progress to the high resolution traffic camera that guarded the lights at Trafalgar Square, I knew who it belonged to.

And it made sense. She'd been present when Coopertown killed his wife and child, during the incident in the cinema and the attack on Dr. Framline. She'd been there when we planned the operation outside the Opera House and she'd arrived with the backup in time to pick up the missing pistol.

Leslie May was my suspect. She was part of it, sequestrated by Henry Pyke as part of his mad play of riot and revenge. I wondered if she'd been part of it from the beginning, from the first night when William Skirmish had his head knocked off and I'd met Nicholas Wallpenny for the first time. Then I remembered Pretty Polly from the Piccini script—the silent girl romanced by Punch after he'd killed his wife and child. He kisses her most audibly while she appears "nothing loth." Then he sings: *If I had all the wives of old King Sol, I would kill them all for my Pretty Poll.*

I hadn't sensed anything from Leslie. Was it possible to mask a *sequestration* or, more likely, maybe I just wasn't as sensitive as I thought I was. Nightingale was always telling me that learning to distinguish *vestigia* from the vagaries of your own senses was a lifetime's endeavor. I'd made an assumption about who was to be trusted—I wasn't going to make the same mistake again.

*   *   *

THERE WAS a mother who lost her son in Covent Garden once. She was very English in an old-fashioned way, good quality print dress, nice bag, down for a shopping trip to the West End and a visit to the London Transport Museum. Got distracted by a window display for a moment and turned back to find her six-year-old son had gone.

I remember very clearly how she looked by the time she found us. A surface veneer of calm, a traditional British stiff upper lip, but her eyes gave her away—darting left and right, she was fighting the impulse to run in all directions at once. I tried to keep her calm while Leslie called it in and started organizing a search. I don't know what I was saying, just calming words, but even while I was speaking I saw that she was shaking almost imperceptibly and I realized that I was watching a human being come apart in front of my eyes. The six-year-old turned up less than a minute later, led up from one of the Piazza's sunken courtyards by a kindly mime. I was looking right at the mother when the son reappeared, saw the relief laid bare on her face and the way the fear was sucked backward into her until only the brisk and practical woman in the sundress and the sensible shoes remained.

Now I understood that fear, not for yourself but for somebody else. Leslie had been sequestrated; Henry Pyke was sitting in her head, had been sitting in there for at least three months. I tried to remember the last time I'd seen her. Had her face looked different? And then I remembered her smile, the big grin showing lots of teeth. Had she smiled at me recently—I thought she might have. If Henry Pyke had activated the *dissimulo* on her, made her over into Punchinella's form, there's no way she could have disguised the ruin of her teeth. I didn't know how to get Henry Pyke out of her head, but if I could get to her before the revenant made her face fall off, then I thought I might know how to stop that at least.

By the time Dr. Walid returned to his office I had a plan.

"What is it?" he asked.

I told him and he thought it was a terrible plan as well.

CHAPTER 11

A Better Class of Riot

THE FIRST task was to find Leslie. This I did by the simple expedient of calling her mobile and asking her where she was.

"We're in Covent Garden," she said. "We" being her and Seawoll and about half the rest of the Murder Team. The Chief Inspector had gone for the time-honored police tradition of when in doubt throw manpower at it approach. They were going to sweep the Piazza and then do a swift check of the Opera House.

"What does he hope to do?" I asked.

"In the first instance, contain any problems," said Leslie. "Beyond that we're waiting on you—remember."

"I may have sorted something out," I said. "But it's important that you don't do anything stupid."

"Hey," she said. "This is me."

If only that were true.

The next thing I needed was wheels, so I called up Beverley on her waterproof mobile and hoped she wasn't swimming lengths under Tower Bridge or whatever it was river nymphs do on their day off. She picked up on the second ring and demanded to know what I'd done to her sister. "She's not happy," she said.

"Never mind your sister," I said. "I need to borrow a motor."

"Only if I get to come along," she said. I'd expected that, in fact I was counting on it. "Or you can walk."

"Fine," I said, feigning reluctance.

She said she'd be over in half an hour.

Third on the list was getting hold of some hard drugs, which proved surprisingly difficult given that I was in a major hospital. The problem was my tame doctor was having ethical qualms.

"You've been watching too much TV," said Dr. Walid. "There's no such thing as a tranquilizer dart."

"Yes there is," I said. "They use them in Africa all the time."

"Let me rephrase that and talk slowly," said Dr. Walid. "There's no such thing as a *safe* tranquilizer dart."

"It doesn't have to be a dart," I said. "Every minute we leave Leslie sequestrated, there's a chance that Henry Pyke's going to make her face fall off. To do magic, your mind has to be working. Shut down the conscious bit of the brain and I'm willing to bet Henry can't do his spell and Leslie's face stays the way God intended."

I could see from Dr. Walid's expression that he thought I was right. "But what then?" he asked. "We can't keep her in a medical coma indefinitely."

"We buy time," I said. "For Nightingale to wake up, for me to get back in the Folly library, for Henry Pyke to die of old age . . . or whatever it is undead people do when they go."

So Dr. Walid went grumbling off and came back a bit later with two disposable syrettes in a sterile packing with a bio-hazard label and a sticker that said, "Keep out of the hands of children."

"Etorphine hydrochloride in solution," he said. "Enough to sedate a human female in the sixty-five-kilogram weight range."

"Is it fast?" I asked.

"It's what they use to trank rhinos," he said and handed me a second package with another two syrettes. "This is the reversing agent, narcan. If you stick yourself with the etorphine then you use this straightaway before you call an ambulance and try to make sure the paramedics get this card."

He handed me a card that was still warm from a lamination machine. In Dr. Walid's neat, all-capitalized handwriting, it said, "Warning: I have been stupid enough to stick myself with etorphine hydrochloride," and listed the procedures the paramedics were to follow; most of them concerned resuscitation and heroic measures to maintain heartbeat and respiration.

I patted my jacket nervously as I rode the lift down to the reception and repeated under my breath that the tranquilizers were on the left side pocket and the reversing agent on the right.

Beverley was waiting for me in the no-waiting zone dressed in khaki cargo pants and a cropped black T-shirt with WINE BACK HERE stenciled across her breasts.

"Ta da!" she said and showed me her car. It was a canary yellow BMW Mini convertible, the Cooper S model with the supercharger at the back and the run-flat tires. It was about as conspicuous a car as you can drive in central London and still fit into a standard parking space. I was happy to let her drive—I've still got some standards.

It was hot for late May, an excellent day for driving a convertible even with the rush hour traffic fumes. Beverley was as averagely terrible a driver as you'd expect in someone who'd passed their test in the last two years. The good thing about London traffic is that your average motorist doesn't get a chance to pick up enough speed to make fatal mistakes. Predictably we ground to a halt at the bottom end of Gower Street and I faced the age-old dilemma of the London traveler—get out and walk or wait and hope.

I called Leslie again but her phone went straight to voice mail. I called Belgravia nick and got them to patch me through to Stephanopoulos's airwave. In case anyone was monitoring the channel, she duly warned me to go home and await instruction before letting me know that she'd last seen Seawoll and Leslie heading for the Opera House. I told her that I was dutifully heading home in a way that wouldn't convince Stephanopoulos or our hypothetical listeners, but at least would look good on any transcript produced in court.

The traffic unclogged once we were past New Oxford Street and I told Beverley to head down Endell Street.

"When we get there you've got to stay away from Leslie," I said.

"You don't think I can take Leslie?"

"I think she might suck out all your magic," I said.

"Really?" asked Beverley.

I was guessing, but a *genii locorum* like Beverley had to be drawing on magic from somewhere and to a revenant like Henry Pyke that must make them attractive victims. Or maybe they had some natural immunity to that sort of thing and I was worrying for nothing, but I didn't think that was the way to bet.

"Really," I said.

"Shit," she said. "I thought we were friends."

I was going to say something comforting, but that was strangled off when Beverley shot out of the one system by the Oasis Sports Center and turned into Endell Street without, as far as I could see, any reference to or indeed awareness of other road users.

"Leslie is your friend," I said. "Henry Pyke is not."

The thank-God-it's-Friday crowds had spilled out of the pubs and cafés onto the pavements and for a little while London had the proper street culture that the people who own villas in Tuscany keep calling for. The narrowing road and the prospect of hitting a pedestrian caused even Beverley to momentarily take her foot off the accelerator.

"Watch the people," I said.

"Ha," said Beverley. "People shouldn't drink and walk at the same time."

We swerved round the mini-roundabout on Longacre, slowed in deference to another crowd of drinkers outside the Kemble's Head on the corner, and accelerated down Bow Street. I couldn't see any police cars, fire engines or other signs of an emergency outside the Opera House, so I figured we might have got there in time. Beverley pulled into the disabled parking space opposite the Opera House.

"Keep the motor running," I said as I got out. I wasn't really anticipating a fast getaway, but I figured it would keep her in the car and out of trouble. "If the police try to move you on, give them my name and say I'm inside on official business."

"Because of course that'll work," said Beverley, but she

stayed in the mini, which was the main thing. I trotted across the road to the main entrance and pushed through one of the glass and mahogany doors. The interior atrium was cool and dark after the sunlight, manikins were mounted in glass cases by the doors, decked out in costumes from previous performances. As I went through the second, interior, set of doors into the lobby, I was met by a sudden rush of people coming the other way. I looked quickly about to see what could be driving them, but, although they were moving briskly and with a sense of urgency, there wasn't any sense of panic. Then I figured it out; it was the interval and these were the smokers heading outside for a cigarette.

Sure enough, there were crowds of people streaming out of the doors marked stalls and heading left, presumably toward the loos and the bar—probably in that order. I stayed where I was and let the people go past—Seawoll at least, because of the sheer size of the man, should be easy to spot. Sartorially, I was disappointed; everyone was dressed expensively, but it was all smart casual with the occasional evening dress to relieve the boredom—I'd expected better of my betters. The crowd thinned and I merged with the flow and let it carry me left, past the cloakroom and up a flight of stairs into the main bar. According to the sign, this was the Balconies restaurant and as far as I could see had been created by throwing several metric tons of stripped pine into a Victorian cast-iron greenhouse. Designed to serve the interval crowd, when a thousand lightly stunned punters would rush in and attempt to drown out the singing with gin and tonics, it featured large open spaces and plain padded furniture with clean brass fittings. Under the vaulted arch of its white iron-and-glass roof it was as if IKEA had been hired to refit St. Pancras station. If Thomas the Tank Engine had been Swedish, his living room would have looked just the same.

Although he probably would have been a lot less cheerful.

There was a balcony six meters up that ran all the way around the room, wide enough for chairs and tables laid with white linen and silver service. The crowds were thinner up there, presumably because most people had headed straight for the bar and as many gin and tonics as they could chuck down their necks before the music started again. I headed for the nearest flight of stairs hoping to get a better look from above. I was halfway up when I realized that the mood of the room was changing. It wasn't much of a sensation, but it was like a dog barking late at night and far away.

"That bitch can fuck off," a woman's voice, shrill from somewhere below me.

It was the same feeling of tension as I'd felt on Neal Street—just before Dr. Framline went psycho on the cycle courier. Somebody dropped a tray, metal clattered on the expensive wooden floor, a couple of glasses smashed. There was an ironic cheer nearby.

I reached the balcony level, stepped between two unoccupied tables and looked out over the crowd.

"Wanker," said a man somewhere below. "You fucking wanker."

I spotted a fit-looking man in his late forties, salt-and-pepper hair, conservative suit, distinctively bushy eyebrows—it was Deputy Assistant Commissioner Folsom—because my life was not complicated enough. I drew back from the balcony railing and as I did, I saw Leslie leaning on the railing of the balcony opposite mine and staring right at me. She looked normal, active, happy, wearing her on-duty leather jacket and slacks. When she was sure that I was watching she gave me a happy little wave and nodded down at the main bar where Seawoll was getting himself a drink.

A voice announced that the performance would be restarting in three minutes.

Down in the main bar, a guy in leather-patched tweed slapped one of the men he was talking to. Somebody shouted, Leslie glanced down and I sprinted down the length of the balcony shoving members of the public out of the way. I glanced over at Leslie, who was staring at me in shock as I rounded the first corner and charged across the balcony that bridged the width of the room. Whoever was doing the thinking in Leslie's head at that moment, her or Henry Pyke, they hadn't expected me to push my way through a crowd of well-dressed worthies. Which is what I was counting on. It's not easy to fumble a syrette full of tranquilizer out of your pocket while forcing your way past protesting opera lovers, but somehow I managed to get everything ready by the time I rounded the last corner and headed straight for Leslie.

She was watching me with quiet amusement, head cocked on one side, and I thought: you can be as cool as you like, because you're going to be sleeping soon enough. By that point members of the public were getting out of my way of their own accord and I had a clear run for the last five meters. Or would have if Seawoll hadn't come up the stairs and hit me in the face. It was like running into a low ceiling beam, I flipped straight over onto my back and found myself contemplating a blurry view of the roof.

Damn but that man could move fast when he wanted to.

Obviously Henry Pyke could influence other people, even hardheaded sods like Seawoll—that couldn't be good.

"I frankly don't care," brayed a woman somewhere to my right. "It's just fucking men singing about fucking men."

A voice announced that the performance would recommence in less than a minute and people should immediately return to their seats. A young man with a Romanian accent and a waiter's uniform told me that I should stay where I was and that the police had been called.

"I am the police, you pillock," I said but it came out muffled on account of the fact that my jaw felt like it was dislocated. I found my warrant card and waved it at him and to be fair he did give me a hand up. The bar was empty except for the staff cleaning up and somebody had stepped on the syrette, crushing it flat. I felt my face. Since I still had all my teeth, Seawoll must have pulled his punches. I asked where the big man had gone and the staff said he'd headed downstairs with the blond woman.

"Into the theater?" I asked, but they didn't know.

I ran down the steps and found myself staring at the long marble counter of the cloakroom. The good thing about Seawoll is that he's hard to miss and difficult to forget—the attendant said he'd headed for the stalls. I went back to the lobby, where a polite young lady tried to block my way. I told her I needed to see the manager and when she tripped off to get him I slipped inside.

The music hit me first in a great gloomy wave and then the scale of the theater. A great horseshoe rising up in tiers of gilt and red velvet. Ahead of me, a sea of heads swept down to the orchestra pit and beyond them the stage. The set depicted the back end of a sailing ship, although the scale was exaggerated to the point where the gunwales towered over the singers. Everything was painted in cool shades of blue, gray and dirty white—a ship adrift in a bitter ocean. The music was equally somber and could really have done with a backbeat or, failing that, a girl in a miniskirt. Men in uniforms and tricorn hats were singing at each other while a blond guy in a white shirt looked on with doe eyes. I had a funny feeling that it wasn't going to end well for the blond guy, or the audience for that matter. I'd just figured that the tenor was playing the captain when the bass, obviously playing the villain of the piece, faltered. I thought at first that this was part of the performance, but the murmur that ran through the audience made it clear it was a mistake. The singer tried to recover, but was obviously having trouble remembering his part. The tenor stepped up and tried to cover, but faltered himself and with a look of pure panic looked off the stage toward the wings. The audience was starting to drown out the orchestra who, having finally twigged that something was up, crashed to a stop.

I started down the aisle toward the orchestra pit although I had no idea how I was going to get to the stage. A few of the audience had stood up and were craning their necks to see what was going on. I reached the edge of the pit and glanced down to see that the musicians were still poised over their instruments. I was close enough to touch a lead violinist. He was trembling and his eyes were glazed. The conductor tapped his baton on his music stand and the musicians started playing again. I recognized the music as the first tune sung by Mr. Punch in the Piccini script; it was "Malbroug s'en va-t-en guerre," an old French folk song, but in the English-speaking world it was "For He's a Jolly Good Fellow."

The tenor playing the captain picked up the refrain first;

Mr. Punch is a jolly good fellow,
His dress is all scarlet and yellow.

The bass and baritone joined in quick succession followed by the company, singing as if they had the song sheet before them.

And if now and then he gets mellow,
It's only amongst good friends.

The singers stamped their feet to the beat of the music. The audience seemed stuck in their seats; I couldn't tell if they were confused, mesmerized or just too appalled to move. Then the front row of the stalls took up the beat with hands and feet. I could feel the compulsion myself, a wash of beer and skittles and pork pies and dancing and not caring a fig for the opinions of others.

With the girls he's a rogue and rover;
He lives, while he can, upon clover;

The clapping and stamping spread back, row by row, from the front of the stalls. In the good acoustics of the Opera House, the stamping was louder than a Highbury crowd and just as contagious. I had to lock my knees to stop my feet from moving.

When he dies—it's only all over:
And there Punch's comedy ends.

Leslie stepped onto the stage and, bold as brass, walked up the steps that took her to the exaggerated poop deck and turned to face the audience. I saw then that in her left hand she carried a silver-topped cane. I recognized it—the bastard had stolen Nightingale's cane. A spotlight stabbed out of the darkness and bathed her in harsh white light. The music and the singing stopped and the stamping trailed away.

"Ladies and gentlemen," called Leslie. "Boys and girls. I present to you today the most tragical comedy and comical tragedy of Mr. Punch as related to that great talent and impresario, Mr. Henry Pyke." She waited for applause and when it didn't come she muttered under her breath and made a curt gesture with the cane. I felt the compulsion roll over me while behind me the audience broke into applause.

Leslie bowed graciously. "Lovely to be here," she said. "My, but this theater is much enlarged since my day. Is anyone else here from the 1790s?"

A solitary whoop floated down from the upper tier, just to prove that there's always one in any crowd.

"Not that I don't believe you, sir, but you're a bloody liar," said Leslie. "But the old ham will be here by and by." She looked out past the lights into the stalls, searching for something. "I know you're out there, you black Irish dog."

She shook her head like a dog. "I'd just like to say it's good to be here in the twenty-first century," she said suddenly. "Lots of things to be grateful for, indoor plumbing. Horseless carriages—a decent life expectancy."

There was no obvious way to get from the stalls to the stage. The orchestra pit was two meters deep and the lip of the stage opposite was higher than a man could reach.

"Tonight, ladies and gentlemen, boys and girls, for your entertainment—my rendition of that lamentable scene from the story of Mr. Punch," said Leslie. "I refer of course to his incarceration and, alas, impending execution."

"No," I yelled. I'd read the script, I knew what was coming next.

Leslie looked straight at me and smiled. "But of course," she said. "The play's the thing." There was a crack of breaking bone and her face changed. As her nose became a hooked blade her voice rose to a piercing, warbling shriek.

"That's the way to do it!" she screeched.

I was too late, but I threw myself into the orchestra pit just the same. The Royal Opera House doesn't mess about with a quartet with a drum machine—you get a full-on orchestra seventy musicians strong and the pit is sized to match. I landed among the horn section, who were not so dazed by the compulsion Henry Pyke had them under that they didn't protest. I pushed my way through the violinists, but it was no good, even with a standing jump, I couldn't get my hands on the stage. One of the violinists asked me what the fuck I thought I was doing and, backed up by a bassist, threatened to kick my head in. They both had that same Friday night mean drunk look in their eyes that I was beginning to associate with Henry Pyke. I'd just grabbed a music stand to hold them at bay when the orchestra started up again. As soon as it did, the two homicidal musicians ignored me, took up their instruments, took their places and, with a great deal of decorum considering they were having a psychotic break, started playing. I could hear the thing wearing Leslie's body singing in its awful high-pitched voice.

Punch when parted from his dear,
Still must sing in doleful tune.

I couldn't see what Leslie was doing, but judging from the song she was acting out the scene where Punch watches a gallows being assembled outside his prison window. There were doors at either end of the orchestra pit; they had to reach backstage one way or the other. I elbowed my way through the musicians toward the nearest door, leaving a trail of squawks, twangs, squeals and crashes behind me. The door led into another narrow breezeblock passageway with other, identical-looking, passageways branching off left and right. Since I'd exited stage left I guessed another left turn would get me backstage. I was right, only the Royal Opera House didn't have a backstage—it had an aircraft hangar. A huge high-ceilinged room at least three times the size of the main stage that you could have parked a zeppelin in. All the stage managers, prompters and whoever else lurks out of sight

during a performance had crowded into the wings—
transfixed by whatever influence Henry Pyke was using on
the audience. Getting away from that influence had given me
a chance to cool down and think. The damage to Leslie had
been done, if I stuck her with my last tranquilizer now her
face would fall off. Rushing onto the stage wasn't going to
help—for all I knew, me blundering in was part of Henry
Pyke's script. I sidled through the stagehands and tried to get
as close to the stage as I could without showing myself.

They hadn't built a gallows. Instead a noose had been lowered from above, as if from a yardarm. Either Henry Pyke
was even more organized than I thought he was or the original opera had involved someone getting hung. Presumably
after a lot of singing.

Leslie, still playing the role of Punch, mimed languishing
behind a barred window. She didn't seem to be following the
Piccini script any longer, but instead was regaling the audience with the life story of one Henry Pyke, aspiring actor,
from his humble beginnings in a small Warwickshire village
to his burgeoning career on the London stage.

"And there I was," declaimed Leslie. "No longer a young
man but a seasoned actor, my God-given gifts augmented by
the years of experience dearly won on the hard and unforgiv-
ing stages of London."

That nobody among the stage managers was even snigger-
ing showed the strength of the compulsion they were under.
Since Nightingale hadn't yet started me on "compulsion for
beginners," I didn't know how much magic it took to hold
over two thousand people in thrall, but I bet it was a lot and
that's when I decided it was probably better for Leslie to have
her face fall off than her brain shrivel up. I looked around;
there had to be a first-aid kit close by. Dr. Walid had said I was
going to need saline solution and bandages to wrap around
her head if I was going to keep her alive long enough for the
ambulance to get there. I spotted the kit mounted on the wall
above a selection of fire extinguishers, contained in an impressively large suitcase of red ballistic plastic that would also
come in handy as an offensive weapon. I got my last syrette

ready and with the first-aid kit in my other hand I sidled into the wings. By the time I got sight of the stage again, Leslie, I couldn't bear to think of her as Punch or Henry Pyke, was giving a full and detailed description of Henry's disappointments. Most of which he blamed on Charles Macklin who, Henry claimed, had turned his hand against him out of spite and when challenged, outside this very theater, had cruelly struck down Henry.

"He should have hung for that," said Leslie. "Just as he should have hung for poor Thomas Hallum that he did for in the Theatre Royal. But he has the luck of the Irish and the gift of the gab."

That's when I realized what Henry Pyke was waiting for. Charles Macklin had been a regular at the Royal Opera until his death. According to legend, Macklin's ghost was supposed to have been seen on numerous occasions in his favorite seat in the stalls. Henry Pyke was trying to draw him out, but I didn't think he was going to turn up. Leslie paced the width of the poop deck, peering out into the stalls.

"Show yourself, Macklin," she called. I thought there was uncertainty in her voice now. The poop deck was a raised section of stage, too high at the sides for me to climb, the only access would be up the stairs at the front—there was no way to sneak up on Leslie. I was going to have to do something stupid.

I boldly stepped onto the stage and then made the mistake of looking out at the audience. I couldn't see much beyond the footlights, but I could see enough to feel the great mass of people staring back at me from the towering darkness. I stumbled over my own feet and caught myself on a prop cannon.

"What's this?" screeched Leslie.

"I am Jack Ketch," I said—too quietly.

"God spare me from fools and amateurs," said Leslie under her breath, then louder. "What's this?"

"I am Jack Ketch," I said, and this time I felt it carry out to the audience. I got a ripple of *vestigia* back, not from the people but the fabric of the auditorium. The theater remembered Jack Ketch, executioner for Charles II, a man famed for being so unrepentantly crap at his job that he once published a pamphlet in which he blamed his victim, Lord Russell, for failing to stay still when he swung the axe. For a century afterward, Ketch was a synonym for the hangman, the murderer and the Devil himself—if ever there were a name to conjure with, then it would be Jack Ketch. Which explained his role in the Punch and Judy show and why this was my best chance to get close enough to Leslie to use the syrette.

"Thank you very much, Mr. Ketch, but I am quite comfortable here," said Leslie.

I hadn't bothered to learn the script by heart, but I knew enough to improvise. "But you must come out," I said. "Come out and be hanged."

"You would not be so cruel," said Leslie.

I knew for a fact that there was supposed to be a load more banter, but since I couldn't remember the words I cut to the action. "Then I must fetch you," I said, and advanced up the stairs to the poop deck. It was hard to make myself look at the ruin of Leslie's face, but I couldn't risk any surprise moves. Her Punch face twisted with irritation, presumably because I was skipping lines, but she went on with the show— just as I'd been hoping she would. This was the part where Jack Ketch seizes Punch and drags him to the noose, at which point the wily wife-murderer tricks Jack Ketch into sticking his own head through the loop and thus hanging himself. No sir, they don't make role models for children like that anymore.

I readied the syrette.

Leslie cowered as I approached. "Mercy, mercy," she squeaked. "I'll never do so again."

"That much is certain," I said, but before I could inject her she whirled and thrust Nightingale's cane in my face. The muscles in my back and shoulders locked and it was all I could do to keep my balance.

"Do you know what this is?" asked Leslie, waving the cane from side to side.

I tried to say "it's a stick" but my jaw muscles were locked up with everything else.

"As Prospero had his book and staff," said Leslie. "So does your master have both those things, but I need only the staff. Being of the spirit world gives one a certain *je ne sais quoi* when dealing with magic, but what one lacks *sans* corporality is the spark of vitality necessary to facilitate one's desires."

Which at least confirmed that Henry Pyke had no intrinsic magic of his own, an observation I'd have found more interesting if I hadn't been sodding paralyzed and at his mercy.

"This is the source of your master's power," said Leslie. "And with his power I can do, well, just about anything I please." She grinned, showing her smashed teeth. "Your line is, 'Now Mr. Punch, no more delay.' "

"Now Mr. Punch, no more delay," I said and gestured at the noose. "Put your head through this loop." The weird thing was, this time I could sense the compulsion almost as if it was a *forma,* a shape in my mind but not of my mind.

"Through there," said Leslie, winking at the audience. "Whatever for?"

"Aye, through there," I said. I sensed it again and this time I was sure, the idea of the shape was external, but the actual shape itself was being formed by my own mind. It was like hypnotism, a suggestion rather than a command.

"What for? I don't know how," said Leslie and struck a pose of deep despair.

"It's very easy," I said grasping the noose, the rope scratchy against my palms. "Only put your head through here."

Leslie leaned forward and, missing the noose entirely, asked, "What so?"

"No, no," I said and pointed at the noose. "Here." If it was a suggestion, I thought, then I should be able to just think it away.

Leslie theatrically missed sticking her head through the noose once more. "So then?" she asked.

I tried to push the shape out of my mind, but found myself saying; "Not so, you fool," and pantomiming exasperation.

So obviously brute force wasn't the way and I was going to have to come up with something, because in less than two lines the character of Jack Ketch was due to stick his own stupid neck through the loop and get himself hung and me with him.

"Mind who you call fool; try and see if you can do it yourself," squeaked Leslie and paused to give the audience a chance to titter in anticipation. "Only show me how and I will do it directly."

I felt my body shift in anticipation of the move that would shove my head into the noose. Which is when I thought that if I couldn't get rid of the compulsion, maybe I could change it enough to break it. I did it like antinoise, where you cancel out a sound wave by broadcasting another sound wave with an inverted phase; it's clever stuff and very counterintuitive, but it works. I was hoping the weird inside-my-head version would work, because I'd only just started making the shape in my mind when my mouth said; "Very well, I will."

My *forma* met the compulsion like the wrong two gearwheels brushing up against each other in a transmission. I thought I could actually feel bits of the *forma* spinning around in my brain and painfully ricocheting off the inside of my skull, but that could have been my imagination. It didn't matter. I felt my body unlock and I yanked my head away from the noose and looked at Leslie in triumph.

"Or maybe I won't," I said.

A huge arm clamped across my chest from behind and a large hand gripped the back my head and pushed it back through the noose. I smelled camelhair and Chanel aftershave—Seawoll must have walked up behind me while I was feeling clever.

"Or maybe you will," said Leslie.

I twisted, but while there are some big men who are surprisingly weak, Seawoll wasn't one of them, so I jammed the syrette into the exposed bit of his hand and gave him the whole dose. Unfortunately, the whole dose had been calibrated for Leslie, who was half Seawoll's size. The pressure never wavered until Leslie yelled, "Hoist away, boys," and I was dragged into the air by my neck.

The only thing that saved my life was the fact that I was being hung in a theatrical noose that had been designed, as a matter of health and safety regulations, *not* to hang the attractive Croatian baritone whose neck was supposed to be in it. The slipknot was a fake and there was a wire reinforcement inside the rope to keep the loop in shape. Undoubtedly there was an eyelet for clipping a tether to the, no doubt artfully concealed, safety harness to be worn by the handsome baritone once he'd made his farewell aria. Unfortunately, I didn't have a harness, so the damn thing half killed me before I managed to get my head out of the loop, scraping the skin off my chin in the process. I got my elbow into the loop for more support, but even with that there was a sudden line of agony down my back.

I had a quick look down and saw that I was a good five meters above the stage. I wasn't going to be letting go any time soon.

Below me, Leslie had turned back to the audience. "So much for the constabulary," she said. Behind her, Seawoll sat down heavily on the stairs and slumped forward like a tired runner—the etorphine hydrochloride kicking in at last.

"See," said Leslie. "One officer of the law kicks his last while another lies sleeping, no doubt stupefied with drink. Thus do we good men of England put our trust in swine barely separate from the villains they purport to chase. How long, ladies and gentlemen, boys and girls, are you prepared to put up with this? Why is it that men of good quality pay their taxes while foreigners pay naught and yet expect the liberties that are an Englishman's hard-won prerogative?"

It was getting harder to maintain a hold, but I didn't fancy my chances letting go. There were drapes on either side of the stage and I wondered if I could swing over far enough to grab one. I changed to a two-handed grip on the loop and started to shift my weight and flex to get momentum going.

"Because who is more oppressed," exclaimed Leslie. "Those

that seek nothing but entitlements for themselves or those that claim for everything, social security, housing benefit, disability and pay for nothing." One thing I did do in history was the reform of the poor laws so I knew then that Henry Pyke must either be using stuff from Leslie's memories or else had been reading the *Daily Mail* for the last two hundred years.

"And are they grateful?" she asked. The audience muttered in response. "Of course they are not," said Leslie. "For they have come to look upon such things as their right."

It wasn't easy keeping the rope from swinging out over the orchestra pit. I tried to correct and ended up describing a figure of eight. I was still several meters short of the scaffolding platform so I put my back into it, jackknifing my legs to cross the gap.

Suddenly the crowd gave a roar and I felt a wave of frustration and anger well up around me like floodwater backing out of a storm drain. I lost concentration at a crucial moment and slammed into the drape. I made the jump, desperately grabbing handfuls of the heavy cloth and trying to get enough between my legs to stop me sliding smack onto the stage.

Then all the lights went out. They didn't spark, flicker, flash or do anything theatrical—they just turned themselves off. Somewhere among the Royal Opera House's sophisticated lighting rig, I reckoned, a couple of microprocessors were crumbling into sand. When you are hanging by your fingernails, down is nearly always the right direction, so I did my best to ignore the pain in my forearms and started working my way down the drape. Out in the darkness I heard the audience not panicking, which, given the circumstances, was much creepier than the alternative.

A cone of white light appeared around Leslie like a spotlight from an invisible lamp. "Ladies and gentlemen," she called. "Boys and girls. I think it's time to go out and play."

One of my mum's uncles once had tickets to Arsenal v Spurs at Highbury and took me when his own son couldn't make it. We were down among season ticket holders, the hardest of the hard-core soccer fans, who went there for the game, not the violence. Being in a crowd like that is like being caught in the tide—you might try going in the other direction, but it drags you along all the same. It was a dull game, stylewise, and looked to be heading for a nil-nil draw, when suddenly in injury time Arsenal made a late surge. As they got into the penalty area I swear the whole stadium, sixty thousand people, held their breath. When the Arsenal forward put it in the back of the net, I found myself screaming with joy along with the rest of the people around me. It was entirely involuntary.

That's what it felt like when Henry Pyke let loose the audience at the Royal Opera House. I must have let go of the drape and fallen the last couple of meters but I only know that I was suddenly lying on the stage with a shooting pain in my ankle and a sudden desire to smash someone's face in. I pulled myself to my feet and found myself face to disfigured face with Leslie.

I flinched. Up close the ruin of Leslie's face was even harder to deal with. My eyes kept sliding away from the grotesque caricature. On either side of her stood the principal cast, all male, all tense and, except for the boyish baritone, much tougher-looking than you'd expect in practitioners of high culture.

"Are you all right?" she squeaked. "You had me worried there."

"You tried to hang me," I said.

"Peter," said Henry Pyke. "I never wanted you dead. Over the last few months, I've come to think of you as less of an archenemy and more as the comic relief, the slightly dim character that comes on with the dog and does a funny turn while the real thespians are getting changed."

"I noticed Charles Macklin didn't make an appearance," I said.

The Punch nose twitched. "No matter," said Leslie. "The gout-ridden bastard can't hide forever."

"And in the meantime we . . . ?" It was a good question. "What are we doing?" I asked.

"We are playing our role," said Leslie. "We are Mr. Punch, the irrepressible spirit of riot and rebellion. It is our nature to cause trouble just as it is your nature to try and stop us."

"You're killing people," I said.

"Alas," said Leslie. "All art requires sacrifice. And take it from one who knows—death is more of a bore than a tragedy."

I was struck suddenly that I wasn't talking to a complete personality. The way the accent bopped around from era to era, the bizarre switches in motive and behavior. This wasn't Henry Pyke, or even Mr. Punch, this was like a patchwork, a personality cobbled together from half-remembered fragments. Maybe all ghosts were like this, a pattern of memory trapped in the fabric of the city like files on a hard drive— slowly getting worn away as each generation of Londoners laid down the pattern of their lives.

"You're not listening," said Leslie. "Here I am taking time out of my busy schedule to gloat and you're in a world of your own."

"Tell me, Henry," I said. "What were the names of your parents?"

"Why, they were Mr. and Mrs. Pyke, of course."

"And their first names?"

Leslie laughed. "You're trying to trick me," she said. "Their names were Father and Mother."

I was right—Henry Pyke, at least the portion of him inside Leslie's head, was literally not all there.

"And tell me all the good things that come into your mind," I said. "About your mother."

Leslie cocked her head to one side. "Now you're just taking me for a fool," she said. She gestured at the principal cast who'd been impassively watching our exchange. "Do you know what the *Times* said about this production?"

"It was gloomy and pointless," I said as I got to my feet. If Leslie was going to monologue I was going to use the opportunity to get up.

"Close," she said. "What the opera critic of the *Times* actually wrote was that the performance had 'all the *gravitas* of a Christmas episode of *Coronation Street.*'"

"That's harsh," I said.

I didn't have any more tranquilizer, but the first-aid kit was still lying in the wings. One blow to the back of the head with the heavy case might be enough to put Leslie down. And then what?

Leslie cocked her head over to the other side—eyes still on me. "Oh look, boys," she said to the principal cast. "It's the opera critic for the *Times*."

I CONSIDERED telling them that I didn't even read the *Times*, but I didn't think they'd listen. I ran for the nearest fire exit on the basis that, by definition, that would be the shortest route out, and, by law, always unlocked. Also, the emergency exit signs were on a different circuit and thus the only source of light.

I got three meters ahead of the singers while crossing the aircraft hangar space behind the stage and didn't slow down as I banged through the first door—which cost a bruised rib but gained me at least a meter. My eyes had already begun to adjust, but even with the next emergency exit sign directly ahead there wasn't enough light to stop me from tripping over a badly parked trolley. I went down clutching my shin and an absurd part of my mind noting that an obstruction like that was a violation of Health and Safety regulations.

A silhouetted figure came charging down the corridor toward me. One of the singers had caught up; it was too dark to see which. I kicked the trolley into his path and he went down on his face next to me. He was a big man and smelled of sweat and stage makeup. He tried to get back up, but I stepped on his back as I climbed to my feet. His friends banged through the door, so I yelled to make sure their attention was focused on me and then ran for it. The yelps as they tripped over their colleague were deeply satisfying.

Bang through another door and the lights were on, separate circuit from the house lights I guessed, and I was back in a blinding labyrinth of narrow corridors that all looked the same. I ran through a room inhabited by nothing but wigs and turned into a corridor whose floor was covered in drifts of ballet shoes. I slipped on one and went skidding into a breezeblock wall. Behind me I could hear the principal cast howling for my blood and the fact that the threats were beautifully articulated was of no comfort at all.

Finally, another fire exit and I found myself by the ground floor toilets next to the cloakroom. I could hear glass smashing from the direction of the main foyer so I headed for the side exit by the ticket office. I ignored the slow wheelchair-accessible revolving door and headed straight for the emergency exits, but what I saw through the glass brought me to a sudden stop.

There was a riot in Bow Street. A really well-dressed mob was looting the hotel opposite, a column of greasy black smoke was rising from a burning car. I recognized the make—it was a canary yellow Mini convertible.

CHAPTER 12

The Last Resort

NOBODY LIKES a riot except looters and journalists. The Metropolitan Police, being the go-ahead and dynamic modern police service that it is, has any number of contingency plans for dealing with civil disturbance. From farmers with truckloads of manure to suburban anarchists on a weekend break and Saturday jihadists. What I suspect they didn't have plans for was just over two thousand enraged opera lovers pouring out of the Royal Opera House and going on a mad rampage through Covent Garden.

I was pretty sure that a smart Londoner like Beverley would have the brains to bail out of her car before the mob torched it, but I knew her mum wouldn't forgive me if I didn't check. I ran out yelling my head off in the hope that everyone else would mistake me for a rioter too.

The noise hit me as soon as I was out the door; it was like an angry pub crowd, but on an enormous scale, all strange half chants and animal hooting noises. It wasn't like a normal riot. In one of those, most of the crowd does nothing except watch and occasionally cheer. Show them a broken shop window and they'll cheerfully liberate the contents, but like most people they don't want to actually get their hands dirty. This was a mob of ringleaders, everyone from the suspiciously well-dressed young man to the matron in an evening gown was mad as hell and ready to break something. I got as close to the burning Mini as I could and was relieved to see no sign of anyone in any of the seats. Beverley had sensibly legged it and I should have followed suit, but I was distracted by the sight of the helicopter hovering directly overhead.

The helicopter overhead meant that GT, the Met's central command, had taken direct operational control of the disturbance. This meant that dozens of ACPO rank officers were having their dinner parties, nights in with a DVD, evenings out with the mistress, interrupted by urgent phone calls by non-ACPO rank officers who were desperate to make sure that they were in no way responsible for anything. I'll bet that GT knew early on that the wheels were coming off the wagon and that as soon as the riot was over, a grand game of musical inquiries would start. Nobody wanted to be the one without a chair when the music stopped.

It was that thought which, ironically, distracted me enough for Deputy Assistant Commissioner Folsom to be able to sneak up behind me. I turned when he called my name and found him stalking toward me. His conservative suit jacket, pinstripe I saw now that he was close up, had lost a sleeve and all its buttons. He was one of those people whose faces twitch when they're angry; they think they're all icy calm, but something always gives them away. In Folsom's case, it was a nasty tic by his left eye.

"Do you know what I hate the most," he shouted. I could see that he'd rather be adopting a sinisterly conversational tone, but unfortunately for him the riot was too loud.

"What's that, sir?" I asked. I could feel the heat from the burning Mini on my back—Folsom had me trapped.

"I hate police constables," he said. "Do you know why?"

"Why, sir?" I edged round to my left, trying to open an escape route.

"Because you never stop moaning," said Folsom. "I joined up in 1982, the good old days, before the PACE, before Macpherson and quality control targets. And you know what? We were shit, we thought we were doing well in an investigation if we arrested anybody at all, let alone the perpetrator; we got the shit kicked out of us from Brixton to Tottenham and fuck me, were we bent? We weren't even that expensive, we'd let some scrote go for two pints of lager and a packet of crisps." He paused for a moment and a look of puzzlement crossed his face, then his eyes fixed back on me and the left one twitched.

"And you," he said, and I wasn't happy with the way he said it. "How long do you think you'd have lasted back then? A locker full of excrement would have just been a warm-up. Odds are, a few of your relief would have taken you to one side and explained, in a rough but friendly manner, just how unwanted you were."

I seriously considered just rushing the guy—anything to make him shut up.

"And don't think your relief inspector would have helped," he said. "He wouldn't have been able to spell racial discrimination on his report, if there had been a report . . ."

I feinted at him to back him up and then darted to my right, away from the burning car and the rest of the riot. It didn't work. Folsom didn't back up and as I went past he gave me a backhander that was like being slapped with a floorboard. It knocked me right back on my arse and I found myself staring up at a seriously enraged senior officer looking to give me a good kicking at the very least. He'd just managed to land one of his size tens on my thigh—I ended up with a purple heel-shaped bruise for a month—when someone clubbed him down from behind.

It was Inspector Neblett, still dressed in his impractical uniform tunic, but carrying an honest to God wooden riot truncheon of the kind phased out in the 1980s for being slightly more lethal than a pickax handle.

"Grant," he said. "What the hell is going on?"

I scrambled over to where Folsom lay facedown on the pavement. "There's been an irretrievable breakdown in public order," I said, while tugging Folsom into the recovery position. My head was still ringing from his backhander, so I wasn't that gentle.

"But why?" he asked. "There wasn't anything scheduled."

Riots are rarely spontaneous, crowds usually have to be assembled and provoked, and a conscientious inspector keeps a weather eye out for problems. Especially when his patch contains a riot magnet like Trafalgar Square. The only half-convincing lie I could think of was that somebody had attacked the Royal Opera House with a psychotropic aerosol, but I figured that might raise more questions than it answered. Not to mention trigger an inappropriate military response. I was just about to risk the truth, that a kind of vampire ghost had put the influence on the entire audience, when Neblett twigged exactly who it was he'd just smacked in the head.

"Oh my God," he said, squatting down for a closer look. "This is Deputy Assistant Commissioner Folsom."

Our eyes met across the twitching form of our senior officer.

"He didn't see you, sir," I said. "If you call an ambulance, we can have him off the scene before he regains consciousness. There was a riot, he was attacked, you rescued him."

"And your role in this?"

"Reliable witness, sir," I said. "As to your timely intervention."

Inspector Neblett gave me a hard look. "I was wrong about you, Grant," he said. "You do have the makings of a proper copper."

"Thank you, sir," I said. I looked around. The riot had moved on—down Floral Street and into the Piazza, I reckoned.

"Where's the TSG?" I asked.

The TSG are the Territorial Support Group. These are the guys that tool around in Mercedes Sprinter vans with equipment lockers stuffed with everything from riot helmets to tasers. Every borough command has a couple of these buzzing around their operational area, especially around closing time, and there's a reserve force held in standby just in case of unexpected events. I suspected that current events counted as unexpected.

"They're staging on Longacre and Russell Street," said Neblett. "It looks like GT's plan is contain them around Covent Garden."

There was a crash from the direction of the Piazza followed by ragged cheering. "What now?" asked Neblett.

"I think they're looting the market."

"Can you get the ambulance?" he asked.

"No sir, I've got orders to find the ringleader," I said.

A Molotov cocktail makes a very distinctive sound. A well-designed one goes crash, thud, whoosh—it's the last, the petrol igniting, that's going to kill you if you let it. I know this because before you graduate from Hendon, you get to spend a fun-filled day having them thrown at you. Which was why Neblett and I both instinctively ducked when we heard them smashing into the tarmac less then fifteen meters down the road.

"It's kicking off," said Neblett.

Looking south, I could see a mob of rioters on the crossroads where Culverhay met Bow Street. Beyond them, I saw flames reflected off blue riot helmets and gray shields.

I still had to get Leslie, subdue her, and get her back to Walid at the UCH. Transport shouldn't be a problem since half the ambulances in London were probably converging on Covent Garden right at that moment—that left finding her. I decided to assume that she was still looking for revenge on Macklin, who'd once had a gin shop on Henrietta Street and was buried at the Actors' Church. That meant getting back into the Piazza, which unfortunately meant either passing through the exciting civil disturbance to the south or running up Floral Street, which contained God knows what in the way of rioters and really bad things.

Fortunately, when they rebuilt the Royal Opera House, one thing they made sure of was that it had a lot of exits. Pausing only to wish Neblett good luck and give Folsom a surreptitious kick in the shins, I ran back inside. Then it was a simple matter to slip past the box office and the company shop and out the other side into the Piazza. At least it would have been, if someone hadn't been looting the shop.

The glass display window was smashed, fractured glass littered the displays of DVDs, holdalls embossed with the Royal Ballet School logo and souvenir pens. Somebody had

torn the silver-and-ivory colored manikin out of the window
and flung it across the corridor with enough force to break it
against the marble wall opposite. I could hear sobbing coming from inside punctuated by the occasional crash. Curiosity got the better of me as I was creeping past and I paused at
the broken entrance to cautiously peer inside.

A middle-aged man sat barefooted on the floor of the shop
surrounded by hundreds of clear plastic wrappers. As I
watched, he grabbed one of the wrappers and ripped it open
to extract a pair of white ballet shoes. Carefully, the tip of his
tongue emerging from the side of his mouth, the man tried to
slip one of the shoes onto his big hairy foot. Unsurprisingly,
the shoe was too small to fit no matter how hard the man
pulled on the straps—until finally he ripped the seams open.
The man held the ruined shoe in front of his face and burst
into tears. When he flung the shoes across the shop and
reached for another pair I left him to it—there are just some
things that man is not meant to know.

The back exit of the Royal Opera House emerges under the
colonnade in the northeast corner of the Piazza. The Paper-
chase on the left had been gutted and shreds of colored paper
were blowing across the stone flags and into the square. On
the right the Disney Store was being enthusiastically looted,
but the Build-a-Bear shop was bizarrely untouched—an oasis
of brightly colored twee and peace. Most of the actual fighting seemed to be down by the church on the west side—that's
where I guessed Leslie would be. I headed for the covered
market, reckoning that I could use it as cover to get close to
the church. I was halfway there when somebody wolf-whistled
at me. It was a proper two fingers in the mouth whistle and
cut right through the noise of the riot.

I zeroed in on the second whistle. It was Beverley, staring
down at me from the pub balcony on the first floor—she
waved when she saw me looking and ran for the stairs. I met
her at the bottom.

"They burned out my car," she said.

"I know," I said.

"My lovely brand new car," she said.

"I know," I said and grabbed her arm. "We've got to get out of here." I tried to drag her back toward the Opera House.

"We can't go back that way," she said.

"Why not?" I asked.

"Because I think there's some people following you," she said.

I turned. The principal cast were back, followed by what I recognized as the orchestra and some people dressed mostly in T-shirts and jeans, whom I took to be the backstage crew. The Royal Opera Company is a world-class institution dedicated to staging some of the biggest operas on an epic scale—they have a very large backstage crew.

"Oh my God," said Beverley. "Is that Leslie?"

Leslie had pushed to the front of the crowd, still wearing her Punch face. She held up her hand and the company paused.

"Run," I said to Beverley.

"Good idea," she said and, grabbing my arm, pulled me backward so hard I almost fell over. Beverley darted down one of the dim brick corridors that led into the heart of the covered market. With evening drawing in, most of the actual shops were closed, but stalls serving drinks and generic ethnic food should have been doing a roaring trade fleecing tourists. But there was nobody in sight, and I was hoping this meant punters and stall holders had already run for safety.

Behind us, I heard the company give a great howl, in good harmony, and above that the high-pitched squeaking laugh of the avatar of riot and rebellion. There was a sudden ominous silence and then the first of the firebombs hit the roof. Leslie had said she didn't want me dead but I was beginning to suspect that she may have been lying.

Beverley swung us round a corridor and into one of the covered courtyards, which is where we found the German family. There were five of them, a stolid dark-haired father, a sharp-faced blond mother and three children between seven and twelve. They must have taken shelter behind a food stall when the riot broke out and were just emerging when they looked up to find me and Beverley barreling toward them. The mother gave a terrified yelp, the eldest daughter screamed and the man squared up. The father didn't want to fight, but by God he was ready to defend his family from dangerous stereotypes whatever the odds. I showed him my warrant card and he deflated in relieved surprise.

"Polizei," he told his wife and then, very politely, asked whether we might help them.

I told them that we'd love to help them, starting by proceeding to the nearest exit and evacuating the area. I was sweating suddenly and I realized that it was from the heat of a fire at my back. The whole rear of the covered market was on fire—I put one hand on the father's back and the other on his eldest son and pushed them in the other direction. *"Raus, raus!"* I yelled, hoping it really did mean "get out."

Beverley led the way toward the so far untouched southwest corner of the market, but we'd barely cleared the second row of stalls when she skidded to a halt and the German family and I slammed into her back. Ahead, a group of rioters were using the western façade of the market to engage in a running battle with police reinforcements.

"We're trapped," said Beverley.

The rioters had their backs to us, but it was only a matter of time before one of them turned round.

One of the nearby shops looked surprisingly unlooted and while running into a building during a fire is generally considered a retrograde step, I didn't see that we had much choice. It wasn't until we'd bundled inside and I found myself crouching behind a manikin wearing nothing but two wisps of silk that I realized we were in a branch of Seraglio. I persuaded the family to sit down behind the counter so they wouldn't be visible from outside.

"Please," asked the mother. "What is happening here?"

"Beats me, sister," said Beverley. "I just work here."

The covered market at Covent Garden has four parallel rows of shops under its iron-and-glass roof. Originally built to house open-fronted fruit and vegetable stalls, they'd been retrofitted with windows and power, but they were still less than three meters across. Into them were shoehorned specialist craft shops, cafés and bijou versions of high street chain boutiques that weren't going to let a little thing like inadequate floorspace get in the way of them gleaning some of that high-spending tourist action. As a result, our haven was crowded with manikins, of the tastefully abstract silver and black kind, wearing distractingly skimpy bits of satin. I hoped the manikins would make us less obvious to anybody who glanced inside.

That was tested when a number of rioters slunk past the windows. Judging from the torn suit jackets and dirty white shirts, these were members of the audience, not the cast. I held my breath as they paused outside, calling to each other in their guttural stockbroker accents.

Strangely, I found I wasn't frightened. Instead I was embarrassed—that this nice family of Von Trapp impersonators had come to my city and instead of being gently relieved of their money they were facing violence, injury and bad manners at the hands of Londoners. It pissed me off no end.

The stockbrokers loped off toward the west.

"Right," I said after a minute. "I'm just going to check the coast is clear."

I slipped out of the shop door and looked around. On the plus side, there were no rioters in sight, but on the minus side, this was probably because everywhere I looked was on fire. I ran a little way toward the closest exit, but I got no more than a few paces before the heat started singing my nostril hair. I quickly ducked back into the shop.

"Beverley," I said. "We're in deep shit." I told her about the fire.

The mother frowned. Obviously she was the linguist in the family. "Is there a problem?" she asked.

The flames were clearly reflected in the shop windows and the blank silver faces of the manikins so it seemed pointless to lie. She looked at her children and then back at me. "Is there nothing you can do?"

I looked at Beverley.

"Can't you do any magic?" she asked.

It was definitely getting hotter. "Can't you?"

"You got to say it's okay," she said.

"What?"

"That's the agreement," said Beverly. "You've got to say it's okay."

One of the window panes cracked. "It's okay," I said. "Do what you have to do."

Beverley threw herself down and pressed her cheek to the floor, I saw her lips moving. I felt something pass through me, a sensation, like rain, like the sound of boys playing football in the distance, the smell of suburban roses and newly washed cars, evening television flickering through net curtains.

"What is she doing?" asked the mother, "She is praying for us, yes?"

"Sort of," I said.

"Sshh," said Beverley sitting up. "I'm listening."

"What for?"

Something flew in through the window, pinged off the wall and fell into my lap—it was the cover off a fire hydrant. Beverley saw me examining it and gave me an apologetic shrug.

"What exactly have you done?" I asked.

"I'm not sure," she said. "I've never actually tried this before."

The smoke thickened, forcing us facedown onto the mercifully cool stone of the shop floor. The middle German child was crying. His mother put her arm around him and pulled him close. The youngest, a girl, seemed remarkably stoical. Her blue eyes were fixed on mine. The father twitched, he was wondering whether he should at least get up and try to do something heroic—however futile. I knew exactly how he felt. The last of the window panes shattered, glass pattered down on my back. I breathed in smoke, coughed, breathed in more smoke. It didn't feel like enough of a breath. I realized that this was it—I was going to die.

Beverley started laughing.

Suddenly it was a hot Sunday morning under unexpectedly blue skies, there's a smell of hot plastic and dust as the paddling pool is rescued from the garden shed and the kids, dressed in swimsuits and underwear are bouncing up and down with excitement. Dad is red-faced from blowing up the pool and Mum is yelling to be careful and the hose is run in through the kitchen window and jammed onto the cold tap. The hose gives a dusty cough and all the children stare at its mouth . . .

The floor began to vibrate and I had just enough time to think—what the fuck—when a wall of water hit the south side of the shop. The door was smashed open and before I could grab hold of something I was lifted by the surge and slammed against the ceiling. The air was blown out of my lungs by the impact and I had to bite down on the instinct to draw in a breath. For a moment the flood cleared enough for me to catch sight of Beverley floating serenely among the debris before the water drained out of the shop fast enough to slap me onto the floor again.

The father, with more presence of mind than I'd shown, had wedged himself and his family against the counter. They assured me they were all okay except for the youngest, who wanted to do it again. Beverley stood in the middle of the shop and did the air-punch.

"Oh yeah," she said. "Let's see Tyburn do something like that."

BEVERLEY'S EUPHORIA lasted long enough for us to get our German family to the nearest ambulance. As far as I could tell from looking around while we walked out, Beverley's wave of water had started somewhere near the center of the covered market and rolled outward to flood the Piazza to a depth of ten centimeters. I reckoned that at a stroke, Beverley had quadrupled the amount of property damage done that night, but I kept that thought to myself. She hadn't managed to extinguish the fire on the roof, but even as we sidled away, the London Fire Brigade were moving in to finish it off.

Beverley got strangely agitated when she saw the firemen and practically dragged me up James Street and away from the market. The riot seemed to be all over, bar the media witch hunt, and TSG officers in full riot gear stood around in groups discussing baton technique and reattaching their ID numbers.

We sat down on the plinth of the sundial column at Seven Dials and watched the emergency vehicles roaring past, with Beverley flinching every time a fire engine went by. Still soaking wet, we were beginning to chill despite the warm evening. Beverley took my hand and squeezed it. "I'm in so much trouble," she said.

I put my arm around her and she took the opportunity to slip one of her cold hands under my shirt and warm it against my ribs. "Thanks a lot," I said.

"Just shut up and think warm thoughts," she said as if that were hard with her breasts brushing up against my side.

"So you burst a few pipes," I said. "How much trouble can you be in?"

"Those were fire hydrants I messed with, which means the cult of Neptune's going to be pissed," she said.

"Cult of Neptune?"

"London Fire Brigade," she said.

"The London Fire Brigade are worshippers of the god Neptune?"

"Not officially, no," she said. "But you know—sailors, Neptune, it's a natural fit."

"The Fire Brigade are sailors?"

"Not now," she said. "But in the old days, when they were looking for disciplined guys who knew about water, ropes, ladders and didn't freak out at altitude. On the other hand, you had a lot of sailors looking for a nice steady career on dry land—marriage made in heaven."

"Still, Neptune," I said. "Roman god of the sea?"

Beverley laid her head on my shoulder. Her hair was wet, but I wasn't complaining. "Sailors are superstitious," she said. "Even the religious ones know you got to have a little respect for the King of the Deeps."

"Have you met Neptune?"

"Don't be silly," she said. "There's no such person. Anyway, I feel bad about the hydrants, but it's Thames Water I'm worried about."

"Don't tell me," I said. "Worshippers of dread Cthulhu."

"I don't think they're very religious at all, but you don't

piss off people who can release raw sewage into your head-waters," she said.

"You know," I said. "I don't think I've ever seen your river."

Beverley turned and made herself comfortable against my chest. "I've got a place off the Kingston bypass," she said. "It's just a semi, but my garden goes all the way down to the water." She lifted her head until her lips were brushing mine. "We could go swimming."

We kissed. She tasted of strawberries and cream and chewing gum. God knows where we might have gone after that, except a Range Rover screeched to a stop right by us and Beverley disengaged so fast that I got lip burn.

A stocky woman in jeans got out of the Range Rover and marched over. She was dark-skinned with a round expressive face that was, on this occasion, expressing a high degree of annoyance. "Beverley," she said barely registering my presence. "You are in so much trouble—get in the car."

Beverley sighed, kissed me on the cheek and got up to meet her sister. I scrambled up myself, ignoring the pain from my bruised back.

"Peter," said Beverley. "This is my sister Fleet."

Fleet gave me a critical once-over. She looked to be in her early thirties, built like a sprinter—broad-shouldered and narrow-waisted with big muscular thighs. She wore a tweed jacket over a black polo neck and wore her hair trimmed down to a thick stubble. Looking at her gave me a weird sense of familiarity, like you get when you meet a minor celebrity whose name you can't remember.

"I'd love to get acquainted, Peter, but now is not the time," said Fleet. She turned to Beverley. "Get in the car."

Beverley gave me a sad little smile and did what she was told.

"Wait," I said. "I know you from somewhere."

"You went to the same school as my kids," she said, and climbed back into her Range Rover. The door had barely closed before Fleet started yelling at Beverley; it was muffled, but the phrase "irresponsible child" was clearly audible. Beverley saw me watching and rolled her eyes. I wondered what it was like to grow up with that many sisters. I thought it might be nice to have someone pick me up in their Range Rover, even if they were going to shout at me all the way home.

It's a funny thing about a London riot, but once you're outside the perimeter, nothing seems to be different. On the minus side, Covent Garden had nearly burned down, but on the positive side there weren't any major bus routes or tube lines affected. It was dark, I was soaked, the Folly was still out of bounds and I didn't fancy spending another night in that chair in Nightingale's hospital room. I did what everyone does when they've run out of options—I went back to the one place where, when you turn up there, they have to let you in.

I MADE the mistake of catching the tube—it was crowded—people heading back from an evening out. Even that late in the evening, it was warm and close inside the coach, but wet, disheveled and slightly ethnic as I was, I got more elbow room than anyone else.

My back and leg hurt, I was tired and I was missing something. I've never trusted the idea of policeman's gut instinct. I'd watched Leslie at work and every time she guessed right, it was because she'd spotted something I'd missed, dug a bit further or thought a little bit harder about a case. If I was going to save her life, I was going to have to do the same.

More people got on at Goodge Street—it got hotter, but at least I was beginning to dry out. A guy in tan slacks and an off-the-rack blue blazer took the space by the connecting door on my right—close enough for me to catch the tinny backbeat from his iPod earpieces. I began to feel reassuringly anonymous again.

None of the references to revenants I'd read had provided a clear idea of how or why an ordinary ghost gained the ability to suck the magic out of other ghosts. My working theory about ghosts was that they were the copies of personalities that had somehow imprinted into the magic residue that accumulated on physical objects—the *vestigia*. I suspected ghosts degraded over time, in the same way that stuff recorded on magnetic tape degrades, unless their signal boosted with more magic, hence the need to suck it out of other ghosts.

We must have picked up a ranting drunk at Warren Street, because after a brief windup he was in full flow by the time we reached Euston. There, I was distracted when a young woman in a pink halter with more cleavage than I thought physically possible got on and leaned against the glass partition opposite me. I looked away before she caught my eye and shifted focus to the nearest advert. I felt the guy in the blue blazer shift position and guessed he was doing the same thing.

A white boy with dreads lurched into my little corner of the train; I caught a whiff of patchouli, tobacco and marijuana. The woman in the halter top hesitated and then moved closer to me—apparently I was the lesser of the two evils.

"The dogs, the dogs," shouted the ranting drunk, from somewhere down the other end of the carriage. "This country is going to the dogs." And the happy train lurched into movement again.

Revenants had to be rare or there'd be no ghosts left for them to feed on, which brought me back to: what made a revenant? Psychological state at the moment of death maybe? Henry Pyke had died a pointless and unjust death even by the lax standards of the eighteenth century, but despite that, his resentment at Charles Macklin and burning disappointment at the sad state of his acting career didn't seem enough motivation to make him want to force poor Bernard Coopertown to beat his wife to death.

"Used to be a fucking paradise," shouted the ranting drunk. He couldn't be talking about Camden Town, which, despite the markets, had never really aspired to much more than shabby respectability.

Camden tube station is where the Northern Line splits into Edgware and High Barnet branches and here loads of people got off and even more people got on. We all crushed up a bit more and I found myself staring at the top of the woman in the halter top's head—she had blond roots and dandruff. The man in the blue blazer got shoved in from the right and between them they had me boxed against the door. We all shuffled about trying to keep our armpits out of each other's faces— just because it's uncomfortable, there's really no excuse for not maintaining standards or making eye contact.

The ranting drunk welcomed everyone aboard. "The more the merrier," he said. "Let's have the whole fucking world in here—why not?"

The smell of the white boy with dreads intensified, urine and excrement, I wondered when he'd last changed his fake combat trousers.

Less than a minute out of Camden Town, the train lurched to a stop. An almost subliminal groan rose from the passengers—especially when the lights dimmed as well. I heard someone chuckling at the other end of the carriage.

There had to be something else behind Henry Pyke, I thought, something much worse than a bitter failed actor.

"Of course there is," shouted the ranting drunk. "That would be me."

I craned my neck to spot the drunk, but my view was blocked by the white boy with dreads, whose face now had an expression of dumb satisfaction. The smell of shit got worse and I realized that the white boy had just relieved himself in his pants. He caught my eye and gave me a big smile of contentment.

"Who are you?" I shouted. I tried to get out of my corner, but the woman in the halter top thrust herself backward and pinned me to the back wall. The lights dimmed further and this time the groan from the passengers was anything but subliminal.

"I'm the demon drink," shouted the ranting drunk. "I'm gin lane and your local crack house. I'm a follower of Captain Swing, Watt Tyler and Oswald Mosley. I'm the grinning face in the window of the hansom cab, I made Dickens long for the countryside and I'm what your masters are afraid of."

I pushed at the woman in the halter top, but my arms felt heavy, useless as if in a nightmare. She started to rub herself against me. The carriage was getting hotter and I began to sweat. A hand suddenly grabbed hold of my backside and squeezed tight—it was the man in the blue blazer. I was so shocked that I froze up. I looked at his face, but he was staring straight forward with the typically bored abstracted expression of a seasoned traveler. The bleed out from his iPod was louder and more irritating than it had been.

I gagged on the smell of shit and shoved the woman in the halter top enough to get a view down the carriage. I saw my ranting drunk—he had the face of Mr. Punch.

The man in the blazer let go of my arse and tried to stick his hand down the back of my jeans, the woman in the halter top ground her hips into my crotch.

"Is this," shouted Mr. Punch, "any way for a young man to live?"

The white boy with dreads leaned toward me and with great deliberation poked me in the face with his index finger. "Poke," he said and giggled. Then he did it again.

There's a point where a human being will lose it, just lash out at everything about them. Some people spend their lives on the edge of that—most of them end up doing time in prison. Some, a lot of them women, get ground down to that point over years until one day, it's hello burning bed and a legal defense of extreme provocation.

I was at that point and I could feel the righteous anger, how wonderful it would feel just to fuck the consequences and let rip. Because sometimes you just want the fucking universe to take some notice—is that too fucking much to ask for?

And then I realized that was what it was all about.

Mr. Punch—the spirit of riot and rebellion—does what it says on the tin. This was him, the guy behind Henry Pyke and he was fucking with my mind.

"I get it," I said. "Henry Pyke, Coopertown, that cycle courier, lots of frustration—but that's everyone in the big city, ain't it, Mr. Punch. And what percentage actually let you in? I bet you've got a piss poor success rate—so you can just fuck off out of it—I'm going home to bed."

At that point I realized that the train was moving again, the lights were up and the man in the blue blazer didn't have his hand down my trousers and the ranting drunk was

silent. Everybody in the carriage was studiously not looking at me.

I bailed at Kentish Town, the very next stop; fortunately, it
was where I wanted to go.

FROM SEPTEMBER 1944 to March 1945, that lovable Nazi
scamp Wernher Von Braun aimed his V2 rockets at the stars
and yet, in the words of the song, somehow hit London instead. When my dad was growing up, the city was dotted
with bomb sites, gaps in the neat rows of houses where
homes had been obliterated. In the postwar years, these sites
were gradually cleared and rebuilt as a series of ghastly architectural mistakes. My dad liked to claim that the mistake
where I grew up was built on a V2 impact site, but I suspect
it was probably just an ordinary cluster of German high ex-
plosive dropped by a conventional bomber.

Still, whatever caused the two-hundred-meter gap in the
Victorian terraces lining Leighton Road, the postwar planners weren't going to pass up an opportunity to make mistakes on this scale. Built in the 1950s, the blocks of the
Peckwater Estate are six stories high, rectangular and built,
as a final aesthetic touch, of a dirty gray brick that weathered
badly. As a result, when the clean air act put an end to the famous London pea-soupers and they started sandblasting the
old buildings clean, the Peckwater Estate came out looking
worse than it had before.

The flats were solidly built, so at least I didn't grow up listening to next door's live docusoap, but they were built on
the dubious assumption, so beloved of postwar planners, that
the London working class was composed entirely of hobbits.
My parents had a third-floor flat with a front door that opened
onto an open air walkway. When I'd been growing up in the
early nineties, the walls had been covered in graffiti and the
stairwell with dogshit. These days, the graffiti was mostly
gone and the dogshit got regularly hosed into the gutter,
which, by the standards of the Peckwater Estate, counted as
gentrification. I still had my front door key, which was just as
well because when I got there, I found my parents were out.

This was unusual enough to give me pause. My dad's in his early seventies and doesn't move about much, I figured it had to be a major occasion, a wedding or a christening, for my mum to dress him up and drag him out of the house. I figured I'd hear all about it when they got home. I made myself a cup of tea with condensed milk and sugar and ate a couple of generic brand biscuits. Thus fortified, I went to my old bedroom to see if there was room for me to sleep in it.

As soon as I'd moved out, and by this I mean about ten minutes after the door had closed behind me, my mum started using my bedroom for storage. It was full of cardboard moving boxes, each one stuffed to capacity and sealed shut with packing tape. I had to move several off the bed just to lie down. They were heavy and smelt of dust. On roughly a two-year cycle, my mum collected clothes, shoes, cooking utensils and nonperishable beauty products, stuffed them into cardboard boxes and shipped them back to her family in Freetown. The fact that a great deal of her immediate family had already immigrated to the UK, the U.S. and, strangely enough, Denmark, never seemed to cause a reduction in the flow. African families are notoriously extended, but from what I could gather, my mum was related to about half the population of Sierra Leone. I'd learned from an early age that anything I owned that I didn't defend was subject to arbitrary seizure and deportation. My Legos, in particular, were the subject of a running battle from my eleventh birthday, when my mum decided that I was too old for such things, to my fourteenth year when they mysteriously vanished while I was on a school trip.

I pried off my shoes, climbed under the covers and was asleep before I could wonder where all my posters had gone.

I woke briefly some hours later to the sound of the bedroom door being stealthily closed and the muffled sound of my dad's voice. My mother said something that made my father laugh and, comforted that everything was all right, I went back to sleep.

I woke again, much later, with the morning sunlight slanting through my bedroom window. I lay on my back feeling refreshed, with a solid erection and the vague memory of an erotic dream about Beverley. What was I going to do about Beverley Brook? That I fancied her was a given, that she fancied me was pretty obvious, that she wasn't entirely human was a worrying possibility. Beverley wanted me to go swimming in her river and I had no idea what that meant, except Isis had warned me against doing it. I had a strong feeling that you didn't shag a daughter of the River Thames without getting out of your depth—literally.

"It's not that I'm scared of commitment," I said to the ceiling. "It's just that I want to know what I'm committing to first."

"Are you awake, then, Peter?" said a soft voice outside my door—my father.

"Yeah, Dad, I'm awake."

"Your mum's left you some lunch," he said.

Lunch, I thought. The day was half done and nothing achieved so far. I rolled out of my bed, squeezed past a stack of cardboard boxes and headed for the shower.

The bathroom was as hobbit-sized as everything else in the flat and it had only been by dint of some serious Polish retro-engineering that a power shower was shoehorned into the gap between the sink and the window. It was me that coughed up the cash for it, so I guarantee I didn't have to duck my head to get it wet. There was a new soap dispenser mounted beside the shower, the kind you find in the toilets of executive office suites, bought or liberated from a cleaning wholesaler. I'd noticed that the toilet paper and the bath towels were much better brands than when I was living at home—Mum was obviously cleaning a much better class of office these days.

I got out and dried myself off with an enormous fluffy towel with *Your Institution Here* embroidered into the corner. My dad was of the "real men don't moisturize" school of dry skin diseases and all my mum had was a wholesale tub of cocoa butter. I've got nothing against using cocoa butter, it's just that you end up smelling like a giant Mars Bar for the rest of the day. My skin taken care of, I nipped back into my old room, where I cracked open some of the boxes at random until I had a change of clothes. One of my distant cousins was just going to have to go without.

The kitchen was a narrow slot that could have been used to train mess crews for Trident submarines. It was just big enough for a sink, stove and a work surface. A door at the far end opened out onto an equally vestigial balcony that at least caught enough sun to dry clothes most of the year round. Curls of blue tobacco smoke drifted in from the balcony, which meant that my father was out there having one of his four precious daily roll-ups.

My mum had left groundnut chicken and about half a kilo of basmati on the stove. I threw both in the microwave and asked my father if he wanted a coffee. He did, so I made two cups using instant from a catering-sized tin of Nescafé. I topped them up with a centimeter of condensed milk to mask the taste.

He looked well, my father, which meant that he'd had his "medicine" sometime this morning. He had a reputation for good grooming in the heyday of his career and my mum liked to keep him respectable: khaki slacks and linen jacket over a pale green shirt. I always thought of it as Empire chic and it obviously did something for my mum. He looked suitably colonial in the sunlight, sitting on a wicker chair that was almost as wide as the balcony. There was just enough room left for a stool and white plastic end table. I put the coffees down on the table by the pub-sized Foster's Lager ashtray and my dad's tin of Golden Virginia.

From our balcony, on a clear day, you could see all the way across the courtyard to the net curtains of our neighbors.

"How's the Filth?" he asked. He always called the police the Filth, although he turned up for my graduation from Hendon and seemed proud enough of me then.

"It's not easy keeping the masses down," I said. "They keep fighting and nicking stuff."

"That's the sad condition of the workingman," said Dad. He sipped his coffee, put the mug down and picked up his tobacco tin. He didn't open it, just placed it on his lap and rested his fingers on it.

I asked whether Mum was okay and where they'd been the night before. She was fine and they'd gone to a wedding. He was hazy as to whose, one of my many cousins, a definition that could range from the child of my aunt to a guy who wandered into my mother's house and didn't leave for two years. Traditionally, a good Sierra Leonean wedding should last several days, as should a funeral, but in deference to the hectic pace of modern British life, the expats liked to keep the celebrations down to just a day, or thirty-six hours—tops. Not counting preparation time.

As he described the music—he was hazy on the food, the clothes and the religion—my dad opened his tobacco tin, took out a packet of Rizlas and, with great care and deliberation, made himself a roll-up. Once it was finished to his satisfaction, he put tobacco, Rizlas and the roll-up itself back in the tin, sealed it up and replaced it on the table. When he picked up his coffee, I saw his hand was trembling. My dad would leave the tin on the table for as long as he could stand it before picking it up and putting it on his lap, then he might remake his roll-up or, if he couldn't stand it any longer, smoke the damn thing. Dad had the early stages of emphysema. The same doctor who supplied him with his heroin had warned him that if he couldn't stop smoking, he should at least keep it down to less than five fags a day.

"Do you believe in magic?" I asked.

"I once heard Dizzy Gillespie play," said Dad. "Does that count?"

"It might do," I said. "Where do you reckon playing like that comes from?"

"In Dizzy? That was all talent and hard work, but I did know a sax player said he got his chops from the devil, made a deal at the crossroads, that sort of thing."

"Don't tell me," I said. "He was from Mississippi?"

"No, Catford," said Dad. "Said he made his deal on Archer Street."

"Was he any good?"

"He wasn't bad," said Dad. "But the poor bastard went blind two weeks later."

"Was that part of the deal?" I asked.

"Apparently so," said Dad. "Your mum thought it was, when I told her. She said that only a fool expects to get something for nothing."

That sounded like Mum, whose principal saying was, "If it doesn't cost something it isn't worth anything." Actually her principal saying was, at least to me, "Don't think you've got so big that I can't still beat you." Not that she ever beat me, a deficiency that she later blamed for my failure to pass my A-levels. Numerous university-bound cousins were held up as shining examples of discipline through physical violence.

My dad picked up his tobacco tin and put it in his lap. I picked up the mugs and washed them in the kitchen sink. I remembered the groundnut chicken and rice in the microwave. I ate the chicken but left most of the rice. I also drank about a liter of cold water, which is a common side effect of eating my mum's food. I seriously considered going back to bed. What else was there for me to do?

I stuck my head out onto the balcony to ask my dad if there was anything he needed. He said he was fine. As I watched, he opened his tin, took out the roll-up and put it in his mouth. He took out his silver-colored paraffin lighter and lit it with the same deliberate ceremony with which he had rolled it. As he inhaled for the first time there was a look of bliss on his face, then he started coughing, nasty wet coughs that sounded like he was bringing up the lining of his lungs. With a practiced twist, he snuffed out the roll-up and waited for the coughing to subside. When it had, he put the roll-up back between his lips and lit up again. I didn't hang about—I knew how it went on from there.

I love my dad. He's a walking caution.

My mum has three landlines. I picked one and called my voice mail service. The first message was from Dr. Walid.

"Peter," he said. "Just to let you know that Thomas is conscious and asking for you."

THE BROADSHEETS called it May Madness, which made it sound like a tea dance, the tabloids called it May Rage, presumably because it had one less syllable to fit across the front page. The TV had some good footage of middle-aged women in long dresses tossing bricks at the police. Nobody had a clue what had happened, so the pundits were out in force, explaining how the riot was caused by whatever sociopolitical factor their latest book was pushing. It was certainly a searing indictment of some aspect of modern society—if only we knew what.

There was a big police presence in the UCH's casualty department, most of them loitering in search of overtime or trying to get statements from victims of the riot. I didn't want to give a statement, so I slipped in the back way by grabbing a mop bucket and passing myself off as a cleaner. I got lost in the upper levels looking for Dr. Walid before stumbling onto a corridor that looked vaguely familiar. I opened doors at random until I found Nightingale's. He didn't really look any better than the last time.

"Inspector," I said. "You wanted to see me."

His eyes opened and flicked toward me. I sat on the edge of the bed so he could see me without moving his head.

"Got shot," he whispered.

"I know," I said. "I was there."

"Shot before," he said.

"Really, when?

"War."

"Which war was that?" I asked.

Nightingale grimaced and shifted in his bed. "Second," he said.

"The Second World War," I said. "What were you in—the baby brigade?" To have enlisted even in 1945, Nightingale would have had to have been born in 1929 and that's if he'd lied about his age. "How old are you?"

"Old," he whispered. "Turn century."

"Turn of the century?" I asked and he nodded. "You were born at the turn of the century—the twentieth century?" He looked like he was in his bluff midforties, which is a neat trick when you're lying half dead in a hospital bed with a machine that goes "ping" at regular intervals. "You're over a hundred years old?"

Nightingale made a wheezing sound that alarmed me for a moment until I realized that it was laughter.

"Is this natural?"

He shook his head.

"Do you know why it's happening?"

"Gift horse," he whispered. "Mouth."

I couldn't argue with that. I didn't want to tire him too much, so I told him about Leslie, the riot and being locked out of the Folly. When I asked him whether Molly could help me track Henry Pyke via hemomancy, he shook his head.

"Dangerous," he said.

"Has to be done," I said. "I don't think he's going to stop until he's stopped."

Slowly, one word at a time, Nightingale told me exactly how it would work—I didn't like the sound of it one bit. It was a terrible plan and it still left the question of how to get back into the Folly.

"Tyburn's mother," said Nightingale.

"You want her to overrule her daughter?" I asked. "What makes you think she'll do that?"

"Pride," said Nightingale.

"You want me to beg?"

"Not her pride," said Nightingale. "Yours."

CHAPTER 13

London Bridge

IT'S NOT easy maneuvering an articulated lorry up the Wapping Wall, so I hired a middle-aged man called Brian to do it. Brian was balding, potbellied and foulmouthed; the only thing missing from the stereotype was a Yorkie Bar and a rolled-up copy of the *Sun*. Still, I hadn't hired him for his erudition and he did get us all the way to Mama Thames's house without any extraneous insurance claims.

We parked up half outside Mama Thames's block and half outside the Prospect of Whitby. The staff must have thought that it was an unexpected delivery because they came tumbling out—I had to tell them it was for a private party and, weirdly, they didn't seem that surprised. I asked Brian to wait and picking up my crate of samples from the cab, I staggered over to the communal entrance. I put it down and rang the doorbell. This time I was met at the door by the same white lady I'd seen among Mama Thames's cronies. She was dressed in a different, but equally nice, twinset and pearls and carried a small black child on her hip.

"Why Constable Grant," she said. "How lovely to see you again."

"Let me guess," I said. "You must be Lea."

"Very good," said Lea. "I do like a young man who has his wits about him." The River Lea rises in the Chilterns northwest of London and skirts the top of the city before making a sharp right-hand turn down the Lea Valley to the Thames.

It's the least urbanized of London's rivers and the largest, so of course it survived the Great Stink. Lea must be one of Oxley's generation of *genii locorum*—if not older.

I pulled a face at the child who looked to be a girl of nursery age; she pulled a face back. "Who's this?" I asked.

"This is Brent," said Lea. "She's the youngest."

"Hello, Brent," I said. She was lighter than her sisters, with brown eyes that might have been called hazel by a good-natured liar, but the belligerent set of her face was unmistakable. She was wearing a miniature red England soccer team's away strip, predictably the number 11 shirt.

"You smell funny," said Brent.

"That's because he's a wizard," Lea told her.

Brent squirmed out of Lea's grip and grabbed my hand. "Come with me," she said and tried to drag me through the door. She was surprisingly strong and I had to brace a little to stay still. "I have to bring my crate," I told her.

"Don't worry, I'll take care of that," said Lea.

I let Brent pull me down the long cool corridor to Mama Thames's flat. Behind me, I heard Lea calling for Uncle Bailiff and if he would be a dear could he take the crate to Mama's flat.

According to Dr. Polidori, *genii locorum "behave as if the imperatives of ceremony are to them as necessary as meat and drink is to man"* and furthermore claimed that they *"anticipate such events with miraculous facility so that they are always appropriately attired and if surprised or somehow prevented show signs of great distress."* Given that he was writing in the late eighteenth century, I like to cut him slack.

They were waiting for me in the throne room and this time I could see it was a throne room, the potted mangrove sheltering the sacred World of Leather executive armchair. There sat Mama Thames, resplendent in her Austrian lace and a headdress of blue-and-white Portuguese beads. Behind her were arrayed her attendants in batik lappas and headscarves and on her left and right hands, forming an aisle down which I had to walk, stood her daughters. I recognized Tyburn and Fleet on my left, standing with a pair of teenaged girls wearing thin braids and cashmere jumpers. Beverley was on my right, look-ing underdressed in Lycra shorts and a purple sweatshirt. When she was sure I was looking, she rolled her eyes. Beside her stood an amazingly tall and slender woman with a fox face, electric blue and blond extensions and elongated nails painted in green, gold and black. That, I guessed, was Effra, another un-derground river, who was obviously moonlighting as the God-dess of Brixton Market. I noticed that it was North London rivers on the left and South London rivers on the right.

Brent let go of my hand, essayed a curtsy in the direction of Mama Thames and then spoiled the effect by skipping over and hurling herself into her mother's lap. There was a brief pause in the ceremony as the little girl squirmed herself into a comfortable position.

Mama Thames turned her full gaze on me and the under-tow of her regard drew me closer to her throne. I had to fight a strong urge to throw myself on my knees and bang my fore-head on the carpet.

"Constable Peter," said Mama Thames. "How nice to see you."

"It's nice to be here. As a token of my respect, I've brought you a gift," I said hoping that it was going to arrive before I ran out of pleasantries. I heard clinking behind me and Uncle Bailiff arrived with my crate. He was a heavyset white man with a skinned head and a faded tattoo of SS lightning bolts on his neck. He set the crate down before Mama Thames, gave her a respectful nod and, with a pitying look at me, left without a word.

One of the cronies stepped forward to pluck a bottle from the crate and show it to Mama Thames. "Star Beer," she said. The core product of the Nigerian Breweries PLC, available in the UK from any good stockist and available in bulk if your mum knows someone who knows someone who owes someone a favor.

"How much has he got out there?" asked Fleet.

"A lorry load," said Lea.

"How big a lorry?" asked Mama Thames, without taking her eyes off me.

"Big lorry," said Brent.

"Is it all Star?" asked Mama Thames.

"I put in some Gulder," I said. "Some Red Stripe for variety, a couple of cases of Bacardi, some Appleton, Cointreau and a few bottles of Bailey's." I'd liquidated my savings doing it, but as my mum says—nothing worth having is free.

"That's a handsome gift," said Mama Thames.

"You can't be serious?" said Tyburn.

"Don't worry, Ty," I said. "I threw in a couple of bottles of Perrier for you."

Someone sniggered—probably Beverley.

"And what can I do for you?" asked Mama Thames.

"It's a small matter," I said. "One of your daughters feels that she has a right to interfere in the business of the Folly. All I ask is that she steps back and lets the proper authorities get on with their jobs."

"Proper authorities," spat Tyburn.

Mama Thames turned her eyes on Tyburn, who stepped before the throne. "You think you have a right to meddle in this?" she asked.

"Mum," said Tyburn. "The Folly is a relic, a Victorian afterthought from the same people who gave us Black Rod and the Lord Mayor's show. Heritage is all very well and good for the tourist industry, but it's no way to run a modern city."

"That is not your decision to make," I said.

"And you think it's yours?"

"I know it's mine," I said. "My duty, my obligation—my decision."

"And you're asking—"

"I am not *asking*," I said, pleasantries were over. "You want to fuck with me, Tyburn, you had better know who you're messing with."

Tyburn took a step back and recovered. "We know who you are," she said. "Your father is a failed musician and your mother cleans offices for a living. You grew up in a council flat and you went to your local comprehensive and you failed your A-levels . . ."

"I am a sworn constable," I said. "And that makes me an

officer of the law. And I am an apprentice, which makes me a keeper of the sacred flame, but most of all I am a free man of London and that makes me a Prince of the City." I jabbed a finger at Tyburn. "No double first from Oxford trumps that."

"You think so?" she said.

"Enough," said Mama Thames. "Let him into his house."

"It's not his house," said Tyburn.

"Do as I say," said Mama Thames.

"But Mum . . ."

"Tyburn!"

Tyburn looked stricken and for a moment I felt genuinely sorry for her, because none of us ever are grown up enough that our mothers don't think they can't beat us. She slipped a slimline Nokia from her pocket and dialed a number without taking her eyes off mine. "Sylvia," she said. "Is the commissioner available? Good. Could I have a quick word?" Then, having made her point to her own satisfaction, she turned and walked from the room. I resisted the urge to gloat, but I did glance over at Beverley to see if she was impressed with me. She gave me a studiously indifferent look that was as good as a blown kiss.

"Peter," said Mama Thames and beckoned me over to her chair. She indicated that she wanted to tell me something private. I tried to bend down with as much dignity as I could, but I found myself, much to Brent's amusement, on my knees before her. She leaned forward and brushed her lips against my forehead.

For a moment it was as if I stood high up on the middle cowling of the Thames Barrier looking east over the mouth of the river. I could feel the towers of Canary Wharf rising triumphantly at my back and beyond them the docks, the White Tower and all the bridges, bells and houses of London town. But ahead of me over the horizon I could feel the storm surge, the fatal combination of high tides, global warming and poor planning, waiting. Ready to drive a wall of water ten meters high up the river and bring down the bridges, towers and Uncle Tom Cobley and all.

"Just so you understand," said Mama Thames. "Where the real power lies."

"Yes, Mama," I said.

"I expect you to sort out my dispute with the Old Man," she said.

"I'll do my best," I said.

"Good boy," she said. "And because of your good manners I have a last gift." She bent her head and whispered a name in my ear—"Tiberius Claudius Verica."

THE PARATROOPERS were gone by the time I got back to Russell Square. I was back in charge of the Folly and also responsible. Toby slammed into my ankles as soon as I was across the threshold, panting and thrashing affectionately, although once he'd established that I wasn't carrying anything edible he lost interest and scampered off. Molly was waiting for me at the foot of the western stairs. I told her that Nightingale was conscious and then lied and said that he'd asked how she was. I told her what I was planning to do and she physically recoiled.

"I'm just going to my room to get some stuff," I said. "I'll be back down in half an hour."

As soon as I reached my room, I pulled out my Latin notes and checked the stuff about Roman names. Which, I'd learned, often have three bits—praenomen, nomen, and cognomen— and, if you can read your own handwriting, tell you a lot about the individual. Verica wasn't a Latin name, I suspected it was British, and Tiberius Claudius were the first two names of Tiberius Claudius Caesar Augustus Germanicus, otherwise known as Emperor Claudius, who was in charge when Britain was first conquered by the Romans. The Empire liked to co-opt the local ruling elite whenever possible—it being easier to get your leg over a country if you fork out for dinner and a dozen roses first. One of the bribes on offer was Roman citizenship and many that took up that offer kept their native name and prefixed the praenomen and nomen of their sponsors—in this case the emperor. Thus, just from the evidence of his name, Tiberius Claudius Verica

was an aristocratic Briton who lived around the time that the
city was founded.

Which meant—nothing, as far as I could tell. If I survived
the next hour or so I planned to have a word with Mama
Thames about it. I had more immediate problems.

IN 1861, William Booth resigned from the Methodists in
Liverpool and headed for London where, in the grand tradition of metropolitan reinvention, he founded his own church
and took Christ, bread and social work to the heathen natives
of East London. In 1878, he declared that he was tired of
being called a volunteer and that he was a regular in the army
of Christ or nothing at all; thus the Salvation Army was born.
But no army, however pure its motives, occupies a foreign
country without resistance and this was provided by the
Skeleton Army. Driven by gin, boneheadedness and growling resentment that being the Victorian working class was
bad enough without being preached at by a bunch of self-
righteous northerners, the Skeleton Army broke up Salvation
Army meetings, disrupted marches and attacked its officer
corps. The emblem of the Skeleton Army was a white skeleton against a black background—a badge worn by right-
thinking ne'er-do-wells from Worthing to Bethnal Green. I'd
spotted one on the ghostly form of Nicholas Wallpenny, a
candidate for the Skeleton Army if there was one, and it was
this badge I recovered from the graveyard of the Actors'
Church. Nightingale had said that I was going to need a spirit
guide and in the absence of mystical bears, coyotes or whatever, a larcenous cockney was going to have to do.

The badge was where I had left it, in the plastic box where
I kept my paper clips. I held it in the palm of my hand; it was
just a cheap little thing, pewter and brass. When I picked it
up and closed my hand around it there was the fleeting taste
of gin, old songs and just a little stab of resentment.

If this was to be a spiritual journey, I wasn't going to need
anything else and I'd put off the moment long enough. I went
reluctantly downstairs to where Molly was waiting for me in
the middle of the atrium. She stood with her head bowed, her

hair a black curtain hiding her face, hands locked in front of her.

"I don't want to do this either," I said.

She raised her head and for the first time looked me directly in the eye.

"Do it," I said.

She moved so fast I didn't see it, throwing herself against me. One arm snaked around my shoulders and grabbed the back of my head, the other around my waist. I could feel her breasts pressing against my chest, her thighs clamping hard around my leg. Her face was buried in the hollow of my neck and I felt her lips against my throat. Fear rolled over me; I tried to pull myself free, but she held me tighter than a lover. I felt her teeth scrape at my neck and then pain, strangely more like a blow rather than a stab, as she bit me hard. I felt the action of her swallowing as she sucked at my blood, but I also felt the connection with the tiles beneath me and the bricks in the walls—the yellow London clay—and then I was falling backward into daylight and the smell of turpentine.

It wasn't like a virtual reality or how you imagine a hologram should work, it was like breathing *vestigia,* like swimming in stone. I found myself in the Folly's own memory of the atrium.

I'd done it—I was in.

THE ATRIUM looked largely as it should, but the colors were muted almost sepia in tone and there was a ringing in my ears like the sensation you get when swimming near the bottom of the deep end. Molly was nowhere to be seen, but I thought I caught a glimpse of Nightingale, or at least the imprint of Nightingale on the stone memory, making his way wearily up the stairs. I unclasped my hand and checked that I was still "holding" the skeleton badge; it was still there and when I closed my fingers back around it, I felt it tug, very gently, toward the south. I turned and made my way toward the side door in Bedford Place, but as I crossed the atrium floor I was suddenly aware of a vast darkness beneath my feet. It was as if solid black-and-white tiles had been rendered transparent and through them I could glimpse a terrible abyss—dark, bottomless and cold. I tried to move faster, but it was like walking into a violent headwind. I had to lean forward and push hard to make progress. It wasn't until I'd carefully steered myself through the narrow servants' quarters under the east stairs that I wondered whether, this being the realm of ghosts after all, I might just walk through the walls. After knocking my forehead a couple of times, I just opened the side door like a normal person.

And stepped out into the 1930s and the stink of horses. I knew it was the thirties because of the double-breasted suits and gangster hats. The cars were nothing but shadows, but the horses were solid and smelt of sweat and manure. There were people walking on the pavements; they looked perfectly normal but for an abstracted look in their eyes. I stepped in front of one man as an experiment, but he just stepped around me as if I were a familiar and inconsequential obstacle. A sharp pain in my neck reminded me that I wasn't here to sightsee.

I let the skeleton badge tug me onward down Bedford Place and toward Bloomsbury Square. Above, the sky seemed strangely ill-defined, blue at one moment, cloudy the next, and then gritty with coal smoke. As I traveled, I noticed that the clothes on the passersby changed, the ghost cars vanished completely and even the skyline began to alter. I realized I was being drawn back in time through the historical record. If I had guessed right, then Nicholas Wallpenny's badge would not only take me to his Covent Garden haunt but to the point in time where he started haunting it.

The most recent book on the subject I could find had been from 1936 and written by a guy called Lucius Brock. He'd speculated that *vestigia* were laid down in layers like archaeological deposits and that different spirits inhabited different layers. I was going to Wallpenny in the late Victorian era and he was going to lead me to Henry Pyke in the late eighteenth century and Pyke, whether he wanted to or not, would reveal his last resting place.

I'd made it as far as the top of Drury Lane when the Victorian era drove me retching to my knees. I'd been getting used to the pervading smell of horseshit, but the 1870s was like sticking your head into a cesspit. It may have been *vestigia,* but it was strong enough to heave my imaginary lunch onto the filthy gutter. I tasted blood in my mouth and realized that some of that was my own—no doubt fueling whatever occult shit Molly was doing to keep me here.

Bow Street was crammed with enormous carts and high-sided vans drawn by horses the size of a midsized family hatchback. This was Covent Garden at its height and I expected Wallpenny's skeleton badge to lead me down Russell Street to the Piazza, but instead it pulled me to the right, up Bow Street, toward the Royal Opera House. Then the carts changed shape and I realized that I was too far back in time and that something had gone wrong with plan A.

As if being cleared for the start of the next scene, the heavy carts vanished from outside the Opera House. The sky dimmed and the street became dark, lit only by torches and oil lamps. The ghost images of gilded carriages drifted past me while bewigged and perfumed ladies and gentlemen promenaded up and down the steps of the old Theatre Royal. A group of three men caught my eye. They seemed to be more solid than the other figures, denser and more real. One of them was a large elderly man in a big wig who walked stiffly with the aid of a stick—this had to be Charles Macklin. The light clung to him as if he were being singled out for a close-up—no prizes for guessing who by.

This, I assumed, was going to be a reenactment of the infamous murder of Henry Pyke by the dastardly Charles Macklin and, right on cue, enter Henry Pyke in velvet coat and a state of high emotion, his wig askew and an outsized stick in his hand.

Only I recognized the face. I'd first seen it on a cold January morning and it had introduced itself as Nicholas Wallpenny—late of the Parish of Covent Garden. But no, not Nicholas Wallpenny, it was Henry Pyke. It was always Henry Pyke, right from the start, from the portico of the Actors' Church, making the most of his chirpy cockney impression. Well, at least it explained why Wallpenny wouldn't show himself in front of Nightingale. It also meant that the scene at the church that led me to my impromptu excavation of a priceless London landmark had been just that, a scene, a performance.

"Help, help," cried one of Macklin's companions. "Murder!"

Some things are universal; birds got to fly, fish got to swim, fools and policemen got to rush in. I managed to restrain myself from shouting "oi" as I ran forward and as a result got within two meters before Henry Pyke saw me coming. I got a very satisfying "oh fuck" expression from him and then his face changed—became the ludicrous quarter-moon caricature that I had come to know as Mr. Punch, spirit of riot and rebellion.

"You know," he squeaked, "you're not nearly as stupid as you look."

Standard operating procedure for dealing with mad fuckers: keep them talking, sidle closer, grab them when they ain't looking.

"So was that you pretending to be Nicholas Wallpenny?"

"No," said Mr. Punch. "I let Henry Pyke do all the deception; lives to act, poor thing, it's all he ever wanted out of life."

"Except he's dead," I said.

"I know," said Mr. Punch. "Isn't the universe wonderful."

"Where's Henry now?"

"He's in your girlfriend's head, having carnal knowledge of her brain," said Mr. Punch and then threw back his head and shrieked with laughter. I lunged, but the slippery bastard turned on his heel and legged it down one of the narrow alleys that connected to Drury Lane.

I took off after him and I'm not saying that I could feel the spirit of every London thief taker flowing through me as I ran, but consider—we did start outside Bow Street's Magistrates' Court and I could no more have not chased him than I could have stopped breathing.

I burst out of the alley onto a winter's Drury Lane; pedestrians were bundled into anonymity, steam rose from the horses and the men who carried the sedan-chairs. In the rush of cold and snow, the city smelt clean and fresh and about to be rid of one irritating revenant spirit. Spring came with stuttering stop-motion swiftness and Mr. Punch led me down grimy side streets that I knew didn't exist anymore, until finally we passed a newly built St. Clements and onto Fleet Street. The Great Fire of London went by too fast for me to register it, just a blast of hot air as if from the open door of an oven. One minute the top of Fleet Street was dominated by St. Paul's and the next, the dome had been replaced by the squared-off Norman tower of the old Cathedral. To a Londoner like me, it was a heretical sight—like suddenly finding a stranger in your bed. The street itself was narrower and crowded by narrow fronted half-timbered houses with overhanging top floors. We were back in the time of Shakespeare and I have to say it didn't smell nearly as bad as the nineteenth century. Mr. Punch was running for his afterlife, but I was gaining.

London was also shrinking. Gaps were opening in the buildings on either side. I could see green pastures with hayricks and herds of cows. Things were losing focus around me. Ahead, the River Fleet appeared and suddenly I was dipping down to cross a stone bridge while on the other side of the valley there were walls—the ancient walls of London. I only just made it through the Ludgate before the actual gates had grown back and barred my way. The old Cathedral was long gone; we'd missed the Anglo-Saxons and what modern go-ahead historians like to call the Sub-Roman period, and paganism was back in fashion.

If I'd been thinking about it, I probably should have stopped and had a good look around, answered a few important questions about life in Londinium, but I didn't because that's when I closed the last couple of meters on Mr. Punch and rugby-tackled the dead fucker to the ground.

"Mr. Punch," I said. "You're nicked."

"Bastard," he said. "Black Irish bastard dog."

"You're not making yourself any friends here, Punch," I said. I got him back on his feet with both his arms jacked far enough up behind his back that he wasn't going anywhere without at least a broken elbow.

He stopped squirming and turned his head until he could watch me with one eye. "So you got me, copper," he said. "What are you going to do with me now?"

It was a good question and a sudden savage pain in the hollow of my throat reminded me that I was running out of time.

"Let's see what the hanging magistrate makes of you," I said.

"De Veil?" asked Mr. Punch. "Yes, please—I'm sure he'll be delicious."

Revenant, spirit of riot and rebellion, I thought: you idiot. He eats ghosts. I needed something stronger. Brock had written that the *genii locorum,* the gods and spirits of a place, were stronger than ghosts. Was there a god of justice? And where would I find him—or maybe her. Then I remembered: a statue of a woman stands atop the dome of the Old Bailey and in one hand she holds a sword and in the other, a set of scales. I didn't know if there was a goddess of justice or not, but I was willing to bet big money that Mr. Punch would know.

"Why don't we go ask the nice lady of the Old Bailey," I said.

He tensed and I knew I'd bet right. He struggled again and slammed his head back aiming for my chin, but that isn't exactly a new one for a policeman, so I had my head back safely out of reach.

"You're going up the steps this time," I said.

Mr. Punch went limp, defeated I thought, but then he began to shake in my grip. At first I thought he was crying and then I realized it was laughter. "You're going to find that a bit difficult," he said. "You seem to have run out of city."

I looked around and saw that he was right. We'd gone back too far and now there was nothing left of London but huts and the wooden stake rampart of the Roman Camp to the north. There was no stonework at all, nothing but the new-cut smell of oak planking and hot pitch. Only one thing stood complete—the bridge. It was less than a hundred meters away, constructed of square-cut timbers. It looked more like a fishing pier that had got ideas above its station and crossed the river in a fit of exuberance.

I could see a crowd halfway across, sunlight flashing off the brass fittings of a file of legionnaires standing at attention. Beyond them was a cluster of civilians in togas chalked to a blinding white for a special occasion, watching a couple of dozen men, women and children in barbaric trousers and brass torques.

And suddenly I understood what it was Mama Thames had been trying to tell me.

I think Mr. Punch understood as well, because he fought me all the way as I dragged him across the bridge and in front of the toga-rated officials. These were more echoes from the past, memories trapped in the fabric of the city—they didn't react when I threw Punch down before them. I was in year five when we did Roman History at school, so we didn't learn a lot of dates, but we did do plenty of group work on what it was like to live in Roman Britain. Which was why I could recognize the officiating priest by the purple-striped stole that covered his head. I could also recognize him by his face, although he looked a lot younger than he had when I'd seen him in the flesh. Plus he was clean-shaven, his hair was black and hung around his shoulders, but it was the same face that I had last seen propping up a fence at the source of the Thames. It was the spirit of the Old Man of the River as a young man.

Suddenly a great many things became clear to me.

"Tiberius Claudius Verica," I called.

Like a man emerging from a daydream the priest turned his eyes to me. When he saw me he broke into a delighted grin. "You must be my gift from the gods," he said.

"Help me, Father Thames," I said.

Verica plucked a pilum from the hands of the nearest legionary—the soldier didn't react—and handed it to me. I smelled freshly cut beech wood and wet iron. I knew what to do, I upended the heavy spear and hesitated. Mr. Punch shrieked and bellowed in the strange reedy high-pitched voice. "Isn't it a pity about pretty pretty Leslie," he squealed. "Will you still love your pretty little Leslie when her face has fallen off!"

This is not a person, I told myself and drove the pilum, drove it into Mr. Punch's chest. There was no blood, but I felt the shock as it pierced skin, muscle and finally the wooden planking of the bridge itself. The revenant spirit of riot and rebellion was pinned like a butterfly in its display case.

And people say modern education is a waste of time.

"I asked the river to give us a sacrifice," said Tiberius Claudius Verica. "And a sacrifice was provided."

"I thought the Romans frowned on human sacrifice," I said.

Verica laughed. "The Romans haven't arrived yet," he said.

I looked around, he was right, there was no trace of London—or the bridge. For a moment, I hung like a cartoon character and then I fell into the river. The Thames was cold and as fresh as any mountain stream.

I CAME up feeling horribly wet and sticky. There was blood smeared over my chest and I'd wet myself at some point, probably when she'd bitten me. I felt drained and voided and numb. I wanted to curl up and pretend that nothing was real.

"That," I said, "is never going to catch on as a tool for historical research."

Somebody was retching, but amazingly it wasn't me. Molly was hunched over, her face turned away and hidden by her hair, vomiting blood onto her nice clean tiles. My blood, I thought and climbed to my feet. I was light-headed but I wasn't falling over—that had to be good sign. I took a step toward Molly to see if she was okay, but she flung out her arm in my direction, palm out and made violent pushing gestures, so I backed off.

I found myself sitting down again without any memory of wanting to. I was short of breath and I could feel my pulse racing in my throat; all symptoms of blood loss. I decided that it would be a good idea to have a little rest—I lay back down on the cool tiles—all the better to maintain the blood flow to my brain. It's surprising how comfortable a hard surface can be when you're tired enough.

The rustle of silk made me turn my head. Molly, still

crouching, had turned away from the slick pool of red vomit and had inched toward me. Her head was tilted to one side and her lips were drawn back to reveal her teeth. I was just about to tell her that I was all right really and didn't need any help when I realized that was probably not what she had in mind.

With a disturbingly spiderlike motion Molly swung one arm over her head and down until her hand slapped down on the tiles in front of her face. The arm tensed and dragged Molly another few centimeters toward me. I looked into her eyes and saw that they were all black, no trace of white at all, and filled with hunger and despair.

"Molly," I said. "I really don't think this is a good idea."

Her head tilted the other way and she made a gurgling hissing sound, halfway between laughter and a sob. Sitting up gave me tunnel vision and dizziness; I fought the urge to lie back down again.

"You think you're conflicted now," I said. "Just think how you'll feel when Nightingale finds out you had me for dinner."

Nightingale's name made her pause, but only for a moment. Then her other hand swept over her head and slapped down right next to my legs. I snatched them away as best as I could and managed to gain a meter in separation.

This just seemed to aggravate her and I watched as she drew her legs up under her torso. I remembered how fast she'd moved when she first bit me and wondered if I'd even see her coming. Still, I wasn't about to sit still and let her take me without a fight. I started putting a fireball together, but the *forma* were suddenly slippery and impossible to imagine.

Molly snorted and her head twisted on its side as if her neck had become as flexible as a snake. I could see the tension building in the curve of her back and the hunch of her shoulders. I think she could sense me trying to do magic and didn't think she was going to give me a chance to succeed. Her mouth opened too wide and displayed too many pointed teeth and the squeaky little mammal in my ancestry started my legs scrambling in a mad attempt to propel myself backward.

A brown shape smelling of damp carpet streaked past me

and came to a halt, claws skidding on the tiles, between me and Molly. It was Toby in full primeval circle of the campfire, man's best friend, oh *that's* why we domesticated the sodding things, mode—barking at Molly so hard that his front paws were bouncing off the floor.

To be honest, Molly probably could have leaned forward and bitten Toby's snout off, but instead she flinched backward. Then she leaned forward again and hissed. This time, Toby flinched, but he kept his ground in the long tradition of small scrappy dogs that are too stupid to know when to back down. Molly reared back on her haunches, her face a mask of anger and then, as if a switch had been pulled, she slumped down on her knees. Her hair fell back down to cover her face and her shoulders shook—I think she might have been sobbing.

I dragged myself to my feet and staggered toward the back door, thinking that it was probably best to put temptation out of harm's way. Toby came trotting after me with his tail wagging. I bounced off the doorjamb and found myself outside in the sunlight facing the wrought-iron staircase that led up to the coach house. I contemplated the stairs and thought that I should have fitted a lift or at least gotten a bigger dog.

I knew something else was wrong when Toby wouldn't come all the way up the stairs. "Stay, boy," I said and he dutifully sat on the landing and let me do the heroics. I considered walking away, but I was just too knackered to care and besides, this was my space with my flat screen TV and I wanted it back.

I stood to one side of the door and pushed it open with my foot before gingerly peering around the jamb to see who was there. It was Leslie, waiting for me on the chaise longue, holding Nightingale's cane across her knees and staring into space. She glanced over as I slipped in.

"You killed me," she said.

"Can't you just go back to wherever it was you came from?"

"Not without my friend," she said. "Not without Mr. Punch. You've murdered me."

I slumped down in the easy chair. "You've been dead for two hundred years, Henry," I said. "I'm fairly certain you can't murder someone who's already dead." If you could, I thought, the Met would have a form for it.

"I beg to differ," said Leslie. "Though it must be said that I have proved a failure on both sides of the veil."

"I don't know," I said. "You had me fooled."

Leslie turned and looked at me. "I did, didn't I," she said.

I could see the thin pale lines of stretch marks around the bridge of Leslie's nose, the fine tracery of broken blood vessels that started around her mouth and climbed like a winter vine to her cheeks. Even the way she spoke was different, the words slurred by broken teeth and by Henry Pyke's need to keep the mouth closed to hide the damage. I had to hide the anger that seemed to boil up through my chest, because this was a hostage situation and the first rule of the hostage negotiator is never get emotionally involved. Or perhaps it was "don't kill the kidnapper until the hostages are released"—it was bound to be one or the other.

"Looking back," I said, "the more remarkable it seems to me that you never slipped up once."

"You never suspected?" asked Leslie happily.

"No," I said. "You were utterly convincing."

"A female role is always a challenge," said Leslie. "And a modern woman doubly so."

"It's too bad she has to die," I said.

"I want you to know that nobody was more surprised than I to find myself occupying this vessel," said Leslie. "I blame it on the Italian, Piccini, a passionate race—they have to incorporate lust into all their endeavors, even their religious works."

I nodded and looked interested. Despite being plugged in, the TV and DVD standby lights were dark. Leslie had been sitting there long enough to drain all my electronics and if they were gone, then surely Leslie's brain was going to be next. I had to get the last remains of Henry Pyke out of her head.

"That's how it is with a play," said Leslie. "The scenes and acts being so much more ordered than in the humdrum world. Unless one takes a care, one can be swept away by the genius of the character. Thus Punchinella made fools of us both."

"But you'd rather Leslie lived?" I asked.

"Is this possible?" she asked.

"Only if you agree," I said.

Leslie leaned forward and took my hand. "Oh, but I do, my boy," she said. "We can't have it be said that Henry Pyke was so ungracious as to inflict his own sad fate upon an innocent."

I really did wonder when he said that if he had any inkling of the trail of death and misery he'd left behind. Perhaps that was a function of being a ghost; perhaps to the dead, the world of the living was a dream and not to be taken too seriously.

"Then let me call my doctor," I said.

"This would be the Scottish Mohammedan?"

"Dr. Walid," I said.

"You believe he can save her?" asked Leslie.

"I believe he can," I said.

"Then by all means summon him," said Leslie.

I went outside onto the staircase, replaced the battery in my spare mobile and called Dr. Walid, who said he would arrive within ten minutes. He gave me some instructions to follow in the meantime. Leslie looked expectant when I returned.

"Can I have Nightingale's staff?" I asked.

Leslie nodded and handed over the silver-topped cane. I placed my hand on the handle as Dr. Walid had suggested, but there was nothing, just the chill of metal—the staff had been completely drained of magic.

"We don't have much time," I said. There was a relatively clean dust sheet over the back of the chaise longue—I grabbed it.

"Truly?" asked Leslie. "Alas, for as the hour grows closer I feel myself reluctant to depart."

I started ripping the sheet into broad strips. "Can I speak to Leslie directly?" I asked.

"Of course, dear boy," said Leslie.

"Are you okay?" There was no outward change that I could see.

"Ha," she said, and I was sure from the tone that this was the real Leslie. "That's a stupid question. It's happened, hasn't it; I can feel it . . ."

She raised her hand to her face, but I took it and gently guided it back down.

"Everything's going to be okay," I said.

"You're such a bad liar," she said. "No wonder I had to do all the talking."

"You had such a natural talent for it," I said.

"It wasn't talent," said Leslie. "It was hard work."

"You always had such a natural talent for hard work," I said.

"Bastard," she said. "I don't remember them telling me when I joined that there was a risk my face might fall off."

"Don't you?" I asked. "Remember Inspector Neblett, old shovel face himself. Maybe that's what happened to him."

"Tell me I'm going to be okay again."

"You're going to be okay," I said. "I'm going to hold your face on with this." I showed her the strips of sheet.

"Oh, well, that fills me with confidence," she said. "You promise you'll be there whatever happens."

"I promise," I said and, following Walid's instructions, started winding a strip of the sheet tightly around her head. She mumbled something and I assured her that I'd cut a hole for her mouth when I'd finished. I secured the sheet the way one of my mum's sisters had taught me to secure a headscarf.

"Oh good," said Leslie once I'd cut the promised hole. "Now I'm the invisible woman." Just to be on the safe side I knotted the material at the back of her neck to maintain the tension. I found a bottle of Evian by the chaise longue and used it to soak the makeshift bandage.

"You're trying to drown me now?" asked Leslie.

"Dr. Walid told me to do this," I said. I didn't tell her that it was to stop the bandage sticking to the wounds.

"It's cold," she said.

"I'm sorry," I said. "I'm going to need Henry back."

Henry Pyke returned with transparent eagerness. "What must I do now?"

I cleared my mind and opened my hand and spoke the word—"*Lux!*" A werelight flowered above my hand. "This is the light that will take you to your place in history," I said.

"Take my hand." He was reluctant. "Don't worry, it won't burn you."

Leslie's hand closed around mine, light leaking out between her fingers. I didn't know how long my magic would last, or even if the whole blood-sucking business with Molly had left me much magic in the first place. Sometimes you just have to hope for the best.

"Listen, Henry," I said. "This is your moment, your big exit; the lights will dim, your voice will fade, but the last thing the audience will see is Leslie's face. Hold on to the image of her face."

"I don't want to go," said Henry Pyke.

"You must," I said. "That's the mark of true greatness in an actor—knowing, down to the precise moment, when to make his exit."

"How wise of you, Peter," said Henry Pyke. "That is the true mark of genius, to give oneself to one's public, but to re-tain that private side, that secret space, that unknowable . . ."

"To leave them wanting more," I said trying to keep the desperation out of my voice.

"Yes," said Henry Pyke. "To leave them wanting more."

And then the mouthy git was gone, right on cue.

I heard heavy footsteps on the iron staircase. Dr. Walid and the cavalry had arrived. Red stains immediately bloomed on the white sheets covering Leslie face, I heard her gurgling and choking as she tried to breathe. A big hand landed on my shoulder and unceremoniously pushed me out of the way.

I let myself fall to the floor—I figured I could catch up on some sleep now.

CHAPTER 14

The Job

THE YOUNG man in the hospital bed was named St. John Giles and he was a rugby eight or rowing six or whatever at Oxford University who'd come into London for a night out. He had floppy blond hair that was stuck to his forehead with sweat.

"I've already told the police what happened, they didn't believe me. Why should you," he said.

"Because we're the people that believe people that other people don't believe," I said.

"How can I know that?" he asked.

"You're just going to have to believe me," I said.

Because the bedsheets covered him up to his chest, there was nothing to see of his injuries, but I found my eyes drifting down toward his groin—it was like a road accident or horrific facial wart. He saw me trying not to look.

"Believe me," he said. "You don't want to see."

I helped myself to one of his grapes. "Why don't you tell me what happened," I said.

He'd been having a night out with some mates and had gone to a nightclub round the back of Leicester Square. There he'd met a nice young woman whom he'd plied with alcohol before persuading her into a dark corner for a snog. Looking back, St. John was willing to admit that perhaps he might have pressed his case a little too fervently, but he could have sworn she was a willing partner, or at least not objecting too strenuously. It was a depressingly familiar story that the officers on Operation Sapphire, the Met's Rape Investigation Unit, must get to hear all the time. At least right up to the point where she bit his dick off.

"With her vagina?" I asked, just to be clear.

"Yep," said St. John.

"You're sure?"

"It's not the sort of thing you make a mistake about," he said.

"And you're sure it was teeth?"

"It felt like teeth," he said. "But to be honest after it happened I really stopped paying attention."

"She didn't cut you with something, a knife or a broken bottle perhaps?"

"I was holding both her hands," he said and made a grasping gesture with his hand. It was vague but I got the gist—he'd pinned her wrists to the wall.

What a prince among men, I thought, and checked the description he'd given at an earlier interview. "You say she had long black hair, black eyes, pale skin and very red lips?"

St. John nodded enthusiastically. "Sort of Japanese-looking without being Japanese," he said. "Beautiful, but she didn't have slanty eyes."

"Did you see her teeth?"

"No man, I already told you . . ."

"Not those teeth," I said. "The ones in her mouth."

"I don't remember," he said. "Is it important?"

"It might be," I said. "Did she say anything?"

"Like what?"

"Like anything at all?"

He looked nonplussed, thought about it and admitted that he didn't think she'd spoken the whole time he'd been with her. After that I asked a few closing questions, but St. John had been too busy bleeding out to notice where his assailant had gone and he never got her name, let alone her phone number.

I told him I thought he was bearing up well, considering. "Right now," he said. "I'm on some really serious medication. I don't like to think about what's going to happen when I come off."

I checked with the doctors on my way out; the missing penis had never been found. Once I'd finished up my notes—this was still an official Metropolitan Police investigation—I checked in on Leslie, who was one floor up. She was still asleep, her face hidden by a swath of bandages. I stood by her bed for a while. Dr. Walid had said that I'd definitely saved her life and possibly increased the chances of successful reconstructive surgery. I couldn't help thinking that hanging out with me had almost killed her. It had been less than six months since she'd gone for coffee and I'd met a ghost and it was terrifying to think that that might have been all the difference there was between me being the one wearing the bandages and the one looking at them.

Less terrifying but much more depressing was figuring out why it had all kicked off back on that cold January night, or more precisely, that sunny winter's day on Hampstead Heath when Toby the dog bit Brandon Coopertown on the nose. That was the same week the Linbury Studio, the Royal Opera House's second, smaller, auditorium had staged a revival of a little-known play entitled *The Married Libertine*, first shown in the main theater in 1761 and never shown again, as far as I could tell, anywhere else in the world—it's author Charles Macklin. The Royal Opera House fell over themselves to give me access to their booking records, presumably in the hope I'd then go away forever, and I found William Skirmish and Brandon Coopertown had attended a performance on the same night. A random set of circumstances is what did it for William Skirmish and all those who were maimed or died after him—like I said, depressing.

If you want to help, Nightingale had told me, study harder, learn faster. Do the job.

I'd have stayed longer, but I was on the clock.

Nightingale, in an adjacent room, was awake and sitting up

and doing the *Telegraph* crossword. We discussed the case of
the missing penis.

"Vagina dentata," said Nightingale. I wasn't sure that I was
reassured by the thought that it was common enough for there
to be a technical term for it. "Could be oriental, something out
of Chinatown," he said.

"Not Japanese," I said. "The victim was quite clear about
that."

Nightingale gave me some titles to look up in the library
when I had a moment. "But not today," he said. "Are you nervous?"

"A lot of things can go wrong," I said.

"Just don't drink anything," he said. "And you'll be fine."

As I walked back home to the Folly, I generated my own
suspicions as to the identity of the phantom dick snatcher. As
soon as I got in, I went looking for Molly, who I found in the
kitchen—chopping up cucumbers.

"Have you been out clubbing recently?" I asked.

She stopped slicing and turned to regard me with solemn
black eyes.

"You sure?"

She shrugged and started chopping again. I decided that I
was going to let Nightingale sort that one out—a clear chain
of command is a wonderful thing.

"Is that what we're having for the trip?" I asked. "Cucum-
ber sandwiches?"

Molly indicated the rest of her ingredients—salami and
liver sausage.

"You're just yanking my chain now, aren't you?"

She gave me a pitying look and handed me a recycled Sains-
bury's bag with a packed lunch in it.

In the garage, there were no less than six suitcases piled beside the Jag. In addition, Beverley had brought a large shoulder
bag that was, I learned later, stuffed with the entire top shelf of
a Peckham hair salon. Beverley had heard all about the countryside and wasn't taking any chances.

"Why me?" she asked, as she watched me loading up the
Jag.

I opened the door for her and she climbed in, buckled up and held her shoulder bag protectively in her lap.

"Because that's the agreement," I said.

"Nobody asked me," said Beverley.

I got in and checked to make sure that I had a couple of Mars bars and a bottle of sparkling in the glove compartment. Satisfied that emergency supplies were laid on, I started up the Jag and pulled out of the garage.

Beverley stayed silent until we passed Junction 3 on the M4.

"That was the Crane," she said.

"Where?" I asked.

"The River Crane," she said. "We just crossed it."

"One of your sisters?"

"Last one on this side of the River," she said.

I merged us onto the M25 at Junction 15 and headed south; traffic was light, which was a mercy. An Airbus A380 on final approach to Heathrow crossed our path, so low I swear I could see faces peering out of the double row of windows.

"How come she wasn't at the meeting?" I asked.

"She's never in the country," said Beverley. "She's always flying off somewhere, sending us text messages from Bali and postcards from Rio. She went swimming in the Ganges, you know," Beverley said, the last in a tone of awed disapproval.

Thanks to the national curriculum, even I knew that the Ganges is one of the most sacred rivers in India, although to be honest I couldn't remember why. Something to do with funeral pyres and chanting. I put it on the list of things that I needed to look into—it was getting to be a long list.

In the end, I'd come up with one of those messy compromises. As Brock had written, you couldn't get the *genii locorum* to do something as simple as negotiate a contract, symbolism had to be involved. An oath of fealty was out of the question and a cross dynastic marriage was too cruel a fate for either Mother or Father Thames. So I suggested an exchange of hostages, a confidence-building measure to cement ties between the two halves of the River, a suitably medieval solution designed to appeal to two people who definitely still believed in divine rights. It was a typically English compromise, held together by string, sealing wax and the old god network. I'd like to say that I remembered the practice of exchanging hostages from school history classes or from stories of precolonial life in Sierra Leone, but the truth was that it came up while playing Dungeons and Dragons when I was thirteen.

"Why does it have to be me?" Beverley had said after she'd found out.

"It can't be Tyburn," I'd said. You don't inflict Tyburn on anyone as a gesture of peace and goodwill. "And Brent is too young." There were other daughters, some who were the spirits of rivers I'd never heard of and one, a plump smiley young woman, whose formal name was the Black Ditch. Not that anyone called her that. I figured that Mama Thames thought Beverley was the least likely to cause her embarrassment among the yokels. The hostage from the other side was called Ash, whose river's principal claim to fame was that it ran past Shepperton Film Studios.

The exchange was scheduled to take place on the evening of June 21, Midsummer—at Runnymede. Our host was Colne Brook, son of Colne who was also the father of Ash— the tributaries of the Thames can get pretty tangled especially after two thousand years of "improvements." I suspected that the real organizational brains would be Oxley—he wouldn't want to leave anything to chance. This was confirmed when a series of handprinted signs appeared beside the road as I negotiated the tricky bit through Hythe End, which guided us neatly down a cul-de-sac lined with semis that terminated in a gate and an impromptu car park.

Isis met us at the gate with a bevy of teenaged boys, all dressed in their Sunday best, who scampered eagerly over to the Jag and demanded to be allowed to carry the luggage. One straw-headed scamp asked for a fiver to guard the Jag itself—I promised him a tenner just to be on the safe side— payable on my return of course.

Isis hugged Beverley, who was finally persuaded to relinquish her death grip on her cosmetics bag, and led her through the gate into the fields beyond. Father Thames had his "throne" near the priory in the shade of an ancient yew tree.

Around him were arrayed his sons, their wives and his grand-children in all their donkey jacket and sideburned glory. All of them silently watched our approach as if Beverley were a reluctant widow in a Bollywood melodrama. The throne it-self was constructed of old-fashioned rectangular hay bales, of the type I happen to know are no longer common in British farming practice, draped with elaborately embroidered horse blankets. For this occasion, the Old Man of the River had been stuffed into his best suit and his beard and hair combed until merely scruffy-looking.

I followed Beverley and Isis as they stepped before the throne. I'd coached her all the day before, but Isis still had to show the way, a deep curtsy with head bowed, before Bever-ley followed suit. The Old Man of the River caught my eye and then, very deliberately, touched his hand to his chest and then extended his arm, palm facing down—the Roman salute. Then he climbed off his throne, took Beverley's hands in his own and raised her up.

He welcomed her in a language I didn't understand and kissed her on both cheeks.

The air was suddenly full of the scent of apple blossom and horse sweat, lemonade and old hose pipes, dusty roads and the sound of children laughing. All of it strong enough to make me take a step backward in surprise. A wiry arm snaked around my shoulders to steady me and Oxley slapped his hand on my chest in a friendly rib-bending fashion.

"Oh, did you feel *that,* Peter?" he asked. "That's the start of something, if I'm not mistaken."

"Start of what?" I asked.

"I have no idea," said Oxley. "But summer is definitely in the air."

I couldn't even see Beverley among the throng of the Old Man's people. Oxley drew me away from the crowd to intro-duce me to the other half of the hostage swap. Ash turned out to be a young man half a head taller than me, broad of shoul-der, clear of eye, noble of brow and empty of thought.

"Have you got all your things?" I asked.

Ash nodded and tapped the satchel that hung at his hip.

Isis emerged from the crowd long enough to give me a sisterly kiss on the cheek and extract a promise that I would come to the theater with her, such things now being possible in this new and glorious summer. I'd have left there and then, but it took Ash's relatives a good part of an hour to say goodbye to him and it was almost dusk when we got away. As Ash and I walked back to the Jag, I turned and saw that Father Thames's people had hung hurricane lamps from the branches of the ancient yew. At least two fiddles were playing and I heard a clackety sound that I can only assume came from a washboard. There were figures loping and dancing in the yellow light and the seductive melancholy music that gets played at any party you haven't been invited to. I wasn't sure, but with a pang I thought I saw Beverley Brook among the dancers.

"Will there be dancing in London?" asked Ash. He sounded as nervous as Beverley had been.

"Definitely," I said.

We got into the Jag and headed down the A308 for the M25 and home.

"Will there be drinking?" asked Ash, displaying a fine sense of priorities.

"Have you ever been to London?" I asked.

"No," said Ash. "I've never even been in town before. Our dad doesn't hold with that sort of thing."

"Don't worry, it's basically just like the country," I said. "Only with more people."